MEMORY'S RANSOM

GRAEME FIFE

Memory's Ransom

Published by The Conrad Press Ltd. in the United Kingdom 2023

Tel: +44(0)1227 472 874

www.theconradpress.com

info@theconradpress.com

ISBN 978-1-914913-55-6

Typesetting and Cover Design by: Charlotte Mouncey, www.bookstyle.co.uk

The book cover uses an image by M-Verlag Berlin / Peter Cornelius supplied by Alamy Stock Photo.

The Conrad Press logo was designed by Maria Priestley.

Printed and bound in Great Britain by Clays Ltd, Elcograf S.p.A.

For Rudolf Strauss 1913 – 2001, my special friend, a generous man of wide culture, deep knowledge, wisdom and good humour and his wife, Hanna, an artist, whose practicality, plain-spokenness and slightly guarded charm gave me Sybille in this book.

The table was laid like an altar with the sacred vessels for the rite of the blood Mass: on a pristine white lawn cloth, three pistols, three grenades, six cyanide pills.

In silence, each of the six young men pulled on black leather gloves and, left hand raised in pledge, right hand over the heart, spoke the Slavic words of the oath in a tone strained by excitement and fever to get on with the job.

'By the Sun which shines on me, by the Earth that feeds me, by God, by the Blood of my forefathers, by my Honour and by my Life: Union or Death.'

Their priest stroked each forehead with the side of his thumb, making the sign of the cross, and muttering: *'In nomine domini, et filii, et spiritus sancti. Amen.'*

As they picked up the weapons and the capsules, their passage to oblivion, a trance between living and almost certain extinction took them over. Better not to feel. Better to disengage from the world. Their testament to those for whom they acted this day would be a world changed, a world they surely would not see but a liberated world of which they'd dreamed.

They walked out into the city, light-headed, stomach congested, all at once sick with fear: decision faced reality. But fear must not count. That they had talked about. Fear did not count. Of the faces in the crowd they saw the features of none. Of the murder written in theirs, how could that, the obvious mark of Cain, pass notice? Resolve and purpose would erase it. Of the voices in the crowd they heard none individually, only a muffled clamour, a dull buzzing in their ears, a vague concussion of sound.

By slow degrees, seriatim, they took position: one stopped, the others walked on. The second stopped, the others walked on, until the sixth was at post and they formed a relay, a gauntlet of six opportunities to obliterate, bomb gives way to pistol gives way to bomb gives way to pistol…

The agonisingly slow-moving hands of the clock plucked at their nerves. Impatience, they'd been warned, impatience is the spawn of purgatory.

The cathedral bell struck the hour, counted out the booming chimes to ten o'clock , a resonance that hung awhile in the still air and then vanished into ever fainter echo and silence.

The crowd on either side looked down the empty boulevard. Suddenly, a great cheering erupted somewhere unseen and there, at the end of the broad avenue, appeared the open car, inching forward, towards them. In procession behind it, other cars. Cheering rippled along, accompanying the cavalcade as it passed up the avenue between the banks of the people waving and shouting.

The first bomb missed its target and exploded on a following car. The detonation still resounding, the lead car lurched on at racing speed.

Half an hour later, as if nothing so shocking had happened, the car came back, the open car, its passengers in plain sight, improbably heedless of more bombs, and drove towards the sixth pistol. The last assassin, scarce believing his luck, raised the gun and fired pointblank at the passengers in the gleaming black, open Double Phaeton, two bullets: one to the man's jugular, the other into the woman's stomach and the foetus she was carrying.

The wounds were beyond any doctor. As death began to close over him, the Archduke, a treason of blood spreading across his white uniform tunic, whispered to his wife: 'Sofie, don't die. Live for the children.'

1

The architectural confection that is Vienna lies in the baking oven-hot sun this torrid June day like a tray of ornately iced cakes.

The air clings, heavy with heat, the lemonade sellers are doing brisk business, the pavements burn to the touch like a hotplate. Viennese society is at its business, being on show, idling in open-air restaurants, listening to brass oompah oompah from bandstands, flirting, gossiping. The youthful captain of the 3rd regiment of Infantry, in full ceremonial uniform of the royal and imperial Austrian army, leans fondly to the young woman holding his arm. She does not so much walk as float, an airy fantasy of sheer muslin. He, a proud member of the aristocracy of arms, has never seen war. She has never fastened one of her own buttons. They stroll down an avenue of linden trees in the Innere Stadt, making for an outdoor cafe. Nothing disturbs their poise. They flit through shade and sun. Time passes, decays, runs out, but not for them. They do not work, they do not *do* anything. They *are*.

Away from the city's grand imperial core, in the tenements, the five and six-storey terraces of apartment blocks, the anonymous living quarters of Vienna's anonymous thousands, Vienna's face is haggard.

Into Vienna streams a teeming goulash of ethnic peoples from across the vast Austro-Hungarian empire dominating Central Europe and the Balkans: from Bohemia to Bosnia, from Poland to the Veneto. People from the central mountains and the valleys, from the Black Sea, Mediterranean and Adriatic coastlines. People from along the mighty Danube, the great waterway which speaks German as an infant, Hungarian in its maturity and delivers its dying utterance in Romanian. From farm and shtetl, village and town, they tramp the roads to Vienna, the city of God, and become that other, careworn face of Vienna where they learn the lesson of silence by the privacies of neglect.

In the late afternoon of this sultry day two young men and two young women, twenty one years old, walked gaily, arm in arm, along Hießgasse, near the canal. They'd just quit the stuffy room in the university after the last of their final degree exams. But, hot as it was in the open air, the suffocating closeness of the exam room had been more oppressive. Pillaging exam-weary brains for the last scrapings of their revision had been an added trial but, oh, the wonderful, exuberant relief when the invigilator called time and they handed in their papers, stripped off the academic gowns and with them the much-overrated (in their view) consolations of philosophy and walked out into the summer, free to enjoy it at last.

They swung along the street, buoyant and careless, chattering, laughing, joking. They were making for an apartment at number 27, home of Georg. Waiting for them there was a celebratory picnic hamper packed with good things.

The straps of their satchels made damp patches on their shirts and the women's tucked blouses.

9

Katharina said: 'I don't believe it. I can't believe it. Pinch me, tell me it's true.'

'It's true, it's true,' said Helga.

'Do you know what I'm looking forward to most?' said Georg. 'Reading a book I do not have to read, that no one has told me I must read.'

'Starting with…?' said Felix.

'Haven't decided. A novel. What about you?'

Katharina laughed. 'Felix will read a theological tract because he will soooooooo miss the long hours of study,' she said.

'Actually, I won't miss them one bit, I shall read…'

'Let me guess,' said Helga. 'Goethe.'

'Wrong.'

'Nietzsche.'

'No.'

'Well?' she said. 'Grimm's Fairy Tales?'

'Why not? Anyway…I don't know. One thing I certainly won't read is the time.'

'Well, I shall not open a book. I shall listen to music,' said Helga. 'Just music, all day long. And I shall do…nothing, for sweet it is to do *nothing*.'

At which Katharina broke free and began to skip. 'And I shall out-sloth the sloth,' she cried. She pulled a lecture note-book out of her satchel and, with a whoop, ran across to the canal, and skimmed it into the water, the pages fluttering like a stricken bird. She ran back, laughing, her long copper hair tumbling about her shoulders. 'Come on you lot,' she said, linking into the line again. She squeezed her elbows tight to her sides, tugged the others into a run and shouted: 'Hurray, hurray, hurray.'

The main room in Georg's apartment, lit by a broad bay window, whose casement he flung up as soon as they arrived, was furnished with an oval dining table, spread with a burgundy velvet cloth, a tapestry-draped chaise longue, two armchairs and a buffet on which stood a radio.

Helga flapped the collar of her blouse to cool herself, Felix polished the lenses of his glasses with a handkerchief. Georg started to unpack the hamper. 'Wine in the cooler, Felix, corkscrew on the side there. Napkins and cutlery in the top drawer over there, Katharina, Helga, plates and glasses in the kitchen dresser, bread board on top, knife in the drawer, I think.'

He began to spread the table with the packets of food, wrapped in waxed paper – sliced ham, a rye loaf bought fresh that morning, a jar of gherkins, cheese and a box of the famous marzipan of Lübeck, to which he was partial. 'Was it not Thomas Aquinas himself who declared that marzipan does not break the fast?' he said, but no one was listening.

The sound of a popping cork announced Felix who came back into the room with the bottle of Gruner Veltiner. 'Glasses?'

'Coming.' Helga emerged from the kitchen.

'Anyone want water?' said Katharina. 'Jug, Georg?'

'Kitchen shelf.'

Katharina made for the kitchen and called out:'Tumblers?'

'In the dresser. Thank you K.'

When the feast was laid out, Felix handed round the wine, Georg said: 'Prost,' and they all clinked glasses. 'Prost.'

'Come, children. Eat, drink, be merry, life may be full of woe but we are not. *Jubilate*. Rejoice. Tuck in.' Georg, master of ceremonies, his element, beamed at them one by one. A ripping of bread, slicing of cheese and sausage, clunk of knife blade on the sycamore board, the rustle of paper, clatter of cutlery on plates, a jingling of glass and laughter, the murmuration of deep contentment. Felix cleared his throat and began to croon *Gaudeamus igitur juvenes dum sumus* and the others joined in *Youth's a time for merriment, let us all then merry be* and cheered.

And then Georg raised his glass and said: 'A solemn toast…'

'No solemnity.' Katharina shuddered.

'No, hear me out. Hear me out. The message is important.' He cleared his throat and assumed a heroic posture. 'In these great times of the apogee of the empire, how can anything be wrong with anything? Is not Vienna always Vienna? And is not Vienna Austria's immortal heart? By my troth, I believe it is. For God, who as we all know, spoke German before he spoke Latin - *or* Greek - is in his heaven, the Emperor is on his throne, the next in line all ready to succeed him, and, lo, our sacred continuum is assured. Worth a hurrah.'

'Hurrah,' they cried.

'An emperor dies, we proclaim: "The emperor is dead, long live the emperor".The same for Austria, even at her umpteenth resurrection. For Austria is not the corpse, Austria is the idea. So, come what may, praise God and pass the champagne. The truth scorches any who come too close. Besides, why drag *death* into it? Death never did anything for anyone. Let the dead bury their dead and we the living celebrate life. Are we to sink into morbid navel-gazing or turn our eyes heavenwards to gaze at the stellar brilliance of which we are a new galaxy? Well, children?'

He circled their eyes with his, burst out laughing and barely spluttered *To hell with them all* before uproarious mirth took him over and they all hooted derision until the hilarity sank into a woozy contentment.

Helga tapped a spoon against her glass, and, as if she were announcing bad news, said: 'And I give you a toast. Confusion to Eisenberg and his ilk, mortal confusion, a plague on all their kind and a fart for their opinions.'

The others chimed in: 'And a fart for their opinions.' More hoots of derision.

Heinrich von Eisenberg, professor of metaphysics, known pederast, short on hygiene, ossified in a rigid state of inertia, was a byword for academic dessication. The eyes half closed, the nose, the cheeks, the doughy lips slack and set as if he were half asleep, the drone of a toneless monologue on an abstraction of idea seeping out of the barely open mouth. Bad breath from foul digestion and carious teeth. 'How on earth does he have the brass neck to lecture us on the nature of *being* when the dreary man is entirely composed of sawdust?' said Katharina. Asked by her, once, why so much of what he dilated on was so depressing, Eisenberg, ever morose, whined 'life is like that'. His sour, hooded look added *and you would do well to remember it, young lady. Frivolity is and will ever be your downfall.*

'Paragons of ennui, every one of them,' said Georg. 'Stewing in envy when we scoff and refuse to surrender to their worn-out creeds. They never questioned anything in their lives. As if the highest accomplishment to which they ever aspired was to become a stolid, bourgeois, complacent citizen of upright standing. Most of them moved from infancy straight to middle age. With desire comes danger, with striving comes risk. Let's be ambitious for the impossible. True to ourselves, true to a determination to cheat Time of its deadening claim on us.' He paused. 'Sorry, am I preaching?'

Katharina and Helga exchanged glances and burst into giggles.

And Felix wondered about that – true to ourselves? - as he wondered, in a perplexity he couldn't shake off, about so much. Who is the I that I'm to be true to? he thought. But that was part of the problem. He was, and knew it, too self-conscious, too beset with doubts, too ridden by conscience. There were always questions, questions and no clear answer. And conscience was an inhibition Georg despised. 'Conscience turns us into cowards, Felix, quote unquote. Conscience and guilt are the senna pods in our coffee. Lead in the soul.' Georg had no such doubts. He was a perfect rationalist.

It was to Georg that Helga had come, in scalding tears, for comfort, when a man had thrown her over. His dismissal had been brutal. 'Why should you complain?' he'd said, with callous chilly dismissal. You were as hot for sex as I was, weren't you? Admit it. Or were you pretending? And I miss that too.'

'Is that all it was to you, a fuck?'

He'd shrugged and half-smiled. 'There was *dinner*. More than one.'

It broke her. She wept, shrank away from him in disgust. 'Heartless bastard. How can you say I was pretending? Unfeeling shit. I wish we'd never *gone* to bed.'

Georg had settled her in the armchair drawn up a dining chair from the table next to it and stroked her hair.

'You men are so fucking predictable,' she'd said to the sodden handkerchief. 'All after one thing, the same thing. Have not hold.'

'And you're not, you *women*?' Georg had said that with a crooked look in his eyes, signal that this was self-deprecation.

14

'We go hard, you go soft and wet. Quite straightforward, in truth.'

'That's where you're wrong, so damned wrong.'

Her anger jolted him. 'Yes. I'm sorry.' He reflected, admitting the flippancy. 'Thoughtless. The passion you give, unrequited, rebounds and crushes you. At least it proves you're alive. That you can feel.'

'Does it?'

'Doesn't it?'

'Right now I don't want to feel,' she whispered. 'It's all there is of me. Damned feeling. Shit.'

'I know. Nothing I can say, much, to help you. I wish there were. I do love you, you know that, Helga, and if it's any consolation, I feel for you. If anyone hurts you, I take it very seriously.'

She looked up. Tears glistened on her cheek. 'You know, I thought…I don't know what I thought. You saying that. I thought you were immune.'

'Immune?'

'You just seem to be able to brush things off.'

'Really?'

'That's why I came to you. You seem so self-contained. Not dangerous.'

He laughed. 'Come on, honey, I may not care in the same way but I care, of course I do. I care about you.'

'Oh, Christ…' propping up her head with one hand. How exhausting grief was. The pain was so sharp. 'How could I have been so naïve? I'm not sure I even liked him. That's no good, is it?'

'Helga, honey, don't blame yourself for your feelings. As for being naïve, well… Maybe it's naïve to expect someone else to feel as strongly as you do. But how do you calculate for that? Plaisir d'amour, chagrin d'amour. Anyway, better to find out he's a nitwit, isn't it? Besides, he's only a man and we're all the same, most of us…fucking predictable.'

She'd laughed for a few seconds and the laughter merged with sobs and ebbed into defeat as she murmured: 'Oh, Georg, I feel such a fool.'

'Don't. Don't. You're not a fool. Far from it. You're real. He didn't deserve you. Someone does, someone will.'

Will they? she'd thought. *Will they?* You're only saying that, to console me. How can I believe it's true?

Katharina lay on the chaise longue twirling a lock of her hair with the fingers of one hand, drained her glass and folded her lips over the wine. Katharina was a mystery, an elegant sphinx. Beautiful, capricious, a brilliant, effortless scholar, she was ungraspable. Dismay seemed never to cloud her. She blinked at disappointment and calamity yet seemed wedded to some unaccountable tragedy. At such times, though, her smile was distant, withdrawn. Things were as they were, she appeared to be thinking, and she could not change them. Why waste energy or emotion trying to change them? She chose not to cry, tears would ruin her composure, tears were a tiresome weakness. Yet, if she showed no hurt, she felt it, still. The wounds were too deep. And who would or could nurse them but her? Once she had let slip her guard when she asked an admirer – they were legion: this one she'd picked for more torment than the others, his vulnerability to hurt being no small part of his charm – she'd asked him: *Do I look pretty today?* And he, poor fool, said with just too much seriousness, 'But you're the most beautiful girl in the world.' It wasn't what she wanted to hear. Looking pretty was a prize, a hold over him, beauty was a responsibility. She did not say *But I need to be told, I need you to say it, because that would prove how much in thrall you are. Instead, you turn the answer to yourself, you deny me my vanity by asserting your own. If I have nothing of you, how can you expect, even dare, to have anything of me?* She turned on him the serene look which was both a seduction and a withholding. Reach out for me, it said, and be assured that I will deny you. It was the face of a child, the mask of her privacy. Love came too close. Adoration maintained a less oppressive distance. Adoration could be held at arm's length. Adoration could be relied on. Asked how she felt after a broken love affair, she said, without any inflection: 'Pretty desperate.'

Georg, leaning back against the chaise longue on which Katharina reclined, said: 'A toast. To us. May we stay us in every sense.'

'To us,' said Katharina with a distracted air, eyes fixed on the ceiling.

'What does that mean, exactly?' said Helga from the armchair scratching an itch on the back of her neck.

'It means that blessed with friendship as we are, we are, by definition, true to each other and therefore intend to remain so.'

Helga blew him a kiss.

'Felix, darling,' said Katharina. 'Would you pass the wine over?'

Felix, sitting at the table, leaned over with the bottle and

17

filled her glass as she extended it.

'How about some music?' said Helga.

Georg stood up and switched on the radio. The valves warmed through to a soft ochre glow showing through the perspex panel, lighting up the frequency indicators. As Georg turned the dial, a crackle of interference was snuffed out by the clear sound of an orchestra playing something classical.

'Find some dance music?' said Helga.

'It's usually on this station,' said Georg.

'We can't dance to that.'

'No reason why not. It's Beethoven,' said Felix. His lips were screwed up. Felix was at contemplation.

Georg turned the dial again through a medley of crackling, hissing, blurted fragments of speech, until he lit on a brass and wind band rollicking through a polka.

'That's more like it,' said Helga, getting up. 'Let's dance.'

'What, here?' said Felix.

'Of course. Don't be so stuffy. Pop some buttons. Come on, let's push the furniture back.'

Suddenly, the music stopped in mid-phrase. A brief gap of silence and then a sombre man's voice spoke.

'Good evening. There follows an official communiqué. This morning, in Sarajevo, during an official visit to the capital of Bosnia, the heir to the royal and imperial throne of Austria-Hungary, the Archduke Ferdinand, and his wife were assassinated by a Serbian terrorist. At this dark moment in our empire's history, we ask all our people to join in mourning their death from this despicable act. Our thoughts must be with the Emperor and his family. *Oesterreich auf immer.* Austria forever.'

The dead march played.

Katharina said: 'Switch it off.'

Georg turned the knob and the radio's light faded out.

It was a while before any of them spoke. Finally, Helga said: 'Why?'

'Poor creatures,' said Katharina. 'Think of their children.'

There was another silence, which Katharina broke. 'What's going to happen?'

Georg sighed. 'They'll bumble through. It's what they're good at. They've had enough practice.'

'Cynical?' said Felix.

'Oh, come on, Felix. The morons in charge? My god, they couldn't run a newspaper stand.'

2

22 September 1915, Italian front. Eastern Alps. Night.

In this quarter of the battle zone, immediately west of the Isonzo river, the Italian trenchworks formed an indented line round the base of a limestone crag. Sandbagged machine gun emplacements sat at intervals commanding a flat expanse of soggy land, some hundred and fifty metres wide, stretching to the riverbank. On the far side of the stream rose a long ridge, not more than a hundred metres high, its forward slopes dotted with dwarf oaks and scrub.

The moon, near full, cast a pale electric light.

On the observation platform in the Italian line, the battalion colonel checked the luminous dial of his watch. A little after midnight. Next to him, his aide peered through a trench periscope across the approach ground. Signals had just received reports of enemy movement along the road north from Gorizia. This road ran parallel to the course of the river below the ridge on its far side, out of sight. The message was timed at 1900 hours.

A drifting pack of clouds obscured the moon. The silhouetted bulk of the ridge merged with the sky's sudden darkness.

The colonel yawned. He'd had two hours sleep before his orderly woke him with the report. The same orderly came out of the command dug-out behind him now and whispered:

'Coffee, sir,' and handed him the mug. He sipped at the bitter-tasting brew, then added a shot of grappa from his pocket flask.

The clouds cleared again. The aide, surveying the empty landscape caught in moonlight, muttered: 'Nothing, sir.'

The colonel whispered to him. 'Nevertheless, pass the word, Canetti. Sentries on full alert, men on standby, possible action imminent.'

Canetti went a short distance along the trench to a scooped hollow of the earthen wall where the battalion runner was sitting, asleep. Seconds after Canetti's hand had jerked him awake, he was on his way down the line.

An hour passed, the moon coming and going behind rags of cloud.

Suddenly, in its full glare, the colonel noticed movement along the skyline of the ridge, a broken line of men. Rifle fire erupted from the trenches, the machine guns opened up. The men on the exposed ridge went to ground.

A bank of cloud extinguished the moon. The colonel, observing through the periscope, called out to the command post signallers on the firestep: 'Flares.'

The men loosed off their flares and reloaded. Blossoms of incandescent light floated down over the ridge illuminating the target. Machine guns and rifles hammered high concentration rapid fire onto the hillside. There was no discernible movement there. The firing stuttered and died out even as the light of the flares began to disperse.

The silence was fraught. Stalemate, endless hours of inaction and boredom punctuated by abrupt explosions of shocking violence had shaved their nerves thin. As the light of the flares dwindled, a stuttering volley of rapid rifle fire broke out from the hillside. Moments later, a second volley and silence again.

The colonel said: 'Platoon strength?'

Canetti agreed. 'No more.'

'What the hell are they playing at? Flares.'

The magnesium rockets burst and rifles and machine guns bruised their light with shocking fury. The light faded once more. There was no answering fire.

The colonel turned to Canetti. 'What do you think?'

'Could be scouts.'

'Too many. And not enough for any sort of attack.' He paused. 'Flares.'

An artificial brilliance hung once more briefly in the sky and merged with the moon's silvery sheen. There was no movement on the slopes of the hill.

Five minutes passed. Nothing. Ten minutes. Nothing. The colonel told Canetti to pass the word: 'Men to stand down. Sentries on full alert.'

Dawn came in a glaze of pink. The new day warmed itself in the rays of a young sun and cast off the chilly night like an overcoat, stiff with mud. A flock of ducks flew past with a chuckle of quacks.

A runner thumped along the duck boards of the trench to the command dug-out.

'Sir?'

The colonel, dozing in a chair, was instantly awake.

'Sir. Message from the observation post, sir. Spotter, sir. Small number of enemy troops holed up at around 75 to 100 metres to the front. About twenty of them, just visible, sir.'

The Colonel scanned the area through his binoculars,

pondered, then said: 'Canetti, pass me the megaphone.'

He stood up on the fire step and shouted over the parapet:

'Soldati Austriachi. Cedete. Darvi. La vostra posizion' è disperato, senza speranza. È inutile.'

He waited, repeated the call to surrender, waited again, handed the megaphone to Canetti who called out, in German: 'You need to surrender,' then watched as a piece of white material, tied to the muzzle of a rifle, rose into the air. The binoculars showed the man holding the rifle getting to his feet, the rifle raised above his coal scuttle helmet, his drab grey uniform daubed with mud. A pair of spectacles, dislodged from one ear, dangled loose against his cheek. He wore a pistol holster. An officer.

The colonel lowered the binoculars and said:

'Take an escort, Canetti. Bring the officer in.'

'Yes, sir. What about the men?'

'Put them under guard. We'll see to them later.'

The colonel went into the command dug-out and ordered the signals corporal to contact Intelligence at Brigade HQ. The corporal took up the receiver, spun a handle on the set, gave a code number when a voice answered and, after a brief pause, handed the colonel the receiver.

'0656 hours, 22 September, Colonel Vittorini, 7th group, sector J, command post 14. We're bringing in a prisoner, Austrian army, in all likelihood a junior officer.'

He listened to the response and replied: 'Small body of men, number as yet undetermined, no more than platoon strength.'

He listened again.

'Very well, sir.' He handed the receiver back to the corporal, left the dug-out, went across to the observation step and watched as Canetti, pistol in hand, marched the captive officer, hands in the air, over the boulders making an erratic splashy path through the shallows of the river. Behind him, on the far bank, the soldiers of the escort, rifles at the ready, had grouped together and surrounded the other prisoners who sat on the ground, shoulders hunched, helmets discarded, packs and weapons in a heap outside the circle.

The Austrian officer appeared on the lip of the parapet. Canetti, behind him, said, in German: 'Down you go.' The prisoner clambered, with some difficulty, down the vertical rungs, his arms and legs cramped with cold and wet. His spectacles still hung loosely from one ear.

When he got to the trench floor, Canetti descending after him, he fumbled at the glasses to replace them on his nose. A small dignity. The lenses were filthy. They can have been no use.

He was a young man of medium height. The outsized coal scuttle helmet lent his grime-streaked face with its blind eyes, a haunted look. The uniform jacket and trousers were clamped with drying earth.

'Tell him to take his pack off.' Canetti translated. 'And hand me that map case.'

The colonel leaned into the dug-out. 'Corporal, bring a chair out here.'

The young Austrian sat on the chair, Canetti offered him a cigarette which he refused, a mug of water which he accepted. He didn't speak. The colonel turned to Canetti.

'Intelligence are sending someone up here to interrogate him. He doesn't look as if he's got the stuffing to try to escape but get one of the men here to guard him.' He checked his watch. 'Tour of inspection in ten minutes. Corporal.'

'Sir?'

'Organise some coffee, pronto. We'll take breakfast after inspection.'

'Sir.'

They left the enemy officer sitting in the trench, an Italian infantryman lounging on the firestep opposite, at the foot of the ladder, his rifle across his knees. The Austrian spoke.

'I need to pee.'

The Italian didn't respond.

'I need to pee, to urinate, to pass water.'

The Italian's expression did not alter. It was neither hostility nor anything definable rather a compound of fatigue, boredom, hunger, discomfort, battered nerves, the sick malaise of war, the squalor.

The Austrian pointed at his crutch. The Italian shifted position and braced his rifle.

The Austrian pointed at his crutch, again, and made a hissing noise through his teeth. The Italian called out: 'Corporal.'

The Corporal appeared.

'I think he wants to piss.'

'Well get a latrine orderly up here with a bucket.'

'I've got orders to guard him.'

'So, take him, under guard, to the piss-house.' He stared hard at the private. 'Jump to it, before he wets himself.'

The private levelled his rifle at the prisoner, nudged him with the barrel and nodded sideways. The Austrian stood up and walked along the duckboards, left down a narrower side trench, cut at right angles, to a makeshift latrine – canvas covering, buckets either open or covered with a lavatory seat, earth floor, stink of excrement and urine, flies.

As they rejoined the main trench, they encountered the colonel and Canetti.

'What the hell are you doing, soldier?'

'Latrine visit, sir. Call of nature. Not pissing about, sir.'

'Get him back there.'

Far along the trench, one of the Italian infantrymen wrote out a new poem in his notebook:

Soldati

Si sta come
d'autunno
sugli alberi
le foglie

Soldiers

We are
Like leaves
On the trees,
In autumn.

The intelligence officer arrived half an hour later. Vittorini handed him the map case and the prisoner's pay book. The Austrian had been given a mug of thin coffee and a slice of bread with two roundels of greasy salami. He sat, now, on a chair in the dug-out. The intelligence subaltern sitting at a table in front of him riffled through the pages of the prisoner's pay book, and spoke to him in German.

'Confirm your name, rank and number.'

'Breitenbach, Felix, Lieutenant, 19932.'

'Third army, 57th division…' He looked up. 'Major General Goiginger, yes?'

'I'm not obliged to say.'

'We'll find out anyway, from one of your men, so…'

'Where are my men? What's happening to them?'

The subaltern didn't reply.

'I demand to know what is happening to my men.'

'You're in no position to demand anything, so I advise you to cooperate. It's in your best interests.' He opened the map case.

'The Monte Santo sector is indicated here, yes?'

The Austrian didn't respond.

'According to this map, it would seem you'd been detailed for the Monte Santo sector. Is that correct?'

There was a long pause before the prisoner nodded.

'That's a kilometre down the valley.'

The prisoner stiffened.

'They sent you to the wrong place, it appears. And this map…where did they get it? A secondhand book stall?' He laughed. 'So, Lieutenant Breitenbach,' he said with obvious contempt, 'what does Major-general Goiginger have in mind? Why were you, or why did you think you were, proceeding to the Monte Santo sector?'

'I'm not obliged to…'

'Lieutenant. You're doing yourself no good, here. The more irritated you make me, the worse it'll be for you. Well?'

The Austrian stared at the map spread out in front of him. The wrong place. They'd sent him to the wrong place. Orders, directions, map, signboard…the wrong place. He chewed at his lip, cleared his throat.

'Yes?' said the subaltern.

'I…' he began but couldn't continue. Fatigue swamped him. He sighed.

The subaltern drummed his fingertips on the map. 'Let's play at police and criminals, shall we? You were ordered to go to the Monte Santo sector and not here. That we've established. Why to that particular sector? To link up with other units of the Austrian army? That seems likely. Over the hill in some vague direction with some vague mission to find the rest of you, somewhere or other. So what's going on, here?'

There was no reply.

The subaltern picked up and dropped the map on the table. He shook his head. 'Are you going to tell me why they sent you into a blind alley?'

The Austrian looked at the floor then at the subaltern. 'What's happening to my men?'

The subaltern stood up, both hands planted on the table and, his face clenched, said: 'We are at war, Lieutenant. You are our prisoner, your men are our prisoners, and that's it, as far as it goes. I suggest you think very hard about it for a while.' He caught the signals corporal's eye. 'Get me Brigade and take this man outside.'

The conversation between the intelligence officer and his superior was brief. Canetti ducked through the dug-out entrance.

'Get anything out of him?'

'Enough. It does no harm to make them think they're holding back on something important.'

'What are we to do with him?'

'They're sending transport up from Brigade. They'll take it

from there.' He put his cap back on and saluted. Leaving the dug-out, he gave the prisoner a hard look and walked off down the trench past look-outs standing on the fire step, other men at rest, playing cards, reading, writing scratched notes in diaries or letters on creased sheets of paper, sleeping.

A skein of geese flew over. There were three rifle shots. An officer shouted. None of the birds was hit.

Two hours later, a second intelligence officer appeared with two military police. They marched the Austrian down the communication trench to an open portal, out into the trees, up the slope of the hill to a muddy track and a small, covered lorry. The driver, standing by the door, threw away his cigarette into the grey dust. The intelligence officer climbed into the cab, the MPs followed the prisoner into the back of the vehicle and sat on the bench opposite him. The engine started and the lorry moved off.

3

Units of the imperial army paraded in glittering pomp through the first district of the city, the magic carpet of Viennese society, towards the cathedral of Saint Stephen for a service of dedication of the colours. At their head walked the archbishop of Vienna accompanied by the deacons of the cathedral. A richly embroidered canopy, its supporting poles borne by lay gentlemen of the city council, flanked by priests bearing candles, sheltered a sacred vessel containing the most holy sacrament, body of Christ.

The emperor-king himself, the elderly Franz Josef I, followed on a chestnut stallion. Behind him, slow-marched his men at a strut, cocks of the walk, disparate regiments from every corner of the empire, tricked out in a flighty array of uniforms from a vast wardrobe. And the Hungarian Hussars. As proud as purple. They knew: a cavalry charge was still the fitting end to any battle, horsemen striking out of the battlefield's gunsmoke like Zeus's lightning bolts out of the storm clouds. If the infantry was the body of the army, the cavalry was its immortal soul. Ask them.

All Vienna, it seemed, had spilled onto the pavements and crowded the sidewalks, waving, fluttering handkerchiefs and parasols, doffing hats, cheering, applauding. Small boys stood agape in wonder, already chafing at the unfair slowness of time that kept them from joining the ranks of the demigods marching past, at the misery of having to wait for the chance to go to war.

Somewhere in the crowd stood Felix, conflicted. It was all very splendid, somehow all very repellent.

Within weeks, brown paper envelopes began to arrive in post boxes across the city and the empire. Each contained a single printed sheet of pale Hapsburg yellow paper with the recipient's name written in ink.

'By command of his Imperial Majesty, Franz Josef I, Emperor of Austria and Apostolic King of Hungary, you [*everyman*] are summoned to…'

One day in mid-October, Felix sat in the library, his habitual escape from the claustrophobia of home. He stared round the room at the floor-to-ceiling shelves lined with books, thousands of books. He took in the earnest researchers sitting at the long tables poring over densely printed pages, other volumes piled at their elbows. He watched the librarians moving about the room like envoys of a silent order deep in contemplation and unspoken orison. He listened to the crackle of pages being turned, the occasional dull soft thud of a book being delivered to a reader, to the scraping of a chair as the occupant got up to take another request slip to the central desk.

He slipped into a daydream. The librarians were queueing up in front of his table, one after the other, delivering book after book, building a barricade round him. Each librarian looked at him with a pitying smile. *It was you who ordered this. It has your name on the slip.* And still more books came, heaped up in front of him, beside him, behind him, next to the chair. He could see the shelves emptying, all the books they contained heading for him.

He blinked and started out of the daze. And, with a hot surge of energy and clarity, said to himself: 'What am I doing here?'

He got up, walked across to the guichet in the central desk and handed in both a book and his immediate future.

He reported a week later at the gates of the Roßauer barracks in the Alsergrund district of the city, not far from the Jewish cemetery. The barracks might have been a prison, a gaunt quadrangle of characterless three storey blocks enclosing an inner parade ground and more blocks of rooms and offices.

A sentry indicated a door at the end of a long internal corridor smelling of carbolic soap, floor polish and fresh paint. An orderly was pushing a large trolley down the corridor. Felix stepped aside to allow it to go past and put his hand onto the wet paint of the wall. He swore.

'Can't you read, four eyes?' said the orderly, indicating a handwritten sign.

'I didn't see it.'

'Jesus,' mumbled the orderly and walked on.

The corridor led to a door upon which was fixed a printed notice RECRUITS. Felix knocked. An orderly opened, asked his name and showed him into the room where rows of chairs across its main body were filled with young men. Felix joined a group of ten other young men standing by the door

Glazed half walls and doors lined one side of the room, visible behind the glass, officers conducting interviews. Opposite, a line of clerks at small square desks, typing. Telephones rang constantly, orderlies bustled to and fro. At the far end of the room, behind a kneehole desk on a low, raised dais, a sergeant sorted through a sheaf of papers, marking each with a stamp and adding it to one of three piles of documents in front of him.

Felix had to wait an hour and a half past the appointed time, long minutes squeezed out by the rheumatic clock on the end wall, and was jerked out of a semi-doze at the sound of his name, and his name repeated. He looked up to see a junior NCO beckoning him forward. He handed Felix a single sheet of paper franked with the official stamp of the royal and imperial Austria-Hungary over the motto 'All nations are subject to Austria'.

The junior NCO led him to one of the office doors and knocked. No response. He knocked again. Another pause. Then a voice: 'Come.' The junior NCO opened the door and ushered Felix into the room.

The officer held out his hand, Felix stepped forward to hand over the page on which were recorded his name, address, age.

'Are these details correct?'

'I didn't check, sir.'

'Good god,' said the officer under his breath and handed the page back. 'Check them.' Felix scanned the page.

'Yes, sir. Correct, sir.' He handed the page back. The officer sniffed. 'Education?'

'University degree in Literature and Philology, sir.'

The officer drew back in his chair. 'Literature and Phil…by jove,' he said, as if Felix had just claimed relationship with the blood royal. 'Well, well, well…university degree in literature and…' he twiddled his pen.

'Philology,' said Felix. 'The study of –'

'I know what it's the study of,' snapped the officer. 'Damn your impertinence.' He pulled a document out of a file and perused it.

'Application for officer training?' He looked up. 'You do know what you are asking for, do you, Breitenbach, in spite of your study of litter-at-chewer?' he asked.

'Yes, sir.'

That I very much doubt, thought the officer. He passed the document to Felix. 'Your orders. You have a month to read the last bit of litcherchewer you are likely to see in a long while.'

'Thank you, sir.'

'Well, what are you waiting for? Coffee and cakes? Dismiss. Next,' he called waving Felix out of the room with a brisk motion of his left hand towards the door. He dipped his pen into the ink cellar and leaned over to mark a tick against Felix's name in a large ledger. *Thank you,* indeed. They're sending us schoolboys and infants, he thought.

4

Well, now, joined the army, have you?

Felix walked away from the barracks in a daze. Signed on for infantry and officer training at the royal and imperial barracks in Klagenfurt, commencing 20 November, 0800 hours. Pinned to the document, a travel warrant.

It was, by now, dusk. Street lamps sputtered alight. The air was chilly. He pulled up the collar on his jacket.

She can't have been much older than him, perhaps younger. She was walking up and down the pavement of the side street in and out of the pallid pools of light cast by the gas lamps, swinging a small reticule in her right hand. She looked bored, faraway, thinking, perhaps, of the village in Ruthenia that had tuned her accent.

Felix approached, fell into step beside her. A tram clanked by, illuminated like a fairground sideshow. The girl glanced quickly at him. Student? More money than sense and randy as hell.

'Miss?'

'How would you know?' She kept walking, the slow pace giving her hips a more pronounced and provocative swing.

'Excuse me.'

She stopped and turned to face him. 'What do you want?'

'What do you think?'

'You tell me.'

'How much?'

'You sure you can afford it?'

'I've just joined the army.'

'Taking boys are they, now?' She cocked her head.

'I can afford it.'

She moved in close to him. 'Well, well, well. Joined the army, have you? Brave soldier boy standing up straight all stiff and erect for king and country, are you?' She cupped her hand on the front of his trousers to feel him. 'So you are, so it is.'

'Bit of a send-off,' he said.

'Know the drill already, do you?'

'Short arm, as far as it goes.'

The laugh was like a gurgle. 'Oh, very *modest*. And just how far does it go?'

'That's for you to find out. Ready, cock, fire.'

'And die for your country?'

'Die for *your cunt*ry.'

'Well, now. That depends on how accurate the gunfire is, doesn't it? The quality of the ammunition…the aim and range.'

'I think you're right. A ranging shot?' He leaned forward and whispered: 'How much?'

She held up one hand with outspread fingers.

He crooked one arm round her waist and drew her to him.

She led him to a garret room at the top of a building a few doors along the street and lit a cheap paraffin candle, sheathed in a glass funnel. The reflection of its flame danced in the pane of the single grimy skylight. The remains of a coal fire glowed in the grate. Black and graying coals, crimson blisters of heat, lent a slight lingering warmth to the tiny room. Felix took out his wallet and laid the notes on a chair as she unbuttoned and stepped out of her dress. She took off her camisole and long knickers as he unbuttoned, kicked off his boots and hoisted his shirt. She lay back on the tousled bed, wetted her fingers with saliva and stroked her vagina. She noted the bald dome of his erection.

'Jewish?' she said.

'Someone has to be.'

He crouched over her. The springs sagged and squealed as they took her weight and then his. They sagged and squeaked in steady rhythm as he went into her, into her, into her, while she groaned and moaned as required. Advice from a tart who'd been long on the game. 'Makes no difference to you, ducky, but they think they're giving you a good time, getting their money's worth and the more you groan the quicker they come, gets it all over quicker.'

Suddenly he shivered all over, gasped and stopped and she groaned, too. The bed-springs let out a tired sough of apparent relief.

She wriggled his weight away and raised herself on one elbow.

'Where are you from?' he said.

She sat up. 'Listen,' she said. 'I'm paid to fuck not supply small talk.'

She rolled away, walked over to her undergarments tossed over the floor pulled them and then her dress on.

She buttoned herself in and watched him pulling on his clothes. When he was dressed again, she went to the door, opened it and said: 'You know the way,' and closed the door behind him. She folded the notes he'd left into her purse and put on her coat. She went out for supper, usual place, and maybe a call during the meal to pay for it.

5

Home

Felix walked out into the dusk. The buildings, grey with dust in the daytime, looked greyer still in the gloom. The gaslight from the street lamps was a sickly yellow. He could feel the girl's damp juice drying on him, her cheap scent clinging to his nostrils. One whore had said 'Strawberries,' when he finished and pulled out of her.

'Strawberries?'

'I always get the taste of fruit in my mouth when I come.'

'You came?'

'Not always.'

'Always strawberries?'

'It varies.'

In the army, he thought. I'm strawberries. Tart, fruit tart. What was he? Elated? Afraid? Dubious? Blank? Whatever it was, he'd handed himself over to Fate.

He turned the corner into Matzleindorferstraße and entered number 129. He walked up the three flights of stairs, opened and closed the door to apartment 15 and called out 'Mother, father, I'm home, it's me,' as if they needed reminding that they had an only son. He walked into the cramped room where his mother and father sat at the table, laid for dinner.

His father bristled. 'Where've you been? You know meal time. We're held up, food getting cold, us getting hungry, worn thin to the bone, as if you cared…'

Felix drew a deep breath. 'I had to go for a medical. It took ages.'

'Medical?'

His mother repeated: 'Medical? Why medical? You got an ailment, a condition, a disease?'

'No. A military doctor.'

'Military?' His father sat back in shock. 'What's with military?'

'I've been…' (he swallowed) 'conscripted.' He paused. 'Into the army.'

'Conscripted?' said his father.

His mother put one hand to her heart. 'The *army?*'

'Just like that you say it,' said his father. 'The army? Like it's nothing more than a hole in a sock.' His tone thickened. 'You burst in here, ages late, and suddenly you're in the army, pardon us for not knowing because you didn't tell us.'

'Yes,' said Felix. 'I should have…'

'Yes, you should have. And what are we supposed to say, your mother and me, as if we don't count in this?'

'Jakov, please, don't get angry.'

'I didn't get angry. I'm asking is what I'm doing. Perfectly reasonable and calm. So maybe, Felix, you'd like to give us some light on the subject.'

'The food is getting cold.'

'The food can wait, darling, till we get this cleared up, first. Well, boy?'

'I got my call-up papers last week. I had to report to the

40

Roßauer barracks this afternoon and…'

'Who cares the name of it, Roßauer barracks? You didn't think to tell us you got your call-up papers?'

'I didn't think that…'

'No. Exactly. Like usual. Where it's us concerned, your father and mother, you didn't think.'

No one spoke. Then his mother said: 'Felix, you're scaring me. What's it mean?'

'It's only a preliminary, mother.'

His father bridled. 'Don't shilly shally, boy. What's with "preliminary"? You *in* the army now, out of the blue, or not?'

His mother plucked at her apron. 'It's casserole and dumplings,' she said. 'The dumplings will go soggy,' she said, trying to smile.

'Never mind the food, now,' said her husband. 'We got to sort this thing out first. Felix, listen to me. All your education, all your books, you still can't talk plain and simple, say what you mean.'

'I've told you. I've been…' He hesitated on the untruth. '… conscripted.'

'Felix, Felix,' said his mother. 'Stop with all these words.'

'So what happened? They just haul you in off the street as you go past?'

'Why you?' said his mother. 'They haven't got enough other people *want* to go into the army?'

'Well…it's duty.'

'Oh, our son the heroic patriot,' said his father, planting both forearms on the table and shaking his head, tsking under his breath.

Felix's mother's face twisted in anguish. The newspaper

41

reports and headlines, fighting on various fronts, casualty lists, and now Felix was going to be part of it?

'Duty…' His father scoffed. 'You see how desperate they are?' He gave a sign of bafflement to the wider audience of the ceiling. 'Taking kids with spectacles who know nothing except from books? Such a state we're in. What are you going to do with a rifle? All your education, they should make you a book-keeper in a nice warm office, no bullets, everything paid for.'

'I've been ordered to report for basic officer training in Klagenfurt. A week from now.'

'Officer?'

'Yes.'

His father looked bug-eyed.

'Felix?' said his mother. 'Why you?'

'I suppose it was my turn. Working through the alphabet.'

'So it's *my* fault, oh pardon me, for having a name beginning B,' said his father.

His mother began to weep, mopping at her face with her handkerchief.

'Mother…please don't cry.'

'Don't tell your mother don't cry. She's upset.'

'The war may be over before I've even finished training.'

'So giving you training is some kind of charade and soon as they put you in uniform, name starts with B, abracadabra, peace is going to break out all over the place? You're not paying attention. The world caving in all round us, being blown to smithereens, and you…? Nose buried in your books like a giraffe, can't, *won't* see all round you what's going on?'

'You mean ostrich.'

'Ostrich? Don't tell me what I mean. What's from ostrich?'

'An ostrich buries its head in the sand…not a…'

His father erupted. 'Ostrich schmostrich. Who cares ostrich or giraffe? You have to pick at nits, pick pick pick, my son the clever one, the smart one, with all the right answers. So lucky I should've been to get the education we paid for for you, went without to pay for, scrimping, saving, no complaint, never. Nothing too good for you only nothing's good enough for you. Ostrich, giraffe, who cares? Camel. Porcupine.'

'Stop it. Stop it. Always ends in arguments between you. Oh, Felix, I can't bear it.' She sobbed.

Felix and his father fell silent and the silence shamed them.

Softly, Jakov said: 'We're upset. Things get said shouldn't be said. No more upset. That's it.' He reflected ' An officer?'

'Seems so, yes.'

Jakov turned to his wife and nodded. 'So now they're making Jews into officers, bright Jews. The education paying off, see, mother? Going to be an officer, our boy.' He pondered a moment and then said: 'Must be getting short of gentiles.'

'Jakov, Jakov, why do you always spoil it, say the wrong thing?'

'It's logical is what it is. You think they hand the pick of the jobs to Jews unless they're forced to? Of course not. Why should they care? Men get shot, blown up, simple: send more. You think they bother who? Walls crashing down round our ears, no work, no trade, no money, no nothing. Only place there's anything guaranteed these days is in the army – food, drink, bed, clothes, everything free, plus paid a wage. All right for some. Goyim, farshtinkener, who cares?'

'The food's all cold. I'll go and put it back on the stove.'

Her husband reached out to stroke her hand. 'That's it,

darling, we can eat and…we can sit together, family, that's it. Break bread and count blessings.'

She brought the casserole, steaming, to the table, served it out and Jakov spoke the grace:

'Bless this food, bless our being, bless our family, we beseech you in your everlasting mercy, O God. Amen.'

They began to eat in a tense silence.

Felix broke the spell. 'It's delicious, mother. Thank you.'

She leaned over and squeezed his hand.

Silence again, which Jakov attempted to jolly into conversation. 'Rosenberg has gone to the wall,' he said.

His wife glared at him. 'I said no more about war.'

'Wall. Wall. Not war. Wall. Bust, finished. Rosenberg. Who's next? Who knows? One goes, he takes others with him.'

'He owes you money?'

'Owed. Owed. What's to pay with? Sure he owed me money, everyone owes me money. I owe everyone else money. How does it end? Same way it always ends.'

6

The following day. Morning. Georg's apartment.

'Felix, dear silly misguided Felix, what *were* you thinking?'
    'How did you know?'
'Felix, please.'

Georg, in shirtsleeves, trousers, slippers, lounged in an armchair. Felix hovered in the doorway, wondering, now, why he'd come.

Georg snapped at him. 'Oh, for goodness' sake come in, help yourself to some coffee and sit down. You're making me fidgety.'

As Felix poured himself a cup of coffee, a young woman emerged from the bedroom. The jade silk dressing gown hung loosely open round her naked breasts. Ignoring the two men, she crossed to the table, removed a cigarette from a mahogany box and fitted it into the long ebony and amber holder she was holding like a wand. 'Georg, darling?' She folded her left arm under her right elbow. 'Do you run to a lighter?'

Georg reached into his pocket, produced a chrome-plated lighter and clicked it into flame. He didn't stir from the chair, hardly spared her a glance, as she leaned down. Smoke curled. Georg clicked the lighter shut and said: 'Claudia, Felix. Felix, Claudia.'

Felix's felt a sudden, idiotic embarrassment. He cleared his throat. 'Pleased to meet you.'

'Are you the one who's joined the army?' she said.

Felix didn't reply.

'Yes,' said Georg.

'How very stupid,' said Claudia. She inhaled deeply on her cigarette, tilted her head back and exhaled a thin stream of smoke. 'I'm going to have a bath,' she said. The voice was husky. 'Is there any coffee?'

'Felix?'

Felix fumbled at the lid of the coffee pot and peered inside. 'Half a cup?'

Claudia sniffed and looked at him, blank as a cat. 'I see *you've* got a cup.' She inhaled once more. The vapour exhaled over her upper lip - pout with smoke-screen. 'Do make some more, Georg. Darling,' she added, without warmth. She turned on a bare heel, wafted off to the bathroom, trailing a scent of sex and cologne, pulled the door to and switched on the bath taps.

Felix observed with mingled curiosity and envy. Style, definite style. Scary. No match for that, Felix, he thought. Out of your vocabulary.

'So, Felix, my dear, muddled friend…'

'Will you make the coffee? Shall I?'

'The coffee can wait. Will you please just tell me, what's this about enlisting? Toss me a cigarette, would you?'

'I don't know.'

'You must know. You must've had a reason.'

'None I can explain.'

'Goddamit, Felix. Reason is what you do, logic *ad absurdum*. What the fuck is going on? I'm very angry with you.'

'It seemed the right thing to do.' It sounded lame, even to him.

A click of the lighter, a freshet of smoke, a new tang of black Russian. 'It seemed the right...to join up? I don't understand you, Felix. Meek, inoffensive, buttoned up bookworm joining the army, own accord. It's daft. They're a bunch of nincompoops, Felix. You're better than that.'

Felix shrugged.

'My god. Why didn't you at least wait to be called up? We could have done something.'

'Such as what?'

'Listen to me. Call up papers can be made to disappear.'

'Well, it's irrelevant, now.' Felix poured the dregs of the coffee pot into his cup.

'Felix, listen. The official answer is: you get called up, you chug along obediently to the address in the papers where the nice people in the recruiting station – no effort spared to put you at your ease – write your name in the book and that's you, a name and a number, on record, in the army, whatever. The *sensible* answer, however, is to ask yourself *Do I wish to be in the army?*' He drew deep on the cigarette and exhaled. 'I'm taking it as an emphatic *no* to that?'

'Probably not. But in the circumstances...'

'In the circumstances be buggered. You make enquiries, friends of people who know people with influence.' He picked a filament of tobacco from his nether lip. 'Claudia, for instance... Her father's in the diplomatic, prime source of plum jobs for bright young intellectuals with a taste for classical learning and the niceties of language.'

Felix sat holding the empty cup and saucer as if it were a dead bird.

The taps in the bathroom were turned off and Claudia's

muffled voice whined: 'Georg, Georg, for god's sake...Where's my coffee? Please...Sweetheart?' She made the afterthought sound like a threat.

'She's very demanding, not that it isn't worth it. Tigress.' He got up, called out *Coming* and went into the kitchen. 'Well, Felix ?' he called out as he clattered with coffee tin, coffee pot, kettle, gas lighter.

'Well, what?'

Georg's head appeared round the frame of the door. 'Felix, don't be obtuse. I've got contacts, all the way up to the War Ministry, if need be. There are countless niches to be filled. Plenty of call for sharp intelligences, all crucial to the war effort, need I say? I'd have had you out of uniform before you'd even put it on. It may still not be too late, hm?'

He dodged back into the kitchen and continued from there. 'I'm only thinking of you, your interests. You're a scholar and a damned good one. Stick to what you're good at, brain not brawn.'

'Short-sighted, puny, Jewish. They'd probably post me to some remote garrison for administrative duties,' Felix called out.

'Oh, for god's sake. The army never sends you where you want to go or can be useful. They do the opposite. I told you. They're morons.'

He came back into the room with replenished pot and fresh cup and saucer. 'Take a look at the paper. Side of your chair. Front page, some flim flam about Serbian forces being pushed back by the gallant troops of our royal and imperial armies who mounted fierce resistance to concerted attacks but responded indomitably with determined counter-attacks, blah blah blah,

Serbian forces flung back to Belgrade. Strategic and moral victory. Of course. And, on the inside pages, some hint of the truth: the casualty figures. After the Court Circular. Somewhat in contradiction to the bombast of the headlines. One thing you can be sure of about a headline, that it's a misconstruction if not a downright lie.'

Claudia howled. 'Georg, you *monster*…I am desperately in need of coffee and a cigarette.'

'Excuse me a minute, the lady calls.' Georg liberated a cigarette from the box and ferried a cup of coffee into the bathroom. Felix heard the door shut and raised voices. Georg reappeared, nonchalant, squeezing his right shirt sleeve which was wet to the elbow. He sat down, thrust his legs full out and laid his arms along the arms of the chair.

'All you had to do was ask, Felix. I'm telling you for your own sake. Felix? Are you listening?'

Felix felt dispirited. 'Yes, I'm listening.'

'Well?'

'I don't know, Georg. It doesn't feel right.'

'What's right got to do with it? Is it *right* for young men to go off to a war not of their making to fight for some mindless point of factitious principle? Who, apart from our august leaders, gives a toss about Serbia, Russia, any of them? Who gives a toss about our so-called national dignity? Ha. The very idea. What dignity? The army which you have so inexplicably signed up to has been fighting the same battles for over a century and it's still peddling the absurd lie that it's bathed in glory when actually it's walked into a shit-pot of disaster over and over again and led by whom? By the stupid bastards who brokered the disaster all along. And they're *still* doing it.

'Why should any of us sacrifice himself on the altar of some imbecile's supposed national pride just because he tells us we ought to? *Right?* What's right about war, under any circumstances? Has no one ever learnt? As the man said, even God struggles in vain against stupidity.'

'Schiller.'

'Yes, Schiller.' He shouted in exasperation. 'Yes, Schiller and...Listen, Felix, I'm deadly serious about this because it is deadly serious. And it's not only about you. What about us?'

'What do you mean?'

'D'you think we – the others, me – could possibly be happy about what you've done?'

'No, of course not. How could anyone be *happy* about it?' He stood up.

'Except that you don't seem to be making any fuss about it which implies that you *are* happy about it.'

'There didn't seem to be any choice.'

'Dammit, Felix ...'

'Any honourable choice.'

'Honourable?' He laughed. 'Since when did honour have anything to do with it? Since when did honour have anything, anything at all, to do with rank bloody-minded arrogant folly? Madness, sheer bloody madness. Honour's graveyard, Felix, honour's graveyard. And there is *always* a choice, a perfectly decent choice.'

'Not a choice I feel able to make. Sorry.'

Georg sniffed and stubbed out the cigarette. He spoke with a growl. 'God, Felix, you can be a real prig, sometimes. I do love you but you are.'

There was a loud hammering at the front door. Georg got

up to answer it.

A woman's voice: 'Bloody hell. Have you heard about Felix?' It was Helga. 'Do you know where he is?' She ran into the room. 'Felix? Oh, for pity's sake, what've you done?'

Felix raised and lowered both arms as if on a thermal current of his own doubt. Helga stared at him, her features working, and suddenly she broke down in tears, her eyes raining anger.

'What in hell were you thinking of? You of all people.'

She turned away, cursing at him, at everything, then, sobbing, she flung her arms round him and clung to him. Felix faltered, then put his own arms round her, not knowing what else to do.

Claudia came in from the bathroom, her hair swagged in a turban of towel. 'Did I miss the party? What's going on?'

Helga pulled away from Felix and shouted: 'Read the fucking papers, you stupid cow. That's what's going on.' She made for the door, brushing past Georg. In the doorway stood Katharina. She'd evidently come with Helga. Felix hesitated. Helga was crying. Katharina expressionless. Helga turned her back to him.

'Helga, please. Don't go. Please. Not like this. It may be…' He touched her shoulder. She flinched and wheeled round.

'It may be *what?* The last time you see me? How dare you. How dare you be so fucking selfish. How dare you make it my fault.' He reached out. She shrank away from him. 'Don't touch me.'

She went into the hallway, Felix following. Katharina tried to catch hold of her. She shook her off. 'No, no, no,' she wailed and slammed the front door behind her.

Felix's head and chest buzzed with hot shame. 'Katharina?' he said.

She reached across and laid a hand on his sleeve, a gesture of spontaneous kindness which spoke, too, of her sorrow and incomprehension, not just about him and what he'd done but about what had been brought down on them all.

Felix looked back into the room. 'I think I should go, Georg...I'm sorry.'

'What's eating them?' said Claudia. Georg mouthed *shut up.* 'Well...?' she persisted. 'Bit histrionic.'

'I think,' said Felix, suddenly furious, 'I think that, since you plainly don't know what you're talking about, you should shut up.'

Claudia gave him a *what's eating you?* look.

Felix calmed himself. 'Georg I know you mean it kindly, more than kindly, and I wish I...but...well, there it is.' He turned away. Katharina said:'I'll walk with you.' The door clicked shut behind them.

Claudia began to rub at her damp hair with the towel. 'I seem to have said the wrong thing.'

'Oh, I don't know,' said Georg. 'They're only my friends, after all.'

'What's that supposed to mean?'

'What do you suppose it means?'

'And where does that leave me?'

'Right now, I don't know. I really don't know.'

He slumped into the chair and gazed into the empty grate. 'It's all starting to fall apart, isn't it?' He paused. 'No bad thing, maybe.'

Outside in the street, Katharina looped her arm in Felix's arm.

'Why?' she said as they walked towards the canal.

'Um…' he said, but all the reasons for what he'd done seemed to him all at once so trite. And was there more than one reason? Any reason at all? He could no longer tell. Georg was right. Reason had deserted him. Reason had disobeyed orders, quit its post and betrayed him.

'I suppose the why doesn't matter, now, though, does it?' she said.

They walked along the side of the canal.

'Do you remember?' she said.

'Remember?'

'That day. After the last exam.'

'Oh. Yes.' He paused. 'It seems an age ago.' He paused again. 'I seem to have done the wrong thing. I'm sorry. Do you remember…what we said? That sort of promise?'

'That we'd be true to ourselves?'

'Yes.' He stared at the pavement.

'And…?'

'It's…you see…I wonder…the thing is…I'm sorry, I'm not being very…'

'It's all right.' She squeezed his arm.

'It must sound so bloody stupid, hardly a reason at all, but the fact is, I've never *done* anything. I wanted to do something.'

She grunted. 'Hm. Well, you've certainly done something'. They walked on.

'You know how you threw the book into the water?' he said.

'Yes. What about it?'

' I thought…at the time, I thought: I wish I could do such a thing. That's what I thought. It was so carefree and boisterous and so enviable. I thought *I wish I had the freedom of spirit to do such a thing.*'

'Really? All I did was chuck away an exercise book I'd never use again. Goodbye and good riddance and off I go.'

'Yes. Exactly that. Goodbye and off I go.'

'And you don't think what you've done is something like that? It seems pretty without thought and lacking in reason to me. Very unlike you. Very…untidy.'

A man walked past, pushing a handcart, the hard tyres rumbled on the cobbles.

Felix said: 'Are you angry?'

'With you or with the whole bloody catastrophe?'

'Both. Either.'

'Not exactly. Disconcerted. Muddled.'

They turned away from the canal.

'Where are we going?' she said.

'Do you mean generally or specifically?' he said.

She laughed. 'Felix always and ever Felix.'

He didn't smile. 'I seem to have put myself out on a limb, though.' He stopped walking. 'It's so important to me.'

'What, what's important?' she said.

He gulped. 'Our friendship, us four. Our lovely friendship.'

'Yes? And…?'

'I don't want to lose it. I couldn't bear that. To lose you.'

She tugged at his sleeve. 'Why should you? Why should you think that?'

'Helga…'

'Helga loves you, that's why she's so upset. Nothing more.'

He didn't reply at once. In proportion as she is angry, he thought, so is her feeling true? If only it were so simple. 'You see,' he said, 'that time, when we were celebrating, and then that radio bulletin, I had a premonition that nothing would ever be the same again.'

'You think we didn't have that too? That I didn't? And look what's happened. All changed and nothing we can do about it.' She paused. 'Pretty desperate.'

He turned to her and smiled. 'As you say...'

Her smile in return was mischievous.

He assumed the hi-falutin tone of the lecture hall. 'Of what, then, in summary, can we be sure? We may say "true to ourselves" yet how can we know, nay, even guess at, what we will be, what will become of us and where we will be and who we will be in that indeterminate circumstance, the future? For that, in conclusion, is another question: *when?* And when, what? Do I make myself obscure?'

'Perfectly opaque. Come on, let's root out a coffee house and you can tell me in grisly detail exactly what it is you've done.'

'And you? What about you?'

'Life drawing. Anatomy. Bones and bods.'

'No, not that. *You.*'

'Well, now, I do have something of a confession to make, too.'

'Oh?'

'Yes. I've fallen in love...and been fallen in love with. Same person, luckily.'

'Oh, wonderful. That's a lovely thing. Anyone I know?'

She laughed.

'What's funny?'

'Oh, Felix, it's wonderfully funny. Can't you guess?'

'No.'

'Helga.'

He stopped dead. 'Helga? *Helga?*'

She looked full at him. Yes.'

'You mean…?'

'Don't be stuffy. Yes.' She giggled. 'Come on. You'll get used to it. I'm only just getting used to it myself.'

7

January 1915. K.u K. Kaserne, Olomouc, Moravia.

The weapons instructor, Sergeant Jessner, a grizzled, burly man of forty whose jutting chin looked as if it had slid down under its own weight and drawn his cheeks after it, glared at the line of recruits with the ingrained disdain of all old soldiers landed with a lumpen mass of subhuman incompetence and slovenliness, an offence to all things military. The army recruit is acknowledged to be the lowest form of human life. The recruit, they say, can crawl under a brick with a top hat on. Jessner would, of course, against all the odds, turn this latest rabble into trained men. For, like Pygmalion, Jessner could breathe life into inanimate matter, even these clods.

'There are two people,' he used to say, a favourite joke, 'two people only who can walk on their own across this parade ground: me and Jesus Christ, and he's only allowed to because I can't see him.'

He stood with a rifle at his side. 'Right,' he shouted at them, his mount Sinai of dignity towering over the arid wilderness of their insignificance. 'Pay close attention. What I tell you now,' he said, 'I'm not going to repeat, so peel your shell-like ears because what I say may, one day - and one day sooner rather than later - save your lives. Whether they're worth saving is another matter.'

He flicked up his rifle, caught it in his left hand and held it slantwise across his body, then swivelled round as if displaying a new-born child to family admirers.

'This Mannlicher 95 rifle delivers a killing force which travels at what we term a muzzle velocity of 500 metres per second. The rifle is zeroed at 410 metres, which is to say for effective range, whereat the bullet will do its work most efficiently. Which means that you may rely on hitting any target at a distance of 410 metres with the rifle set as it is. However, it not being the general inclination of the enemy to oblige the opposition by placing himself at a regulation distance of 410 metres, adjustment of the range may be needed. That is achieved through altering the adjustable lifting sight at the rear of your weapon by means of the gnurl. As here…'

He flipped up the sight, flipped it back, flipped it up again and indicated the gnurl.

And so it went on, day after day, more numbers, more counting, more adjustment by one species of gnurl or another: of time, of parade, of duty, of lecture, of physical fitness, of the rare gaps for relaxation.

Thus by marginal computations they girded their loins for the march to war. They marched out of the barracks and they marched back into the barracks, in all weathers, every step of the way, every beat of the time, made aware, intravenously aware, of the great military truism *In your barracks is Austria.*

Laden with kit and rifle, they felt their senses dulled by the monotonous muffled thump of army boots trudging in time – left, right, left, right – over compacted snow along a frozen road, the sunless sky sagging under an awning of pewter-grey, lint-like cloud. The day, bent only on decease, wore on. The men wore on. Their warm breath spurted in a glacial mist and evaporated. The pine forest to either side of the road formed a dark labyrinth of tree trunks. The NCOs marched alongside the column, chivvying as the mood took them. Magpies barked in dispute across the brittle forest air.

Kilometres out, kilometres back, every kilometre taking them nearer the moment when they would be tramping up to the front, marking off the final kilometres of whatever their doom might be. Blisters, back ache, boredom and marrow-deep fatigue shaping them into fighting men, the Emperor's men, the *Kaiserlich und Königlich*, imperial and royal, men.

In a dusty barracks hut Felix was writing a letter.

'Dear Father and Mother
I hope you're well....'

He sat on the edge of his bunk staring out of the window of the crowded room. Creaky iron beds, hard mattresses, draughty windows, chancy heat from a leaky stove, no privacy, bad food and little of it, an endless tedium of drill, regimental history (epic fiction), antiquated tactics that had been discredited over and over again, the protocols of military organisation, bugle calls for everything, from reveille, get out of bed, tired out, to lights out, go to bed, tired out. March to cookhouse, parade to chapel, and a medley of signals for engagement and manoeuvre in battle, all dinned in and committed to memory.

He resumed writing.

'We do everything by numbers, here. I've become quite

the accountant. We're identified individually by name but primarily by our service number, which always precedes the name. So I'm 19932 *Soldat* Breitenbach of first section, fourth platoon, second company, later to be swallowed up in the 101st regiment and whatever number of army swallows up that regiment. All these numbers add up to one…me. We also eat, drink and sleep by numbers on the clock face. We parade, march and halt by fours and so frequently do we do this that it's become the permanent rhythm of my breathing – 1, 2, 3, 4, breathe in, 1, 2, 3, 4 breathe out. I imagine I snore in the same time signature.'

All around him buzzed the chatter of the other recruits, one or two cleaning their Mannlicher M95 rifles – *the infantry rifle is not only your weapon it is your friend,* the *Manual of Instruction* told them, *treat it well and it will treat you well, treat it badly and it will fail you and should it fail you, you will have failed yourself, your comrades, your superior officers, the army and the emperor.*

Others were playing cards, some back from fatigues huddled at the feeble stove, warming frozen fingers, others tidying lockers, polishing boots, dozing, one or two reading…an empress had once said that she didn't care what her soldiers read, so long as they fought like lions.

'And there's the question of identification. We're like birds marked out by an entire palette of different colours worn as regimental flashes, patches and buttons, nine colours in all, and twenty-eight shades. Ten shades of red, two of brown, three of yellow, six of green, five blues but only one white and one black. An assortment of these colours in different combinations with buttons and patches make a sort of chart which gives the identity of the various units and woe betide us if we muddle them.

'I'm in pretty good spirits. I've been detailed for officer training at the Kaserne in Klagenfurt quite soon.

'I send my love. Your son, Felix.'

As he folded the sheets of paper and put them in an envelope, a fat, dark-jowled farm-boy, nineteen years old, from Swabia, called out across the barrack room:

'Breitenbach has written a love letter.'

Felix ignored him.

'Given her one yet, eh, city boy?'

Felix licked the envelope flap and closed it.

'You should shag her on straw in a barn – that way she gets a prick both sides.' He guffawed.

Felix made for the door but the Swabian lumbered off his bed and cut him off. 'Give us a read, then.' He grabbed for the envelope. Felix looked him square in the eye. 'Actually, it's to my parents.'

The man made a lahdy-bloody-dah face and, mimicking Felix's Viennese accent poorly, said: 'Ooooh. Mummy's precious little bundle. Feeling homesick, are we?'

Another voice intervened: 'Oh, for god's sake, shut up. Leave the sad little Jew alone.'

The door crashed open. The Corporal stood on the threshold. 'Room inspection. Stand by your beds.'

And so it went on, the old and new testaments of duty: *Duty is your god, a god who tolerates no blasphemy.*

And then it was their last day. On the vast drill square, a line of their officers in front of them, Felix and the other men swore the oath of allegiance:

'I swear by Almighty God that I will be faithful and true to His Majesty Franz Josef, imperial and royal monarch of Austria-Hungary, to his heirs and successors, and that I will, as in duty bound, honestly defend His Majesty, in Person, Crown and Dignity against all enemies, and will obey the orders of His Majesty and of the generals and officers set over me above all other claims on my life and liberty. So help me God.'

The regimental chaplain blessed them in Latin and sprinkled holy water over them. The battalion band played the Radetsky March, the sacred hymn of the Austro-Hungarian army, as they paraded past the podium, where the depot commander took the salute. And they were soldiers. They marched off the square and on to death or glory, for it had ever been so.

8

Three months later, officer training depot, Klagenfurt.

Felix and his classmates sat at wooden, schoolroom desks, as Captain Grüner concluded his lecture on the precepts of their new existence.

'Gentlemen, as von Clausewitz in his *On War* writes, above all, be decisive. Especially in the fog of war, the impetus to action must be clear-sighted and prompt. Better to act and make a mistake than to let the moment pass at the cost of worse consequence.'

He paused and looked round the room. 'And remember: everything in war is simple, but, in war, even the simplest thing becomes difficult. Good luck to you all and godspeed.'

The new officers of the imperial and royal army stood up and cheered, Felix, for one, wondering what they were to make of *Everything in war is simple, but, in war, even the simplest thing becomes difficult...*

The four days home leave he was permitted before joining the unit to which he'd been assigned, on the Italian Front, were sticky. He and his parents managed a sort of truce by avoiding the issue of his departure, all too pressing. Conversation at the family meal was stilted, prayers in the synagogue sharpened the apprehension, a walk into town to show off Felix's uniform was an embarrassment to him, a fussy pride to them.

His mother veered from incipient tears to a struggle for cheerfulness. How agonizing it was going to be to wave good-bye to him, her son, knowing that she might lose him forever, on some faraway patch of ground churned to ruin by the horrors of war.

And Jakov, caught between envy of his son and the bellig-erence of his own nature, would not, could not, admit to weakness of any kind. Jakov Breitenbach, businessman of this Burg, bankrupt or not, would survive, just to spite them all.

The leave-taking itself was a tragicomic charade of brave faces, attempts at light-heartedness, awkward pauses, untenable promises and fake good cheer.

Felix boarded the crowded troop train heading south, his relief laden with guilt. Crammed into the carriage with other junior officers, enjoying the privilege of a seat, he reflected on what was happening to him. Suddenly time had stopped. They were all the same age, now, the same distance away from death.

He watched the city recede through the grimy window of the carriage as the train steamed slowly out of the station and on through the outer suburbs of Vienna. The hinterland of all that had been familiar to him for so very long, now become strange and disconnected. He'd crossed a threshold into an abstracted Homeland, a mythic version of Austria, to defend it, or else to irrigate it with his blood.

He'd purposely seen none of his friends. The sorrow that would have thrown up was unimaginable, he could not even think of it.

And now, in a cocoon of his own musing, dumb and unde-monstrative, he wondered at how raucous they'd been, the enlisted men on the train, waving to the girls on the platform waving back at them, all smiles, a few tears, jubilant hysteria. Men scarcely more than boys, they'd strutted away from the recruiting stations, grinning like circus loons, with a ticket in their hatband: US THEY'VE GOT. For who'd not ache to be part of the great adventure? It was their destiny. Not their fate. God had bestowed on them the chance of a lifetime and they'd seized it with gratitude and pride. Here, in this great moment, was their manhood singled out and summoned to the flag.

Farewell, Vienna, goodbye you girls of Vienna, wait for us and we'll be home again soon, hot and ready for you, never fear. Wait for us.

Twelve weeks later, the newly gazetted Lieutenant Breitenbach in parade dress: blue tunic with stand-up collar, a yellow and black sash with fixings for the ceremonial parade sword, grey slacks, glossy black pull-on boots, peaked black shako with the silver badge - Imperial double eagle surmounted by moon disc and a fan of ostrich feathers - reported to the office of the 101st regiment's adjutant at divisional headquarters at Görz, on the Slovenian border with the Venezia region of north-east Italy.

The adjutant, Captain von Benda, belonged to an aristocratic elite which scorned to acknowledge the existence of the parvenus who'd been drummed into the hallowed ranks of the army. They themselves had been born to status, influence, power, and were impervious to mental clutter. Exhibition of emotion was for the vulgar. Faced with a hopeless situation, the vulgar will panic, lose control, funk, while the gentleman remains nerveless. Whatever the situation, the gentleman will get by, see things through. For the gentleman is not burdened with that bitter impediment to clarity in such a predicament: imagination.

The adjutant waved Felix to wait and continued his study of a bulging dossier. For some ten minutes, he turned page after page, making occasional marginal notes, ignoring the man standing at attention in front of his desk. He finished scanning the last page, arranged the papers into a neat pile which he put back into the folder and the folder into a drawer of his desk. He screwed the cap back on his fountain pen and looked up.

'Profound apologies for keeping you waiting, Lieutenant. You are…?'

'Lieutenant Breitenbach reporting for duty, sir.'

Von Benda leaned back in his swivel chair. 'Ah, Breitenbach.' He reached forward for a docket in his in-tray, read down the page and looked up again. 'Gazetted…13 May, is that it?'

'Yes, sir.' He remained at attention.

'Lieutenant,' the captain said. 'Do stand at ease. This isn't a court martial.' Felix removed his shako and tucked it under his left arm.

'Welcome to Görz.' Von Benda plucked another slim file from his in-tray and consulted the top page of the contents. 'Let's see….aha.' He spoke to Felix over the top of the page. 'And how did you find Klagenfurt?'

'Sir?'

'This isn't an interrogation, Lieutenant. I wonder how you enjoyed, or not, your time in Klagenfurt. Hm?'

'Yes, sir. I did, sir. Enjoy it, sir. Thank you.'

'You passed, anyway. Rather well in map-reading and tactical theory, not so well in gymnastics. Moderate in weapon drill. Top marks in regimental history. You were told the results, I take it?'

'No, sir.'

'Remiss of them.' He set the file aside and, leaning back in his chair once more, said: 'Can you see without your glasses?'

'See, sir?'

'It's a simple enough question. Can you see without your glasses?'

'Not very well, sir. I'm short-sighted.'

'Don't function so well in rain, then. What languages do you have?'

'Latin and Greek, sir, and...'

'Latin and Greek. I see. Bang up to date on military manoeuvres, then, Julius Caesar and all that.' He leaned forward. '*Useful* languages, I mean. Languages that people speak.'

'Some French, from school, sir.'

'French. Well, it's not likely that that will come in, not down here at any rate, but who can tell? No Russian? No Czech? Hungarian?'

'I'm afraid not, sir.'

'You haven't travelled much.'

'No, sir, Vienna and the environs.'

'And Klagenfurt, of course.'

'Oh...' Felix said, 'Klagenfurt, yes, sir. And Olomouc, infantry training.'

'You mean Olmütz, surely? Or is Olomouc the extent of your grasp of Czech?'

'Yes, sir, I suppose it is.'

Von Benda stared at him for a while. The ice-blue eyes did not blink. 'Are you proud to be an officer in the imperial and royal Austro-Hungarian army, Lieutenant?'

'Yes, sir, very proud.'

'You volunteered? Why?'

'I felt it right, sir. In the circumstances.' He breathed in. 'The nation under threat, sir.'

'There's no need to over-egg it. We have a fine tradition, Lieutenant, and whatever else you do when you're wearing this uniform, we expect you to uphold that tradition. The great victories, Leipzig, Solferino…a lot to live up to.'

'Yes, sir.' Felix coughed nervously. Calling Solferino any kind of Austrian victory was stretching the facts more than somewhat.

'We'll find out, won't we? And I hope for your sake, as well as ours, that we find out before it's too late to change our minds about you.' He called out. 'Sergeant?'

The door to the office opened and a man with three stars on his braided collar tabs marched in, stamped to attention alongside Felix and saluted.

'At ease, sergeant. Lieutenant Breitenbach, Master Sergeant Jaschke, Sergeant Jaschke, Lieutenant Breitenbach, your new platoon commander.'

'Yes, sir. Thankyou, sir.' The sergeant's eyes, muscles, limbs, hands were locked, immobile.

'Lieutenant Breitenbach has just arrived from the imperial barracks training depot in Klagenfurt.' He made it sound like a discouraging appraisal of what they might expect from him. 'You'll show him to his quarters, point out the officers' mess, quartermaster's stores and so on, acquaint him with regimental procedure here, daily timetable, training schedules etc introduce him to the men of his command…'

'Yes, sir.' Jaschke came once more to attention, saluted made for the door and opened it.

'Oh, Breitenbach, one thing…' said the adjutant.

'Yes, sir?'

'You may find it prudent to keep a short length of string handy.'

'String, sir?'

'To secure your spectacles. When you're running, for example. We don't want them falling off, now, do we?'

9

The men under your command

Jaschke stopped outside a wooden hut the size of a railway carriage, opened the door, walked into a dingy vestibule and pushed open an internal door to reveal what might be a square boxroom, furnished with a table and a chair. He flicked a switch. A single dusty light bulb suspended over the table cast a bilious glow.

On one wall, a chart gave a hierarchical diagram of the battalion's units, combatant and auxiliary. Next to it, another chart, headed *Regimental Orders*, listed duties for the day and was, each day, updated.

'Your office, sir.'

Felix walked in and peered out of the grimy window at a narrow throughfare, on its far side, the main barrack block. He turned to face Jaschke.

'Do stand at ease, sergeant. First, the men under my command.'

Jaschke removed his cap and wiped his brow.

'Cap on when you're addressing an officer,' said Felix, immediately thinking *how pompous I must sound…it's the strangeness of all this.*

'Sir…' said Jaschke, replacing his cap. 'Sir, Fourth Platoon is made up of fifteen Austrians, six Magyars, two each Ruthenian,

Czech, Bohemian, thirteen Poles, four Bosnians, five Croats – one of which, infantryman Bogdan, is your orderly, sir – plus one Serb and one Italian. The list of names on the sheet on your table, sir. In alphabetical order, sir. By name rather than nationality. Nationality marked at the side, sir.'

Felix scanned the page.

'And who is our interpreter?'

'Corporal Schiefner, sir. Native German, speaks German, obviously, also Slovak and some Hungarian.'

'Some Hungarian?'

'More of a smattering, sir. Notoriously hard language, Hungarian, sir. But adequate, sir. He gets by. I myself have Polish and Russian, sir.'

'Adequate?'

'More like fluent, sir.' He smirked.

'And where did you acquire this fluency in Russian and Polish?'

'In the service, sir. Russian at a language course, special assignment, being as how I'd shown a flair, sir. Plus, I'm married to a Polish lady. Best way to learn, that, sir.' He ventured a faint leer and an involuntary wink. Felix did not react. The leer dissolved.

'Am I to understand that although we have both Croatian and Italian personnel, we have no way of communicating with them, other than through basic German?'

'Pesenti is from the Trentino, sir. On our side, that is, so he's got fluent German. '

'On our side? I should hope he is.'

'I meant of the Trentino, sir. The German side of the Trentino.'

'Does he speak any Italian?'

'Possibly, sir, enough to…'

'…get by. I see.' Felix looked down at the list of names. 'I take it that the other members of the platoon are also on our side?'

Jaschke's brow wrinkled. 'Sir?'

Felix looked up.

'Ah, yes sir, I see what you mean. Most amusing, sir. The Poles, by and large, have workable German, also some of the Slovaks. The Magyars…' He paused. 'The Magyars by and large are reluctant to answer to anything except Hungarian.'

'What?'

'The Magyars, sir. Stick to Hungarian.'

'You mean they haven't learnt the basic commands in German?'

'They've learnt them, only…it's a question of national pride with them, sir. They're rather defensive on the subject.'

'Defensive? Goddammit, this is an army preparing to go to war not a…a school gymkhana.'

'Yes, sir.' Jaschke once more evoked the implacable effigy.

'They'll just have to learn to accommodate their sensitivities won't they?'

'Yes, sir.' He shifted as if he had an itch. New officer. Green as cabbage. Knows less than the square root of fuck-all. Thinks he can change things by snapping his fingers and giving an order. Everyone knew about the Hungarians. How could he not know about the Hungarians? 'The thing is, sir,' he said, ' it's a bit of a longstanding thing, sir. Mists of time, and all that …they're different, sir.'

'*Different?*'

'Doesn't affect the way they fight. Deserved reputation for being a bit of a handful. Demons for a battle, sir. And loyal. Never any doubts about that, sir. Except that veez arh vee the Austro-Hungarian Army, sir, they stress the *Hungarian* part of the army over the Austrian.'

'We'll see about that.'

'Yes, sir.' Of course we will, he thought. You turn up, first day, and magic the stubbornest bastards in the entire army into pussy cats overnight. Why hadn't anyone thought of it before? All it took was to say: *Right, you Hungarians, party's over, you've had your time, so, listen up - this is how it's going to be in future: Shut it.*

'Very well.' Felix placed both hands on the table. 'Parade the men tomorrow morning at 0700 hours. Field marching order, packs, helmets and rifles. Full waterbottles.'

'Sir?'

'Something you don't understand?'

'No, sir. That is, yes sir, absolutely. 0700 hours, platoon on parade, field marching order, packs, helmets and rifles, full waterbottles.' He paused added 'Sir,' then: 'If I may speak, sir.'

'What is it?'

'If I may suggest, with the greatest respect, sir...'

'Jaschke, don't prevaricate. Spit it out.'

'Sir. Only that it might be more to your advantage if you was not to meet the men for the first time on what sounds like a punishment parade, sir, even if that's not what you intended.' He stared at the window above Felix's head.

'And what do you propose?'

'Parade after breakfast, sir. When they've got full stomachs, sir.'

Felix stood up, consulted the list of regimental orders on the wall. 'Breakfast is at 0800 hours.'

Jaschke remained impassive. 'Yes, sir.'

'In that case, they can work up an appetite. 0700 hours.'

Jaschke sucked in his cheeks. 'Sir.'

'Very well, sergeant. That'll be all.'

'Yes, sir.' He saluted, about-turned and marched out of the office.

Next morning, Felix surveyed them, the forty men of B Platoon for whose lives and well-being he was responsible: the new men who'd just joined, others who'd been drafted from different units depleted in combat, the regulars who'd signed up long before the war.

The new men, him included, had undergone a transformation that none of them could ever have foreseen or prepared for. Men living ordinary, workaday lives as tradesmen, farm and building labourers, clerks, shop assistants, waiters, barmen, cooks, tram drivers, railway workers, drovers, market traders, bank tellers, schoolteachers, ticket collectors, postmen, valets, transmogrified into trained killers.

What would they say, if they survived to go home at the end of the war? Would they say *I killed a lot of men?* Would they say it with pride, with regret, with horror, with disbelief? *Was that me?* they might ask and *Who was I then?*

The numbers and names on a page, an arithmetic of 'platoon strength', stood there in bold actuality in front of him. Some of them almost certainly destined to become a very different sort of statistic as casualties of war.

They would look to him to keep a cool head in the yet

ungauged terrors of battle, him a veteran of no worse violence than heated argument. Violence was now to be the norm of their existence. Violence calculated to prolong their existence.

He scanned the faces in front of him, then began to read out the names in alphabetical order on the muster list, glancing upwards to see who responded.

'Lind?'

'Sir.

Lind was a short, big-chested man with a bushy moustache, florid complexion, deep-set eyes.

'Where are you from, Lind?'

'Hopfgarten, sir. East Tirol.'

'And what do you do in Hopfgarten?'

'Was, am, hope to be again, sir, bar tender. Wife and three children, sir.'

Hope to be again, thought Felix. He looked at the next name. *Płaschiński.* He called out: '*Plashinskee.*'

There was no response. Jaschke, standing at his side, leaned over and whispered 'Pwash-chee-yn-ski, sir'.

'Pwashchinski?' he whispered in his turn.

'Pwash-chee-*yn*-ski.'

'Pwash-chee-yn-ski?'

'Yes, sir.'

Felix called out 'Płaschiński?'

A tallish, swarthy man with thick brown eyebrows and heavy lips, answered from the third rank.

'Sir. From Upper Silesia, moved to Lower Silesia when I was a nipper. Coalminer, sir.'

'Coalminer? You didn't think to take your skills to the Sappers?'

'No, sir. Glad to be topside, sir, out in the fresh air.'

And so he proceeded to the bottom of the page.

On a route march, three weeks later, Felix marched alongside them and listened to the banter they used to leaven the monotony of the hours of tramping out to nowhere and back to the somewhere they'd started from.

'Who are you?' yelled the caller.

'Valiant Austrian soldiers,' yelled the rest.

The Magyars supplemented that with 'Hungarian soldiers' to routine sarcastic jeers from the others.

'Where are you going?'

'To slaughter the Lombard weasel, to slay the Venetian fox, to butcher the Piedmontese pig, each and every one.'

'And why are you going to war, to war, and why are you going to WAR?'

'Because Italy tries to shake off the yoke, because Italy tries to leave the fold, to leave the fold of brotherhood…'

'Some hopes,' interpolated one wag.

They continued, regardless: '…because the Italian devil wants to keep his macaroni to himself, because the Italian devil knows how hungry we are, how famished.'

'And what if you are slaughtered, then?'

'We'll not be hungry any more.'

'And what if you're taken prisoner?'

'We'll be given bread, fresh bread.'

'And if you win a victory?'

'We'll enter the city and eat macaroni till we can eat no more, no more, we'll drink good wine and we'll get gold.'

'And where is your homeland?'

'Anywhere we can eat.'

At the end of the litany, the ritual execration *Fuck the Eyeties* and hoots of laughter followed by a bonhomie of low chuckle and murmur and the clump clump, clump of boots marching.

Felix spoke to Jaschke. 'Very well, Sergeant. Final kilometre to barracks. Silence in the ranks, march at attention,.'

'Sir.' He gave the order. The men braced and marched as if they were at a review. They felt the stirring of pride, that vital juice of their manhood.

10

21 September 1915. Görz. Divisional Headquarters, 57th Infantry Division commanded by Major-general Goiginger.

Colonel Brückner entered the operations room to address his regimental battalion and company officers. They all stood. Brückner walked across to the desk at the front and picked up a long, map pointer. On the end wall, behind him, hung a large map of the territories lining the Austrian-Italian border.

'Gentlemen, do sit down.' He contemplated the map for a few moments, then turned.

'Much depends on you. I'm sure that you're determined to perform your job with that distinction to which the men of the imperial and royal army have always aspired and for which the men under my command are known.'

He regarded the map once more and, punctuating his discourse by jabbing at the map with the pointer, summarised.

'The Italian Front. A six hundred kilometre chain of mountains from the Tirol *here* to the Julian Alps *here* forms a natural defensive barrier, our ramparts, if you will. They keep the Italians in Italy and bar them from the heartland of the Empire.'

He paused and scanned the room.

'It's paramount that Görz should remain in our possession. It's a crucial base of our operations in this sector.

'The Isonzo valley makes a corridor through the Alpine wall between two high plateaux, the Bainsizza *here* and the Corso *here*.' He plonked the pointer in front of him, butt end on the floor, like a billiard cue.

'The Corso has been described as a howling wilderness of stones sharp as knives. Not only inhospitable, therefore, but singularly bad terrain for a scrap.

'The flat basin west of the Isonzo and those flanking plateaux are our responsibility, gentlemen. Here is the area covered by our Third Army, 57th Infantry Division. On our southern flank, the 94th Infantry Division under Lieutenant-fieldmarshal Kuczera. To the north, *here*, the 93rd Infantry Division commanded by Brigadier General von Boog.

'Facing us, a considerable number of Italian divisions, infantry and motorized.

'You know what you have to do. Every small success adds to the momentum towards a large success and eventual victory. That is all, gentlemen. We move out tomorrow.'

An orderly came across, took the pointer and handed Brückner a flimsy sheet of paper. The colonel read: 'By order of Major-general Goiginger, commander 57th division, attention all platoon commanders, 4th Battalion. Platoons will parade in marching order at 1600 hours, 22 September, prior to departure to main marshalling zone at Görz railway depot. Iron rations and ammunition to be issued, Quartermaster's Store, from 1300h, platoons by number. Following morning muster, men to be permitted free time.'

He folded the page and looked round the room. 'Very well, gentlemen. There you have it. Good fortune go with you. The Emperor.'

They stood, sang out in unison: *The Emperor.*
They dispersed.

11

22 September, afternoon and evening.

Felix tightened the straps on his field pack and looked round the room. Everything, he thought, had become temporary. On the side table stood an open cardboard box containing the books, sketch pad and pencils, he couldn't take with him. The box, addressed to his parents, also contained a note, undated and without address.

> My dear Mother and Father. I'm in good spirits. I'm not allowed to say anything more. I think of you. Your loving, affectionate son, Felix.

He picked up the one book he was taking, a favourite volume of Goethe's poems. He opened it to *Prometheus*. Prometheus, who stole fire from heaven as a gift to mankind, and was punished for it by the Olympian gods, chides them:

> I should honour you? And why?
> Did you ease my pain in my grief?
> Did you dry my tears in my distress?
> Was I not forged into human shape
> By all-conquering Time and eternal Destiny,
> To which I must bow, as also must you?

That's it, they all bowed to Time and Destiny, and, now,

Time and Destiny took on a much more sinister aspect. Felix stowed the book in the haversack at his side, put on his pack, shouldered his rifle, hooked the helmet strap over its barrel, picked up the box and left without closing the door on a room empty of him as he was of it.

He deposited the box with the Despatch Section clerk at the headquarters building and made his way across to the parade ground. It was 1557 hours.

As he approached, Jaschke called the men to attention.

'Officer on parade, atten...SHUN.' A sharp smack of boot heels on the hard surface of the drill square. Jaschke wheeled round and saluted.

'Platoon present and correct, sir.'

Felix returned the salute. 'Stand the men at ease, Sergeant.'

Felix addressed them. 'I know you've all been chomping with impatience to see action. Well, now we're going into action. We proceed from here to the marshalling zone from where we go on to the Front, tonight. You probably face a long march, so brace up.'

Some of them affected a groan. Jaschke hissed for silence.

Felix continued.

'Whatever happens from now on, make no mistake, you will have to call on everything you've learnt in training. You'll need fortitude, resolution and courage. The consequences of what each man does affects us all. Very well, sergeant, let's get moving.'

'Sir. Platoon...platoon...SHUN. To the right...right... TURN. In column of fours, by the left, forward...MARCH.'

Outside the railway depot, on the broad concrete apron

generally used for unloading trucks and stacking supplies and matériel, they joined other elements of the battalion to await their turn for the off. So much of their life in the army had been spent waiting, even as they tramped the roads, cleaned their weapons, queued for food, forever waiting, practising, preparing. It had been a pretend sort of existence. Now, at last, the real thing, and they brooded on it, still waiting. They lounged on the ground, talked or did not talk, dozed.

The day darkened and, with it, the sky. A swell of rat grey cloud blustered in from the Gulf of Trieste and swarmed in the sky over the town. The lamp standards round the perimeter of the yard blinked alight. The whole area resembled a prison compound. It began to rain. Men cursed, unrolled the heavy waterproof capes from the bundle under their pack, heaved them on and squatted like miniature tents.

At 1930 hours, a young soldier carrying a clip board walked up to Felix.

'Sir? Regimental orderly Fritsch, sir, 3rd Army Divisional Headquarters Staff. If you'd confirm your name and unit, please, sir.'

'Lieutenant Breitenbach, B Platoon, 4th Battalion, for the Monte Santo sector.'

Fritsch plied torchlight at the talc-covered document on the board. 'Monte Santo. You have a rendezvous with the liaison officer some distance north of town, sir. I'll set you on your way, sir.'

The platoon formed up and they marched out of Görz, the road awash with rain, loose grit, mud, along the east bank of the Isonzo river, its southbound stream growing ever wider as it neared its rendezvous with the waters of the Adriatic.

From lines strung overhead, hung long, thin metal wafers no more than a metre apart, to camouflage troop movements from observers on high ground overlooking the valley.

At a crossroads on the outskirts of town, Fritsch said: 'If you'd stop the men here, sir…'

Felix called out: 'Platoon… HALT.'

'The rendezvous point is 3.7 kilometres along this road, sir,' said Fritsch. 'The Lieutenant-colonel liaison officer will be waiting for you there.'

They marched on, rifles upended against the rain, Felix at the head of the column, the interpreter at his side, Jaschke at the rear, the corporal on one flank. The ribbon of wet, earthen road glistened in the pallid light of a moon wreathed in thin cloud. Rain trickled in under the collars of their capes. Damp seeped into their boots. One man had a hacking cough – he'd reported to the sickbay that morning complaining of a recurrent lung infection, come back, couldn't shake it off, had had to be hospitalised before…The medic officer gave him some pink pills and told him to report for duty.

Darkness, intermittent moonlight and constant rain swept over them for over an hour before a torch ahead of the column flashed several times and a voice called out: 'Halt and identify'.

'B Platoon, 4th Battalion, 57th Division, Lieutenant Breitenbach. For Monte Santo sector.'

A sentry approached. 'Come with me, sir.'

He led Felix to the liaison post, a small canvas booth at the side of the road. Felix could just discern the vague silhouette of a man, standing in the dry shelter of its doorway. The glowing end of a cigar flared and Felix caught the aroma of expensive tobacco.

The sentry stopped and said: 'Platoon for Monte Santo sector, sir.'

'Thankyou, corporal. You are…?' said the Lieutenant-colonel in a distinctive languid, patrician drawl. His face was obscured, his body a statue of shadow.

'Lieutenant Breitenbach, sir.'

The cigar flared again. 'A filthy night. Are you wet through?'

'Not quite, sir.'

A pause. 'Have you seen action before, Lieutenant?'

'No, sir.'

The cigar flared again. 'You're facing rather a baptism of fire, then. You've been briefed, you know what you have to do?'

'Yes, sir. To make contact with other units of our forces already in position, on the line of the Isonzo. Before daybreak, if possible.'

'There's no *if* about it, Lieutenant. That's what you've been told to do and that's what you must do. Is that perfectly clear?'

'Yes, sir.' Felix tugged out the map case from under his cape and held it under the light of the lantern, the transparent water-proof cover yellowing with age,. The officer nodded. He paused to draw on the cigar. 'Follow this road to a left hand junction at around five kilometres. The turn is clearly indicated by a white marker board. From there you proceed two kilometres or so north-north-west, over the ridge of Monte Santo, and down to reinforce our units already in position. I cannot stress too strongly how vital it is that you make that contact with them as swiftly as is humanly possible.

'We cannot afford to leave a breach in our defensive line, Lieutenant. You are the plug in that breach. Do you understand?'

'Yes, sir.'

A pause. The aroma of the cigar, the stale smell of rain and sodden earth, the impenetrable darkness.

'We're expecting a lot of you but that's why you're here. A vital link in the chain.'

'Sir.'

'Good luck.'

'Thank you sir.' Rain spattered on the canvas tilt like gravel on glass, sounding, incongruously, like applause. Felix turned and went back to the platoon. 'Sergeant Jaschke?'

He wiped his glasses again. Jaschke presented himself.

'Off we go, sergeant.'

12

The night march

They'd been marching for about an hour when the rain stopped, the sky cleared and a brilliant, gibbous moon broke through to reveal higher ground ahead of them. A short way on they came to the marker board. A track branched to the left. Felix called halt.

'Remove your capes. Listen to me. We'll be crossing broken ground. It's essential that you maintain formation. As soon as we reach the high ground we'll be exposed so we need to get off the ridge ith the utmost despatch. A bullet in the breech. Safety catches on. Runner, Corporal Habe, I want you both with me. From here on, no talking. Quiet as you can.'

They moved onto the lower slope in orderly formation. Picking their way up the steep hillside, the column elongated as the slower among them struggled to keep pace. Jaschke, bringing up the rear, chivvied the stragglers on.

They stumbled through clumps of vegetation, tripped over boulders, ruts and hummocks of the uneven ground. Men cursed. Felix and Jaschke hissed *quiet* at them. A man fell over with a loud clatter of equipment, water bottle, helmet. Jaschke heaved him back on his feet. He'd sprained his ankle. He hobbled on.

They broached the top of the slope onto the skyline, began to make their way across the bare summit of the ridge, in the moon's limelight, to where the ground began to fall away. They could make out a sparse scattering of stunted trees, some hundred metres down the far slope.

Felix gestured right and left with a circling sweep of his arm. The men fanned out to form a ragged line for the advance.

Suddenly, rifle fire broke out from across the valley. Spurts of muzzle flame pierced the blackness below them, like the wink of glow-worms. Seconds later, a machine gun opened up, then another and a third.

They hit the ground, too late for seven of the men who toppled over, caught in the opening fusillade. A drifting cloud began to extinguish the moon. In the new darkness, a flare fizzed up into the sky and burst in a dazzle of ghostly white. They were in full view on the open ground.

A harsh staccato of bullets jabbered overhead. Felix peered at the open ground in front of them. It was dotted with stunted shrubs, clumps of rock, not much cover, but some. As the light of the flare died, he called out: 'Head downhill by stages. Two volleys of rapid fire, then run like hell for any sort of cover. Wait for my order. Hear me: in three, rapid fire. One, two, three, fire.'

The rifles opened up, two ragged volleys, Felix cried out: 'On the double, go.'

In the first dash, three more men went down, four, five. Felix dropped behind a small bush and looked round as others flopped to the ground. When they were all in, he called out again: 'Rapid fire, two volleys, ready: fire.'

The rifles spoke again, the men raced forward, hunched

over, lurching under the weight of their packs. The ground was beginning to flatten out, now. Another flare soared into the night and blossomed into a spectral glow. The machine guns opened up again. Felix saw another three men go down as the rest blundered into the sparse shelter. Felix looked back up the slope. There was no one moving. He could see the black shapes of the men who'd been shot, lying motionless. Dead? Wounded?

The machine guns stopped. They waited for them to open up again. Nothing. In the fraught silence, Felix whispered: 'Sergeant Jaschke? Jaschke?'

A tremulous voice answered in Polish.

'Wydaje me się, że nie żyje, panie poruczniku.'

'What? What did you say?'

'Wydaje me się, że nie żyje, panie poruczniku. Kopnął w kalendarz. Kaput.'

'Is that Płaschiński?'

Another voice answered. 'Over here, sir. Said he thinks he's dead, sir. Kaput, sir.'

Felix whispered again. 'Corporal Habe?' He could hear a man whimpering. 'Corporal Habe?'

There was no response. Then a voice in German: 'I saw him go down, sir.'

Dead. No interpreter.

Thin, horse-tail clouds drifted across the face of the moon. Felix lifted his head cautiously above the cover. There was little to see and less to be sure of. Where were the other units of the army? It surely can't have been them firing at us, he thought. No, not possible. The enemy. He and his men were expecting us. So where in hell were they?

There was no option but to stay put and wait for daybreak.

Felix spoke in a hoarse whisper: 'Listen to me. Every one of you. We're going to…' He didn't finish. Another flare burst, artificial day, and they all clung in terror to the yielding soil, scrabbling for pointless grip in it. An extended volley of bullets followed. It lasted about a minute and then stopped. There was deathly quiet again.

Felix had a dilemma. To try to withdraw was suicide. The order to link up with other units must be paramount but what did they risk by staying where they were? No time for that. He whispered again. 'We stay put until light. Check ammunition. No noise.'

There was a soft sound of fumbling for some minutes and then, in the unbroken still of the night, the survivors of a platoon cut to half its strength lay inert, wet and cold in the mud of the Isonzo watershed.

It was, by now, a little after four in the morning. Some of them sank into a washed out sleep, others lay in a confused anguish.

Felix lay awake, Private Mantler curled up miserably alongside him.

Must stay awake, he told himself, must stay alert but, after a while, straining after every slightest noise, he fell asleep. He woke with a start, a rush of adrenalin. He strained to hear something. Nothing.

Dawn came in a glaze of pink. The new day warmed itself in the rays of a young sun and cast off the chilly night like an overcoat, stiff with mud. A flock of ducks flew past with a chuckle of quacks.

Felix stifled a ravenous yawn and glanced round. He saw a number of his men scattered about, prone, motionless. To the front, a flat river meadow. On the far side, shallow slopes below a tall cliff. Along the foot of the slopes, a low line of earthen fortifications. Two small lights that might have been eyes winked and were gone. Silence. Then the sound of a voice with a metallic tone floated across to them.

'Soldati Austriachi. Cedete. Darvi. La vostra posizion' è disperato, senza speranza. È inutile.'

Silence.

Felix croaked: 'Pesenti? Pesenti?'

There was no reply.

'Pesenti? Pesenti?'

A sleep-drugged voice answered in a mumble. 'Sir?'

'What did he say?'

'I don't know, sir.'

'I thought you were Italian.'

'From the northern bit, sir. Don't speak it.'

'But I thought…'

The voice called out again: *'Soldati Austriachi. Cedete. Darvi. La vostra posizion' è disperato, senza speranza. È inutile.'* There was a pause. Then, in German: 'You need to surrender.'

Felix felt drained. He suppressed an agony of indecision. He had no choice. He prodded Mantler, still curled up tight next to him, cringing, like a dog flinching from a whip. He was clutching his rifle as if for comfort, like a teddy bear.

'Mantler. Give me your rifle.'

Mantler's blank, terrifed eyes stared at him. Felix reached out to pull the weapon away. Mantler shook his head, babbling *no no no* in an asthmatic rasp. Felix leaned closer and said: 'It's

91

all right, Mantler, I'm here. I'll take care of you. Don't worry. You're all right. I just need your rifle, now. Please? There's a good boy.'

He pulled the rifle gently out of Mantler's hands, took a handkerchief out of his pocket, knotted it to the end of the rifle's muzzle and hoisted it above his head. He waited a few seconds and, with trepidation, scrambled to his feet. In doing so, he dislodged his spectacles.

13

The covered truck bumped and lurched down the steep track, branches of trees slapping at the canvas roof cover. Felix clung fast to a metal upright in the framework supporting the canvas. The vehicle swung sharp left onto a broader track along the flat path through the forest. It drove out of and away from the forest along a serpentine country road for about half an hour into a small town where it drew up on a main piazza thronged with Italian military personnel. A sign hanging over the entrance of a large building on one side of the square, indicated Hospital. A nurse was walking up the steps to the main entrance. She ignored the priest who emerged from it.

The Italian officer appeared at the back of the truck and ordered Felix and the two MPs out. All four walked over towards a municipal building at the far end of the square, past a line of ten soldiers with rifles aiming at a man in army uniform, hatless, his hands tied behind his back, standing against the wall of the church. An officer in attendance snapped an order, the rifles fired, the man crumpled and went down. The officer strode across, pulling his pistol out of its holster and fired a single shot into the man's head. The execution party sloped arms and marched off, leaving the dead man where he lay.

The senior intelligence officer was sitting behind a desk in a large, noisy room occupied by clerks either busy at a long refectory table or bustling in and out with files, papers, messages. Army runners came and went. A high-ranking infantry officer emerged through a door at the end of the room and left the building.

The Subaltern approached his superior's desk, saluted and spoke. The senior man looked past him to where the two MPs flanked Felix, then said something to the Subaltern. The four men, prisoner and escort, made their way out of the building across the piazza to the low door of what might have been a private house. A sign *Carabinieri* on the wall indicated the police station.

The cell door was made of thick oak, a tiny barred window admitted no more than a glimmer of light into the cell itself – barely three metres long and two wide, furnished with a latrine pail, a narrow wooden bench and a pillow-sized straw-filled meal sack. The door thumped shut. The key grated in the lock.

Felix sat on the bench. They'd taken his pack, his pay-book, his watch. Effectively, he no longer existed. He was a common prisoner in a common gaol, in a timeless nowhere. He felt a crushing weight of fatigue, his mind and body contorted in a stress of misery such as he'd never experienced. He lay on the hard boards of the bench, in cramps of agitation, longing for the release of sleep, but sleep would not come. His nerves held him up in consciousness, like tight strung ropes of a hammock, until at last they slackened and he drifted into a blessed oblivion.

Almost at once, the cell door thumped open, startling him

awake, taut, his head ringing, his throat dry, his body aching all over. An unshaven policeman in a shabby blue uniform jacket dumped a metal plate and a tin mug on the cell floor – on the plate, a dollop of yellowish porridge, in the mug, water. The door thumped shut once more.

On the fourth morning of his confinement, the junior intelligence officer entered the cell.

'Come with me.'

Felix, unshaven, unwashed, his throat dry and sore, his head throbbing, his body and limbs stiff from largely sleepless nights on the wooden boards, had to lean against the wall for support.

'Why am I being held here?' he croaked. 'I'm a prisoner of war. You have no right to keep me in a dungeon.'

The Subaltern raised his eyebrows and said nothing. He stood aside, waved Felix through the doorway into the corridor and led him out of the building through the front office where the slovenly policeman sat behind a desk, reading a newspaper. He looked up for a moment, then resumed reading.

An open-topped military car stood outside, the driver in place. The Subaltern indicated the front seat, next to the driver and then climbed into the back seat, next to Felix's pack.

The vehicle drove off out of town in the opposite direction from the way they'd come in. To all Felix's questions and protest – *Where are you taking me? What happened to my men? Where are they being held? How many were killed, wounded, captured? I demand to know what has happened to them* – the Subaltern made no reply.

They drove through a flat agricultural landscape largely composed of meadows and vineyards, dotted with low-roofed farm-houses and barns. They passed tiny villages of no more than ten houses, stretches of woodland, ruined glebe, glum horses in paddocks spare of grass, scrawny cattle mooching in fields. Here a church adjoining a cemetery within a low walled enclosure, black cypress trees in mournful attendance, there an albergo by the side of the road, shuttered against the glare of the sun, already climbing to its zenith. There was no one to be seen, no human activity apparent anywhere.

After about two hours, they crossed a broad river whose stream was diffracted in a network of lesser streams. They drove on through a large town. Felix looked for any sign of what it was called but there was none. Further on, in open farmland, they drew up. Felix was allowed to get out to stretch his legs, the driver refuelled the vehicle with a spare can of gasoline, the officer smoked a cigarette. They drove on.

Another hour brought them to a bridge across another big river, its course also split into capillaries. Eventually, the car turned right onto a long avenue lined with sentinel walnut trees leading to a small palazzo girded by a high, precinct wall. Large wrought-iron gates in front of a paved courtyard stood open. The car drove through the gates and halted outside the main door of the house. The masonry of the façade was flaked and scabbed with age and weather, the paintwork of the shutters and window frames peeling and sun-bleached, the stones of the courtyard itself sprouting weed and grass at their seams.

There were no sign boards indicating that this was a military establishment, no vehicles parked, no sentries. The place looked deserted.

The subaltern alighted from the car, gestured Felix out, handed him his pack, accompanied him up the small flight of steps leading to the main door of the house and knocked. The door opened and an elderly man appeared in its frame. Slightly stooped, balding, he wore shabby drugget trousers, scuffed leather boots, and, under a clean white apron, a voluminous dark blue shirt from whose open collar at the neck protruded a downy flue of white chest hair.

The officer handed him a sheet of paper and held out a pen. 'Receipt of prisoner, Lieutenant Breitenbach, Felix, Austrian army. Sign here.'

The old man scribbled on the paper, handed it back to the subaltern then led the way through a hallway starved of light and on up a flight of shallow, stone steps set into the bare wall, its plaster marred by cracks and grazes where damp had peeled away the lime render, past two half landings to an upper landing with a continuation of the stone balustrade on the open side, three doors set in the side walls. There were no paintings, no hangings, only a simple wooden crucifix hanging above the central door.

It was this door that the old man unlocked with a large key to reveal a smallish, oblong room. The subaltern gestured Felix in. The old man hovered in the doorway. The air in the room was musty.

'Empty your pack.'

Felix began to unpack his belongings – the military issue clothing, wash bag, eating irons and mess tins, first aid kit, felt pouch for spare buttons, needle and thread, the book of poems...

He watched as the subaltern rummaged, poking at the detritus of Felix's existence with his pistol barrel. He reached for the Goethe, opened at the frontispiece and seemed to be debating whether or not to confiscate it.

'May I keep it? Please?'

The subaltern, not listening, shut the book and dropped it back on the bed. Next he picked up a notebook, riffled through the pages, the first quarter filled with writing, the rest as yet empty, tossed it back on the bed. He pocketed the sewing kit.

Felix said: 'Where am I?'

No answer.

'Where am I? What is this place?'

'You're a prisoner of the Italian army. Beyond that you don't need to know anything. Don't think of escape. Should you try to escape, I promise you the consequences will be most unpleasant. My advice to you, Lieutenant, is to count yourself lucky that you're alive.'

'Am I alone here?'

The Italian, who was staring out of the window, didn't respond.

'I want to know what has happened to the men under my command.'

Again, silence.

'Why am I not in a prison camp?'

The subaltern sniffed. 'We have, of course, informed your commanders, through the normal channels, that you're alive and being held prisoner. They'll inform your family.'

'What is this place?'

'You may write to your family, only your family. Bear in mind that your letters will be censored. We'll supply you with writing paper, one sheet at a time.'

He turned to go.

Felix said: 'Are there any books?'

'Books?' said the Italian, as if it were the most bizarre question anyone could ask, a frank idiocy. He scoffed and left the room even as Felix was saying: 'Where's my watch?' The door closed behind him, the key turned in the lock.

14

The Italian officer walked down into the entrance hallway, the old man trailing him.

'Domenico, isn't it?'

'Brentani, Domenico, yes.'

'The prisoner is to be given breakfast, lunch and supper. Nothing more. No wine. Exercise periods I leave to you. Up to two hours per day. Otherwise, the room is to be locked at all times as must every door leading out of the building, save into the inner courtyard. You will remain with the prisoner throughout the exercise period. There will be some provision made by the army for the purchase of food and necessities – soap…' He seemed unable to think of what other necessities might consist. He handed over an envelope. 'The first payment, which is to last a month. Spend it carefully. I or someone will come back in twenty eight days, or so. Meanwhile, you bear total responsibility for the welfare and safe custody of the prisoner. Is that clear?'

The old man nodded. There was a long pause. The officer looked him straight in the face. 'Total responsibility, do you hear?'

'Yes, sir.'

In the room on the upper landing, Felix looked round the room. It was furnished with a chair, a plain wooden table, a metal washstand, a narrow bed, a small chest of drawers. The single window looked out over an inner quadrangle. There were no guards, no sign of any military presence. What had this place been? he thought. Were there other prisoners here? It must be a holding place before he was transferred to a prison camp.

He looked out of the window at the only view he'd see until he was moved or released: high walls that shut out every vestige of the world he knew, enclosing him in complete isolation, the only links with his former life a book of poems, a few clothes and memory.

He went over to the bed, gathered up the spare under-clothes, a woollen sweater, the second pair of socks, folded them and put them in drawers. He saw a bedpan under the bed, pulled it out. There was no cover. It gave off a faint odour of carbolic.

The wash bag he put by the washstand. The Goethe he laid on top of the chest of drawers. The notebook and pencil he placed neatly on the table, then fussily changed their position. He shifted the table so that it sat under the window. The pack he put on the floor by the chest of drawers, thought again and pushed it under the iron frame of the bed. He felt the bed. The mattress was thin, the blankets worn, darned here and there, the sheets were clean. He tested the springs. They were tired.

He got up and paced the room, measuring its dimensions. He pulled the chair up to the table and sat down. He stared out of the window for a while, then opened the notebook and smoothed the first blank page. He took up the pencil, stared out of the window again. He wasn't even sure of the date. After long deliberation he wrote 'Day One' and felt sick.

The old man sat at the scrubbed wooden table in the kitchen, opened the envelope and counted the money it contained. Not enough to feed a bird. He put the money back. And what strangeness it was, all this. So long living on his own, grown used to his own company, now he had someone else to think about, not a guest, a prisoner. Not a nice word *prisoner*, he thought, makes it into a prison, the house, all the good feelings in it locked up, shut away, forbidden.

The case clock in the corner of the room chimed four o'clock. The old man got up and made for the room on the landing. He turned the key in the lock, suddenly wondering if he should knock. Did total responsibility cover just opening the door and barging in? He knocked, didn't wait for a reply, went into the room and locked the door behind him. And what was to protect him from being overpowered by a young man desperate to escape and tied up, even killed? Shouldn't he have a gun? He stood close to the door.

'I am Domenico,' he said in Italian. His prisoner was sitting on the chair by the table.

'I will give you food three times a day.'

Felix frowned.

Domenico wondered what to say next. Felix had nothing to say. It was a pantomime of mutual incomprehension, if not suspicion, comical were it not pathetic. After a long pause, suddenly inspired, Domenico said: 'Eat,' and mimed eating, 'drink,' and mimed drinking.

Felix nodded.

Domenico said: 'Seven o'clock.' He said it again and held up seven fingers.

Something clicked in Felix's mind: sette…septem, Sieben,

sept seven. He said 'sette'.

Domenico nodded, faltered, waggled the key, unlocked the door and left the room.

As the door closed and the key turned, Felix walked across to the window.

Solitary confinement with light, he thought.

He felt a choking burden of guilt: he'd surrendered and in so doing abandoned – been forced to abandon – his men. He'd failed in his duty.

No books. All I can do without interruption is think. There's no way of stopping thought. There'll be no peace, no calm. No music. Time will drag and halter me with its dragging. But safe. Safe, yes, but that only sharpened the sense of guilt.

This was it, then, he thought, everything so alien. A room about eight metres by six. No fireplace. It'll get very cold when winter comes. Winter will come and after winter, spring, and spring will lead to summer and summer to…a year. And in a few words he'd used up a whole year of days, days like this one, Day One. What hope? Hope is possibility. This room, therefore, is not my end, it's a beginning. I will pave it with the streets of my memory and the open spaces, the parks, the streets and boulevards of my imagination. Yes, he thought, that's what I'll do. Yes. And, looking down into the empty courtyard, as it were into a dried up stone cistern, misery assailed him, the first corruption of despair, the terror of solitude. Is this what it was going to be like? Fine words, Felix, streets of memory blah blah. How? How?

Two hours later, with resignation, he opened the notebook and wrote, under Day One, 'food and drink at sette'.

15

Day 33

Three men. He didn't recognize them. Probably old. They looked half asleep. Apart from that, the evidence for senility was scant. A white moustache, stooping shoulders. Sitting at a trestle table. Smoking cigars.

It was outside somewhere. Freezing. Light snow falling. It was the inner quadrangle, though, he suddenly recognized it, absolutely it was the inner quadrangle, platelets of ice on the flagstones, streaks of white pigeon shit staining the wall and the imperial insignia, double eagle thing, hanging from a hook. Juppiter's eagle grasping a viper in its talons, was it? What made him think of that? Oh, come on, Felix, don't be a slouch. Symbolism. Because he couldn't move, of course, tight cords bound him, arms and legs, to the chair. Gripped. And there's a fourth man, gliding in front of him from the side, in a white carnival half mask, no eyeholes. He starts speaking. That voice, that voice, that voice by the roadside, lazy drawl, sounding as if he was half cut, sending him straight into the trap, much as to say *fuck off, why don't you, Lieutenant Brightbox?* Then he's turning round and pointing a finger. *It wasn't my fault,* forms in your throat but it sticks there. The mask tilts up. The wearer speaks:

'I accuse you of cowardice in the face of the enemy, I accuse you of being a worm, I accuse you of gross unspeakableness and disgusting habits, a disgrace to the uniform, a pig. Also Jewish. Is it any wonder? Pork. Odious toad. Reptile. Perfectly simple instructions, all said and done, a cretin could have followed them: march up the road, join the others, follow orders. But, oh no. Didn't do it. Didn't do any of it. Sneaked off, ratted, scuttled over to the enemy, hands up, pleading (rabbit): "Don't shoot, I'll come quietly, no ammunition, see?"

'Whining and cringing, where's your pride?

'So, "What do you say?" you say to them, the *enemy*, wheedling, "here's an idea: what if I surrender, in exchange for a room in a hotel, sit it out, waited on hand and foot? Can't do any harm, can it?"

'No harm? Harm is what we're here for, to inflict harm. *What about your men?* "What about them?" I hear you say. "They're grown ups. Am I my brother's keeper? I didn't ask for them. They didn't ask for me. Back where we started, nothing to do with me. Can I go now?" No you cannot. Filth.'

The trio at the table grunted.

The carnival mask spoke again.

'I accuse you of being a craven, yellow-bellied, gutless apology for an officer in the imperial and royal, all that, taken as read. Are you getting all this down?' he said to the trio at the table. 'I can't speak any slower. It's not an affectation, it's the way I've always talked.' He resumed his diatribe. 'Ferret, girl, tin of milk, apology for a gentleman, no no no no, not close. Honour? Pah. Incidentally,' he said, turning to the trio at the table, 'do you know that one: "She offered her honour, he honoured her offer, and all night long he was on her and off her"? Eh?'

'We've told you before, no ribaldry, no smut,' said one of

105

the men at the table 'No obscenity'.

'He's an obscenity,' the man said, pointing at Felix without deigning to look.

'That I grant you. Have you finished?'

'No.'

'Then pray proceed. I'm gagging for a drink.' The others snuffled in agreement and shifted in their seats. 'Come on, get on with it.'

'Yes your justiceship. To conclude. I'm almost lost for words.' He wheeled round and the eyeless mask stared at Felix. 'Damnation, man, this is mortally serious. The damage you caused. And not a sign, not a glimmer, not a flicker of any conscience, regret, remorse, sense of shame, no evidence of having a spine. Exposed as a traitor.' He stopped for a moment. Felix felt the valve of his bladder beginning to loosen. 'In the circumstances: Death, that's it. And what else could it be?' The mask turned away to address the three men at the table, their faces part obscured by the heavy fume of the cigars. There was a sudden hush. The trio formed a huddle. There was some low whispering. Then they sat up. The man in the middle said: 'What do you say?'

'Say?' said white mask.

'The charge. Cowardice or desertion.'

'Both.'

'No no no, must be one or the other.'

'I'm not following you.'

'It's a point of procedure. We don't want him to waltz away scot free on a legal nicety.'

'They both merit death, don't they?'

'That's a point. Let's call it desertion, then, shall we?' he said, first to the man to his right, who nodded, next to the man on his left, who also nodded. 'Desertion, then, all agreed, nem con. We'll write it down as treasonous desertion. All right with you?'

'Absolutely, sir.'

'Firing squad, would you say?'

'Ready and waiting, sir,' the mask called out: 'Load, aim, fire.'

Not safe at all.

BANG

Felix woke with a jolt, his limbs locked in a rigid spasm as from an electric shock. He was conscious of a giddiness, a nauseating throb of blood in his brain and then his father's voice, thick, as if clotted with chocolate, saying: 'Felix, Felix, come on, boy, be reasonable.'

His limbs slackened, his whole body ached. He could hear only the keening of the wind, the rattling window.

Fully dressed, huddled under the thin covers, he shivered with cold and lay awake till dawn. Thought trudged through a desert of sense. The daylight came slowly like an exhausted, sick old man struggling vainly to get out of bed.

Later, Felix wrote in his log:

'Day 33. Nightmare. Cold start. Beware lethargy. Must not rage.'

That afternoon, the intelligence officer reappeared. If it was to check on the welfare of his prisoner it didn't show. The questions were perfunctory.

When he'd finished, Felix steeled himself.

'May I have books?'

'Why?'

'I'd like to be able to read. As a distraction. I've...always had books.'

The officer gave him a cold look.

'I'd be very grateful.'

The officer thought for a moment then left the room and went down to the hallway where Domenico was waiting.

'Do you have any books here?' he said.

Domenico nodded. 'Yes, sir. Lots of books. In the library.'

'Show me.'

They walked along the corridor to a door which opened on a room lined with shelves, crammed with books, floor to ceiling. The officer inspected one shelf, took a book down, opened it, thought for a moment, put it back on the shelf, then took it off the shelf again and handed it to Domenico.

'Give the prisoner this. When he's finished with it, you may replace it.'

He left the building and Domenico walked up the stairs holding the book.

It was a large, illustrated volume, *Animali Commestibili dei mari d'Italia*. That was easy enough to decipher. So, Felix thought, I'm to become a student of the edible fish and crustacea of the seas round Italy. In Italian. But, it was a book, a small break-through, a relaxation of the rules. He smiled at Domenico and said: 'Thank you.'

Domenico smiled back and said: 'Welcome,' and lay one hand on his heart. He then mimed what could happen next by taking the book, going through the pages, closing the book and handing the book back. He said: 'Finish. Number two,' and held up two fingers.

And so began Felix's rifling of the library. From the higgledy-piggledy selection of books Domenico brought him, he picked out words here and there with similarity to Latin and French and slowly assembled a strange monosyllabic maca-roni, squashing both languages together with Italian. He asked Domenico for a Bible. It took some time to establish what he was asking for – the German and Italian were so different – but a sketch of a book with a large cross on the cover did the trick. Domenico clapped his hands together, went downstairs and, five minutes later, came back with a Bible.

Felix, in his turn, applauded. Now he could begin to learn the language with more confidence by matching his own recall of the German to the Italian – Genesis, Psalms, Proverbs… it was, perhaps, the key he needed. In the beginning…in the beginning…

16

Domenico's story

The more or less invariable routine of his confinement became established, from Domenico's first turn of the key in the lock each morning to its last turn at night. There were no other prisoners. Felix lived in a silence broken only by the noises made by the building, birdsong, the sough of the wind, rain, a crack of thunder, and Domenico's voice.

He came and went with trays bearing the three daily meals, at 7 o'clock, noon and 7pm. As he got to know Felix better and the rapport between them strengthened, the elderly Italian quite often extended his visits. He brought a second chair into the room. He brought an extra cup for coffee. He and Felix talked for a while. It was obvious that Domenico was as glad to have the younger man's company as Felix was glad of his.

Felix learned to speak a serviceable if eccentric Italian, in what soon became easygoing, amiable conversation with Domenico, who showed a remarkable patience and willingness to encourage his pupil. The two men might not have had much in common, on the face of it, but it soon became clear that what they did have in common was a growing affection. They became friends. Felix felt less and less a prisoner, although the reality reminded him that he was and could be nothing else. Domenico locked the room morning and night, performing the required function of a warder, but there was only and ever benevolence in his manner.

Six months after he was given the first book, Felix asked the inspecting officer if he might have books in German. The officer said nothing and appeared wholly indifferent but, on his next visit, he arrived with a copy of a collection of stories by E.T.A. Hoffmann, *The Brothers Serapion*. Felix was overjoyed. He thanked the officer and got the first sign of any kind of interest, a slight bow.

Much encouraged, next time, Felix asked for a sketch pad, pencils and water colours.

The man was suspicious. 'Why? To make plans of the palazzo?'

'No. And I'll show you everything I draw. It's only because I enjoy sketching.'

The sketch pad and water colours arrived, a further relief of tedium.

He'd considered, and dismissed, the idea of escape. Escape to where? To what? For what? And how? By killing or injuring Domenico? Such a thing was unimaginable. The old man's kindness had saved him from going under. What frigid maxims of duty, what abstract code of honour could outweigh the human debt he owed to Domenico's magnanimity? Besides, he'd surrendered, hadn't he? He was already an outcast from any sacrosanct notions of duty and honour. There was nothing, no one, to be loyal to, now, except his own instincts and Domenico. He owed it to him and to himself, did he not, to put humanity before the aggressive spirit that war required of him? Of course that darker stirring of conscience taunted him with cowardice: your bounden duty to escape or die in the attempt. And for what extravagance of futility? he replied.

One morning, after breakfast, the old man related how he'd come to be the custodian of the cavernous empty house. He said nothing about where it was.

'See, Felix, we work the land, my mother, my father, two older brothers, me soon as I could walk. *Vai lavorare, piccino*, my father say, quite rough. Get to work, kid. *Subito subito*, no time to waste. Always jobs to do on a farm even for young peoples, is still an extra pair of hands, carrying, fetching, fetching, carrying, far back as I remember, far back. School? Not so much. In the countryside is too much work to do for any time from school. The priest teach us numbers and letters, God and the Mass, but mostly what the church got to say about right and wrong.' He snorted. 'All we hear about God is that he is father and we are his children and we all know that means punish.

'And he's not so much interested in lessons, the priest, not in books like you are, Felix. He's more interested in telling us, very strict, "Ask forgiveness to God. On your knees, tell him you're a bad boy and how bad you been and how many times you been a bad boy". Shaking his finger and all angry in the face, even when you don't feel a bad boy, you done nothing wrong. But you have to say you done something wrong, make it up, because the priest tells you you got to and "Say Ave Maria all through ten times," to punish. Because punishment is cleaning, he says.

'Now, I know cleaning, I done cleaning a lot in my life and one thing Ave Maria is not is cleaning.' His eyes widened and he chuckled. 'And the priest has housekeeper, so what does he know about cleaning? Not so much. Housekeeper, she knows cleaning and Hail Mary. And everybody knows, too, what kind housekeeper for the priest.' He winked.

'When I was maybe eleven, twelve, something young, I arrive to here. My mother says to my father: "Time Domenico did something more than work on farm. Time he got to learn some other thing." See, my two brothers they'd have the farm one day after our mother and father die or get too old to work because it's hard – from time you get up, time you go to bed, all in between, work work work, no stop.

'But my brothers quarrel a lot, too. So, maybe there's going to be big argument: who's in charge of the farm? They fight like dogs so much, so much. Real fight. Fists. Me? I stay out of the way. That kind of thing...*è stupido, stupido.*' He shook his head, slipping back in memory for a moment to the drudgery and torn tempers of that time.

'So they send me to the palazzo. We walk here, my Mamma and me, and when I see such a big house and all gardens and driveway and horse and carriages and walls and gates, I think *Got to be very rich peoples live there. Important peoples.*

'I start as kitchen boy. Still carrying, fetching, running about, but not outside, not summer hot sun and dust, not flies and stinky, not winter rain and cold and mud. I do cleaning and sweeping inside. The man here teach me how to sweep.' He beamed. 'You think no one needs to learn to sweep, is simple, broom and sweep? Ah, no, not so true, Felix. Like in most things, there's right way and wrong way and I learnt right way, from old Francesco who worked here. He tell me *You got to keep the head of the broom down when you push the dust across the floor or any what's there, keep the head down, like this* – and he showed me, push the broom, keep it head low and that way not so much dust gets thrown up. See, Felix? Even sweeping there's a right and a wrong. It's a lesson. Always a lesson you think you don't need to learn but you do.

'Mostly, that early days I was here, they were seeing if they like me, so I can maybe stay and be useful and not be nuisance. And I was, I was useful and they seem to like me and I found a different sort of life here, a happy life, no quarrels. And I learn a little bits cooking, too. The cook tell me "now you do this, next you do that", and me watching what she done. It's good, Felix, that way you learn. You keep your eyes your ears open. You pay attention.' He tapped the side of his temple. 'We got an expression: "*Se ascolto, imparo, se vedo, ricordo, ma se faccio, capisco.*" See?'

'If I hear I…*imparo?*'

'Not…' He made the rocking motion with his hand.

'Not sure?'

'Si. Not sure. *Se vedo…*'

'If I see I remember but if I do - *ma se faccio* - I understand. That it?'

'Bravo, bravo. That's the way proper learning is. And I live in a little room up in the top, under the roof, quite high up, right at the top of a long wooden stairs, creak creak when you go up, like my knees now.' He laughed and slapped his thighs. 'First time I ever sleep on my own, in a room. I was a little bit scared to begin, all quiet mostly with small noises, which is the building getting settle for the night, and in the dark on my own. But I get used and like it because it's mine that little room, all for me, and a bed not to share and have to squeeze

114

up. And the peoples I work with was friendly, like us, now, Felix, friends, see? Is the best way.'

He smiled, let the pleasant thought sink in. Felix smiled, too. He was happy, and for the first time conscious of the fact that he was happy, against expectation and, without doubt, against orders. Happy and he didn't question it.

'Could be kept on toes, too. The cook tells me "Domenico, you gotta do this, Domenico, you gotta do that and quick, hurry, hurry, this day can't wait for you to rub sleep out of your eyes and people who sleeps don't catch fish…*chi dorme non piglia pesce*, but not angry, never boil over, angry. It's working together, same as I learnt from the farm, but more *amicabile*. Not like my father. With him, it was furious, always furious. He had heavy hands and a quick boil. Hit me for being lazy. Hit me for being slow. Hit me for being get something wrong. Then hit me when I cry because he say I'm windy and like a girl. "The boy's like a girl, too soft," he say. "Always bursts into tears. Needs to courage up." I see the look on his face, like he was in pain, too. And mother says nothing, but she knows I don't like quarrels and fights and shouting, like men. No. I always had a smile. He didn't like that, my father. Think I was laughing at him, poking fun.' He paused.

'A smile is like an open pistacchio nut,' he said. 'You ever hear that, Felix?'

'No.'

Domenico laughed. 'My father never smiles. Work on a farm is can grind a man's goodwill out of him, like millstones on grain. I could understand. Some ways, not his fault except…' He didn't finish.

'Not my mother. My mother was, you know she put up with

a lot. Not so happy with how her life was turn out. You need only look, could see all the sadness in her face and eyes. But her nature was kind. She was very gentle, very warm here.' He held both hands over his heart. 'But the way my father was, the way my brothers came out so like him, it hurt, it hung very heavy on her heart. All bad temper men around her. Lots of anger. No joy, Felix, no joy. No laughing. Maybe she was happy once, in love with my father, when they was young and just starting. Before children came, which is more work, when just the two of them. Then…?' Once more he stopped, shook his head.

'The priest tell us that work is praying, but there wasn't so much praying in our house, apart to praying for work to stop. All that changes for me here, my new life. And one day the man in charge of us, Giacomo, a big, tall man, smart black trouser and short jacket, always a shirt white as a swan's feather, he call me and say: "Domenico, how old you are now?" I lift my hands like this, and my shoulder, and say I'm maybe fifteen…? I just begin to shave. And he says: "How do you like to learn the garden?" "Learn the garden?" I say. And he says: "You know Salvo who work in the garden, getting the vegetables and the fruits, the herbs and the flowers?" Of course I know Salvo from when he comes to the kitchen with a big basket full of vegetables but I didn't know he took any notice of me. Anyway, then Giacomo says: "Salvo says you are ready, maybe, to start there, learn the garden from him, all his knowledge."

'*Learn the garden?* I think, and my eyes are wide like an owl's, because that's something I would never dream of, not think I might get such a luck. And so I start in the garden with Salvo who was old, old as I am now, maybe, old as I see in the mirror. Makes no difference. Only time, years, what we're given.

116

'I like work with Salvo. He knew everything from soil and how to grow and put seeds. He was a very patient man. He teaches me everything, and I learn it by bit, like things growing. The seeds goes in the ground, you can't see them. Then they come up little green whisker, and rain and sunshine and they grow bigger, stronger, bigger till they're ripe. And picking is knowing the learning, after the teaching.

'I tell you, we grow tomatoes sweeter than you ever ate before. That right, Felix?'

'It's right.'

'Good Italian tomatoes. Trick is not give them too much water else all they fill with is water, not *dolcezza*, not sweetness. We grow lemons and oranges, zucchini and melanzane, all sorts things, green stuffs, grapes for wine and grappa, lovely flowers for the house table when Giacomo comes to say they need to fill the vases because visitors. Always had visitors. Not exactly always but, you know, plenty. And for the funerals, flowers for the coffins.'

He lapsed into a brief reverie. Then:

'And the people die, first man, then woman. They have one children, a son who goes off to Milan, somewhere, to be in a bank, something high up. He came back for the funerals. Salvo, he died, too, long time before, and I was in charge, me, Domenico, head gardener. My mother and father died when I was something thirty, I think, and my Francesca had the baby. All dead. All dead now.' The words stifled him. He gulped. 'Only one left is me. In the empty house seemed nobody wanted.' The smile ached with sorrow, but before Felix could say anything, he continued:

'One day…and I carry on working here, because I don't

know anything else and where am I going to go? My broth-ers...?' He shook his head and didn't pursue that.

'One day, a man comes with a fold of papers. Drives up in a pony and trap, a very self-importance man, talks to me like servant when I never saw him before. He tells me the house is being inherit by the son. This I expect, no surprise. Only wonder if the son wants to keep me head gardener, you know? Nobody to eat what I grow, what's to do with all the flowers...? And I ask when is he coming, the son, and the man say that's not his business and it's not mine either and goes off, nose in the air, like frog in a pail of water. And you know who owns the house, Felix? You know who owns the house, now?'

'I've no idea. You?' and he laughed.

Domenico laughed, too. 'Yes, me, can you believe? Me. Because the son comes to see me and says that he doesn't need the house, he doesn't like the country and slow way of life we got and he's have too much work in the city all the time and a wife and a family, then he tells me...we're sitting in the library, and he looks at me, takes a paper out of his pocket and holds it up. "Do you know what this is, Domenico?" No, I say. "It's a deeds," he says. A deeds? I say. And he smiles and says that his mother and father like me so much they tell him if he does not want the house then I can have it till I die, just keep it, only for me, and then it goes back to the son. Can you believe that, Felix? How it all comes out. What would my Mamma say? She came to see me here sometimes, when she can got the possibility. And she feel so happy here, so happy. I could see some pleasure in her eyes, how her body all go loose and relax like she's put down a heavy load and can sit to rest for a while. So happy here. And happy for me. And for ...' He stopped, folded both lips under and wiped his eye.

'And at start of the war,' he said, 'the government people come to tell me they have to use the house as some word I didn't know and…here you are and here I am.'

He got to his feet, wheezed and coughed to clear his throat. 'What the cook say, "Now, Domenico, this day can't wait for you to rub sleep out of your eyes, things to do," so I got things to do.'

He gathered up the empty cups, loaded the tray and, giving Felix a big wink, went to the door and left the room.

Felix sat reflecting. He looked out of the window at the great emptiness of the sky – strange the comfort in its changes, colour, scudding clouds, sun shadow. Then he opened the latest volume he'd been brought to read, another of Hoffman's books, to read in the warm air by the open window.

'*How wonderful these human beings are who find a meaning in the meaningless, who read the words which have never been written, who bind like masters the tangled skeins of things and still trace paths in the eternal dark.*'

17

Day 365

Felix, standing by the window, heard a light tap on the door and called out: 'Good morning, Domenico.' The key turned in the lock, the door swung open, and there was his friendly gaoler, bending down to pick up the tray carrying cups, battered tin coffee jug, two slices of bread, a dish of jam. 'Is homemade, Felix,' Domenico told him when he'd brought in the first pot months past.

'Another thing I learn years ago. Not so much sugar but is got lots of fruit in. This is berries from the woods.' He put the tray on the table and went back to the doorway to pick up a book he had laid on the floor.

Felix said: 'You know, it's a year since I was brought here.'

The old man's eyes widened. 'How do you know that, Felix?'

Felix held up his journal. Another relaxation in the regime – replacement notebooks. 'It's my calendar and silent clock.'

'You been counting?'

Felix smiled. 'It's what prisoners do, isn't it?'

Domenico shifted the new book in his hands. 'I'm sorry you have to be prisoner, Felix, young man, locked up, not so nice.'

'Oh, Domenico, you've made it as manageable as it could be in the circumstances.'

'But, some ways lucky. No fighting here.' He smiled. 'Good

name you got Felix, is what we say *Felice*, lucky.' He looked at the book on the table. The stream of reading had swollen and books came more frequently than the monthly deliveries. Felix could even make requests, now, and Domenico arrived at the door, like a bookseller.

'How you read all these books, hundreds books, seems like, makes me wear out just to carry them, all they got inside them, heavy like full flowerpots, and you put all that in your head, Felice? You don't get headache, all that weight of books inside your brain? This one…' as he mimed the weight of it, '…got to be double weight of normal.'

He peered at the writing on the spine.

'Can't read what it says here. Is no words I know. Even looking what words you write down for me, on your list, the books you want, when a book comes, I got to see if it's the same as the words on your list. Mamma mia, makes me dizzy, sometimes. Eyes not so good now. And brain…' He tapped one temple and made a rueful face.

'I'm sorry, Domenico. You know how very grateful I am.'

The old man wagged his finger. 'No, no, no. Keeps me on toes. A book you ask for, you write down the name. A book comes, I look the words and see if it's the one and I draw a line through the name of the book on the list, that's how it works. System, see?'

Felix bowed with exaggerated deference and, with the flourish of a courtier to a duke, said: 'Your humble servant, with extreme gratitude.'

The old man laughed and said: 'A year ago today you come here? Really? *Incredibile* …Things change, meanwhile, no? Things a bit better for you now. With books. Makes you happier?' He clicked his tongue. 'Some things don't change – same room, same day by day, same food and not much… is the war.'

'You do your best, Domenico. I know that.'

The old man waved a disclaiming hand. 'Kind you say so, but go to market, no this, no that, empty tables, little bit this, little bit that. Lucky I still got the garden.

'Beginning of war, I buy as much dry pasta as I can and flour to make pasta, sugar for jam, salt – the war comes, I say to myself, we're going to cry a lot so needs salt.' He laughed. 'Best to make joking. Complain don't change nothing and only makes you feel bad, worse. Is like you take poison and expect someone else to die. And I make lots tomato sauce, for the store room. Good crops onions, aubergine, apples, grape, all in the dark and cool. And seeds for next year out of all what I grow this year. Such tiny, small as crumbs, the seeds, and all that food in them to come. A miracle, you say? And, army gives me bits here, bits there.' He sighed. 'Same for everyone. Only…' He leaned towards Felix. 'Only, I tell you one thing.'

'Yes?'

'You think the mayor sits down to empty plates in the *Municipio*? The government people, the generals, the Pope in Rome, the high-ups? You think they pull their belts tight? Nah…You think I come down with rain out of a cloud? Pah. Fat, high-up peoples, bigwigs…give them a finger they take an arm. Always the same. *We* don't get. *They* get.'

'It's the way of the world, Domenico.' Felix rubbed his index finger and thumb together.

Domenico chuckled. 'You got it, Felix, you got it exact. A den of thiefs and thiefs that got everything hid up and cellar away.' He blew his nose. 'What can we do? Isn't proper Italian hospitality like it should be hospitality. Even in prison. Still has to be a prison, sure, but still it shouldn't make bad manners. You aren't no criminal, Felice. Just got caught on the wrong side is all.'

'Yes.' Felix paused and suddenly felt overwhelmed with longing for home. He shook his head.

Domenico fell silent, and then said: 'Don't hold back feelings, Felix. Need to feel and not be embarrass. Like a rain butt gets full, the water has to spill over. Is the same. Has to flow over. All that sorrow you try to keep inside? Can't do it. Have to let your feelings go.'

'Thing is, I'm not sure what they are. I've got books, your company, food. I'm safe, in no danger, and I ought not to have it so easy.' He glanced for a moment at the uniform jacket hanging on the door, a tawdry reminder of what had been expected of him and what he'd failed in.

Domenico saw the ache of the dilemma in the young man and said nothing. He reached across and patted Felix's hand.

Felix recovered himself. 'I've even got used to coffee made with acorns,' he said.

Domenico, all feigned shock, expostulated. 'Acorns, Felix? Not just ordinary acorns anyone picks. Is *roasted* acorns. *Roasted* acorns.'

'Ah, of course roasted. How could I be so thoughtless?'

'Yes, you ungrateful.' He laughed but Felix had fallen silent, thinking of that most potent symbol of home, the aroma of real coffee in a Viennese café.

Domenico caught his mood. 'You miss home.'

'Yes.'

'Tell me all what you miss. No good pretending you don't miss things, Felix. Or, you become a saint this past year?'

Felix sighed. 'Oh, God, the idea...'

He stared out of the window for a few seconds and, speaking to the enclosed world outside the panes of glass, said: 'I miss the coffee of a Viennese Kaffeehaus. I wonder if there's anything like it anywhere else in the world. Perhaps because it goes with the smell of fresh baking - warm sponge cakes, Sacher torte, Linzer torte, Kuchen, Kipfen, Strudel, Stollen. We grow up with those aromas. In the cafés where we go to meet friends, read the newspapers, exchange news, the buzz of talk all round, the coils of smoke from cigarettes of black tobacco, the clink of cups in saucers, people coming and going. Vienna and coffee and Kuchen...one scent of that coffee, those cakes, and, well, it's home, you see.' He smiled.

Domenico gave him a knowing look. 'And home makes you think of girls, maybe? One girl particular?'

'No, there's no girl.'

'You got no special girl?'

'No.'

'Well, maybe not such a bad thing. Time enough to get settle. And we got a saying.' His face crinkled with glee. 'Hair on a woman's, you know,' he pointed at his crutch, 'got more strength to pull a man than an oxcart.'

Felix blushed.

'Now, I got not much experiencing here – I only went ever with one woman but she was...she was...' He didn't continue. 'But you only have to get scent of a rose once to know it has sweet perfume. So, I can tell you, truth is, women don't like too much thinking not enough laughing, not young women, specially, not too serious. Like you got no time for them, too much in yourself. Better make her laugh, make her feel good inside herself. You don't feel good about your self, what chance you got? You get all furrowed here,' he tapped his forehead, 'and pity me? You make *them* all furrow brow and *that's* a pity. Don't get nowhere. You *been* with a woman?'

Felix stared once more out of the window. 'Yes, I have.'

Domenico looked across at him and pondered.

'Maybe missing lots, here, Felix, but isn't no one trying to shoot you, blow you up. Is something not so bad, I think. Something what a lot of young men your age cold under the ground now – came out to war like you and boom, bullet, big gun, their life goes finish, like a match blown out – they had an offer of what there is here, you know what they'd say? Course you know what they'd say. Ah, *basta*, enough me babbling like a priest in the pulpit.'

'It's what I think about more than anything, the one thing I can't shake off. My men.'

The old man sighed and leaned back in the chair. 'I know. Sure thing, think about your men…but think too much, maybe. Worry don't change nothing.'

'No. Still, it's hard *not* to worry.'

Domenico said: 'Yes, is hard.' He folded his arms. 'You're a good boy, Felice, a good sensible boy and you talk all right. The only people I know was reading books before I know you was lawyers and priests, and what they get out of books doesn't do people like me much good. So I got my suspicions about them. Not you, though, which makes me think different. Only, one thing I say is, maybe can be too much in books, isn't so good for you. World outside, too, got to see what's going on there, listen and look. Not like some monks in a monastery all shut in from the outside, might as well be a prison.'

'Except that I don't have much choice, do I?'

'There I go, put my big boots in it, talking not thinking. Not fair on you. What choice you got?'

'You connect me with the outside, a bit of it, anyway.'

'I don't bring nothing so special. Nothing I can say to you so much, not stories what you got there. Just every day what happens things.'

'Even so, stops me from going crazy.'

Domenico glanced sideways, then out of the window again. 'Not crazy, Felix.' He flipped the latest book open at the title page. 'Take you a long time, I think, Felix, to read all this. Maybe you even won't finish before they open the door and say "Free, now. Peace got signed. Off you go home." Then…' He paused and didn't have to go on.

They both fell silent.

Felix broke off a piece of the bread Domenico had brought, spread some jam, and said: 'One thing I do know. I'll never be ungrateful for anything, ever again.'

'You don't act ungrateful, Felix, no no no.' He took a sip of coffee. 'What they tell you happened to them?'

Felix licked a crumb off his lip. 'My men?'

'Yes.'

'Nothing. Told me it wasn't my concern any more. Except it is. Has to be.'

'They don't understand that.'

'I gave up asking. So you go round in circles wondering how many were killed, how many were wounded. Did they get looked after? Are the others being treated well? Don't ask questions, they told us, all the way through training. Do what you're told. Shut up and get on with it. Well, I didn't do what I was told to do and I go on asking questions. Some kind of officer.'

'Doesn't do no good, to think like that, Felix, even if you feel.' He leaned back on the chair. 'Say you ask me: "Domenico, who you choose? You choose an officer going to tell you to get yourself killed to be a good soldier, or you choose the officer who tells you, listen boys, no sense in going on fighting here, just so you can die, we got no chance, sensible thing is to stop?" You ask me which one I choose, eh?'

'That's not a choice we're allowed to make.'

'But you make it for yourself.'

'That's just the trouble. It's not how they think.'

'Think, you call it?'

'The fact is, it was my duty to look after my men and I didn't.'

Domenico snorted. 'Felix, please, course you did. You look after them, you save them. Why you go on tormenting yourself?'

Felix toyed with the knife, pushing at the flecks of jam and the crumbs on the plate. 'I don't need to,' he said. 'It's just that I keep hearing that voice in my head, that officer at the side of the road. Then I go back over that march, the dark and the rain, the attack, men calling out and me so-called in charge and completely at a loss. On the razor's edge, isn't that what you say? And here I am, safe and cared for, reading books, sometimes I feel…I don't know, rather ashamed.'

'Ashamed?'

'Yes…'

127

'Felix, listen to me. You got absolute no reason to feel shame. That's what *they* do to you, put shame on you. Like punishing a child by telling him guilt. Easy done by grown-ups, only pass on punishment what they got when they was kids. Any weak person has bad time as kid, they put the hurt they suffer back on kids. Never faced up to what happen to them, never been strong and put it aside.

'That man giving orders, saying what *you* had to do, what did *he* do? Just stood, no danger, by the side of the road. They got nothing to lose, they put it all on you. Any man got nothing to lose, you got to be careful of him. Their feelings get blunt like an old chisel, if they ever had feelings, see? Probably cry when they get beat by their fathers, but the more they get hit it goes two ways. They wear out any feeling or it get too much and they suffer, always suffer. Is a tricky thing, feelings, but you gotta know, Felix, some people don't got many, some people don't got any. They get thick skin, don't notice things. And it's what we say is, a man don't go through some bad time and pay attention to what's happen, he stays a baby all his life.'

He scratched his head. 'Comes a war, the Devil builds more Hell. You got caught in it and you come out alive. But what you got to remember, one thing they got no room for, the men tell you orders, they got no sense here,' he said, tapping his heart. 'Only duty and no consequence. A man spends his life in uniform, he thinks in uniform. But you, you got other ideas, and now you got a memory goes round and round in your head like the hands on a clock, can't stop it, and, I know, no good saying don't wind the clock, Felix. Maybe one day, maybe one day, the clock unwinds itself. Got to hope so.'

Felix didn't reply.

'You got a warm heart, Felix, and you're a decent man. War isn't no place for you. Isn't no place for any man, you ask me. And you ask me why so many wars? I say, so many wars because that's what some men like, they like wars. Till they go. Then they find out… maybe, and maybe not. Now, I got to go. Cold out today. You need a coat for exercise walk.'

He loaded the tray with the remnants of breakfast, and, as he walked over to the door, Felix said: 'Domenico…?'

Domenico turned and said: 'See you later.' He left the room and turned the key in the lock.

Felix went over to the wash basin and gazed into the mirror, the silvering flaking on one edge, a faint crack across one corner. And another echo came in his head: the sermon on honour as preached by Klausewitz.

"Of all the passions that inspire a man in a battle," he wrote, "none, we have to admit, is so powerful and so constant as the longing for honour and renown.

"Obstinacy is a fault of temperament. Stubbornness and intolerance of contradiction result from a special kind of egotism, which elevates above everything else the pleasure of its autonomous intellect, to which others must bow."

He reached for his toothbrush and the tin of chalky tooth powder. If only it were so easy to brush his memory clean.

A week later, an afternoon of November chill and overcast sky, the room of the door swung open and the Italian liaison officer marched in with two young soldiers, each carrying a rifle. Felix was sitting at the table. The officer walked across, laid a creased telegram form in front of Felix, then nodded to the two soldiers, who began to ransack Felix's belongings. They turned the mattress over, strewed his clothes on the floor, upturned his kit bag to check that it was empty. The officer himself shook the pages of the book Felix was reading, picked up his sketchbook and went through it. Then his notebook. He flicked through, stopped at a page, read, sniffed, turned more pages, read another extract, closed the book and tossed it onto the table.

The two soldiers were standing by the door, their search completed. Felix was staring at: 'Lieutenant Breitenbach, Felix. Regret to inform. Death of mother. Signed: Captain Paul Rosen. Adjutant.' It was dated 3 August.

He looked up at the Italian officer. 'When did this arrive?'

The Italian shrugged.

'Why have you done this?' Felix gestured at the ruins of his minuscule territory.

'You're being fed adequately, Lieutenant, you have the exceptional privilege of books and so on. Good day.'

The three Italians left the room and the door slammed shut. The key turned in the lock.

Downstairs, the officer sought out Domenico.

'The door to the room was left unlocked. You left the room unlocked.'

'I'm sorry. I must have forgot.'

'You were given strict orders to keep the room locked at all times, except for the purpose of allowing the prisoner to take exercise.'

'Yes, sir.'

'Make sure you comply in future, or else the consequences will be hard on you, and your prisoner. Do you understand?'

'Yes sir.'

The military trio drove off.

Felix looked again at the hateful news.

When Domenico brought the evening meal – a bowl of vegetable soup, a square of coarse brown bread, a small bowl of raisins, a glass of water – he found Felix, his head bowed, sitting on the floor, leaning against the wall, the disorder of the room still untouched. His cheeks were streaked with dried tears.

Domenico put the tray on the table. 'Felix?'

Felix glanced up.

'What they done? What's happen?'

Felix shook his head and let the telegram slip from his fingers onto the floor.

'You got bad news?'

Felix nodded and whispered something inaudible.

Domenico went over and crouched on one knee in front of him. Felix whispered again, coughed and in a quiet, clear voice said: 'My mother died. I don't know how or when. They don't say. Just, she died.'

Domenico paused a moment then reached across and patted Felix on the shoulder.

'Heavy loss, Felix. All you say about her, your mother, heavy loss. Sorry. Sorry.'

Felix didn't speak. He regarded the old man for a stunned interval and whispered: 'Thank you.'

18

Vienna. That same afternoon.

Georg and Claudia walked, arm in arm, along the Mariahilferstrasse. They'd been shopping in the Stafa department store, where Georg bought her a silk scarf, and then spent an hour in Dobner's café, wreathed in those aromas for which Felix so hankered.

It was a clear, bright winter's day. A crowded streetcar clanked by. An overspill of passengers crammed the open platforms – men in bowler hats, a couple of infantrymen in uniform, women muffled up against the cold, the conductress perched on the platform step, holding onto the side rail.

The uniforms prompted thoughts of Felix. It had taken some finagling, words in ears, polite pressure, tiptoe and whisper along the usual channels, to get any inkling of what had happened to him, but Georg was nothing if not resourceful. Breitenbach, Felix, last known, posted to the Front on the Isonzo, early September 1915. No further information on record.

'You remember Felix?' he said.

'The one who joined the army?'

'Yes.'

'What about him?'

'I'm worried about him.'

'From what I recall he didn't have to join the army and you were pretty shirty about it at the time.'

'Yes, I was. Even so. He's my friend.'

'Well, if he's been killed or wounded, it'd be reported, wouldn't it? Casualty lists? So, if there isn't, he's a prisoner, isn't he? Bored out of his mind, thin as a stick and sex-starved, but safe.' Her voice was flat, dismissive.

'You don't really do sympathy, do you?'

'I'm just saying what's likely to be the case. Sorry if you don't approve of being realistic.'

He paused. 'It's not that I don't…oh, to hell with it. I just hope he's all right, that's all. It'd be nice if you shared my concern. You know? Moral support?'

She didn't reply. He said: 'I need to go back to the office.'

'I thought you had the rest of the day off?'

'I did, but a pile of work came in this morning, apparently. Requisitions. It's urgent, They phoned.'

She was suspicious. 'When did they phone?'

'This morning. First thing. You were in the bath.'

She sulked. 'Why does it have to be you?'

'Don't be grumpy.'

'I'm not being grumpy.'

'There is a war on.'

'It'll get on perfectly well without you.'

'Darling, you're not listening.'

'*Dah*ling,' she said in mockery, unlinking her arm from his. 'I know you. You're going back to the office because you want to go back to the office so don't pretend otherwise. It insults my intelligence. What are you waiting for? Go on. Go.'

'Claudia…'

'No. I shall be perfectly content painting my toenails, knowing that you are up to your delicate sensibilities in paperwork, contributing valuable expertise to the war effort. Or should it be War. Effort?'

'Don't be such a shrew.'

'Your shrew.'

How many times, he thought, how many times had they been trapped in the stalemate of her caprice and his frustration, and every time how he cursed the seeming inevitability of it. Perhaps she, too.

'Listen,' he said, 'I'll be back as soon as I can and we can...'

She was ignoring him. 'Does that rather sad little button-nose creature with the froth of baby curls and the dimple still trot in and out with the coffee?'

'What are you getting at?'

'She looks far too young to be doing anything so grown up.'

'What...?'

'What was her name? Thumbelina?'

'What are you insinuating?'

'Nothing, nothing at all.'

'God, you can be infuriating.'

'Grumpy again,' she said, looping her arm through his. It unnerved him. She snuggled against him, in a mercurial switch of mood, a change of tactic, rather than a gesture of peace.

'Why do you do this?' he said again.

She dug her elbow in his side. *Because of you, why else?* They walked on without speaking.

'How long will you be?' she said after a long deliberation about what to say next.

'I don't know.' He was tight-lipped.

'I thought we were going to have a nice time. You promised.'

He took a deep breath. Gentle surrender. 'Darling, I'm sorry.'

'You said so. *I've got a free day*, you said. *The war can wait.*' She paused. 'That's what you said.

He didn't reply at first. She crooked her arm tighter and pinched him.

'Ouch. I know,' he said, 'and I wouldn't go in if it weren't pressing, I promise.'

She didn't answer.

'We'll have a nice time later, there'll be treats.'

'You and your treats.' She didn't smile. 'You can be such a bore, you know, such a lump.'

'Leave it, Claudia, leave it. Let's just…be at peace.'

'But there's a war on. You said it.'

He lost his temper. 'I know there's a fucking war on, but that's not the fucking point. Don't be so fucking obtuse.'

She bowed her head, thoughts tumbling, with him, without him, trust and mistrust, the impossibility of knowing, depending, being sure, and the paradox of kindness and cruelty wearing the same mask… Now that it is winter, I'll put you in a passion, and fan your rage to fever pitch with taunt and provocation. When you're stoked up, blazing hot, I'll cease my raillery, and draw up close, to toast my toes and fingers on your fury. She stole a glance sideways at him. Almost instinctively, her eyelashes fluttered, but the charm was spent.

They reached the apartment. Her face was set, the familiar blank intense look of dismay, apprehension, her eyes as expressionless as a cat's. He'd once more thrown her, pushed her, driven her into the dead-end of rejection, that's how it felt, the hollows of loneliness, the ruins of shattered confidence. Could he, could anyone, possibly ever know how dark and painful it was, this solitude she had to endure, how frightening the panic that tightened in her breast at the very hint of abandonment?

He unhooked his arm. 'I'll be as quick as I can,' he said, knowing the signs of her fragmentation, trying to reassure her. She didn't speak. 'Darling…?' Her expression didn't change. He pulled her to him. She hung in his arms as it were lifeless, and then cleaved to him. 'As quick as I can,' he whispered and kissed her cheek and gingerly, not to let her fall, pulled away. He looked into her eyes, touched his lips and walked off.

As he approached the corner where the various tram lines intersected and made a sort of cat's cradle of rails, a young woman in an elegant, slim-fitting, ankle-length coat with a fur collar buttoned under the chin, called out behind them: 'Georg?'

He turned round. 'Katharina. Goodness gracious. How are you? It's been ages. I thought you and Helga were in…' He couldn't remember. Somewhere in the country. Fresh air. They'd gone there for Helga to convalesce.

Katharina didn't react to his kiss. She stood quite still, in obvious distress.

'Katharina? What's wrong?' She clenched her fists, struggling for control. 'What's happened?'

He held Katharina by the shoulders. Her head sank.

'Darling…?' he said. She shook her head. 'Oh, damn,' he said. 'Is it Helga?'

The name seemed to punch into her with solid force. She gulped, sobbed and began to weep.

'But they said…they said she'd recovered…'

'They *said*. Oh, yes, they *said* she'd be all right. Diphtheria? No, no, there's nothing to worry about. Liars, fucking liars. We were going to…when she got better…we were going to leave this…this bloody place for good. This damned vacuous little city. This seedy mendacious small-minded stagnant pond.' She scraped at her eyes.

'What happened?' he said, overborne by disbelief, taking hold of her.

Katharina looked at him. 'What happened?' She pulled away and stared in horror. 'She died, died died fucking died. *That's* what happened. She died. The only person I ever truly loved, who loved me.' The tears came back and split her apart, heart and reason.

Georg's head buzzed with the brutal finality of it. 'Oh fuck,' he said.

Katharina almost smiled 'And now there's no point. She's dead and everything died with her.'

'Katharina, come on…don't say that.'

The look was venomous. She growled: 'Don't tell me what to say. How would you know? Jesus.'

'Katharina, I'm so so sorry. She was…is there anything I can do?'

'*Do?*' She laughed. 'What can anyone do?'

'Are you…are you going, coming, back to the apartment?'

'That's why I'm here. To scour the place out, nothing left, all gone. Empty the whole damned lot.'

'But where are you going to go?'

Katharina began to walk off. He called after her.

'Katharina? Where are you going? K?'

She stopped and turned round. 'Anywhere. Nowhere. Who

cares? Away from here. As far away from this damned miserable heartless place as possible. Without her. Without … any of you.' She walked away.

'Shit,' he said, staring after her, the shoulders hunched, feet striking the pavement as if there might be some alleviation of the grief in stamping it into the stone to crush it. 'Shit.'

19

October, 1918

Felix looked through the grimy pane. How he longed to see anything other than weather-stained stonework, a slanting fold of roof tiles, a blank canvas of sky of varying colour, pale or cobalt blue, mud white, lampblack or, as now, autumnal grey, the wash lined with scrawls of cloud, strips of thin vapour, or stamped with an anaemic sun, a fluctuating moon, an appliqué of stars. A skein of geese flew across, their hoarse honks of apparent threnody fading as they diminished in view and were gone. Then he heard a rumble of thunder in the east. The sky gave no hint of storm. The thunder persisted but came no nearer.

The day waned. Felix did nothing. It was one of those times when the energy drained from him. To think or not to think, that's just the pain of it, no choice in either. The key in the door squeaked, the handle snicked and Domenico came in with the supper tray which he put down on the table. Felix waved in acknowledgement.

'There must have been a storm nearby,' he said.

Domenico echoed: 'Storm, Felix?'

'I heard thunder.'

The old man didn't respond but pointed at the tray. 'Is cheese. Local.' He clicked his teeth. 'Is not so easy now these days.' He looked at Felix and tapped his nose with a finger, smiling and said: 'Is all I can say.'

And the more that he could not say was that on the way back from the house belonging to the couple who made the cheese he'd seen columns of Italian soldiers on the road, moving eastwards. Trucks, field guns, limbers, drove past, followed by ambulances.

Domenico stood in a small group of villagers by the roadside and watched. Soldiers waved at him. He heard one of them shout 'Piave or death'. Others echoed him: 'Piave or death,' and they cheered and waved their helmets.

A man standing next to Domenico nudged him. 'Piave or death,' he said and tapped the ground with his walking stick. Domenico didn't know what Piave meant. 'It's the mountain over there,' said another man, pointing in the direction of the march. 'No, it's the river. Piave is the river.' The other man snarled. 'What do you know?' A third man intervened. 'Ignoramus. It's the river. Between us and them. That's where it'll be.' 'Where what'll be?' said he of the mountain theory. 'The battle. That's where.' 'Who can fight on a river?' said the mountains theorist and, to prove his opinion said: 'On a mountain you can fight.'

Domenico left them to it. River, mountain, what did it matter? The thunder was guns, that's what the thunder was, guns, ours or theirs. And maybe the storm the thunder announced was the Austrian army swarming over the mountain or across the river to swallow them all up. He set off back to the palazzo.

A month later, Felix sat drawing. In the course of the year, he'd made studies of the room entire, the room in detail, the door, the floor, the window with different patterns of the sky visible through it. He'd drawn the bed, the washbasin, the table on which lay the books, the chair. This mid-morning in the third winter of his confinement, he was drawing the courtyard below the window. And with every drawing came a nuanced perspective expressive of his mood, fluctuations of light and of line – now sharp, now impressionistic, now clumsy and without touch – always introverted. In the shifting acres of his imagination he roved, often like a newcomer.

His concentration on line with the pencil switched into reverie and thoughts of the men out there, the soldiers:

What did you do all that time, Felix? All that time we were fighting, killing, being killed, constantly shot at and blown to smithereens of flesh and bone, living in the filthy, stinking wet, the biting icy cold, sloshing day after long miserable day through mud, snow, rain, shit, blood, piss, what were you doing? Where were you when we were struggling back to the lines with the loaded stretchers, the wounded, the maimed and crippled, the dead, the legions of the dead? Comrades and strangers alike. What were you scoffing and drinking when we were drinking swill and sucking at our belts for a taste of meat?

'Me? I was staring out of a window, down onto a deserted stone quadrangle with grass and weeds lining the joints in the paving. And into the quadrangle, once a week, a girl came to hang out the washing. She wasn't pretty. She had coarse features, straggling reddish hair, brawny arms, shoulders like shelves and her hips hung off her waist like a bushel sack of meal. She wore heavy wooden clogs and a dress of what looked like burlap. Every Monday morning at about ten o'clock she dumped the washing basket on the ground and pulled out the linen, some of it my sheets. I can hear you spitting, *clean fucking linen?* And when she bent over, her great stolid arse went up, and I imagined…you can guess what I imagined, boys. And what about you, all this time? Did you have to imagine or could you do it?

'In the long hours of monotony, of this pared down existence, I filleted the pages of books. I read about love, about passion and desire, requited and unrequited, about hatred and revenge, about longing and loneliness and solace and comfort, and how the world goes as men and women make it go, more often than not by cussed persistence in folly or guesswork. I read and had no part in it.

'I thought about the violence, the barbarities that humankind is capable of, the mindless cruelties that war excuses. And in this cell of a room, cut off from the world and the inhumanity you suffered and inflicted, because you had orders to, did I, effectively a hermit, somehow become something different? More innocent? Suffering no harm? Inflicting no harm? Divorced from that inhumanity? Causing no pain? Somehow less culpable? Am I, have I become, less than or more than you for what I have not done? Does inaction condemn me forever to making excuses for my lack of shame?

'Eating at one end and shitting at the other, we are a composite of plenty and waste. Even the saint in pious seclusion has to defecate and wrestle with his demons. Didn't Luther do both at the same time?

'There's a story about a man who locks himself away from the world, away from the stink and disease of mankind, to live a life of perfect virtue. Then Death comes for him and Death says: "Blind fool, I'll teach you to value and be worthy of life just once, before I take you, by introducing you to pain, the pain of loss, of grief, of betrayal, the pain of *being human*."

'And that's about the sum of it, boys. I philosophised myself into blind alleys. Through arguments this way and arguments that way, I came to what promised to be enlightenment, only to see it vanish, like a dream on waking. I thought I had enlightenment cornered once, but then my brain gave out and it was gone, like Tantalus's feast.

'I ate, I slept. I spent my time in a palazzo inhabited by a kindly Italian and me, sole occupants. Sound fantastical? I read umpteen books and I gazed at a stone quadrangle round which, for two hours every day, I was allowed to walk and look at the open sky or stone walls perforated with shuttered windows. I saw no trees, no flowers, no sign of life beyond the high walls. Conversation apart, I heard nothing but the wind, the building's own peculiar creakings, sometimes a bird, the splash and gurgle of water from a tap.

'I walked up and down the room, up and down, up and down, round and round. From time to time I stood over the chamber pot and masturbated, pretty well the only other physical exertion open to me. That way I had all the women I've ever had, over and over again. And every time, it meant nothing, as it had always meant nothing, as lying with them for the brief time it took never meant anything.'

The bells of the church began to ring, a tuneless, two-note boing boing.

'I chased the wraiths of reality. I lived in memory. I paced the margins of my existence and pretended.

'As for what you did, boys, I'm not sure if I'd have been up to it, in truth. One thing is sure: I shall never find out, now. I made a mess of the only action I saw, I failed, I escaped unscathed into gaol. I had, and have, no way of redeeming myself.'

As he cross-hatched and smudged the lines of the soft pencil to shade in the angle of a small buttress in the sketch, he heard footsteps on the landing outside the room, the key turning in the lock, Domenico's voice 'Felix, Felix…'

The door opened. Domenico stood there, grinning.

'Felix… Hear the bells? War is over. Finish.' He all but sang it.

'What?'

'Yes, yes, you hear right. Finish.' He half closed his eyes and rocked his head from side to side, brimming over with the pleasure of the news.

Felix laid the sketch pad and pencil on the table. He whispered: 'But that means…'

'Yes.' The old man stopped. 'Yes, it means go home, maybe soon, maybe not so soon but final, go home.' The implications of this were not lost on either of them.

'Felix?' said the old man. 'You happy?'

'I don't know. I ought to be.'

Neither spoke. What hadn't come with the long-awaited news was knowing how to accommodate it.

At last Domenico said: 'You feel like going out, maybe?'

'Out?'

'Sure.' He pointed vaguely. 'Nice day.'

'You mean outside, right outside?'

'I don't know that, maybe not yet, but outside, and no time limit. Enjoy the sun.'

In the weeks that followed, no official communiqué arrived. The visiting subaltern did not come. The war might well have ended but the daily routine in the palazzo remained as it had been throughout the captivity. Inevitably, one thing did change. Conversation with Domenico became tentative, even evasive. Each man shied away from the inevitable consequence of the peace: the farewell. They knew that once the day of Felix's release came, it was almost certain that they'd never see each other again.

So, they talked about nothing much at all, skirting the one thought which preoccupied them both. And still the key turned in the lock.

'Very sorry, Felix. Got no orders not. You understand?'

'I understand.'

20

Vae victis...

At last, one morning of sharp frost in February, the Italian subaltern came, very full of himself, his unbuttoned uniform overcoat freshly pressed, the boots glistening. He did not need to say *woe to the vanquished*, his bullish manner said it for him.

He strode into the room, a slim, leather attaché case under one arm. Felix was lying on the bed, reading. He sat up and swung his legs over the side.

The Italian laid the case on the table and pulled off his gloves, finger by finger.

'Lieutenant Breitenbach. I have good news for you. You're free to go home.'

'Why have I had to wait so damned long?'

The Italian raised his eyebrows.

'Come, now, no need to get worked up,' his hands gesturing *softly, softly*. 'You have to appreciate, there were complications of administration which made arranging it any sooner impossible.'

'The war finished over three months ago, didn't it?'

The Italian, in the happy position of being able to brush this off, said: 'There were formalities which had to be observed. Protocols.'

Felix wasn't listening. He stood up. 'Three months. I'm the only one here. So why did it…?'

The subaltern swivelled round. 'Lieutenant Breitenbach, a war does not just stop. Think of trying to extricate yourself from a thicket of brambles. Things don't return to normal over night. You think all it takes is goodbye and good luck?'

'No.' Felix sat back down on the bed.

'I understand your frustration and I sympathise.'

'Do you really?'

'Lieutenant Breitenbach, let us understand each other. I'm trying to make this as easy as it can be and I'd remind you, you're still our prisoner and we did win the war against your armies. In the circumstances, we might be rather less generous. I apologise for what must seem to you a needless prolongation of your confinement here. Blame the logistical and administrative chaos that ensued on the armistice. We've done all we had to do as fast as we could. There were many, very many, *other* prisoners besides you to deal with.'

He opened the document case, took out a small sheaf of papers and laid it on the table. One sheet he held out to Felix.

'This is authority for your immediate repatriation as well as forms for your official release from our custody as a prisoner-of-war of the *victorious* Italian Land Forces over those of Austria-Hungary.'

He organised the documents on the table, removed a pen from his tunic pocket, unscrewed the cap and held the pen out to Felix.

'If you'll sign here…here…and here. Excellent.' He took the pen back. 'A cart is waiting to take you to the railway station at Treviso and from there by train to Vienna.'

'Treviso?'

The officer didn't respond. He checked that the ink on the signatures was dry, handed one page to Felix.

'This is for you. Your *laissez passer*.' He shuffled the other pages back into a pile, put them back in the case and the case under his arm. He picked up his gloves.

'And now you speak Italian. Good luck, Lieutenant, in peacetime. War was not so unkind to you. You leave in half an hour.' He sketched a salute and left the room without closing the door.

Felix looked round the room, the unlocked room.

There was a light knock. Domenico stood in the open doorway.

'Felix...you're going home.'

'It seems so.'

The old man came in, looked round, blew his nose and stuffed the red handkerchief, big as a napkin, into his pocket. 'You got everything?'

Felix stood up and walked over to the table. He picked up his sketch book.

'I want you to keep this, Domenico.' He held out the book. Domenico took it, opened it, looked at Felix, puzzlement in his face.

'But, Felix...is all your drawings. All you drew in here.'

'To remember me by.'

'Felix, friend...you think I ever forget you, my officer with the books?'

Felix shook his head. 'Thank you, Domenico. Me, too.'

Domenico opened the book again, turned a couple of pages, closed it. A short silence, then he said: 'Thousand thank yous,

Felix, bottom of my heart.' He bunched the finger tips of his right hand and put them to his lips. Then he frowned. 'But I got nothing to give you.'

'You already did, Domenico, more than you can ever know.'

Domenico wiped at his eyes, straightened up. 'You want help packing?'

'No, it's all right, there isn't much.'

'You sure?'

Felix nodded.

'I wait for you downstairs. With the cart.'

'I won't be long.'

Domenico lingered in the doorway. 'Something I like to show you before you go. Just something.' He left.

Felix looked round the room. How different from that other room he'd vacated before all this happened. How full of him it was, this unlikely prison he'd inhabited for so long. How replete with memory. The discomfort of being a captive paled before the kindness, the humanity, he'd found there. The sadness of leaving was compromised by a pricked sense of what he ought to feel - gratitude. But a vivid sunset does not dampen its glory because someone is dying in its light. Freedom cannot exist without the coexistence of chains.

Felix's bag loaded on the cart by the open gates of the Palazzo, a light dusting of snow on the ground, the driver muffled in a khaki greatcoat, woollen hat and gloves, Domenico said: 'Five minutes, five minutes…'

The driver shrugged.

Domenico led Felix round the far side of the house to a walled enclosure, its interior perimeter lined with dark cypress trees. They passed through a wrought iron gate into what had

149

been the private cemetery of the Gabrieli family.

'Palazzo da *Gabrieli*,' said Domenico, 'now you can know. No more secret.'

He walked over to one corner of the little graveyard crowded with shrines adorned with elaborately carved pediments and inscriptions, some with long epitaphs. He stopped in front of a small cast iron rectangular plaque set into the wall. It was quite clean, neither tarnished with rust nor coated with verdigris, evidently cared for. Domenico clasped his hands together and bowed.

On the stone, Felix read:
Brentani, Francesca 1868-1896
Brentani, Giulia 1889-96
Requiescant in pace

Domenico whispered: 'Hello my dear dears,' then turned to Felix. 'It was fever, some sort of very bad fever. Spared me. Don't know why. Who knows why?'

Felix mumbled:'I don't know what to say.'

'Then don't say nothing,' said Domenico, kindly and, without looking, patted Felix on the shoulder.

21

Vienna. April, 1919.

Felix alighted from the train at Vienna's Sudbahnhof into a compressed smell of steam and coal-dust from the engine, wheezing from its exertions. Other passengers, mostly civilians, straggled along the platform, a few soldiers amongst them, all worn out by the long, stop-start journey. *And in this faceless crowd,* he thought, *my shame in multitudes.*

He walked out into the city wishing he were invisible, dreading the moment when someone might call out *Felix, is that you? Felix...?* He wanted, instead, to pass unnoticed in the well-trodden streets, flit like a shadow, a nameless being fused with the wider anonymity.

The sadness of his mother's death flooded him. And what life was he coming back to, like a prodigal who'd returned only because there was nowhere else to go? There'd be little happiness here and he brought none with him.

And what label would they plant on him? Coward? Deserter? Traitor? Would they revile him: *Austria was defeated because of spineless shits like you. So, what are you doing back here? There's no place for you. We don't need you or any of your lily-livered sort. Great Austria has been brought to her knees, reduced to penury, sold down the river, because gutless individuals like you wouldn't stand up for her when she needed them. She called on you for help and what did you do? You ran.*

He was wearing the now threadbare battle dress, many times cleaned and washed, in which he'd gone to the Front. He might have been just another soldier of so many coming home from the war, unkempt, hollow-eyed, undernourished. Nothing marked him out as a prisoner. Domenico had given him shirts and an old pair of baggy, gardener's trousers to wear, and these he'd packed in his kitbag. A memento.

Vienna was barely recognisable as the exuberant city he'd left almost five years ago. The streets were littered with refuse. Bedraggled men, women, children scavenged through garbage for scraps of food. Paupers, beggars, crippled war veterans, men who'd survived the horrors of war and come back to the privations of peace, haunted street corners like harbingers of a wider doom. They wore signs asking for work, help, a few coins to eke out their absolute impoverishment. Shops were boarded up, with nothing to sell and no customers to buy. Windows of other shops had been smashed by looters and not replaced. The walks of a park, once a pleasure ground, were heaped with rubbish. The roads were, most of the time, clear of traffic, motor-driven or horse-drawn. A tram clanked by, the rickety noise of it like an asthmatic straining for breath. Vienna stank of decay and destitution.

He walked past the open door of a café and saw a dismal tableau of inertia. One man pored over a newspaper, looking for any sort of job. Another stared in morose disaffection. A woman dabbed at her eyes with a handkerchief. Another plucked at a tangle of wool, an unravelled garment, material for a pair of socks. There was no smell of coffee, only a sour pall of chicory.

Had he, then, left roasted acorns and come back to roasted acorns?

The steps leading up to the landing outside the family apartment might have been a treadmill. The effort of climbing them creased him and he was out of breath before he'd got even halfway. His gloom intensified the closer he got. Liberated from one confinement into that other confinement, the prison of his childhood and younger self.

He knocked at the door and waited. He knocked again. Then, his father's voice from inside the apartment:

'All right, already, all right, my God. You don't have to break the door down. Hammer, hammer, hammer.'

The door swung to. His father stood in the open doorway. He didn't speak, trying to work it out, this apparition. *My son? Felix? What are you doing here so sudden? You didn't think to warn me, tell me in advance the shock that was coming? Another shock. What next?*

Then, as if he wasn't sure, he said: 'Felix?'

An hour later, they sat at the table in the kitchen, spooning up mouthfuls of insipid broth, chewing at stale bread, the silence broken only by the clack of the spoons against the chipped china plates.

Felix finished the meal and watched his father, head bowed over the bowl, slurping the tasteless liquid.

Felix said: 'How did mother die?'

His father rasped: 'One minute she's alive, next minute she's dead, that's how she died, same as anyone dies. You were in a war, you have to ask?'

'I mean, what did she die of?'

'Then say what you mean, straight off. Don't prevaricate, for god's sake.'

Felix took a deep breath. 'What, then? What did she die of?'

His father sat back in the chair. 'As if it makes any difference.' He was shouting. 'Dead is dead. You can't be satisfied with that, you have to rake it all up? A broken heart is what she died of.'

'Father, no one dies of a broken heart.'

His father sat up, banged the handle of the spoon on the table, the plates rattled. Livid with pain, he said: 'So suddenly you're a medical expert, too, on top of everything? *She* did. Your *mother* did. A broken heart.'

'I'm sorry, father.'

The reply shot back. 'What are you sorry about?'

'It must have been awful for you.'

'Awful for me? Awful for me?' He scoffed. Spittle flecked his lip. 'What you don't understand, never could understand, all your smart thinking, things happens, you get on with it, you have to be strong, face up to things, you're on your own. No good kvetching, makes no difference. A man bleats how he needs a helping hand? Feh. Look at the end of your own strong right arm, boy, there's the helping hand, only one you can rely on. Your mother broke her heart, over you, over the war, over everything dropped down on top of her like a roof falling in. She got crushed. Crushed. That was her nature, her sweet nature. Too nice for this world. She broke her heart.' He resumed his fretful splashing at the soup.

'I got the telegram months late.'

'That changes things? What difference does it make, when?'

'None, I suppose. Only…'

'None, you suppose. None, you suppose. Pah.' There was a long, loaded pause. 'So…what are you going to do now?'

'I don't know.'

'Well, let me tell you, there's nothing left here. Not for me, not for you, not for anybody. They saw to that. First they bankrupt the Jews, then they bankrupt the whole country. Now Austria is finding out what it's like to be put out of business.'

'I have my arrears of pay…'

His father sat up, incredulous. How could he have sired such a no-hope klutz, a naïve schoolboy? 'Arrears of pay?' he said shaking his head, and, with contempt: 'In your pocket, those *arrears of pay?*'

'Not yet. I have to make a claim.'

'That what they told you, *make a claim?*' He sniggered. 'And you believed them?' He looked at him, this dopey son of his. 'Nah nah nah, Felix, boy. Too trusting. Just like your mother. You should learn to be a bit more sceptical.'

'I'll go to the War Office in the morning. I also need to find out what happened to my men.'

'What men?'

'Father, I told you what happened.'

'And why should you worry? Did they worry about you?' He laughed.

'Father, that's not the point.'

'Of course it's the point. You spent four years locked up. You don't owe them anything.'

'I feel guilty about them.'

'Oh, guilty. You've got a natural talent for it. Lucky you can afford the luxury of guilty.'

'Father, until I'm officially exonerated, I won't have any peace

155

of mind. I can't just let it rest.'

'Rest? You've had four years rest. Four years peace of mind.'

'Damn it, father. Is it so difficult? Don't you understand?'

'Nah, Felix, I don't understand. It's not in you to talk plain and simple, explain yourself, say what you mean clear straight out. You got a pathometric aversion to clear.'

'I *need* to find out what happened to them. They were under my command…'

His father thumped the table and shouted. 'You *know* what happened. You were there. And *here*, you know what happened? Your mother can't sleep at night for worry. Short of food and clothes and everything like you wouldn't believe. No fuel to get any kind of heat. No money. We get a card, a piece of card with some sort of army address which is no sort of address – you're safe, that's it. That's what happened here. Peace of mind? My God… Peace of mind doesn't exist. If it ever did, it doesn't now, not for any of us, so make your mind up on that one.'

22

The War Ministry

At ten o'clock the next day, Felix arrived at the offices of the War Ministry to be directed to the Records Department, where he joined some twenty other people, mostly women, young and middle-aged, in a cramped waiting room. All the chairs were taken. He stood against the wall. Inured to the practices of boredom, he slipped into a pensive free fall.

What of Georg? he thought. *What of Helga, Katharina, the others? Who would they be, now, to him? Who would he be to them? Everything would be changed, wouldn't it? How would it be to meet almost as a stranger someone he'd known as a friend? Should he search them out? Leave it to chance, a chance meeting? And how was he to face them? How was he to smoke out the termites of his conscience and suppress the more complex hungers of his spirit? Loneliness, grief, an inability to place the experience of the captivity in any rational compass...so much of what had been familiar was unfamiliar in this new, dilapidated Vienna. It was too many things at once and he felt powerless to comprehend.*

He waited his turn for over an hour as people left and more came. The room was muggy with the odours of unlaundered linen and unwashed bodies.

At last it was his turn. He went into the office to find a

sergeant clerk in uniform seated at a large desk. Reading from a prepared form, the clerk asked and recorded his age, address, marital status when enlisted, date of call-up, regiment, rank, details of posting, date of release from custody by the authorities of the Italian High Command…

'And…?' said the clerk, laying down his pen. 'What's the nature of your enquiry?'

'Claiming pay arrears.'

The clerk pulled out another form from one of the bank of drawers behind his desk.

'Deliver this to the Cashiers Department.'

'Thank you.'

'What are you waiting for?'

'There's something else.'

Felix explained. The clerk made no notes and looked bored. When Felix had finished, the clerk leaned back in the chair and snorted. He'd heard it all before, all too often, from civilians turned so-called soldiers.

'And what d'you expect me to do?' he said.

Felix explained. The clerk was, of course, far too busy to enquire into such an obscure event tucked away in an obscure action in the course of four years of war. But Felix persisted and the man finally agreed *to look into it*.

'Come back,' he said, flicking the pages of the large appointments book, 'Friday. *Next* Friday, not *this* Friday.'

'What time?'

'Makes no difference. You wait your turn with everyone else.'

The clerks in the Cashiers Department were harassed and unobliging. Nevertheless, Felix exited from the Ministry four hours after he'd entered it but with an official requisition form, signed and stamped, entitling him to a percentage of the back pay due to him. The cashier explained, as he had explained to so many of them, that he was not entitled to the full amount, because of circumstances which he wasn't empowered to overlook, namely a curtailed active service and lack of proof of whereabouts in the interim between capture and repatriation.

'Why should that make any difference?' Felix asked.

'Don't ask me. I don't make up the rules, I just apply them. Besides,' he added 'we haven't got the money. No one's got the money and now you haven't got the money. Think yourself lucky to get what you've got. That's it. So, off you trot… Lieutenant,' pleased to be imparting bad news.

Returning to the same office to which he'd gone the previous week, Felix found a different clerk rubber stamping a large pile of papers. The clerk didn't look up. 'Yes? What is it?'

'I came last Monday. I was told to come back today.'

The man continued his stamping. 'Were you?'

'The sergeant clerk who was here promised that he'd check the records. I'm Breitenbach, Felix, Lieutenant.'

The rubber stamp fell silent. The man glanced up. 'Which records?'

'I was taken prisoner with my men and…'

The man cocked his head to one side. 'Well, that's a start.' The sarcasm was humourless.

Felix let it pass. 'It was on the Isonzo river.'

'The Isonzo river.'

'Italian Front.'

'Italian Front? What do you know? The Isonzo river being

159

in Italy? Well, there's a thing.'

'Please, would you check?'

The clerk resumed his scanning of the papers, hammered the rubber stamp three more times – thump, page to one side, thump, page to one side, thump, page to one side, and put the stamp down.

'The Italian Front,' he said, looking up, the expression caught between distaste and boredom.

'The Isonzo river. Would you check for me, please? I'd be very grateful.'

'Sergeant…what did you say your name was?'

'Lieutenant. Breitenbach, Felix. I gave details of my unit and the date. Last week. The sergeant recorded them in a register.'

'Ah, Lieutenant. There I go, demoting you. What register would that be?'

'I have no idea. One of yours?'

The clerk leaned forward over the desk. 'I don't have to do this, you know.'

'I'm sorry. I'm a bit…I'm sorry.'

'Last Monday?' The clerk made a show of checking the three ledgers piled on the desk. 'Nothing here that I can see and I've got a lot of work to do.'

This was the game: lowly clerk enjoying unwonted power over the officer. Felix smiled. 'I really would be most grateful.'

The man gave Felix a long hard look then got up and went over to a row of filing cabinets, walked his fingers down the labels, opened a drawer and flicked through a line of folders, muttering: 'Isonzo… Isonzo battles…five between June 1915 and March 1916…'

'It was September 1915.'

The clerk paid no heed and spoke to the files. 'May 1916, Austrian counter-offensive. Followed by another six battles August 1916 to August 1917. Final breakthrough by combined German and Austro-Hungarian forces, November 1917, twelfth battle of the Isonzo, also known as the Battle of Caporetto, Italian retreat across Piave, June 1918, final battle, November 1918, Austrians pushed back towards the Isonzo.' He turned round. 'There you have it, potted history of the Italian Front, Isonzo, battles of the.'

'I was taken prisoner in September 1915.'

The man ignored him, flipped along the files again. 'Some time round the third battle, then. What do you want to know about it?'

'I want to know what happened to the men under command. Monte Santo sector.'

'You said Isonzo sector.'

'It was part of the Isonzo sector. I suppose you'd call it a sector within a sector, a sub-sector.'

The clerk whistled and pushed the drawer shut. 'And you want to know what happened to your men? Just that, what happened to your men.' He slammed the drawer of the filing cabinet shut.

'Yes.'

'You've come to the wrong department, then. We deal with official records, unclassified, Campaigns and Battles. You might try Personnel: Other ranks. Room 420. Along the corridor, down two floors, second, no, I tell a lie, third corridor on the right. Corporal Streffleur.'

'Thank you. Room 420?'

In room 420, Corporal Streffleur was sitting with his feet on a desk, reading a book. Felix waited. Streffleur turned a page and continued reading. Felix coughed. Streffleur continued to read and muttered:

'Yes?'

'I'm Lieutenant Breitenbach. I was sent here by Corporal Grüber.'

'Why?'

Felix explained.

Streffleur glanced sideways and peered over his wire-framed spectacles. 'Why did he send you down here? Personnel records have been relocated to the Military Archive. Across the road. Corporal Friedl.'

'Do you have a room number?'

Streffleur turned another page and said: 'I'm not a telephone directory.'

Felix tracked down Corporal Friedl in the warren of corridors of the military records building. He was typing. Felix stood to wait. Friedl stopped typing. 'Yes?' Felix made his request. Friedl listened with a dutiful patience, explained the situation and then indicated a filing cabinet containing 'all the records available for that sector of operations' and left him to it.

Felix could find nothing. He went back to Friedl.

'Sorry, but are these all the files you have?'

Friedl stopped typing. 'I told you, Lieutenant. We have a million files scattered about this archive. I showed you the files you asked for.'

'Well, there's nothing in them that I can find that's relevant,' Felix said, the exasperation surfacing.

Friedl waited. Felix continued.

'I've looked through battalion orders, casualty lists, missing in action, prisoners of war, repatriation…everything that might have a bearing. There's nothing.'

'And what conclusion do you draw from that, Lieutenant? Possibly that if there's nothing there, there's isn't anything?'

'Please, Corporal. It may not be important to you but it's very important, indeed, to me.'

Friedl laid his arms on the desk top on either side of the typewriter. 'Which files did you ask for?'

'Third Army, Isonzo river, September 1915.'

'What does it say on the labels of those files?'

'Third Army, Isonzo river, September 1915.'

Friedl feigned satisfaction and resumed typing.

'But there's no record in here of the men under my com…' The corporal cut him off.

'*Must* I spell it out…*sir?* If the record isn't in there the record does not exist. What do you want me to do? Make something up?'

'There must, surely, be some record somewhere? Are you telling me my men didn't exist?'

'I'm not telling you anything. If the record exists, it's in those files. And if it's not it doesn't. Now. Are we done?'

Felix refused to budge. 'I can remember some of their names, there was…'

Friedl was angry: 'Have you any idea what you are asking? Sir. Registry of lives and deaths? Please. What are the dates on the documents in those files?'

'August to November 1915.'

'Including September 1915?'

'Yes.'

'Well, then.'

'Are you sure there isn't somewhere else I might look?'

'You know the way out.'

'Where else can I look?'

'Try the door.' He started typing again. The chatter of the keys reawakened memories of the muted stammer of a machine gun.

Waiting outside the door was a captain in the Intelligence Corps. 'Lieutenant Breitenbach?'

'Yes?'

'Come with me, would you?' He led the way along the corridor, down a flight of stairs, along another corridor, down another flight of stairs and across a landing to a door which he opened.' He ushered Felix into what must be his office. He closed the door.

'Do take a seat,' he said and sat down behind a large desk. 'Now, a few routine questions to establish the basic scenario we have here.' He went through the questions put to Felix by the sergeant clerk on his first visit to the building. When he came to 'date of capture?' Felix didn't answer.

'Lieutenant? Did you not hear me? The date when you say you were taken prisoner was…?'

Felix was taken aback. The date *when you say* you were taken prisoner. Didn't they believe him?

'Lieutenant. You do remember, do you?'

Felix shook his head. 'I'm afraid I don't. Not exactly. Not after all this time. It was September. Late September. In 1915.'

The intelligence officer interlaced the fingers of both hands. 'Odd, that, not to remember when something so obviously traumatic occurred to you. I'd have thought that day would be etched deep in your memory.'

'It is.'

'But not the date of the day? The precise moment when the forces against whom the Austrian army, in which you served as a junior officer,' he tapped the file on the desk, 'of that at least we can be more or less certain, not the terrible moment when you were taken prisoner by the Italians.'

'No sir. I'm sorry, I don't. The exact day? Twenty something September? I can't see that it matters, particularly.'

'Allow me to be the judge of that. You see my quandary? You say you spent three years as a prisoner of the Italians but you can produce no proof of the fact. And if you cannot prove it, there's only one conclusion we can draw. That it's entirely possible that you deserted.' Felix protested. The officer held up his hand and went on: 'And, now that the war is over, you come back, bold as a burglar, and even claim back pay.'

'Sir,' said Felix, 'this is absurd. You have the details of my regiment, my posting, it should be easy enough to corroborate what I'm saying.'

The officer raised his eyebrows, pouted his lips and sighed in query. 'Is it true that you've spent some time in several departments in the War Ministry seeking to find out, I quote your words, as reported to me, "what happened to my men"?'

'It is, yes. I wanted to find...'

'With what result?'

Felix lowered his head and said nothing.

The officer continued: 'With no result, exactly. A resounding negative, a complete blank. Nothing known. All vanished. Whereabouts untraced.' He paused. 'Convenient, wouldn't you say?'

'I was taken prisoner by the Italians near the river Isonzo, north of Görz...'

The officer interrupted. 'Now in Italian hands, following our humiliating defeat, and known to them as Gorizia.' The slant was obvious: the humiliation laid at the door of men like this Breitenbach.

Felix cleared his throat. 'I was separated from my men, forcibly separated. I asked again and again what had happened to them and was told nothing.'

The officer did not speak at first. He sat back in his chair. 'Where were you held prisoner?'

Felix looked back at him and didn't reply. The officer repeated the question. Felix bowed his head and said, in a low voice: 'I don't know. Somewhere near Treviso. A large house, a palazzo...'

' "Somewhere near Treviso." In a prison camp? A civil gaol?'

'No.'

'No. "In a palazzo". That's Italian for palace, isn't it?'

And so it went on. Incredulity. Suspicion. Contempt. Sneers. The same questions all over again until Felix hardly knew or cared what he was saying.

'So,' said the officer. 'Where do we go from here?'

Felix felt cornered, battered but defiant. 'Everything I've told you is true,' he said. 'It's beyond me to prove absolutely beyond doubt that it is true. Equally, it's beyond you to prove that it's untrue.' The officer cocked an eyebrow. Felix persisted. 'I volunteered for the army because I felt it was my duty. My patriotic duty and yes, I'm a Jew. To my eternal regret, I unwittingly led my men into a trap because the directions I was given – at night, in the pouring rain - were inaccurate. As a result of that blunder, I have no idea what happened to my men and I spent over three years in solitary confinement even if not under military guard as such and for that I can find no reason because none was given me. That's how it was. I can't make excuses for it. I remember now, the name of the place I was held in. It was the Palazzo da Gabrieli.'

'Which you did not mention before.'

'Because you cut me off before I could tell you and then… it slipped my mind.'

The officer turned his attention to a file on his desk and, without looking up, said: 'What did you say it was called?'

'The Palazzo da Gabrieli.'

The officer stood up, walked across the room and opened the door. He called out: 'Sergeant? Sergeant, take this man to the Guard Room and hold him there until I call for you.'

The Sergeant lifted Felix by one elbow and led him out of the office to a small room in the basement where he was given a cup of watery, lukewarm, ersatz coffee and told to sit on a bench. He was given no food nor any more coffee.

Ten hours later, another Sergeant appeared and escorted him back to the Intelligence officer.

'Lieutenant Breitenbach,' he said. 'We've made some enquiries. It seems feasible that what you've told me is, in some respects, at least, compatible with the circumstances.' Felix was too tired to respond. 'Given that we are overwhelmed with the work of tying up a million loose ends after such a…' He didn't finish. 'Needless to say, there are many more pressing calls on my time than delving into charges against a possible – I say possible, in regard to your insistence that what you've told me is true – a possible deserter. In which case, we are minded to let you go. However, in the light of what is an overall unsatisfactory, if not fanciful, account of how you spent three years of the war in a private house, we have annulled any claim you may already have made for arrears of pay. Without appeal. Have you anything to say?'

There was much to say and Felix felt the words reeling in his mind, a torrent of protest, disbelief, anguish, the pent up tension of his relief at being released and fury at the ill usage it had brought him. He said, however, nothing.

'Very well. You're free to go.' That an Austrian officer should be saying the same words that an Italian, an enemy, officer had said to him not so long before was an irony which, briefly, made this disgraceful interlude seem absurd, even ludicrous.

He walked out into the night.

23

Georg

The following morning, he went to the apartment where Georg had lived. He'd moved. The occupant gave him the address Georg had left, for forwarding mail. It was on the other side of the city. Felix walked there, in a muddle about what it would be like, to see his friend again, to be reunited with the others, to relate all that had happened to them, the four friends, in the long separation they'd gone through, and, when he saw the nameplate under the bell – Georg Strauss - his nerve failed. A silence between friends is only a conversation interrupted, isn't it? Now he was not sure how to broach that.

Doubt and indecision tore at him. What would *he* say? The very least he'd feel was embarrassment at the complete bodge he'd made of his 'patriotic duty'. What would *Georg* say? Welcome home? It would have to begin with banalities, wouldn't it? There was too much to address simply to plunge in. The promises of their younger selves had been sucked into an oblivion for which none of them could have prepared. This tawdry present was what their future had become. How were they to resume living in a world they no longer recognized, a world cobbled together out of defeat and the destruction of all they'd known? Now we are nothing, he thought. We may have been slight in thinking, tender in experience, wildly optimistic in ambition or aspiration before all this happened, when we stood on the brink of our limitless future, but we were never *nothing*. We were *friends*, Helga, Katharina, Georg and Felix, and we'd promised to remain friends. They'd told him he was misguided, idiotic, to join up and see how he'd proved them right. Felix Breitenbach went to war and the war said 'I have no need of you, Herr Breitenbach, so toddle off, why don't you, back into your corner, safe and sound? War is for grown ups.'

And then, a gust of self-mockery raced through him, and like a dog shaking off water, he shook himself awake. He'd faced bullets. All he had to do was press a doorbell.

A voice behind him said: 'Felix?'

He turned round. It was Georg.

'And Katharina?' Felix didn't, couldn't, ask immediately. The news about Helga's death, all that time ago, now, was too much to absorb, too ghastly to encompass. Sweet-natured Helga, bursting with energy and joie de vivre, passionate, concerned. He thought, with a sticky feeling in his throat, of that last time he'd seen her, that bruising envoi. The fiery rage which had rocked him, rattled him so badly, as if he'd only then understood how the need to love in her warred with disappointment, with ruined expectation. How could he have missed that? And then she'd found Katharina, they'd found each other, although, of course, they'd both been there all along, but undiscovered. It was when Katharina told him about her and Helga that day, near comical, the oddity of it, the unexpected delight in it. How had it happened between them, the discovery, the realization? The obvious and open love that had eluded them both and now surfaced in each of them like fresh health after a debilitating illness? Sweet Helga *dead*? Death, one way or another, had dug its talons into them all.

Georg brooded. Had Felix changed, he asked himself. That was stupid. Of course he'd changed, as had they all changed. That wasn't to be avoided. But, deep down, the centre of him, was that changed? The smile was the same, if a little tired. The intensity of those eyes, the blink which indicated some switch in his thought processes. Thinner, naturally, but still brimming with a febrile need to know.

'Katharina?' he said. 'That day, when I saw her, I asked where she was going. She didn't know or else wouldn't say. Too hurt. Too lost. I'd never seen her so distraught. She was so angry.'

'Angry?'

'I know. Not like her, not like her at all. It was…' but he couldn't think of a word that could bear the weight of the suffering he'd seen in her, the savage grief he'd felt. 'I watched her. Going. Not a backward glance. Throwing everything off, everything familiar. You know? Us, all we'd shared, the war, possibility, the happiness she'd enjoyed, briefly enjoyed. Her and Helga. Throwing it all off like a shirt of fire. It was so sad. So…' He drew a deep breath and exhaled. 'So very sad.'

'And…?'

'What happened to her? Give me a refill, would you?' Felix reached for the decanter and poured whisky into the tumbler. 'Thanks. She'd been at art school. Did you know?'

'Yes. Just before I left.'

Georg half laughed. 'You all left. I'm the only one who stayed. I was never known for my constancy, was I?' Now he did laugh.

'That's just fishing for a compliment.'

171

'So what?' He laughed again but was suddenly grim, torn by the irony.

'Friendship, though. You're good at that.' With a nervous sniff, Felix changed the subject. 'You were saying. About Katharina.'

'She nursed Helga, of course. But I said that.'

'When was she taken ill?'

'Hm…I think that March. 1916. Some time around then. Early spring, anyway. As the blossom came out.' He sipped the whisky. 'Apparently your throat closes up with a membrane, so you can't breathe. Sorry, Katharina. She nursed Helga and after she died – they'd gone away to the country, for Helga to get well, when in reality she was…it was all leaking away.'

'Did she go back there, Katharina? After you saw her?'

Georg shook his head. 'She didn't say. Rather gave the impression not. Not anywhere where the memory was too livid.'

'But didn't you…?'

'Ask?' said Georg, interrupting. 'At the time? No. The war, you know. We may not have been in danger but it was eating us alive, so to speak. You can imagine.'

'Not really.' The wry expression betrayed the fact that he was taking a rise out of himself, the same old Felix. 'You haven't any news of her at all?'

'I wrote to her parents in Lienz but never got a reply. And, I rather feel that if she'd wanted to get in touch she would have done. You know how private she was, in some ways. I imagine she's…oh, I don't know what I imagine. Found a new life? I hope so. Wherever she is. To Katharina.' He raised his glass, Felix reciprocated. 'To Katharina.'

'And what about you?' Georg said after a short silence.

'Me?' Again, Felix couldn't respond at once. He made a *where do I start?* noise, sank into silent question, gathered himself and told the story. 'So that's it,' he said. 'The potted biography of ex-lieutenant Felix Breitenbach, imperial and royal army.'

Georg evinced surprise. 'And there was no record of your men?'

'None. Hangs on me like a prison sentence.'

Georg stood up and paced across the room. 'Don't you think you're being a little melodramatic, Felix?' he said.

'What do you mean?'

'It's over. The war is over.'

'But not the mess it left us with.'

'And you intend to roll about in that mess, do you, Felix? That's what it looks like.'

Felix was taken aback. 'I only want to find out what happened.'

'Felix, listen to me,' Georg said at last, in a softer tone. He'd gone back to the chair and sat down. He leaned forward, elbows on knees, and, looking directly at his friend, he knitted his brow. 'I think you do actually know the answer to this. But you're very clever, that brain of yours, as elusive as a kingfisher. You've always got an answer, but answers are easy, it's the questions we have to ask of ourselves that are the hard thing. You can always come up with some way of dodging the issue, shirking what you know deep down and won't face.'

'And what's that?' Felix felt provoked.

'That it's not your fault, any of it, and the longer you go on with this self-flagellation, the more difficult it'll be to let the whole bloody thing drop. It's out of your hands, Felix. It always

173

was. Putting it bluntly, you didn't fuck up, someone else did, or circumstance did, or I don't know what. It's not doing you any favours any of this. Give it up.'

Felix had shrunk inside himself.

Georg folded his hands together. 'All I'm saying is that you can choose to let this morbid obsession go on festering or you can lance it.'

'What?' Felix was nettled.

'Just climb down, ditch the pride you're taking in making it all your responsibility. Just accept that it's part of the mess we've all been left with and you can choose either to get on with your life in spite of it, or you can drag your life after you into the sorry damned mess to wallow. And be thankful, maybe, that it wasn't a leg you lost.'

'That easy?'

'Oh, for gods' sake, Felix, no, not that easy. You see? Always an answer. Nothing worth doing is easy. Doesn't make it undesirable or undoable, now, does it?'

'You think I can just forget?'

'Of course not. And there, that's what I mean – you've always got a counter-argument. Stop being so damned ready to *know*. Forgetting isn't the issue. Living with it *is*. We've all got things clogging our memory. Who's to say you have more troublesome stuff than me? Felix, listen. I know what you're saying and please don't say I don't or can't possibly. The fact is, you can ride your guilt for ever and a day if you choose to. Guilt is inexhaustible if you feed it constantly with submission. Or… or, you can walk away.' He paused. 'You'll probably have to try more than once for it to work.' He smiled. Felix clearly did not want to smile. Georg tilted his head forward as if to say *Your turn.*

Felix's initial instinct was to resist. His face worked. His arms tingled with tension. Neither spoke for a while, Georg sunk in deep seriousness – *had he gone too far?* – Felix struggling to comprehend. Then he blew out air and made a drabbling sound with his lips. 'Walk away,' he said, more to himself than to Georg.

Georg picked up his tumbler of whisky, leaned back in his chair, and said: 'From one who has none, to one who has too much, my dear friend.' He raised the glass.

Felix responded and then said, puzzlement on his face: 'None? Too much?'

Georg smiled. No answer there, no sign of evasion. 'Guilt,' he said. He grinned. 'Remember what your favourite old boy von Hoffmansthal says, hm? "Thought is the end of life and happy those who never think." Worth a thought.'

Neither of them spoke for a while. They lapsed into an uneasy silence, uneasy because the past had closed on them and neither could yet see how they might proceed from here into whatever must come next.

Then Georg said: 'And what will you do now?'

Felix tapped his upper lip with an index finger and said, with vague disinterest: 'Architectural drawing? It's been on my mind. Along with a lot of other things. Something to do, rather than think about?' He smiled. 'Along with a lot of other things,' he repeated as if he needed to plod through his loose reasoning, 'other things rather less useful. Or...' He didn't finish.

'Or?' Georg said.

'Oh, nothing. I think I can do that. Architectural drawing.' He said it as if saying it would make it sound more positive.

'Architectural drawing…you remember what old Griensteidl used to say?'

'Griensteidl the cake man?'

Georg nodded. 'The five liberal arts comprise painting, literature, sculpture, music and cookery, of which architecture is a branch.'

Felix checked a moment, caught the slight uplift of Georg's nose and said: 'Are you taking a rise, Georg?'

Georg burst out laughing. Felix shook his head. Why did he even have to ask?

'Do you know anyone, a firm?' Georg said.

'Do you?'

Georg cocked his head. How he loved this man, this muddled man. 'Of course.'

The introduction was made and Felix began his training.

24

Vienna, end of January, 1923. The Café Central.

The clock over the counter chimed five o'clock. Men and women crowded the large open room, sitting at tables, conversing, reading newspapers, a few men played chess. Waiters performed their snake hips dance through the weave of spaces between the tables, carrying trays loaded with coffee pots, cups, cakes.

At his usual table sat the satirist Karl Kraus. At another table, Richard Wagner had once sat to compose. Here, in the Café Central, beneath the gilded balcony and ornate balustraded stairs, the world stood still, even as change swirled through like an odourless gas.

Austria, once bloated with empire, had shrunk to the size of a county and Vienna had been reduced to the status of an obscure parish, but the ghosts of what Kraus had called that burdensome companion, the imperial and royal trappings and paraphernalia, still haunted the revenant, Austria herself.

Kraus unfolded the morning's edition of the *Neue Freie Presse* and pondered a large advertisement for "Battlefield Round Trips by Automobile" organized by the Basel News. He sipped his coffee, scribbled a note in his working journal: 'Promotional Trips to Hell. Nostalgic warmongers, out of a job, shepherding gormless tourists round the scenes of their catastrophes.

Belligerent idiots, braying like donkeys, hankering for the good old days when the world was their playground and they had power over life and death, gorging themselves on blood by day and drinking themselves into a stupor by night.' He pondered awhile and added two lines: 'In this land no one is uncouth, Except the man who tells the truth.'

At another table, sat Georg. Unlike most of his colleagues in the law firm, he had no moustache – on the advice of an old hand at law, 'lack of a moustache makes you look ingenuous, the clients like that, the fools think you're a soft touch so they can take advantage'. Wearing a well-cut, three piece suit, Georg sported a gold watch chain slung across the front of the waistcoat attached to a gold watch, inherited from his grandfather, in its fob.

He looked up from his paper and saw, across the room, Felix in the doorway, polishing the lenses of his glasses, smeared and impastoed as ever. Putting the spectacles back on, he saw Georg. Georg waved, he waved back, went over to the table, sat down, and plonked his brief case by the side of the chair.

'Phew. I'm so sorry I'm late.'

'You didn't miss anything. Relax.'

'A client. Wouldn't stop talking, changing his mind, droning on. Have you ordered?'

'I was waiting for you.'

Felix swivelled round to gesticulate for a waiter. 'What will you have?'

'Felix, do calm down.' He signalled to a waiter who shimmied across to the table. 'Coffee and Sacher torte for me. Felix?'

'Yes. For me, too.'

The waiter left. Georg leaned forward, smiled a knowing

smile and said: 'Now, do tell. How's it going?'

'They want a summerhouse in the garden, Russian dacha style. I've told them that with the space they have and the shortage of materials and the…'

Georg waved him quiet. 'I'm not interested in plans for summerhouses. I meant Claudia. How's it going? Have you…?'

Felix bit his lip, plucked at a napkin, sniffed. 'It's not. Going. Wasn't interested. She, I mean, wasn't interested.'

Georg's amazement was a full *commedia dell'arte* gawp. 'Not interested? Claudia?' He laughed.

'Apparently not. Not interested in me, that is. Anyway, I don't want to talk about it.'

Georg pursued it. 'Your mind too much on summerhouses? Intersecting members, stress quotients…? That busy brain of yours?'

'Georg…please.'

'Hardly the best way to a girl's baser instincts, blueprints.'

'Georg, just drop it.'

'Sorry,' he said. He wasn't sorry and it showed. 'Cupid still shooting poisoned darts at you?'

Felix reacted with anger. 'Where did you get that from?'

'Oh, come on, Felix. Claudia and I go back a long way.'

Felix flushed with embarrassment. Georg put up both hands.

'All right, truce, change subject. Though you may be better off out of it, as things go. Besides, paying for sex is generally a lot cheaper than getting it so-called free, one way and another. Some women do charge very high rent for sporadic occupation.'

The waiter glided up and unloaded the tray. Felix searched for some money. Georg put out a hand to prevent him.

'On me, please.'

As they both turned their attention to the coffee and cake, Georg said: 'Do you really intend to spend the rest of your life drawing up plans for bourgeois outhouses and interior conversions of dreary attic floor rooms?'

'I don't know. It's a living...'

'"It's a living..." Really, Felix. You call that living? Where's your ambition?'

Felix bristled. 'And what about you? What happened to the radical spirit, reforming lawyer, fearless champion of popular liberty?'

If Georg was taken aback at this outburst, he didn't show it. He stirred his coffee. 'He grew wise, dear friend. No money in it, Felix, and precious little gratitude or progress, either. The lumpen proletariat is just that, lumpen. I got tired of trying to kick some life, any life, out of the oiks. That's all.'

'Honestly, Georg...'

Georg butted in. 'Come off it, dear boy. They're quick enough to take to the streets when some lunatic demagogue rouses them out of their terminal torpor and the mood takes them to smash whatever they can lay their hands on – oh sure, they can tear the place down all right when they're fired up for some wanton mayhem but afterwards? Do they ever rebuild it? Do they hell. Reconstruction? Beyond them, not a clue. Argue amongst themselves, on the other hand? Oh, they can do that, *sine die*. I did my best, so far as it went, but it was like trying to talk sense into a bunch of petulant kids. They all shout liberty in unison and then resolutely refuse to agree amongst themselves of what liberty actually consists. Altercation, that's what they excel at, courting chaos, bleating abstractions – justice, equality, rights…blah blah blah.

'The old aristocracy had its own version of our celebrated propensity for shilly-shallying and to what end? The proletariat replaced it with their own bodged up version and where has that got us? The same damned mess. You can thank me for the quality of this torte, by the way, moist to perfection. I complained last time. I do so fucking hate it dry.'

Felix cut a slice of the torte. 'You're a cynic, Georg.'

Georg smiled. 'And you're a prig. So what? You're bent on improving the civic fabric, domestic architecture and what not, I specialise in litigation for the rich, adjusting the social fabric. The sacrosanct world of the Dual Monarchy has gone forever, Europe has committed suicide and imploded and we have to pick our way through the rubble as best we can.'

'Everyone for himself and to hell with the rest?'

'You're not turning into a Bolshevik, are you, Felix? It rather sounds as if you are.'

'I thought we could do better, that's all. After centuries of getting it wrong, all we had to do was something different, wasn't it?'

'I thought the same, so I did. Truly. I did. But, I find that all we can do, my friend, is to read the world in which we find ourselves. We can't change it. If disaster approaches, what do you recommend: try to block it, head on, or step out of the way? Think avalanche. Some things don't change, Felix. Austria, even without spreading over half the map of Europe, is still the same fatuous, muddle-headed poltroon it ever was. In a drab suit. No more ostrich feathers. Ichabod, Ichabod, the glory is departed and there's not a grain of sense in mooning after it. We just have to make do with what we've got.'

They fell silent, concentrating on the cake. After a long hiatus, Felix broke the silence. 'I've been thinking about going into theatre.'

'Well, there's a thing. There's a very thing. What as?'

'Set design.'

'Not on the boards?'

'Be serious, Georg. I've been thinking about it for a while.'

Georg nodded. 'I see. Turning your back on the real for the make-believe?'

'That's glib.'

Georg flicked a shoulder. 'True, though. Isn't it?'

Felix sat back in his chair. 'No. Allow me to complicate it. After all, that's what I'm good at, isn't it?'

He smiled in self-mockery. Georg chuckled.

'Take theatre as a representation of what's real: human action, emotion, thought, the swirl of the mind. That's not illusion. Even a puppet show. Costumes, scenery, lighting, all artificial, but they do no more than provide a setting, a frame. Dare I say microcosm?'

'If you must.' Georg stabbed a piece of torte.

'The pasteboard wall of a stage dining room doesn't make what people seated at its dining table say any less true.'

'Ah, truth. Pontius Pilate - *What is truth?* Your point?'

'My point is that for all its surface artificiality, the theatre deals with the very real illusions which afflict people outside the theatre. Us, before the war, for instance. We lived in a world which was a sham. An Emperor who had the personality and intellect of a goldfish ruling over a supposedly unified empire which was, in fact, a ragbag conglomerate of peoples with as much inclination to unity as a bunch of feral cats to fireside tranquillity. All it took was a ludicrous myth of the Emperor's sacred powers of kingship going back to Charlemagne, plus the obstupefying capacity of his subjects to forget their differences - the differences they would have died for if it was left to them - and bow the knee to a fantasm of glory. As if that made everything acceptable and all's right with the world. A majestic confidence trick.'

He paused.

Georg said: 'Ob- stupy what did you say?'

'I'm being serious, Georg. I'd appreciate it if you'd take it seriously, too, else this conversation is over.'

'Felix, I know. Don't get your dander up. Only sometimes your serious is so very serious it borders on the hilarious.'

Felix quizzed Georg's blank Pierrot expression. 'Are you taking a rise?'

'Me. Wouldn't dream of it.' He laughed. And then Felix laughed, too. Whatever else he'd learned in those years of captivity it was a broader sense of himself, a willingness to acknowledge the stiffness in his spirit.

'I know, I know, too solemn by half. My genius for feeling uncomfortable and imposing it on others. But...'

'But?'

'There's always a but, there's always got to be a but. And what's changed? Have we dispensed with the hypocrisy, the absurd posturing, the self-delusion? I didn't much like that other reality and I don't much like the squalid version of it we have now.'

'Either way, you're going to have to put up with it. We're sort of stuck with it...aren't we? *Plus ça change* and all that.'

Felix peered into his empty cup as if the grounds might speak prophesy. 'If you believe something, it's not made up, is it? And if you don't believe it, then it's a fairy tale.' He looked up.

'Steady on, Felix. You'll choke on your own paradox.'

'It's not mine.'

'Beware, then.' He poured more coffee.

Felix went on. 'The war may have destroyed the world we knew, but it exposed the monstrous deceit of our supposed greatness. All blown to bits. An antique tableau of former glory pushed face down in the mud of a million bomb craters. And what happens? Back to the lies. Austria still clings to its birthright the way a professional criminal harps on a false alibi. The lands may be gone, the subject peoples subject to other tyrannies, but Austria continues to exist, a great deal withered, frayed and depleted, but business as usual. Hurray. Rejoice. We survived. We came through the inferno. Vienna, City of Dreams, once more full of life and gaiety…the social unrest, unemployment, bankruptcy, governmental chaos and incompetence neither here nor there, so carry on dreaming, Vienna. The nightmare was no more than a lurid interval. Curtain up.'

'Goodness me. Bravo, Felix. We'll make a cynic of you, yet. Doesn't alter the fact that, however melancholy the truth may be, that's the reality we're stuck with. The same old compromise between façade and substance.'

'You're right. Sorry for blasting off.'

'Oh, come on. We mustn't be glum, Felix. Situation desperate not serious, remember? Now, changing the subject, what about this major shift in direction of yours?'

'I'm thinking about it, quite seriously.'

'Let me know, then. Theatre, much more your line, I'd say. You could do with a bit of flamboyance. I've got some contacts.

By the way, what's the new apartment like?' Before Felix had time to answer, Georg had spotted a young woman making her way through the room towards them, looking round as if for a friend. He called out: 'Sybille…Sybille.'

She was a woman in her early twenties, with scalloped bay red hair. Her features had a Slavic cast. Her figure was svelte, the hands slender, the legs shapely. She came across.

'Sybille, join us, won't you? My friend Felix.' Felix stood up and bowed.

'Hello Felix,' she said and glanced round the room and said: 'Sorry, Georg, I'm joining friends.'

'How are you?'

Distracted, she said: 'I'm well. But I'm late. Another time.' She went off to sit with a couple in the far corner of the busy room.

Felix watched her walking away, the balletic swing of her hips, the smooth float of her movement, and said: 'Who's she?'

'Hungarian. Not for you. Next to her Claudia is a pussy cat.'

'I'm sure I recognise her. Do I?'

'Sybille Karolyi.'

'The actress?'

'I told you I had contacts.'

'She's…stunning.'

'Felix, take my advice, don't even think about it. She eats men like you for breakfast. How's the new apartment?'

'I don't know. It doesn't much feel like home. But, then, I have a rather confused idea of what home might be. Not altogether sure where my roots are. I've always felt somewhat uprooted.'

'I completely understand why you didn't stay in… your…

Too many bad associations.'

'Yes. After father died…it was…the place was infected with his gloom, somehow. There'd been too much unhappiness there. And, after I got back I was carrying too much…too much discontent. I couldn't help it. He was never an easy man and I know I irritated the hell out of him. Not on purpose. It was, I don't know…he couldn't fathom me, I didn't understand him. Fact is, he didn't have what I needed and I couldn't give him anything he wanted – he wouldn't take material help, kindness, any sort of sympathy, he was too entrenched in his own self-regarding depression. I don't criticise him for that. He was just bloody lonely, you know? Bereft. Felt as if life had passed him by, I think, kicked him into the gutter. Nothing I could say, nothing I could do. I think he just gave up.

'I was glad to lock the door on it, and the memories.' He fiddled with the teaspoon in the saucer. 'You know, it occurs to me - that room I had to live in, on my own…' He laughed. Humour once more flashed in his face. 'It's probably why I decided to be an architect, to create space. Odd thing is, though, I was as happy there as I've been anywhere. Domenico, of course. Kindness rather unsettles you…if you're not used to it.'

'Hmm, pass on that. By the way, are you coming to the Carnival Ball?'

'Claudia did mention it.'

Georg sighed. 'Does that mean you're *not* coming? Listen, if you can't manoeuvre her into bed at Carnival, well, I despair. We're all meeting at the Reiss Bar.'

'Ah. Who's *we?*'

'Usual crowd. Me, Claudia, Virginia, Augustus, a few others.'

'Who's Virginia? Your latest?'

Georg lidded his eyes. 'Felix, don't be vulgar.'

'Sorry.'

'So? You'll come?'

'Oh, probably.'

'Felix, come on. Show some enthusiasm. We may not be very good at improving the world about us but we do occasionally do a good time. Reiss café. Be there. Now, how about moving on, brandy and a cigar?'

Felix tapped his brief case. 'I really ought to finish this work.'

'Of course you should. Shall we go?'

As ever, Felix felt the tussle – relaxation and lightness of mood and heart…the loneliness of crowded rooms…the sense that, having spent so many years in solitude, he'd lost what little social grace he'd ever pretended to…He stood up, gave his friend a wistful look and said: 'I suppose so.'

As they made for the door, he turned to glance across the room to where Sybille sat, in animated conversation with her friends. And in that brief moment, even as he looked across, she half swung round and the twin beams of her eyes homed in on him. He shrank, turned away, blushing. He'd been found out.

25

Reiss Café. Carnival Eve, 1922.

They gathered in the café – Claudia, Felix, Georg and Virginia, his lover.

Georg beckoned a waiter. 'Champagne.'

Claudia excused herself and went to the powder room.

'Felix, meet Virginia, Virginia, Felix.'

Felix bowed. 'Georg has told me about you.'

'Have you?' she said to Georg.

'All very complimentary.'

'How very sweet of you, darling.'

Virginia was striking. She gave the impression of a woman who is intimidated by nothing and no one, twin to the Ice Maiden, sure of herself to the point of indifference to what others made of her. ('Bewitching,' Georg had said, his face suffused with a sort of proud wonder. 'Runs rings round me. Delicious. Upper crust. Father's a von.')

She acknowledged Felix with a slight widening of her eyes and a faint cock of her head as if she were adjusting focus.

Claudia returned and sat down opposite Felix, next to Georg. 'Where's Augustus?'

'You know Augustus,' said Georg. 'He's always late. Ah…' The waiter arrived with the champagne and flutes. He uncorked, poured, Georg raised his glass and said: 'Friendship.' He turned to peck Virginia on her cheek and then to smile at Claudia.

When he ended their affair, there'd been anger, desperation, tears, pleading. She'd withdrawn in inconsolable distress to brood over yet another betrayal by yet another trustless man. But, it passed and they became friends. For, if she found intimacy so troubling – at once desirable and repellent – and love only a brief respite from biting mistrust, she had a singular gift for friendship. Through friendship, she could express the warmth and affection of a generous heart which sex complicated by demanding too much. Whatever hurts she and Georg had inflicted on each other, their mutual fondness and liking endured.

For this carnival celebration in the boisterous tradition of Old Vienna, the two men were in evening dress, Virginia in a cobalt blue ball-gown, Claudia in the pale jade green of a Lalique ornament. The women carried the customary masks. Until midnight, the high moment of the ball, when they took off the masks to reveal their identity, like fledglings bursting from the shell, it was a tradition that the women must pursue the men. In Vienna, the social zoology might differ, but, as in the wild where the female selects her mate, at the Viennese Carnival Ball, women led the dance.

Augustus arrived, at last, a loose-limbed man with pursed embouchure, black curly hair and dimpled rouged cheeks. He was wearing an Empire line dress of pink velvet whose low neck emphasized the impressive swell of his false top hamper, a short, feathered cape and headdress and heeled patent leather shoes on his large ('*such* a bore') feet. He carried his mask looped round one wrist, on the other, a diamante-speckled reticule. He flounced up to the table and, flopping into the chair, sighed like a deflating balloon and stared at the ceiling, as if he'd just escaped from the jaws of a wolfhound. He spoke in a torrent: 'I'm sorry, darlings, very very very sorry to be so very very late but it was not in my control. I cannot begin to recount the ordeal I've just been through. I felt, at one point, as if I were simply falling to pieces, all in bits, and would never ever be put back together again. Shreds and fragments.' He fluttered his fingers in illustration. 'Crisis of crises. I had to tell myself to get a hold. "Get a hold, 'gustus," I said, "pull yourself together," remembering darling mother. Mother could always haul herself back from the brink and where Mother was concerned, there were more than a few brinks, let me tell you. She had *oodles* of practice there.

'So…quite against all the odds, here I am. Now…' taking a ladylike sip of the champagne Georg handed him, 'do you like my frock? Honest opinion. I wasn't sure. That was the root of the trouble, you see. I got into such a tizz. I thought I was going to burst with frustration, desperation, hesitation, all the –ations in a massive con*glom*eration. The appalling prospect of having absolutely nothing to wear, just a slummy old number from the rail, last year's.' He sighed again and looked at them in appeal.

Claudia crossed both hands over her upper breast and said: 'I think your frock is perfectly lovely, darling, so very *you*.'

'And quite perfectly your colour, divine,' added Virginia.

'Do you think so? Really? You can go so *badly* wrong with colour, can't you?' He leaned forward and, in a husky whisker: 'I mean, just *look* at that poor ginger creature over there - no *don't* turn round – in cerise and turquoise? What was she thinking of? The clash. Thank God *you've* got taste, girls. Inspires a person, no end. And I just love your frocks. Très chic, I mean it, très chic, understated but very alluring, very... *sexy.*' He giggled.

Now that Augustus had settled in, Claudia held up her glass: 'Georg, darling, empty.'

Augustus leaned over to pat Claudia's hand and said: 'Claudia, yours...do tell, where did you find it?'

'Secret.'

'Oh, don't be a meanie.'

'Family. Hand me down.'

'Depends on the family, of course,' said Virginia.

Claudia raised her eyebrows.

'Doesn't matter, darling,' said Augustus, waving as if at a wasp. 'It shows the pedigree of class and tradition and what's tradition but another word for hand-me-down.' The others laughed, Georg topped up the glasses. 'Thank you, Georg, poppet, so very attentive. You'd make a lovely husband for somebody.' He batted his heavily azured eye lids.

They left the café to catch the tram to the Opera House, all Vienna going that way, the streetcars packed with men and women, young and old, in evening suits, ball gowns or fancy dress, bound for the temple of earthly delights on the eve of the Lenten fast, like celebrants of an ancient Dionysia, heading for the ritual dances of the Bacchanal.

Electric bulbs burned in chandeliers and wall brackets making an Aladdin's cave of the Opera's great Baroque vault, the glint of an incalculable treasure of light, goblin treasure winking round the tiers of the upper galleries, the great hall itself, the foyer. The orchestra on stage played waltzes, Ländler, galops, polkas, with occasional sallies into the rustic stomp of folk dances from Bohemia, Hungary, the Tirol, but the Waltz King, Johann Strauss the younger, held sway, the triple time bars counted in a beat of one, fast and impelling. Even the more inexpert of the teeming numbers of couples could twirl in a semblance of poise, spinning tops generating a hectic energy.

The bars in the side halls were lined at the back with banks of mirrors, a press of customers on one side, the thin line of barmen on the other scurrying back and forth, like the beleaguered defenders of a fort holding the battlements against attack.

The party of friends contemplated the shifting tides of the crowd and managed to worm their way through to the shoal of the side promenade. Claudia glanced about, this way, that way, eyes twitching.

'Are you hunting?' Felix asked.

She didn't look at him. 'I'm always hunting,' she said.

Felix wondered why on earth he'd agreed to come. 'Shall we dance?' he said, as if that was what was expected.

'What?'

'Shall we dance?'

'Dance?' she said.

'It's a ball,' he said. 'Why we came. Isn't it?'

'Can you dance?' she said.

'Can you?' he said, matching the tart edge in her voice.

'My shoes are pinching,' she said, as if that settled the matter.

Shoes pinching? he thought. She was just saying it, making an excuse. She didn't want to be here with him. Perhaps she didn't want to be here at all. They'd have that in common, at least. What an ungrateful strain it all was.

'Why did you wear them, then?' he said.

She frowned. 'What do you mean, *why did I wear them?*'

'A bit odd to wear shoes that pinch. To a ball.'

'They didn't pinch when I put them on.'

'You must have known. Haven't you worn them before?'

Claudia suddenly whooped with delight and started to wave.

'Oh, good lord.'

'What?'

She ignored him and called out across the density of the crowd: 'Rudolf.'

She pushed forward and accosted a man wearing an extravagant multi-coloured harlequin motley costume with a half mask on which was planted a stubby length of wooden dowel. He'd come, as always, as Pinocchio.

Claudia lifted her mask so that he could recognise her. He threw his arms out and they embraced. A rapid exchange of conversation, each leaning into the other's ear to be heard above the music. Then she was half turning, giving a cursory wave to Felix before going off with her puppet.

Felix sought out Georg: 'Who's Rudolf? D'you know?' Georg knew very well who Rudolf was but didn't think it appropriate to say – married, ex-lover, always ready to console with a friendly hour in bed. Felix had enough on his plate already without extra helpings of indigestible truth. 'No idea, dear boy,' he said and had a brief exchange with Virginia who listened impassively and then waggled her head, *comme ci comme ça.*

Claudia and Rudolf had disappeared in the throng, but Felix had had the sour feeling he felt so often with her, a sneaking jealousy. He'd concluded that this was how it would always be.

Georg intervened. 'Listen, Felix, why don't you give Virginia a twirl whilst I go and fetch us a bottle? Muster point under the banner,' pointing to the large red and white Austrian flag hanging limp from the balcony overhead. 'I won't be long. Now, Augustus, come with me, there's someone I want you to meet.'

'Single and available?'

'You'll have to ask her.'

'Her?' His nose wrinkled.

'Him, dear, him. Come on, off we trot. See you two shortly.'

'What does he do?' said Augustus, conspiratorial lean towards Georg.

'He's in import-export.'

'Trade? Oh dearie dear.' Augustus winced.

'Don't be such a snob.'

Augustus, contrite, put an index finger to his lips and then whispered: 'Best behaviour, promise. All the stops out. Mum is definitely the word.'

'Don't overdo it. Try to play a bit hard to get, if you can possibly manage that. And do wake up, Augustus. When I say import-export I mean *import-export*... black market, he's loaded. Come on. Won't be long, *Liebchen*,' blowing a kiss to Virginia.

Felix turned to Virginia. 'Would you care to dance?' he said.

After momentary hesitation she said: 'Why not?'

Well, thought Felix, as he showed the way, like an usher, this is going to be a lot of fun. They walked along the arcaded promenade through a press of other people to the steps leading down to the dance floor. As they inched their way through the crush, they were jostled by a man and a woman, hand in hand, shouldering their way past, shrieking with raucous laughter. Virginia almost fell and, in catching her, Felix stumbled backwards and collided with a tall middle-aged man standing in an archway to one side of the packed stream of revellers, one of a circle of three of similar age, late thirties, drinking champagne and smoking cigars. The man's glass jolted out of his hand, fell to the floor and smashed. Virginia skipped nimbly into the archway, Felix clung to the pier of the arch and stared in paralysed embarrassment at the ground then at the man. He pushed the broken shards of the glass together with one foot, stammering apology.

'I'm most dreadfully, dreadfully sorry. I'll get you another glass. Please forgive me. It wasn't intentional. I'll get you another glass.'

The man's expression was haughty, severe. He said: 'No need. It's of no consequence. Pay attention, rather, to your charming companion.' He bowed, a slight movement of the upper chest, to Virginia who returned the kind of look that would have made the Gorgon think she had a fight on.

'I'm sure,' the man continued, 'she was looking forward to the dance.' He turned back to his two companions.

Virginia brushed past the other men: 'Felix, are you coming?' but Felix was transfixed, oblivious to her, to the music. Addressing the man whose glass he'd just shattered, he gabbled: 'The Isonzo River. Monte Santo sector. Late September 1915. It was raining, pitch dark.'

'I beg your pardon?'

'Outside Görz. You gave me orders, B Platoon, 4th Battalion commanded by Colonel Brückner.'

'Are you drunk, sir?' and to Virginia, 'I suggest your companion needs some fresh air, perhaps?'

'You were the mustering officer, 3rd Army, 57th Infantry

Division under Major-general Goiginger. The Italian Front. September 1915. Monte Santo sector. You gave me my orders. At the side of the road.'

'You're raving, sir.'

'No. That's where it was.' He swung round. 'Virginia, I...' but she'd gone.

'You were there weren't you? I recognise your voice.' The swill of all the anguish which he'd managed to forget for so long, all at once rose in his gorge, a vile, sick feeling.

There was a heavy pause. The man drew on his cigar and exchanged covert looks with the other men. He turned to Felix and said: 'What do you want from me, sir?'

'It *was* you. By the side of the road. I know it was. I recognize your voice.'

The man drew once more on his cigar. Felix stared at him, willing him to speak. After studied deliberation, he did.

'And if I *was* there?'

'I believe you were.' He could feel anger, reproved himself, *no anger, be calm.* 'I know you were,' he said in a controlled, level tone of voice.

'Do you indeed?' said the man. 'And on what do you base this assumption?'

Felix said: 'May I talk to you in private? It's important to me.'

The man looked dubious.

Felix was flustered. 'I'll explain. Please, sir.'

The man hesitated, made a sign to his friends – do excuse me, back soon - and led the way to an alcove in the inner promenade, clear of people. There were chairs. He didn't sit down.

He was of medium height, middle-aged, lean of build, sparse brown hair with a sabre scar on his right cheek, the cut made by the *Schläger*, the formal duel which was a brand of honour among Vienna's student fraternities - a nick of the sword blade testified to manly virtue in the chivalric tradition.

Felix was tight with nerves.

The man said: 'Make it brief.' He drew on the cigar.

But Felix couldn't think. After all this time, the man of the voice stood in front of him, unmasked. He spoke in a rush and concluded:

'I surrendered. I spent three and a half years in captivity. I still don't know what happened to my men…' His voice trailed off. It all sounded so very lame.

'Sir,' said the man, 'I don't know what earth you're talking about or what this can possibly have to do with me.'

Felix stumbled through the facts of the story again. It all sounded so surreal. The man's impenetrable silence even made him wonder if he wasn't, perhaps, making the whole thing up.

The man stubbed out the butt of his cigar in an ash tray.

'The Isonzo you say?' There it was, the insouciant, aristocratic drawl.

'Yes.'

'It may have been me, it may not. Either way, I don't understand why you're in such a lather about it.' He paused and reflected. 'If what you say *is* true, the order was passed down a long chain of command, from the higher echelons of the army, at the end of which someone, possibly me, delivered it to you.'

'I just want to know what happened to the men under my command. It's weighed on my conscience…'

'Conscience?' The man tutted with impatience. 'You claim to have been an officer? Then behave like one. Conscience? In war? My god.'

'We were told that an officer's first duty of care was for his men.'

'Care doesn't come into it. Your first duty was to inflict damage on the enemy, whatever the cost to you and your men... Besides, it was a long time ago.'

'I felt I'd betrayed them.'

'You're talking like an adolescent. If we'd all caved in after every setback as you appear to have done, what then?'

'But…'

'No. Enough. I'm going to rejoin my friends and I suggest you do the same.' He made to walk away.

'I apologise for troubling you.'

The man stopped. 'No one, sir, comes home from a war unscathed.' He reached into his pocket for the leather case, took out another cigar and lit it. That same aroma. 'You survived the war. Many young men did not. Be grateful.' Felix tried to interrupt. 'No, listen to me. Whatever happened to you in the engagement about which you are so fixated, it has nothing to do with me. If it's the case that I did give you an order - and I dimly recall that I was in that sector about that time - I was no more than passing on an order given to me. War is confused. The circumstances it throws up are unpredictable.'

'Your directions …'

'The circumstances it throws up are unpredictable,' he repeated. It was a polite way of saying *shut up*. 'If it was a mistake that led you to the wrong place, it was a mistake replicated hundreds, if not thousands, of times all through the war, every day, on every front. I repeat, be thankful that you came away unscathed.' He straightened, the Colonel once more. 'You say you were a Lieutenant?'

'Yes.'

'Then let me assure you, Lieutenant, if the army no longer knows what you and your men did or did not do on a dark night on the Italian Front in September 1916, your anxiety is groundless.'

'It was 1915.'

'The date is of no consequence.'

'But it is.'

'My god. What an inflated view you have of yourself. You and droves of other very junior people like you throughout the war were not that important, not at the time, certainly not now. You were insignificant. Do you understand? Caught up in events which not even our generals could direct as they chose, which not even the entire apparatus of the army could change, you, in spite of your pathetic and inflated opinion to the contrary, did not count. Now, good night, sir.'

'What's your name?' Felix called out to the man's back. The man walked on.

26

Felix stood in the alcove, his mind in turmoil, with no clear sense of where he was or who he was. The nightmare had reawakened. He slumped into a chair. Indistinct shapes of dancing couples roiled past in a constant swim of motion. Men and women on the sidelines stood around like crowd extras waiting to be called. A fuzz of loud sounds outside his head, a staccato of echoes inside: a key turning in a lock…men shouting, crying out…the snap snap snap of bullets…a sick migraine of fear…

He tried to let go, to be subsumed in the rhythms, the wordless swing of the music, so that his mind might sink into an infancy of perception where there was no thought, no reason, no contention, no memory.

He stared into the mill-race of the dance, the orchestra playing at impetuous speed, whipping the dancers round and round like leaves in a wind, skittering, skipping, the couples grinning at each other, their faces bright with perspiration and hilarity, spinning and whirling.

Suddenly, the thump of a chord like a door slammed shut brought the fast tempo to a halt and a swoony slow measure took over. The dancers swayed into the dreamy lilt. They exchanged seductive looks, knowing smiles, winks and whispers for what might come later at moth time, when the dancing was done, the lights went out and velvety blackness swallowed all secrets. Promises tacit and promises spoken, promises made in the caprice of the moment, promises that would be kept, promises that would be withheld. The music swung in the light breeze of their reverie but they all knew what was coming. Expectancy simmered. It would come as no surprise but it would arrive like a surprise, a second thump of a chord, like a door slamming in the wind, the music racing back to speed, faster, faster, how fast can we go? How fast can you go and stay on your feet, hands slippery with sweat and not lose hold?

Felix watched, wrapped in the sound, trying to make sense of the encounter. Was that it? And what now? He was tired of it, this riddle come back to poison him, sick and tired of it. And like a light going off, in the midst of all the noise around him, there was quiet. Nothing resolved but the renewed possibility of surrender to incomprehension.

The dance finished to a rapturous burst of applause and cheering, a thunder of stamping feet.

27

A man appeared in the archway of the alcove. He was around sixty years old, the flesh of his face slack, pasty and much lined with wrinkles, the purpling nose swollen and pocked, the hair sparse, the eyes watery and lugubrious, the brow pilled with sweat. He was wearing fishnet stockings, a sateen bustier, high heels, a sequinned toque with a feather. His cheeks were raddled with inexpert daubs of madder and powder. He was very drunk. He gripped the side of the archway and stared with bleary eyes at Felix.

'Hello,' he said.

'Hello,' said Felix.

'I'm looking for my girl, Austria,' said the man. 'Have you seen her?' He belched. 'You can't miss her. She's in a sexy red and white silk...' he hiccupped, 'number. Eye-catching. Her summer fruits and cream, I call it.'

Felix didn't reply. The man wasn't listening, anyway.

'I've got the sneaking suspicion that she's dumped me again,' he said. 'Gone off whoring. Bit of a tart, got to confess, always was. Loveable, but a tart. I always forgive her, though. Can't help myself. And she always comes back...' he hiccupped, '...eventually, and all she needs then is a bit of a smacked botty. She's a bit giddy, y'see, bit fickle, goes for bright lights, money, glitz, all that. Can't help herself. Every time, hook line and sinker. Folly derh gran-dewer. They play her a snatch of schmaltz music, off she waltzes, till the latest Casa...' he belched, '-nova gets tired of her and she trails back to uncle, all tearful and apo-apo-pology, her mascara running, two black eyes, and I see her lovely face all in ruins, and I'm done for, again. Try to resist, I try to be...' he wiped his nose with the back of his hand. 'Try to be angry with her, but...' He shook his head, belched, wiped his face. He nodded at Felix, tried to smile, lapsed, briefly, into a fuddled absence, sighed again and closed his eyes. He opened them again, bright and feverish for a moment, then soft and glazed as he let go a long, sonorous fart. 'Sorry pardon,' and wrinkled his nose.

'Buxom party, she is. Blonde, darling eyes, blue as cornflowers. Shtreemely blue. You'd know her if you saw her. Gorgeous embonpoint. That's part of the trouble. She...' He paused, snatching at a memory. 'She can't get enough of it. And, fact is, she's – oh god – she's irresist-erb,' he hiccupped, '-ible.'

He leaned forward. 'And I can't keep my hands off her, either. Nor can anyone else, though, that's the problem. She flaunts herself and I can't blame her. You've got it, flaunt it. Why not? But trouble is, trouble is, she can't discrim...discrim...in... hold back. She's so wil...' He found this bit hard. 'So wil... ful. Every Heins Fritz and Werner who tips her the wink and plops a schilling down her cleavage, off she goes. It's not good for her self-esteem, you see? And she doesn't need to. Lots of good things at home, with uncle.'

He sniffed, wiped his eyes again, sighed. 'She was so demure. When she was young. When I met her. Been together ever since. So demure. It all changed with...' He looked back over his shoulder, in case anyone else was listening. 'It all changed with *sex*. After the first time. Opened up the sluices. Insatiable. I couldn't keep up. Lovely fuck she was, too, lovely, innocent, willing to…well, you know…' He was crying now. 'Oh God.'

Through the sobs, he said: 'Oh dear, come on uncle, come on…' He cleared his throat, blew his nose sideways with one finger blocking a nostril.

'She always comes back but you know, I wonder, every time - you do, don't you, you wonder? Maybe this time she won't, maybe get so deep into bad company, end up …doesn't bear thinking about. All she needs, you see, all she needs is a gentle little smack on her lovely bum, pull her skirt up and…' miming the smack. 'You've been a very bad girl.' He murmured to himself, '…a very *naughty* girl.' He closed his eyes for a moment as if he'd dropped off then came to and said: 'Seen her, have you? Buxom party. Blonde. If you do, tell her I'm…over there, will you?' He pointed without clear direction over his shoulder, swivelled round and lurched off into the crowd.

Felix watched him go and thought: *I've got to get out of here.*

It was, by now, approaching midnight. The orchestra was taking a short break, the noise of the crowd rose in volume. People were making their way towards the bars, to dark corners for whatever they could get away with, to any available chairs for a rest.

Suddenly a group of people swarmed into the alcove where Felix was sitting, the women shrieking with laughter at a shared joke. One of the men planted a wet kiss on the bare shoulder of one of them as he encircled her body with his arm, just under her breasts. She spun round, a look of fury in her face, pushed at him with both fists and slapped his cheek hard, before collapsing in the chair next to Felix in a fit of loud giggles. The man crooked his finger and walked towards her with feigned menace. Still giggling, she squirmed in her chair, turned to Felix and said: 'All alonesome?'

'I'm just leaving.'

'Leaving?'

'Yes.' He got up, sidestepped the advancing man who planted himself on the girl's lap and bounced lightly up and down.

'Surrender?' he said.

'Surrender,' she said, her voice muffled behind his back, then reached under him and squeezed his testicles hard. He leapt up.

'You cow. That bloody hurt.'

She laughed.

Felix began to make his way through the press of people towards the main door. Out of the crowd appeared Claudia. She saw him and bore down. She pulled at his sleeve. She was tipsy.

'Felix, why aren't you dancing with me?'

'There's no music.'

'Well, hum. What's wrong with you?'

'I'm sorry, I don't feel like it.' He pulled away from her.

'You don't feel like it?' She pushed at him. 'What d'you mean, you don't feel like it?'

'I'm sorry.'

'Goddamn it, Felix, you're always whining sorry, sorry, sorry about some damn thing.'

'It's…I can't explain.'

'It's what? Surprise me.' She pushed at him again, then tugged him towards her. 'Oh, come on, Felix, let yourself go for once.' She brushed his chest with both hands, pressed into him, looped an arm round his waist to pull him closer. 'Felix… Felix, why aren't you dancing with me? You're neglecting me and I don't care to be neglected, Felix. Don't you fancy me?

Come on, come on.'

'Not now, sorry.'

She pulled away, pushed at him. 'Bloody hell. What's wrong with you, hiding behind the glass screen of those bloody spectacles?'

He shrugged.

'Oh, for God's sake, loosen up. For me…?' she said, wheedling, then erupted in exasperation. 'What are you so afraid of? Why don't you just spill yourself out of your damned corsets for once in your life?'

She tore at his sleeve again. He shrank away. 'Claudia, please, I'm not…'

'Not what? In the mood?' She punched his arm then thrust at him with both hands. 'Christ. It's Carnival for God's sake. You damned trussed up killjoy Jewish Jesuit.' She burst out laughing. 'Yes, that's what you are, a Jewish fucking Jesuit, a sanctimonious bloody pseudo-virgin. For god's sake if not mine, show some spunk.'

She wrenched at his jacket and shook him. 'Christ, how do I get a rise out of you?'

'I'm sorry to disappoint you. I can't…'

She broke him off. 'Can't? Won't. Oh come on, fuck me, Felix, ravish me, do the business, get it out of your system, we'll both feel a lot better for it. Do the business.'

Tight-lipped and without humour, he said: 'What happened to Rudolf?'

She glared at him, slapped him hard round the face and stepped away. 'You bastard. You unfeeling bastard.'

Georg appeared behind her. 'Now, now, children,' he said.

Claudia turned on him. 'Oh fuck off, Georg,' and she was

gone.

Georg watched her go. 'Well, temper,' he said. 'What was all that about? Felix?'

Felix was in a daze. 'What?' he said.

'What was all that about?'

Felix shook his head.

'Anything wrong?'

'Do you mean generally or specifically?' Felix smiled. 'Actually, I don't know, I don't know. But you know what? I don't care, either. I just don't care. Good night. I'm off.'

'Felix?'

28

April 1925, an office in Vienna

Felix walked up a narrow wooden staircase in a large edifice overlooking Stephansplatz in central Vienna. He was carrying a portfolio of projected theatre designs – sketches, full drawings, diagrams. He walked along the second floor landing and stopped outside a door. On the wall, next to the door, a brass plaque was inscribed *Heinrich Wittig, Impresario*.

He drew a deep breath, braced himself for a plunge into the unknown and knocked on the door. A muffled voice answered. He went into the room.

It was a confined hallway, little bigger than a parlour ante-chamber, furnished with a hat-stand, a bulbous Ali Baba jar for umbrellas and canes, a potted aspidistra. The walls were dotted with grainy photographs of actors and actresses, a few in costume, most signed. The receptionist sat behind a desk, typing. The carriage of the Adler machine hit the end of a line, she zinged it back to the start of a new line and looked up. She was about forty years old, her greying hair pinned with elaborate care. Her complexion was sallow, her figure rather too lean, her features were sharp, and years of unsmiling attention to detail had pinched them sharper. Her job was to dot the i and cross the t. As to why the i and the t were there in the first place, was not her responsibility. Her expression suggested that any intrusion was, of itself, unwelcome.

'Good afternoon. Can I help you?' she said.

'Felix Breitenbach. To see Herr Wittig.'

'You have an appointment?'

'Yes. Two o'clock.'

She glanced up at a clock on the wall. 'It's only just twenty-three minutes to.' She consulted her appointments book. 'There's nothing here under that name. Freitag, did you say?'

'Breitenbach.'

She turned several pages over, peered at them, turned back to the first page and, from behind the bunker of her desk, said: 'No, I don't have anything under that name either. With whom did you make the appointment? Not with myself.'

'No, not with yourself.'

'If not with me, not with anyone.' Her nose wrinkled.

'Ah,' he said. 'I'm sorry.'

'I can't answer for Herr Wittig.'

'I imagine not.'

'Herr Wittig is a very busy man.'

'I'm sure.'

'What is it concerning…this appointment of which I have no written record?' Her face clenched tight.

'As I said, it's with Herr Wittig. To discuss...work.'

'Because I need to know,' she said. 'If anyone comes through that door,' she said, 'it's my job to know who they are and why they're here. To keep track. Otherwise…' The consequences of not keeping track were clearly too horrible to enlarge on. She pursed her lips, folded her arms and dared him to explain himself, as if she suspected him of stealing biscuits from her personal tin.

'Well, the appointment was arranged with Herr Wittig, and I assumed…'

'You assumed.'

'I assumed he would…erm…put it on record.'

'Well, he didn't.'

'An oversight, I imagine.'

She was affronted and it showed. 'Herr Wittig leaves all that side of things to me. He can't saddle himself with day-to-day trivialities like recording appointments.'

'Yes, I can see that.'

Her expression suggested toothache.

'Perhaps I could wait?' said Felix. 'Until Herr Wittig arrives?'

'He's not due into the office until two o'clock at the earliest.'

'I don't mind waiting.'

She didn't say anything. She didn't need to. 'I have work to do.' She resumed typing.

'Of course. I'm sorry to have interrupted.' She carried on typing. 'Except that…'

She stopped typing and glared.

'I do have an appointment.' He took a small diary from his pocket, opened it and pointed to a page. 'Here. You see?'

'That's your handwriting?'

'Predictably.'

She arched both eyebrows. 'I shall have to confirm it with Herr Wittig when he comes back. He has a lot on his mind. That's why I'm here, to save him from unscheduled interruptions.'

'Thank you. I'd really be most grateful.'

'He's out of the office in a meeting at present.'

'I don't mind waiting.'

She glanced up at the clock again.

'I brought a book.'

The typewriter started up again, the keys clack-clack-clacking to counterpoint her displeasure.

'Excuse me. I'm terribly sorry to bother you again, but…'

She stopped typing. 'What is it now?'

'Might there be a chair?'

'A chair.'

'Whilst I wait. I…don't want to get in your way.'

'You already have. There's a chair downstairs, in the foyer.'

'Ah, thanks so much.' He paused at the door. 'You won't forget that I'm there?'

She stopped typing. 'You're asking quite a lot for someone of whose apparent business in this office with Herr Wittig I have no written or verbal record.'

She watched him make for the door. It opened and there, in a long velveteen coat with a fur collar, stood the woman from the Café Central. Felix felt a shivery rush of nerves.

'Fraülein Karolyi.'

She was plainly quite used to being accosted by strangers. 'Yes?'

'We met.'

'Did we?'

'At the Central Café…'

'The Central Café?'

'In January. I was there with a friend of yours. Georg…'

'Georg Strauss…' she said, her eyes narrowing.

'Yes.'

'It's…?'

'Felix.'

'Felix.' She held out her hand, he took it with light pressure in his.

'You were in a hurry.'

'I was meeting friends.'

'One mustn't keep friends waiting.'

'No.'

The receptionist coughed.

Felix said: 'Perhaps …I wonder, might we meet? If that appeals. When you're not in a hurry?'

This sparked interest rather than surprise. She thought before saying: 'When you do you suggest?'

He was taken aback. He didn't expect her even to consider it. 'This afternoon?' he said.

'*This* afternoon?'

He cut her off. 'Sorry, it's a bit importunate.'

'What time?'

He gulped. *What time? This afternoon?* 'Erm, I have an appointment here at two o'clock.'

'Shall we say four o'clock?'

'Yes. Four o'clock. You have an appointment, too?'

Again, she narrowed her eyes. 'No, but what I have to say doesn't require an appointment.' She smiled.

The receptionist was fussing with a new page and a sheet of carbon paper. Footsteps sounded outside along the landing and through the open doorway came a portly man of fifty or so, with florid complexion, in a heavy overcoat with an astrakhan collar, silver-topped cane and bowler hat. He bustled into the room, saw Sybille and an involuntary flash of dismay oozed instantly into a sycophantic leer.

'Sybille, my dear.'

'Don't *my dear* me. I'm not here for pleasantries. You promised me full wages during the rehearsal period. I've been rehearsing for a week. I've received no money.'

'Have you not?'

'Until I do receive the money due to me, in full, I cease rehearsals. I have ceased rehearsals.'

'But…'

'No.'

'It must be a misunderstanding.'

'Not by me. You made a promise, you've renegued on it.'

'I'll alert the accountant straight away. Heidi?' The receptionist reached for a note pad.

'It's not the accountant you need to alert, it's the cashier. Between the accountant and the cashier, according to both the cashier and the accountant on separate occasions, in lengthy and irritable exchanges with me, they both insist that there's no record of your undertaking to pay me. *How can this be?* I ask myself. *Am I being toyed with? By honest Herr Gassenbauer? Surely not.*' Her smile shifted to a piercing stare. 'Because, it appears, they each require – the accountant *and* the cashier – your authorisation of your promise to me.' She paused. 'I'll take cash and I'll take it now.'

'The banks…'

'What about the banks?'

'They're not open.'

'Neither will your play be.'

'Sybille, Sybille, *darling*…I'm sure we can sort something out.'

'I'm sure you can. You've got ten minutes. After which I'm leaving.'

Gassenbauer whined, he wrung his hands, a manoeuvre at which only highly evolved members of the species *Pecksniffii*, it seems, are adept.

'Sybille, please...'

'Ten minutes.'

Gassenbauer muttered: 'I'll make a call.'

She checked her watch.

He disappeared into his office even as another man walked into the entrance room. Felix looked as if he'd been slapped. It was the man from the ball, the officer at the roadside in Italy. He stared straight through Felix, gave no hint of recognition.

Felix stammered: 'You don't remember me.'

'Should I?'

'The Carnival ball. We talked. The Isonzo.'

The man's expression did not alter. He said: 'Ah,' and with a faint inclination of his head to greet the receptionist who'd stood up and was gazing at him in adoration, he went into the inner office and closed the door. Muffled voices announced the exchange with Gassenbauer. The door opened again and Gassenbauer himself emerged once more.

'Sybille, Sybille, dear lady. A dreadful mistake, for which I can but apologise. I did give instructions but they were overlooked. So much going on. But, my fault, I should have checked. Here, with my humble er...appreciation.' He handed her a fat envelope. 'With a small honorarium, a bonus, to make amends? It won't happen again.'

'It had better not,' she said, taking the money.

'I promise.'

She didn't respond.

'You'll start rehearsals again?'

'Tomorrow,' she said putting the envelope in her bag. She turned to go and smiled at Felix.

'I'll come down with you,' he said.

At the foot of the stairs, Sybille said: 'I'll see you at four o'clock,' and left the building as a man with a passing resemblance to Bela Lugosi entered the foyer. He stepped aside with a flourish to bow to her.

'Fräulein Karolyi.'

'Herr Wittig.' She left the building, Wittig made for the stairs. Felix said: 'Herr Wittig?'

'Sorry, I can't stop.'

'We have an appointment.'

'An appointment?'

'At two o'clock?'

'You are...?'

'Felix Breitenbach.'

'Herr Breitenbach...of course. Two o'clock? Yes. I shouldn't be long. If you don't mind. A couple of things to attend to.' He set off up the stairs.

29

Café Central

Wittiger kept Felix waiting for over an hour, until the Medusa in the ante-room called down the stairwell: 'Herr Breitenbach? Herr Wittig will see you now.' She peered with baleful distaste at him over the Adler typewriter, as he came into the room and walked past towards the office door.

It was almost four o'clock when Wittig leaned across his desk, shook Felix by the hand and said, in a low voice, as if he were betraying a secret: 'Thank you. I look forward to our collaboration.'

Felix hared down the stairs out into the Platz, just missed a tram, set off running, heard another tram heading for the next stop, a hundred metres away and, as it overtook him, he raced for the stop as fast as he could go. Just as he got there, the tram pulled away, the clank of its wheels on the rails and the pneumonic wheeze of its electric lungs mocking his own gasps for breath.

He continued on foot and walked into the café half an hour late, overheated and embarrassed. He caught sight of her at once, sitting at a table in the far corner, reading a newspaper. He mopped his face with his handkerchief and walked across She looked up. 'Felix,' she said, folding the paper.

'Fräulein Karolyi. I'm very sorry to have kept you waiting.'

'It's Sybille, and of course one mustn't keep friends waiting.'
The smile was arch.

'I'm very sorry. It wasn't my…'

'Well, you're here now.'

'You must think me very impolite.'

She ignored this. 'You look as if you've been running.'

'Yes. I have. I…' Oh, goodness, he thought, she's so beautiful. He felt like the urchin peeping through the curtains at the queen.

'You must be pooped. Sit down. Drink some water.' She poured a glass from a jug on the table.

He put his case next to the chair, sat down, drank the water, felt a trickle down his chin, put down the glass, reached for his handkerchief and dabbed. He blushed. His glasses were misted over.

'Oh dear,' he said. 'What an introduction.' He took his glasses off to polish them with the damp handkerchief. She looked on with amusement. When he'd put his glasses back on, she said:

'That's the introduction out of the way, then. Now, I want to know what you are cooking up with the egregious Herr Wittig. I assume he kept you waiting? Let me advise you: make sure you get everything in writing. He's a snake. Well…?'

'I've made design sketches for one of his productions.'

'You're a theatre designer? Well, now…'

'Not exactly. Not yet. It's my first commission.'

'Congratulations. What have you been doing until now?'

'I was an architect.'

'And…?'

'I decided some while ago that I didn't want to be an architect

217

for the rest of my life. Certainly not doing the journeyman work I was doing, pretty much all I could get. Not much of it, either.'

'So you decided to move into the capricious world of theatre where the wellsprings of work are even less dependable.'

'Something like that. Except that…'

'Except that what?'

'I realised, if I didn't want to be an architect all my life, I'd have to stop being an architect. So, I stopped. I didn't want to live with any regret about not stopping.' He paused, she said nothing, he wondered what she was thinking. Did she disapprove, think him an idiot, wonder what he was talking about? He staggered into a saving question. 'Have you always been an actress?'

'Yes, and are you planning to rebuke me for not stopping?'

'No, of course not, no. Not at all.'

She held up a hand to excuse him. 'It's all I can do, all I've ever done. Beyond that, I couldn't say. Nothing else is of the slightest interest to me and the best that any of us can say is *so far so good*. Isn't it?'

'Did anyone try to dissuade you?' he said. 'At the beginning? Knowing how risky it might be?'

'A few tried. I ignored them. I'd decided to be an actress and it was like jumping off a diving board into water. As soon as my feet lifted, it was too late to change my mind.' Her eyes opened wide.

'And since…?'

'That I made the wrong decision? No. What kind of comment on my life would that be?'

He cleared his throat and peered into the glass now empty

of water. 'I've seen you on stage.'

'And is that why you're here? Why you proposed a rendez-vous in the Café Central?'

He was wrong-footed. 'I don't understand.'

'You're a stage door admirer?'

He drank in the unblinking full stare, a strange cock-eyed, birdlike look in her oval grey eyes, the lips sucked tight at the line of the mouth. 'No. I mean, that's not to say I don't admire your work but it's not...' He swallowed on a dry throat and reddened. 'It's not why I asked to meet you.'

Her expression softened. 'Come. I was teasing. D'you think I'd have agreed if I thought all you were after was my autograph and the offchance of a candid picture of you and me appearing on the society page of a newspaper?'

'I'm sure...that is, I hope not.'

'Well, then...I came because I chose to. Now, what about some coffee?'

Flustered, apologetic, Felix was pitched into sudden disquiet. 'Of course. What bad manners. I'm sorry.'

'Why should you be sorry?'

'I should have thought to order.'

'Felix...you're happy for me to call you Felix?'

'Of course.'

'Then, Felix, if I, Sybille, had wanted coffee I'd have asked for coffee.'

As he swivelled in the chair to locate a waiter, she clicked her fingers with a smart crack and a waiter, catching her eye, glided across the room to their table, even as she asked Felix: 'What have you seen me in?'

'That play by Gassenbauer? Last year? I don't remember what

it was…'

'Oh, god. *Chivalry is not Dead?*'

'Yes. I thought you were…'

'Over-compensating for the embarrassment of being in it?'

'I was going to say I thought you were directed out of it.'

'I suppose that's a compliment.'

'No, I mean they didn't leave you anywhere to go. It was all a bit…tramlines.'

'Stagey? Vapid? Pre…*dic*table?'

He laughed. 'Something like that. I must confess I didn't think much of the play, either.'

'It was terrible. I've seen operettas more subtle. Gassenbauer is a hack. Sugary excess, no substance.'

'Then why did you agree to do it?'

'Good question. It wasn't for the money. I was doing my agent a favour – she'd negotiated a juicy contract for me in another production, out of town. Her daughter was desperate to go on stage. Tread the boards, I think she said. Oh dear… Anyway, I agreed to do the play in exchange for, let's say, persuading Gassenbauer to induce the management to engage her for the ingénue role. I rather think Gassenbauer thought he could wheedle me into bed. She played the maid. What did you make of her?'

He blushed.

'You're not going to hurt my feelings.'

'I confess I didn't register.'

'Poor thing. Still, bruising as the experience must have been for her, it wasn't wasted. She found out that the theatre isn't for her. As let downs go it was relatively soft and it scratched an itch before she got the idea that she had any sort of future…

on the boards.'

'Gassenbauer wasn't impressed?'

'The only thing that impresses Gassenbauer is Gassenbauer. I imagine he made a pass and I imagine she was too frightened even to register. But what did you discuss with Wittiger?'

'The Nestroy revival. This summer.'

'Ah.'

The waiter arrived with the coffee and laid out cups, saucers, pot, jug, bowl, a plate of almond biscuits.

'Why don't you show me?' She poured coffee.

'Show you…?'

'What you showed Wittiger.' She indicated the portfolio.

'They're only sketches.'

'Doesn't matter.'

He pulled the drawings out, laid them on the case and watched nervously as she leafed through the pages.

'Do you like them?'

'Is that important?

'I'd be glad if you liked them.'

She looked at the top page for a long time and sat up. 'I do.' She took a sip of coffee and nibbled at a biscuit.

'Thank you.'

'For what?'

'I'm…well, I'm new to all this.'

She nodded. 'I understand. I think they will do very well. Oh, and I'm playing the lead.'

He put down his cup with a clatter. Coffee spilled. 'Good heavens.'

'So we'd better stay friends, hadn't we?'

'I…yes. Good heavens. What a coincidence.'

'Coincidence or…' She didn't finish. She took a sip of coffee and, over the rim of the cup, asked: 'Now, what is it about von Fessl?'

'Who's von Fessl?'

She was puzzled. 'The man who walked into the office before we left?'

'Von Fessl?'

'Yes. Why did you look as if he'd jilted your sister?'

'I haven't got a sister.'

'You know what I mean. You looked affronted and you went very pale.'

'Oh.'

'What did he do to you?'

He drew a deep breath. 'It's rather a long story.'

'I'm not going anywhere and we can order more coffee. Well?'

'Von Fessl, you say?'

'You didn't know his name?'

'No.'

'More and more mysterious. What's going on?'

He hesitated. 'How do you know him?'

'Heinrich von Fessl, architect, designing the new studio theatre. A scaled down version of Bayreuth, by all accounts. The idea.'

'He's an architect?'

'Yes. With a conceit of himself way beyond his ability. Men like him went back into the woodwork after the débâcle of the war and crept out again when the coast was clear. They get where they get through shifty influence and spurious pedigree. I don't say he's not competent at his job but plenty of people without the same connexions are a lot better. So, where does he come in?'

Felix told the story.

When he'd finished, she pondered a while before saying:

'Do you know why he still rattles you?'

'No, I don't. I haven't worked it out.' He stopped. She waited. 'Seeing him again… Perhaps it has something to do with him appearing in that office, when I was going for an interview which could change my life. Is that it? I don't know.' Again he stopped. Again she waited. Her calm, her quiet, her candour, gave him the feeling that she could see right into him.

He shrugged. 'When I encountered him at the…' He checked. '*Encountered*, isn't that the word? We didn't meet, it was an *encounter*, like, I don't know, like the first time you're confronted with the Greek alphabet and you think you'll never be able to learn it or how it forms into words. Something impenetrable, at first.'

'The Greek alphabet is, and will probably remain, a mystery to me.'

He laughed, but it was nervous. 'Sorry. But do you know what I mean?'

'Yes. Like menstruation.'

'Like…?'

'It's what every young girl has to cope with. Out of the blue, suddenly everything goes wrong with your body, it all gets out of kilter. That's an encounter, isn't it?'

He was astounded at her bluntness. She smiled at his discomfiture. He cleared his throat.

'Have I embarrassed you?' she said.

'Well, I…I suppose you have, did, which is silly, isn't it?'

She laughed.

'It was,' she said, 'rather intriguing, I must say, that look on your face. When he walked in.'

'Ah…' He smiled. 'I suppose the puzzle is, does it mean anything or nothing?'

'That's for you to decide, isn't it?'

'That's more or less what Domenico said.'

'Domenico.'

'The old Italian who…'

'Ah, yes.' Looking at him with a candour he found unsettling, she nodded. 'He meant a lot to you.'

'Yes. He was… Domenico gave me permission to be at a loss, to be broken.' He paused and gathered himself and spoke in a near whisper, recollecting… 'He was very kind.'

She had a sudden insight. It was like unlocking a meaning which had foxed her, in a line in a play, a key to how to place her character. 'You find kindness difficult, don't you?'

He felt pushed backwards, away from what he knew into what he couldn't explain, or maybe had never tried hard enough to explain. Another revelation? Was she right? Why would anyone find kindness difficult? It was the nature of kindness to be gentle, to offer warmth and understanding, wasn't it? But that was it, kindness may expose a buried hurt – the absence of kindness itself.

'Well, don't you?' she asked again.

'I suppose I do.'

'It starts with being kind to yourself,' she said.

How does that work? he asked himself.

She finished the dregs of her coffee, grimaced, it was cold.

'Do you know your own worth?' she said. 'I imagine you do. It showed in the way you try to hide your pleasure at showing me the sketches. For all the self-effacing gestures.'

'I don't understand.'

'Listen, we're accused, I mean we actors, of being vain, egocentric show-offs, good at being other people without a clue as to who *we* are. Well, in some ways, it's true. Not in every case. I've concentrated very hard on trying to know myself. But, in general…And we're prone, of course, to all manner of flaws and failings, like anyone else, but, and you may find it odd, telling untruths isn't one. This may come out as ingenuousness. Isn't the common perception that drama is fiction, fantasy? Pasteboard, cosmetics and make believe? The best drama, though…the best drama cuts to the roots of that great mystery, ourselves, doesn't it?'

Yes. Yes. What he'd said to Georg, except that in the way she expressed it, it made bedrock sense, instead of being mere theory. It prompted the question:

'How do you know Georg?'

She looked surprised. 'That's something of a non-sequitur. Were you trying to change the subject?'

'No, not at all. It's just that I recently had a conversation with him on the same subject.'

'Did you?' The look betrayed the curiosity.

'So how do you know him?

She swallowed a laugh. 'No mystery. Everyone knows Georg and Georg knows everyone. He makes it his business. And one doesn't really know Georg. We know his opinions but who knows what or who he is?'

This touched a nerve. 'He was very radical at the university.'

'Is that where you met?'

'Yes. Here in Vienna. Classics with allied subjects. And extra-curricular radical socialism. He was known as Red Strauss at one point.'

'And what about now?' It was clear she knew the answer to that.

He let out a deep breath and toyed with the spoon in his saucer. 'No. But I think he'd call it maturity.'

'Is that what he'd call it?' She smiled. He saw a delightful merriment in her. 'So, where do we go from here, Herr Theatre Designer?'

Again, a question which unbalanced him rather. Did she mean a walk, a cinema, another café? 'I don't know. Where would...'

'Because I'm ready for some more coffee and...a cake. What about you?'

'I think that would be...' He couldn't think of a word. She'd robbed him of words. He finally lit on 'ideal.'

'Ideal. Do you think it would be *ideal*? Why do you think it would be *ideal*? She was shifting towards him. 'Define *ideal* in the context, Herr Theatre Designer, Felix?'

He was too hoarse to reply.

'Silence gives consent, isn't that the saying? Felix? Unless you protest, object? Shall we order some *Kuchen*?'

'I...yes, let's...some...'

But she had leaned close and brought her lips to his cheek beside his lips and the soft brush of them on his skin thrilled him, sent a tremor through him unlike any he'd ever felt before.

Neither of them knew or could remember who it was who first said *I love you* nor when nor where. On the long walk through the woods outside Vienna that summer afternoon when it must have seemed so obvious to them both, as obvious as sun and shadow, that it hardly needed to be said? That day in June when they made love for the first time and the swimmy squint in her right eye, her beautiful face relaxed in the swamping pleasure of their sex, disarmed him utterly? When she came back from a short engagement in Salzburg and he was there, waiting for her on the platform at the station and the pain of absence, of missing each other so acutely, fell away? After the opening night of the play in which she played the lead on a set which he'd designed? Neither could recall, except that, in its repetition, *I love you* excited the same bright astonishment, every time, at *who was this I?* and *who is this you? We are so much one.* And, as the astonishment between them persisted, so did the simple fact of it persist, of them, of being one. Wasn't it, isn't it, hasn't it from the start been obvious? they might have said and in *I love you* made it plain enough. That astonishment they did continue to register. And perhaps that's what prompted it, that first time of saying it, the amused act of stating the obvious, no more than that? Do you suppose? he said to her later. Do you suppose that's why?

As to when he said *Will you marry me?* to which she replied *Of course,* that was after they'd raced, hand in hand, for a tram and scrambled inside, even as it pulled away from the stop and he, between snatched breaths, posed the question and she, suffused with hilarity, replied and they both giggled like children and could not stop giggling, to the bemusement of the other passengers who, of course, could not see the joke, and to their astonishment at such childish behaviour in public. But astonishment it was between them that marked every fresh realisation that they'd fallen in love, fallen right in, all the way and, knowing that it could not be otherwise between them yet wondered how it could have come to them, the timeless, outlandish, astonishing luck to find each other without trying or looking and then, so naturally, to fall in love.

30

That bright autumn morning, Felix and Sybille sat at their dining table in the small apartment looking out on Singerstraße, across from the Renaissance Bar, Karl Grunwald's soft furnishings, the keymaker, a detective agency. They were both out of a job. Work and love affairs tend to be such transitory holdings in the world of theatre, but they had been married, and content, for seven years.

Sybille had her nose in a book, Felix was reading the *Neue Freie Presse*. 'There's a piece about Hitler,' he said.

'Oh? What about him?' she said, without looking up. 'Nasty little German.'

'He's Austrian.'

'I thought he was German.'

'No, Austrian.'

'Still German.'

'Let's not disagree about that.'

'So, what about him?'

'They're quoting what he wrote, about us, Austria.'

'Tell me.'

'From *our special correspondent in Berlin*. Quote: "Herr Adolf Hitler, leader of the Nationalsozialistische Deutsche Arbeiterpartei, who was elected Chancellor in Germany earlier this year…" January, wasn't it?'

'Was it?'

'I think it was.'

'Doesn't matter. And…?'

'…"has recently been reported, by undisclosed sources, as having voiced his opinion that Austria's true place is as part of greater Germany. However, taken in the context of his more strident opinion as recorded in *Mein Kampf*, we must conclude that his intentions towards Austria do not preclude aggression. This is not the first time that he has hinted at such a course of action and they quote him: "In my early youth I arrived at the fundamental insight which has stayed with me ever since, that *Germantum*, true German identity, could be kept pure only were Austria to be destroyed. Moreover…" etc etc. What are we to make of that?' He folded the paper and put it on the table. 'I know someone who met him. Well, half met him.'

'How can you half meet someone?'

'On a train. From Berlin. He left his compartment and went into the corridor to smoke by the window. Watch the scenery go past. And, just along the corridor was another man standing by the window, looking out. It was Hitler.'

'So?'

'He got a good look at him and he decided that there's nothing to fear from him, he's a manic depressive, he won't last long, off colour and warped ideas or not.'

'And you believe him?'

'Well, it's an interesting theory.'

'Is it so? What a benefit, if not a comfort, to us all it would be if the future of European politics were dependent on casual intuition.'

The phone rang. Sybille glanced at Felix, reached for the paper and cracked its pages open. Felix got up to answer. He listened for some time, put the receiver down and didn't speak.

'Who was it?'

He returned to the table and sat down. 'Max Reinhardt. He wants me to go in, "to discuss my work".'

'Oh.' Sybille, who'd not been called for audition for two months, was caught between opposing tugs of envy and pleasure. She had little time for the grand showman and his bloated views on ostentatious productions in the name of art. Equally, the prestige of working at his theatre in Josefstadt counted as a sort of professional beatification. How could she not be happy for her husband?

'When does he want to see you?' she said.

'This afternoon.'

'He must know you've got no work on.'

'Sybille…'

'Sorry, a little piqued. You know how it is.'

'Yes, I know how it is. There'll be something soon, darling.'

'It's very good news, Felix, and no more than you deserve.'

'Let's go out to lunch, on the strength of the money I haven't yet earned.'

'Good idea. Where?'

'I thought B's.'

'We went there last week and it was crushingly disappointing.'

'I thought you were on good form.'

'And you weren't, but that's not what I meant. The whole experience, food, service, atmosphere, was unutterable, devoid of style.'

'We've been before and you haven't complained.'

'That's because it wasn't limp. Last week it was limp.'

'Perhaps you were out of sorts.'

She didn't reply.

'Where do you suggest, then?' he said.

'Where do you suggest?'

'Not B's...'

'I said not B's.'

'Where, then?'

'I don't know. You choose. I can't be bothered to think about it any more. Make a decision.'

Pause.

'What about M's?'

'They never really pull out the stops, either, do they? Oh, dammit. Let's just say, I don't know...D's?'

'D's. Very well. One o'clock? I'm going for a haircut at noon.' He looked at his watch. 'Damn, I'm late. '

'You can't possibly get there by one o'clock. He'll keep you waiting. Half past.'

'Half past. See you then.' He kissed her upturned cheek.

'Herr Breitenbach,' said Reinhardt, standing to shake Felix's hand, 'thank you for coming at such short notice. Do take a seat.'

The room was wood-panelled, perfumed by the flowers in a large vase on a side table.

Reinhardt had an ease of bonhomie, a gentle tone of speech, a marked theatrical flourish, a suave manner. His features, the fleshy face, the intense eyes, even the gloss of his wavy dark hair, suggested a man of immense charm, a man quite willing to apply that charm as pressure to get the best out of people, in short, to get what he wanted.

'Your wife, Sybille Karolyi…?'

'Yes.'

'How is she? I've always admired her work, never had the pleasure of working with her. Perhaps one day. For the moment…' He steepled his fingers. 'I saw your designs for the Büchner in the spring at the…where was it?'

'The Burgtheater.'

'The Burgtheater, yes. What was the play, remind me?'

'*Woyzeck*.'

'Of course, *Woyzeck*. Very bold, very daring, your contribution, in a production which was…well never mind that.'

'I'm glad you think so.'

'So, then…' Reinhardt contemplated his right hand – were the nails a bit long, now? 'So, then, Herr Breitenbach, I wonder, in the light of that work, whether you might be interested in working on a production here, at our theatre in Josefstadt? You may need to think it over, deliberate. My tastes are not everyone's. Certainly not those of the Nazis. Barbarians. You heard, I imagine?'

'That you had to leave the Deutsches Theater in Berlin?'

'No. I didn't *have* to leave. I opted to leave. I saw no future there. Besides, being a Jew in Germany these days…I wrote to the Nazi government, to say that I bequeathed my theatrical legacy in Germany to them. I can't believe they saw the irony in that. It was like leaving the decoration of the Sistine chapel to a house painter. Anyway, there is still work to be done. I venture to say that I've made a difference, loosened things up from the rather starched posturing of the past, extended possibilities, involved audiences in a new way, affording them an intimacy of theatrical experience even when the overt nature of the production itself might seem to preclude it. People don't see beyond that. Some critics say it's all too lavish on the surface. But it's what lies beneath the surface that draws me, the subliminal power.'

The easy flow of his speech was punctuated by little spurts of nervous energy when his face lit up with a sudden electric excitement.

'Consider the great tragic dramas of ancient Athens – the setting, a vast, open-air amphitheatre, the actors far away from the spectators sitting in the upper rows of seats, diminutive in size but large in their presence. And yet, the acoustic is so fine that they could be heard, quite clearly, even at a whisper. I've striven to recapture that depth of intimacy, you see? To draw the spectators into the beating heart of the action. To *feel* the whisper, as it were.

'The Greeks taught us so much – and so much that has been ignored for so very long, probably only because their stage apparatus was primitive by comparison to the resources we can call on. But they brought into play the vital force of imagination. And in what a setting: the perspective of the open sky enveloping the theatre, the landscape receding in layered shades of darkening colour all around, the late afternoon sun tinging the crowns of the distant hills violet. And the sun itself, now obscured by dark cloud, its bright rays winking at the edges of what the ancients thought of as the harbingers of thunder, the purple chariots of Zeus himself. What magnificence of natural effect. That's it, you see, humans caught up in the huge drama of nature's primal forces.

'And, for example, without scenery or props, they visualised the Bay of Salamis, where the great battle for Greek freedom was fought. You know *The Persians?* Astonishing, bold work. Aeschylus conjures an image of the Greek and Persian fleets, the fury and chaos of the fighting, the Athenians killing the shipwrecked Persians in the water, spearing them with broken oar shafts, "like tunny fish in the boiling foam of the sea in which they floundered", he wrote, to evoke the terror, the desperation, the shock of the boats colliding, the frenzy of the fighting. And with what a simple device: using the firsthand description of the event by the messenger who reports back to the queen at the royal Persian court in Susa, to tell of the annihilation of the fleet sent by the greatest empire on earth to crush the supposedly feeble Greeks.

'What a spectacle it must have been, what an amazing theatrical experience - the poetry and song, the music, the choric dances, all in concert...and that's just what my team and I are trying to recreate here, with all the technical sophistication at our disposal, to make "total theatre". The great tragic dramas sprang out of the soil of their time, so to speak. There were men in the audience for Aeschylus's play who had fought that day – including Aeschylus himself. The entire able-bodied male population of the Athens, aboard two hundred oared ships, chanted their warsong for victory, as they rowed out past a headland into clear view of the huge Persian armada. Imagine how they must have felt in that theatre, ten years after the battle, to see that play performed for the first time.

'I believe that our theatre must also be firmly rooted in the Zeitgeist. However ancient the theme, it must have modern resonance. For example: Sophocles's Oedipus explores the dark labyrinths of human feeling, in which lurk our response to the machinations of the gods. In other words, what nowadays we call our psychological landscape, as if we'd stumbled onto new territory. In fact, it's ground first ploughed centuries past. My aim, if you like, is to recreate the whisper of the Greek amphitheatre, but with very different resources, by a subtle interplay of all that the eyes see and the ears hear. Every sob, every intake of breath. Every extraneous noise on stage and backstage. Every gesture, every movement, every shift of light. Every intonation, every rise and fall in the emotional temperature, orchestrated in the same way that a symphony builds and fluctuates. And then on top there is the magic of what light can produce...ah, it's a large claim but why should we bow to the possibility of failure before we grasp at the perfection?'

He stopped and, his hands in an attitude of prayer, he propped up his chin and looked over the desk at Felix.

'Might you, then, be interested, Herr Breitenbach?'

'I...' Felix's throat constricted. He swallowed hard. 'Um... yes.'

'Good.' Reinhardt stood and held out his hand. 'We'll be in touch. For sometime in the new year. Until then.'

Felix shook Reinhardt's hand and heard himself saying *thank you*, as if it were someone else.

'We're not settled on which play, there are several possibilities but, of course, we'll let you know as soon as the decision is made. Ah, how liberating work is, don't you find? So many people complain of the drudgery of work and it doesn't surprise me, but it does sadden me. Aren't we fortunate? To be spared that? The secret is in the word, is it not? *Play.*'

Felix left the office and walked home. He passed a prostitute. She was elfin slim, very attractive. She blew him a kiss. He tipped his hat and walked on, his mind leaping and racing with possibility, amazement…*Reinhardt wants me to work for him?*

As he walked past the flowerbeds along one side of the square in front of the parish church of Antonius von Padua, there surfaced in the teem of his mind that story about the mason at work on a cathedral steeple in the middle ages. He'd slipped from the scaffolding and, as he fell, he cried out: 'Saint Antony, save me.' A disembodied voice answered: 'Which Saint Antony?' The man croaked 'Saint Antony of the Desert?' 'Sorry,' said the voice of Saint Antony of Padua, 'wrong one.' The Greeks had their gods, he mused, we have our saints, and we both have our illusions about their real power.

Felix met Sybille coming down the stairs from their apartment.

'Darling,' she said. 'I want to hear all about it.' She linked her arms through his. They set off. 'How did it go?'

31

11 September 1933. Trotting race course, Vienna

The new chancellor of Austria, Engelbert Dollfuss addressed a rally of his Christian Socialist supporters. Forty years old, five feet tall, Dollfuss had the look of an eager schoolboy. Diminutive in stature, grand in ambition, he saw himself as a knight of the Grail come to reclaim the ancient and mystic inheritance of the Holy Roman Empire. He wore the uniform of an officer in the old Imperial Alpine Regiment.

Drawn up below the dais were rank upon rank of Austrian patriots: boy scout troops, home defence militia, Tyrolean defence volunteers, contingents of the Austrian army in the uniforms of the former Imperial army. Agents for Dollfuss's administration had scoured the country and bought up the uniforms at considerable expense from veterans, redundant army stores, secondhand shops. Retired staff officers had rescued their stagy dress clutter from mothballs to march through Vienna, buffed and polished spurs and ceremonial sabres glinting, along streets paved with reawakened dreams.

As Dollfuss stepped up to the microphone, a thunderous cheer went up from the crowd, hailing him saviour of the nation: *Heil Dollfuss…Heil Dollfuss…Heil Dollfuss…*

There were opponents in the crowd: Austrian Nazis, hot for assimilation with Germany, the Fatherland, and Social

Democrats who wanted the same but not while Hitler was in power.

Dollfuss began.

'My fellow Austrians, we gather today to herald a new dawn in the noble history of our nation. Austria occupies a crucial pivot between east and west, north and south. We have always been and remain at Europe's hub. Are we, then, meekly to surrender our decisive influence in the affairs of Europe? The empire, of which Austria is and always has been the beating heart, sprang from the mystic unity of God's kingdom on earth and the Roman Empire. Pax Romana was reborn as Pax Austriana. And, just as the Crusaders fought to drive the enemies of Christ from the holy city of Jerusalem, so, today, must we be ready to preserve our sacred nation, free and independent.

'Our language may be German but our nation is not German, our people are not German, our inheritance is not German. Those who seek to impose German identity upon us would crush Austria to a mere cipher. But Austria's unique identity is rooted in centuries of a cultural tradition moulded by a rich combination of the genius of the Romance peoples with the genius of the Slavonic peoples and the genius of the Germanic peoples. What other nation on earth can boast such illustrious antecedents? Are we to betray that heritage, by becoming an annexe of Germany, a mere fledgling by comparison?'

He paused. They shouted: 'Never.'

'Our legitimacy is vouchsafed by the historic continuity which even the dismantling of the Empire could not interrupt. Look around you. You see it today. Austria is eternally Austria, *your* Austria, rising like a phoenix from the flames of supposed defeat.'

They cheered.

'And on this great day, we proclaim and endorse the manifesto of the Empire reborn through a government that will not waver or flinch, absolute in unity, absolute in authority. Political freedoms must take second place to the greater good of national identity. The people must acknowledge and submit to the superior will of those elected to govern them. Not in discord but in harmony. Did the king and emperor seek the opinion of his peoples? No. Did that diminish his fatherly love for them? No. He ruled always with their best interests at heart and uppermost in his concern. He bore the heavy burden of rule in order to spare his people its onerous responsibility. By so doing, he left all the many and disparate peoples of the great Austrian empire free to live in the shelter of his enduring vision of peace.

'This was how he secured stability and order. For to what does the violence of divided opinion lead but anarchy, enmity, internal strife and impoverishment? Are we to stand back and watch while mobs of one political stripe or another turn our law-abiding streets into a battlefield, and, in the process, tear apart our beloved society's natural bonds? No. We must put the common good above self interest and political dogma.

'For Austria to be renewed and reinvigorated as the nation she once was and *will* be again, Austria must reawaken the principals of her glorious past to forge that independence which should be sacred to us all.

'Fellow Austrians, I today declare myself willing and determined to take up the Cross in a new crusade for that independence. I will lead and ask you to follow, in the name of our cherished country. Austria, from this day forth, will submit to a benevolent, paternal authority such as our peoples once enjoyed. It will be a state administered by a body of laws dedicated, in mutual consent, to the prosperity of every single citizen in common, to the happiness of every citizen in common, to their peaceful co-existence. People of Austria, I salute you.'

The regimental band drawn up beneath the podium broke into the national anthem and the people sang:

> Blessing be upon you ever,
> Richness of our homeland's soil.
> Dark green pines and golden wheatfields
> Gracefully adorn your earth.
> German toil intense and noble,
> German love both soft and tender,
> Fatherland, thou glorious,
> God with you, my Austria.

32

12 September.

Felix returned from the shops with a bag of coffee, a loaf of bread and the day's newspaper. The front page carried a report of the rally under a headline *Austro-Fascism, a new epoch*, a bombastic eulogy to what it called 'the bright new dawn of a reemergent great Austria, homeland in name, empire in spirit…'.

In the lobby of the apartment building, he met the postman.

Otto, not yet forty, beaten down by a gaggle of unruly children, a shrew of a wife, the tedium of his job, nursed, with intensive care, the incurable pessimism of a Jeremiah. He seized any opportunity to bemoan the ongoing travail of a life scarce lived, like a cat waiting for a mouse to pounce on. Ask after Otto's health and Otto would oblige with prolix chapter and verse of an invalid's canticle. It was a question which Felix didn't often risk, knowing the answer would exhaust his patience. Even a cheery greeting ran close to a prompt for the latest bulletin on Otto's ailments. After ''morning, Otto,' Felix cut in quickly. 'Any mail?'

'A letter.'

'Thanks, Otto. Lovely day.'

Otto walked off, his leaden spirit dragging at him like a miscarriage of justice.

The letter was a short note from Georg. Felix looked up from reading it.

'He's invited us to dinner.'

'When?'

'This Friday. Says he has some news to impart. Not to tell us, to *impart*.'

'You don't suppose he's getting married?' she said.

'Stranger things have happened.'

'Name one.'

Georg was already seated at the table in the restaurant. He rose to greet them.

'On your own?' asked Sybille.

'No longer, dear friends, for you are here. How very good to see you.'

'What happened to…?' Felix couldn't think of her name.

'Adele?'

'Adele.'

'Ah, the lovely Adele. Rather young, of course, deliciously giddy, lots of fun, but…Anyway, she rather boringly took up with a colleague of mine. Fell in love, she said. Bit of a drip – known privately as the Handbag,' and, to Sybille's enquiring look, added, 'convenient accessory. But wealthy, you know. What price romance? It was all fairly bloody at the time, you can imagine, sharing an office and whatnot. Being usurped by a youth of extremely modest attainment and a fat wallet. And, no sooner married than a baby on the way. What do you know? That was always going to be the fly in the ointment with us, me – marriage and babies. Well, she's happy, by all accounts, bless her, and I'm enjoying my liberty, for the time being. Call it an interim. A guiltless freedom from obligation. Strange business, life, wouldn't you say? The ups and downs? Mustn't be downhearted, though, nor do I intend to be. Champagne?' He clicked his fingers and the waiter, already primed, brought a bottle in an ice bucket.

The waiter was a Piccolo – he came up to shoulder height, only. He was fresh-faced with unbearded cheeks and chin, his hands were those of a young girl, but his practised dexterity with the champagne cork belied any impression that he was too young even to be out so late on his own, let alone at work.

He'd come from Lilliputstadt, a popular attraction in Vienna after the war, an amusement park populated by Piccolos like him, small people strolling, promenading, eating and drinking in cafes and restaurants, served by men who looked like giants beside them. Austria had shrunk and so had some of her entertainers.

After midget town closed down, a number of bars and cafés in Vienna employed the displaced Piccolos as a novelty. They made excellent waiters. Perhaps it was, as Georg suggested, that a low centre of gravity enhanced the poise. Sybille thought, as she ever thought, *what a queer lot these Austrians are*.

'Cheers,' said Georg.

They clinked glasses.

'You said you had some news to *impart*,' said Felix.

'Did I?'

'In your note.'

'Ah, yes. Sorry to have made it sound so portentous. Gets to be a habit, from dashing off official communiqués, numbingly dull diplomatese. It's nothing world-shattering. I'm off to Paris.'

'Holiday?' said Sybille.

'No, darling. Posting. To our embassy. As an attaché. Up a rank or two, in fact.'

'Why Paris?' Sybille asked. 'You don't speak French, do you?'

'*Un tout petit peu...*' He rubbed his index finger and thumb together. 'One of the conditions, crash course in the lingo. Anyway, I needed a change and tired old Vienna has run out of possibilities, no more surprises. I'm rather weary of the painted and powdered old quean and the in-fighting of her sickly spawn.'

'And you think Paris will be so different?' said Felix. 'The French will be in just as much of a basket of crabs as we are.'

Georg put his glass down and twisted it at the stem. 'Well, I shall find out soon enough and report.' He peered into the glass as if to read the signs in the bubbles. 'The fact is, I've had my fill of this Ruritanian backwater, the posturing, the petty politicking, the low factionalism, the crust of schmaltz. Vienna, faded star of her own moribund operetta – spin her a tale of boy wins girl, play her some cheap music and she's in sentimental heaven. The hankering for the overbright sunshine of the good old days, when everything in the garden was rosy and all was right with the world. An etiolate caricature. Even the waiters are shrinking.'

'Opium of the masses?' said Felix.

'That's religion.'

'You are, of course,' said Sybille, 'heading for the home of real operetta...Offenbach?'

'He, at least, had the grace and wit to be satirical. Anyway, enough of this, what are we going to eat?'

Georg finished his meal, drained the last of the claret into the crystal goblets and sat back in his chair.

'I shall keep the apartment. No idea when I'll come back. I may hate it and yearn for the slummy delights of home again. Who knows? Uncertain times, *n'est ce pas?*'

'What exactly will you be doing?' asked Sybille.

'Political advisor. Negotiating nice points of diplomatic protocol, moving softly, treading lightly, manoeuvring. Oiling the cogs.'

'Admirably suited, then,' she said.

'*Touché.*'

'I mean it. The unpractised fox must be outfoxed by a slyer fox.'

Georg lounged back in his chair, took stock, achieved what might be loosely described as a knowing smile, and said: 'Your compliments always come with the barb of ruthless candour, Sybille.'

'You'd prefer flattery?'

'Not in the least. You say no more than I already know.'

Her smile was disarming.

'I shall miss you, of course,' he said. 'You are two of the best people it's my privilege to know.'

He raised his glass and tipped his head forward in obeisance.

'You, too, Georg,' said Felix. 'We value your friendship. Oh, and I have some news, too. *Pace* Sybille's opinion about him, Max Reinhardt has offered me a designing job.'

'Darling, I have no objection to that. He's quite the man to be working for. I don't suspend my critical judgement, however, on his general approach, which I find overblown. That's all.'

'I know and I rather share your feelings, but, as you say…'

'My dear friend,' said Georg in delight. 'What? When?'

'I don't know, yet. Some time next year, he said.'

'Excellent. I'm so pleased. There's one concrete reason already for a return trip from Paris. Bravo. Here's to it.' He raised his glass. 'Now, what are you going to have for pudding?'

Felix said: 'When do you leave for the city of light?' but Georg was muttering over the menu. 'Profiteroles for me, I fancy, yes,' he looked up. 'Sorry, did you say something?'

'When do you leave for Paris?'

'End of the month. They're giving me two weeks leave. I may go away. Autumn by the Black Sea, a trip down the Danube… the Carpathians…I've never been.'

The Piccolo came with the puddings.

'I shall miss you,' said Felix. 'We'll miss you.' He glanced at Sybille. She smiled.

'And I shall miss you, too. But I'll be back on mission, from time to time, smuggling fine lingerie and perfumes in the diplomatic bag, that sort of thing.' His knife bit into the choux and the chocolate filling oozed. Addressing the profiterole he said, in a low voice: ' I wonder. Is it all going to fizzle out?'

'What?'

'National socialism.'

'You mean Hitler?'

'I mean Hitler.'

Sybille took a spoonful of her sorbet. 'I fear him. Partly because everyone else, the Germans in particular, appear not to. And, I don't know…there's an alarming shiftless feel about everything, don't you think? As if we're all waiting for something to happen, and at the same time rather apprehensive… that we're not going to like whatever it is, when it does happen.'

'One thing is certain,' said Georg. 'You can bet on it – if it all gets out of hand, Austria will, as usual, kick and scream and stamp her foot like a spoiled infant and howl for something to be done, so long as it's not by her. And what one lot puts up the other lot will tear down. Sluttish Austria, true to type - mess and muddle.'

Sybille said: 'What price patriotism?'

'Patriotism is what has driven us into every mess since...I don't know. Look at Felix...'

Felix scooped at the last of his ice cream. 'Yes yes yes, we've done that.'

'Good patriot, what reward?'

'I wouldn't call myself a good patriot, even a middling patriot. Unthinking, possibly.'

'You did more than I did.'

'And I was supposed to do rather more but didn't.' He shook his head. 'Anyway, it wasn't so bad, really, and I met a man I shall never forget. Forever important to me.'

'Felix, dear, do you have a cigarette?' Sybille laid her hand on his forearm.

He produced a packet of black Russian and a lighter. She bent to the flame, the tip of the cigarette took fire and glowed, she inhaled and blew the smoke out in a fine jet. She hooded her eyes and looked at both men with a Sphinx-like impassivity and inhaled again. She held the cigarette at an angle above her shoulder, between index and middle finger, the other fingers loosely crooked as if in the gesture of a Latin blessing.

Felix looked across and felt the thrill of her, still, the same frisson that he'd felt the first time they kissed, the silken snares of her exquisite enchantment looping round him. There was also the mystifying silence into which she sank, sometimes, withdrawing into herself, locking out everyone, everything. She'd stare, eyes blank, unfocussed, and, for a while, she was unreachable. The first time this happened, he'd felt excluded, interpreted it as an irate huff. What was wrong? Had he said something, done something? Why should you think anything was wrong? she'd said. Don't you ever just stop, empty out? It's not as if I'm puzzling over the nature of existence. I just don't want to think or talk about anything.

The three of them walked out arm in arm into a balmy late evening. Vienna was still wide awake, the pavements were thronged with people, the roads crowded with automobiles.

A gang of youths in Tyrolean hats, black raincoats, long, white socks, barged along the pavement towards them, pushing and shoving pedestrians out of their way.

Sybille tugged Felix and Georg into a shop doorway.

The Nazis pushed past. One jabbed Felix hard in the chest with his elbow - he was winded, coughed and wheezed, gasping for breath.

Georg said: 'Are you all right?'

Felix yelped. 'Yes.'

'Look at it, the porcine face of new Austria.'

But Sybille's cheeks were running with tears. She whispered 'I want to go home,' though where any sort of home was, any more, she did not know.

33

19 February 1934

Felix wrote to Georg in Paris.

'My dear friend. I hope this finds you well and in good spirits, warm and well-fed. Spare us a thought as we shiver and pretend not to be hungry. Snow falls pretty well every day, and ice forms within hours. That leaves us with a tundra of frozen ruts to negotiate when we go to the shops, to see if any food has come. We waddle about in overcoats, scarves, gloves and hats, sometimes even indoors. Bed is the only relatively warm place but not enough to enjoy. There's no coal to speak of. The weather is as sullen as our spirits.

'And now this latest flare up. About a month ago, the police launched a massive house-to-house search for caches of weapons stockpiled by the socialist militias. (Dollfuss has banned them.) They raided a working-men's club in Linz and ran straight into a nest of the militia. There was a gunfight, the police stormed the place, and when news of it got out late that afternoon – quite a few militia men were either killed or wounded - the socialists called a general strike in protest. Services, power, transport, everything shut down.

'I was walking back to the apartment, along Währingstraße, when the city went dark. The street had been closed off by a barbed wire barrier, manned by the army and units of the home defence, spoiling for a fight, that was obvious. I had to go the long way round. There were lorry-loads of police in steel helmets everywhere, trams standing empty where they'd stopped when the electricity went off, shopkeepers pulling down their shutters. I heard the clatter of machine guns some-where. A sound I never expected to hear again.

'Later on, there was artillery fire - the army was shelling the workers' apartment blocks in the suburbs. The militia fought back, so it's said, till their ammunition ran out. Most of them fled and the rest surrendered.

'Dollfuss was strutting about in his general's uniform, talking tough, as if he could impress the socialists into submission.

'Fighting went on for three weeks, all told, till it petered out, but the divisions between left and right are even more bitter than they were. Dollfuss is out on a limb, politically. After all his blather about common good.

'You were smart. You got out. On a lighter note, I'm going to see Reinhardt next week with preliminary designs for the show – von Kleist's *Broken Jug*. Eminent judge seduces inno-cent serving maid, abandons her, gets found out. Broken jug, lost virginity, you get the picture. I'm nervous, of course. But, Sybille tells me he wouldn't have asked me if he wasn't confi-dent I could come up with the goods. I know she's right, only I don't find it easy. Pathetic, I know.

'She's playing a comedy in Baden. All froth, she says, and the production creaks but the money persuades her to be cheerfully, as well as gainfully, resigned. She'll be home next week but I know she sends her love, as do I.

'Think of us in cold Vienna.

'Your affectionate friend, Felix.'

Felix walked into Max Reinhardt's office with a folder full of sketches which he spread on a table at the side of the room.

'I thought the stage might have steps leading to the floor,' said Felix, 'a sort of apron at the front, playing on the idea of judgement delivered on high, that is from the stage. The higher authority – namely truth – can then be represented in some form of overhead, concealed lighting.

'The steps can extend the perspective into the background, to lend a symbolic sense of depth, hinting at the dark secret hidden behind the duplicity. The stage can double as courtroom and garden.'

'A garden?'

'Eden? Innocence spoiled, the flower choked by poisonous weeds?'

Reinhardt's expression didn't change.

Felix cleared his throat.

'If the stage and steps are painted a neutral colour, that would offset a palette of strong primary colours, for the costumes and whatever furnishings are needed. The judge might wear a scarlet robe, for instance. Which gives an ironic allusion to the scarlet woman, to the shame he's visited upon the innocent country girl. The darker currents in the background and surround will be in a more subdued spectrum – violet, black, ochre, midnight blue...

'I've framed the proscenium arch with forest green foliage, to suggest both a rustic setting and the tree of the knowledge of good and evil.

'The arch can also serve as an entrance to the underworld, layers of deepening dark at the back of the stage, quite quat-trocento, enhanced by a play of light and shadow, suggesting the way the lie is pushed into the sub-conscious, and how it has to be brought to light. If it's not too far-fetched, I thought the vivid primary colours might stand for the absolutes of law and the fusion of the more sombre hues the, um, less defined shades of truth. Er…justice.' He stood back from the table. 'That's as far as I've got.'

Reinhardt riffled through the pages of sketches, each page lined on both margins with Felix's explanatory notes in his impatient scrawl, crossings out, arrows, amendments, a jumble of words, often illegible.

Reinhardt shuffled the pages back into order and tapped the pile. 'Good. We have something to work on here. I'm pleased, Herr Breitenbach, very pleased. You'll have to make full design sketches, and draw up a shopping list of materials by the beginning of April. Our workshop manager and the accountant will work out a budget. I have nothing to do with any of that.' He stood up. 'We start rehearsals in the early summer. Does that fit in with your schedule?'

Felix didn't have a schedule. He'd even begun to seek out architectural work, to earn some money, without any luck. It had felt like an admission of failure. But, there was Domenico telling him:

No good trying to fight against Fate, Felix, does no good. Not a fight you can ever win and fighting it feels like being strong but it's only weak, takes away energy we need to work out how to get round what happens to us. Does no good. Can't be done. Only bury yourself deeper. Got to adapt, Felix. That the word?

Yes, Domenico, he thought. That *is* the word.

He delivered the final sketches at the end of March and, one late afternoon, in the first week of April, Reinhardt took him along to the theatre workshops to meet the production team and the people, nearly all women, who worked in the costume department, assembled round a patterns table on which sat the model Felix had made of the set.

Reinhardt beamed, patted Felix on the back and said: 'Ladies and gentlemen, your designer, Felix Breitenbach.'

They applauded, Felix blinked, Reinhardt turned to him and clapped, then addressed the gathered company. 'So, then. We have an excellent design, a first rate team − as you have proved, over and over again − and, need I remind you? I think not - we also have a *deadline*.' They all laughed and applauded once more. Reinhardt leaned forward and whispered in Felix's ear. Then, as the company dispersed to their tables and benches, Reinhardt beckoned one of the men forward.

'Felix, meet Rainer Schulze. He's in charge of the workshop, manager of the entire operation. Rainer, Felix.' The two men shook hands. 'Rainer will introduce you to everyone. He'll be your first port of call. Liaison is the key. We must all be kept in the know. Rainer?' Schulze nodded. 'I'll leave you to it, then,' said Reinhardt. 'Felix, I'm always available. It's a team effort,' and he left.

'Felix,' said Schulze,'first let me say, I think it's a very interesting design. Lots of challenges there but that's as it should be, it brings out the best in everyone.We're all looking forward to seeing the finished result. Our guiding principle here is *the work comes first*. We don't go in for pettish behaviour, tantrums, "artistic temperament". I hope you'll enjoy working with us. We want the best for you. That's our job.'

Felix was moved. Such appreciation was something he'd

rarely experienced in clients.

Schulze added: 'If anyone has a question they'll ask it, if anyone has a suggestion they'll make it. Collaboration is the key. And, Felix, the same goes for you – your input is important to us. Now, let's meet everyone.'

At 5.30 a bell rang signalling the official end of the working day. A few people quit their desk, drawing board, workbench and left, most stayed to finish something. Schulze said to Felix: 'Well, that's it. You'll get to know everyone. Now, if you'll excuse me, I have some paperwork to see to. You can find your way out?'

'Of course. Thank you, thank you very much. It's all, well... I'm thrilled.'

'Good.'

As Felix made his way along the corridor towards the Stage Door, a man walked up beside him and spoke.

'Herr Breitenbach?'

'Yes?' He stopped.

'I don't mean to intrude. I'm one of the carpenters.'

'Not at all. No intrusion. I can't tell you how pleased I am. I'm looking forward to seeing it all take shape.'

'Yes,' said the man and paused. 'Do you mind if I ask you a question?'

'Of course.'

'It's not about the designs,' said the man. 'I'm Hans, by the way.'

'Hans.' They shook hands.

'The thing is, I wanted to ask you...'

'Yes…?'

'I wanted to ask you if, by any chance, you served in the War.'

Felix was puzzled. 'Yes. In a manner of speaking. Why?'

'On the Italian Front? Isonzo?'

The word stabbed at him. This was too much. His head rang, his stomach lurched. The man's eyes were fixed on him. He continued. 'I don't expect you recognise me.'

'I…no, I, I'm afraid I don't. Do we, are we…?'

'B platoon, 4th Battalion…?'

Felix couldn't speak at first. He muttered: 'Migod.'

Both remained silent for long seconds. Hans's expression didn't alter. Then he said: 'We thought they'd shot you. We heard three shots. We thought *why*? And what's going to happen to us?'

'Migod.' This wasn't a dream it was a frightening subversion of reason.

'It was a bit like seeing a ghost, sir, you can imagine, earlier on.' He chuckled. 'You see? Even calling you sir?' He shook his head in disbelief.

'Migod. What's your second name?'

'Eichhorn. Hans Eichhorn. Private soldier, joiner from Kapfenberg which I bet you'd never heard of.'

Eichhorn, thought Felix, Eichhorn. Was the name familiar? A short, sable-haired man with broken teeth, a cleft chin, and wire-rimmed glasses. 'I'm sorry,' he said. 'It's so long ago and…' He looked hard at the man again, the quizzical look, amused, hopeful. *Did* he recognise him or did he *want* to recognise him? 'I'm sorry,' he said. 'I think I remember but…how disgraceful of me. I can't be sure, except that…'

'It's all right, sir, Herr Breitenbach.'

'Please, Felix,' he said, except that first name terms sounded awkward, not entirely comfortable, caught as they were between the collective geniality of the workshop and the context, albeit redundant, of a military hierarchy where the one had been subordinate to the other.

'It's all right,' Hans said. 'I wouldn't expect you to recognise me. I didn't wear glasses in them days, for one thing.'

Then, Felix had a flash of insight. 'You were the one who could walk on your hands.'

The man's face lit up. 'Could and still can.' He laughed.

Felix felt a deep relief but a pang, too, of embarrassment which compounded his awkwardness in asking: 'What happened to you? To you all?'

'What happened to us?'

'Yes. I never knew, never found out. They refused to tell me. I even went to the War Ministry here when I got back – there was no trace. I didn't know how many of you survived the attack, nothing. You can imagine.'

Hans Eichhorn smiled. 'Prison camp. Twenty three of us. There were eight wounded – the rest got killed, must have. They were taken…that's to say we all hoped they were taken, to hospital. The rest of us wound up in a place called Forte Bramafan, all the way across north Italy, near a town called Bardo something. They had us working on the big railway tunnel under the Alps. Amazing bit of engineering. We were on repair and maintenance work. Long days. A lot of the time in the dark with oil lamps. We used to come out into the daylight blinking like moles. The food was pretty thin and not what you'd call a meal for a day's labouring. Other than that, not so bad – we had football games, prisoners versus the guards - but who wants to be in prison? No drink, not much in the way of smokes. No women. But that's a funny thing. All the blokes used to say things like 'second thing I'm going to do when I get back home to the missus, I'm going to take my pack off'. But really, we didn't think about that so much, it was mostly never being full fed, longing for decent food. Still, on the up side, we were out of it, out of it before we were hardly in it. I suppose we'd all wanted to do our bit. That soon wore off. ' He tutted. 'A few of the blokes got ill – broke down, by the hard work, couldn't take it, not used to it, desk jobs, can't blame them. Worse for them. Had a rotten time. The Italians were mostly all right. It wasn't in their interests to give us too much of a hard time. They needed us – free labour – and the railway was important. Keeping the tunnel in working order. Still, I was more than glad to get out - you know the feeling, I'm sure. And what happened to you?'

When Felix got home that night, he took Sybille in his arms, pressed her lovely giving body close to his, stroked her back and said: 'Darling, the most extraordinary coincidence...'

34

Summer 1934

Vienna baked in the cloudless days of early July. Felix and Sybille attended the opening night of *The Broken Jug*. When the curtain went up to reveal the set, Reinhardt, sitting a few seats along from Felix, winked at him, clasped both hands together and shook them – *a triumph, bravo*. The single most pleasing effect was created by a line of revetted copper panels across the back of the stage. By a subtle play of side lighting, the outer face of each panel took on a lustrous golden sheen, the reverse face a velvety purple hue…a chequer of shimmering sunlight and soft moonlight.

As the citizens of Vienna clapped and cheered inside the theatre at the fall of the curtain, on the sweltering streets the atmosphere tightened as another curtain went up on quite another scenario. The city was like a crane fly caught fat in the sticky silk filaments of a spider's web, struggling to get free.

May brought vivid, arsenic green leaves to the trees in the garden and parks. The Nazis, banned by Dollfuss, burgeoned, too. Gangs of youth marched insolently through the streets, shunting into passers by, chanting the party anthem…*the banner high, the ranks in tight formation, the Storm troops march with steady measured step…clear the streets for our brown shirt battalions…and hail the swastika, the hope of millions.*

Their numbers grew. The message was clear: *We are the only party in control. Not only do we own the ballot box, now, we also make the ballot box count for nothing..*

The police didn't intervene. The municipal authority did nothing. Georg had been right.

It was rumoured that some members of the assembly, even in Dollfuss's administration, had a sneaking regard for the Nazis. Disaffected and impatient with the pocket dictator's failure to deliver on the airy promises he'd made for a new Austria, they were, it was said, colluding with the Nazi campaign to establish real fascism in place of the airy-fairy Austrian version. Something needed to be done to shake the government out of its inertia, the Nazis promised a firm grip and a firm grip was what Austria, after a decade and a half of factional rivalry and fudge, desperately needed.

On 25 July, ten members of the Austrian 89th SS regiment marched into the Chancellery, searched out Dollfuss and gunned him down. The killers were arrested but, against all expectation, the Austrian Nazis made no further move, they did nothing. In the event, Dollfuss exercised more authority in death than he had in life. Indignation at the murder galvanised action in the quiescent mass of people. Loyal Dollfuss supporters, prodded out of their lethargy, gave voice to their outrage. Timidity found a spine.

The pomp of his funeral was as grandiose as an emperor's. Busts and portraits of liberty's martyr appeared all over the city. Towns across the nation dedicated squares, streets, chapels, altar icon, effigies to Dollfuss. It was the turn of patriotic young men to take to the streets. We, Austria's youth, they

sang, stand ready to march with Dollfuss into a great future….
Dollfuss's own future having marched straight into the loaded
barrels of Nazi guns.

'Dear Georg,' wrote Felix, 'the new chancellor is a supercilious
cold fish, a lawyer. His father was a general. Probably beat
any spark of humour there might have been out of him when
he was a child. However, he's stepped in to fill a dangerous
vacuum and he's getting on with the job. The Nazis have scuttled back into their nests. It's not likely they'll give up, though.
As some wag put it, the Nazis generate more plots than the
city's graveyards.

'The run of *The Broken Jug* has finished but it was reckoned
a success. Audiences were enthusiastic. Reinhardt was full of
praise but that's rather a theatre thing, I think, all that post-
show basking in the glow of attention. Anyway, Reinhardt has
asked me to assist on a grand production of *Faust*. Isn't that
good?'

He looked over to the chaise longue where Sybille, in a loose,
cotton robe, her breasts half covered, one leg raised, her shapely
feet naked, lay like Manet's *Olympe*, deep in a book.

'What are you reading?' he said.

She glanced up and held his eye, languid, sultry, thoughtful.
'Roth,' she said. '*The Radetsky March*.'

'Ah.'

'I'm trying to fathom out what it is with you Austrians that
makes you so complicated and such damnable simpletons at
one and the same time.' She revolved an index finger at one
temple.

'Any luck so far?'

'Too early to say.'

'Are you enjoying it?'

'As a novel or an illuminating text?'

'Both, I hope.'

'Who are you writing to?'

'Georg.'

'Ah,' she said, and resumed reading.

'Let me know if you reach any meaningful conclusion.'

'I will.'

'Because I haven't, yet,' he said.

35

The photo album

Photographs record episodes of Felix and Sybille's life.

Felix is seen at work on the designs for Reinhardt's spectacular production of *Faust*, for the staging of which he demanded an entire Fauststadt, a Faust town on a revolve, in and around which the enormous cast of characters might move, live, work, suffer, let off steam, rage, give vent to joy, fall in and out of love...Felix sits at a drawing board in an office adjacent to one of the Josefstadt Theater's workshops...he stands in the workshop itself, talking to carpenters. Scene painters are at work in the background...here he is shaking hands with Hans Georg Eichhorn. They're both smiling broadly. Hans is holding a small box, his present from the cast and crew to say goodbye and best of luck in your new job. Another picture shows what appears, from the taut expressions, the awkward body language, to be a disagreement between Reinhardt and his assistant director. Felix stands next to them with an expression of mild discomfiture on his face.

In the tableau, taken before the show opened, of the regiment of backstage staff and cast – actors and actresses, the production unit, set, lightning and costume designers and technicians, scene-painters, costume-makers, limelight manipulators, dressers, scene- shifters, under-machinists, male and female extras, musicians, cleaners, programme-sellers, Felix is just distinguishable, standing at the end of the third row, his glasses showing as two shiny blind discs in the photographer's magnesium flash.

Sybille and Felix appear together in different locations in Vienna – sitting in cafés, waiting in a queue to the Kino, walking in the Prater and here they are in bathing dress by the shore of a lake, probably in the countryside to the west of the city. There is no note of either date or location.

She sits, leaning to the side on one arm, looking directly at the lens, he lies down, his ankles crossed, head propped up on his hand, his glasses off so that he squints myopically as if into direct light. With them, an unidentified woman. She is fully dressed in a floral dress, and peers out from below a wide-brimmed summer hat which she holds with one hand at the edge. It's difficult to say what age she is. A small hamper sits beside a cloth spread out on the grass, scattered with the remnants of a picnic. There are four glasses. There's no inscription on the back of the photo to say who took it.

In the water behind them, a man is swimming out to the diving platform moored in the centre of the lake. Is it his wife, his daughter, his girlfriend or a stranger who sits on the side of the platform with her legs dangling in the water?

Several photographs show Sybille in various roles in a variety of dresses, once in a trouser role.

The photograph taken during the short holiday they spent in Baden in late July 1936, shows them seated at a café table in front of the casino. They each wear dark glasses and appear rather solemn. Perhaps they've just read the disturbing news that by decree of the Chancellor, Schuschnigg, Nazis imprisoned for civil disorder had been released and Nazi newspapers were now to be allowed into the country, although the Nazi party still remained under ban in Austria. Another paradoxical farce.

Sybille was, at the time, growing more and more uneasy. 'You see how they're treating Jews in Germany? How long before it comes to you, to us?'

'They're clowns,' he said.

'Dangerous clowns,' she said. 'Wake up, Felix. Can't you see what's coming? They're not going to give up.'

The photograph bears the ink-stamp of a professional studio photographer, one Siegmund Fluss. The portrait was taken just over a year before Sybille arrived home from an engagement in Graz, in late September 1937, and told Felix that she'd had a brief fling.

'What?' He went white. Then a sudden heat burst at his cheeks.

'I'm sorry,' she said. 'It should never have happened. It didn't mean anything.'

'It didn't mean anything…?' He was stunned. 'Don't you love me any more?'

'Oh, Felix, it had nothing to do with you.'

Nothing to do with me? he thought. *How did it not have something to do with me, with us?* The words came with a wrench. 'That's pretty hard to stomach.'

'I love you, I've never stopped loving you. That's why I told you, why I'm…'

He could think of nothing to say, nothing either resolute or just. Nor did she speak for a long time. A dreadful alteration that seemed beyond entreaty lay between them like a mill race. The mutual silence was loaded with threat, uncertainty, antagonism. Finally she spoke.

'I didn't want to hurt you,' she said.

'You chose a strange way of going about it.'

'I'm sorry. I'm so sorry.'

'A bit late for sorry.'

'Don't say that, please don't say that.'

He fell silent. He stood up and paced away from her. She sat at the table, her hands in her lap.

'How did it happen?' Much as he did not want to hear the answer, he asked in an innocuous tone, as one might say 'did you sleep well?'

'Oh, Felix, does it really matter? It happened, I don't know why and I regret it bitterly.'

'In Salzburg?'

She nodded.

'I want to hear it from you.'

She looked up and, distracted with anger at what she'd done and at him for pursuing detail like a common gossip, said: 'Yes, in Salzburg.'

'And everyone else knew, but not me.'

'No. That's not true. We were discreet.' How very stupid it sounded, how infantile, she thought, a feeble excuse, a childish justification...*I didn't mean to*.

'You were *discreet*. An actor, I presume.'

'Yes.'

'I can't hear you.'

'Yes,' she said. It came at him like spit. 'Yes, an actor.' She felt numb. The more questions asked, the more bloated they were with a cargo of rebuke. Lonely, flattered by attention, lured like a chit of a girl into feeling sorry for a vulnerable man, except that it wasn't vulnerability, it was pathetic neediness. He'd made it quite clear that he wanted her, and, for reasons less complicated than she chose to believe at the time, she'd allowed herself to be wanted, to give in to a temptation of risk, a ridiculous desire not to be herself, to be some other Sybille no one had ever known. Yes, and how unlike her to be so misled by the taste of a sweet curd of girlish feelings.

'Who?'

'Nobody. What difference does it make *who?*'

'I have a right to know.'

'Jószef Gárdonyi. Better?'

What could possibly make it better? 'Hungarian. Hungarian?' She nodded.

'He seduced you?'

Her eyes brimmed with tears. She cried out: 'Why are you being so cruel?'

And now some foul impulse drove him to worsen the agony. Cruel? He thought. And, casting aside any inclination to forgive or overlook, thought *what is cruel about the truth?*

'But you went to bed with him,' he said, 'spread your legs for him, took him inside you.'

'Oh, Felix, ' her anguish coiled at the brutality of his obvious determination to bruise and punish her. 'Why are you doing this?'

'What do you expect me to do? What else is there to do?'

'I don't know.'

Passion, anger and hurt, their shared agony broke at a pitch and sank in a diminuendo of feeling to a sort of paralysis. For a long time neither could break out of the tense silence. They sat apart, his accusation and her remorse dividing them, the wound too raw to touch, even the touch of forgiveness. Sybille felt her heart bursting.

'Forgive me, please, forgive me, I'm so sorry. I can't bear it.'

'Why did you tell me?' That was the essence of the cruelty: mind and conscience conspiring against the true instincts of the heart.

'I thought you deserved to know.'

'What had I done?'

She shook her head. 'Nothing.' She couldn't think. Her mind split into fragments of memory, instalments of question without answer, answer without question, a rubbish heap of ill-sorted words trying and failing to lasso feelings, to snare meaning. She was tired, so very tired. The stress of no longer being able to articulate any sense, buckled her. 'I've never stopped loving you.'

Was that, he thought, in the vacancy of feeling, in the ruin of his self-esteem, an excuse? Why does not love that inspires us to do what is pleasing also prevent us from doing what is hateful and irreparable? Love? Oh, what havoc, what bloody disasters have been generated by love.

She was crying. 'What do you want me to say?'

'What is there to say?'

She made a gesture of complete desolation. 'What can I do?'

In the flush of his own pain, he didn't stop to think what misery his reply would cause them both.

'I want you to leave.'

'Leave?'

'I shall go out and I don't want to find you here when I come back.'

He left the room. The front door opened and closed with

a faint double click which she heard only because she was listening so hard for it, tortured by disbelief. But there were no footsteps coming back to her, no second thoughts, no forgiveness. There was only an empty apartment, an empty hope, an empty suitcase.

Felix walked with no idea where he was going. There was nowhere he wanted to go, nowhere he would choose to be. Everywhere he'd find the same chaos. Everything broken, the trust and care, all that was vital to him, the certainty on which he'd depended, irrevocably spoiled. All the clocks had been smashed. Time's continuum had snapped. He felt the life being squeezed out of him. From being with Sybille, he was in a vacuum without Sybille. She'd been supplanted by an incubus of jealousy, of diseased imagination. Nor could he repress that most repugnant of grief's companions, self-pity. Any kindness eluded him.

He felt, once more, disconnected, alone, alienated. It was a dislocation all too familiar and what hurt most of all was the sense that having emerged all tight bound from his chrysalis of self-sufficiency to become a creature of free flight, he was being forced back into the pupa, the wings torn in the process, the body twisted, the delicate antennae bent and rendered useless. All that remained of him, the man he'd striven to be and finally become, through the love of a remarkable woman, was, because of that same woman, broken.

Resentment whipped at his bruised ego.

There was no one he could talk to. He and Sybille had become all-sufficient to each other. The interdependence, the mutual reliance, the intimacy of their friendship was an essential part of their being together, the keystone of their partnership. They didn't function very well without each other. The loneliness he felt now was, accordingly, doubly hurtful. When he'd known no such intimacy, being alone had its own pitiable compensation – he was spared any demands of mutual reliance or need and the commonplace lesions of a shared life. But to find himself excluded from the intimacy of their *friendship?* It was the hardest thing of all to lose.

Perhaps she was right, that it didn't matter, didn't count for anything, precisely because of their friendship. Hadn't her admission come out of respect for him, for his friendship? He could bring no magnanimity to bear on that.

He traipsed on, not noticing where he was, until he found himself walking along Kärntnerstraße. The road was crammed with vehicles, open-topped and saloon automobiles, crowded omnibuses, a motorcycle or two, fewer horse-drawn carts, these days. The pavement carried a steady two-way flow of amblers, people on hurried errands, window-shoppers, men and women content to be together, men and women at a frosty stand-off, the distance between both sets of couples the same, the demeanour eloquent of very contrasted states of mind.

He turned down a side street towards the Reiss-Bar and went in. Why there? He didn't know. Because it was familiar? Maybe that. He had, for the moment, no sense of direct purpose.

The mahogany counter top of the bar itself, the ample chromium and glass of mirrors, windows, fittings, trim, caught the glow of the lamps and the rays of the sun and filled the interior with a glaze and interplay of sparkling light.

It was late afternoon. There were very few people in as yet. The smart set had come and gone off to lunch. It was too early for the high-class horizontals of the demi-monde, the women who earn the clothes on their back by lying on it. But, seated at one of the marble-topped, gilt-wood tables, in conversation with a demure young woman with a pointed chin and a button nose, wearing an eau-de-nil cloche hat and shirt-front dress, sat von Fessl. Even as Felix caught sight of him, he turned to look in Felix's direction, as if by subconscious prompting. The recognition, the frown, the look of stagey contempt, was instantaneous. He turned back to his companion.

Felix sat down at a table and sneaked a look across the room at the couple. Why now? he thought. In this place where he'd been that night of the ball? Why should he appear when Felix was at another cross-roads in his life? Could it be that he was, after all, an agent of Fate, Fate's messenger and disclaimer?

What lunacy, he thought. It was chance, no more than that, mere chance. He'd spent too many years listening for the turn of the key in the lock.

He got up from the table, even as the waiter approached, and left the bar without looking back.

He walked up the stairs to the apartment in a terrible uncertainty. What did he want to find there? He wanted to find that none of this had happened and this was him returning from a meeting to spend a companionable evening with Sybille in their cosy living room, to discover that he hadn't said, hadn't felt compelled to say, *I neither want to see you nor hear from you.*

He put his key in the lock, twisted it round, pushed the door open and walked into an absolute silence.

She'd left a note on the table: *I've gone to stay with Hanna in Fünfhaus 79.B Mariahilfer Straße. S*

Hanna opened the door. Sybille was standing outside on the landing, from the look of her, unsure whether she'd be welcome, speechless, distraught.

'Sybille? What's wrong? Come in.' She stood aside as Sybille picked up the small suitcase, entered the apartment and stood in the main room, like a reluctant traveller undecided about boarding a train. She focussed on a photograph, one of several, on the mantelpiece. It showed her and Felix in swimming costumes by a lake, with them, a woman in a floral dress, peering out from below a wide-brimmed summer hat... Hanna. Hanna who'd translated that Chekhov play she'd been in. Hanna, arguing about interpretation of the Russian with a director who had no Russian. Furious and subtle of mind at once, she'd managed to stroke his ego, at the same time getting her way with the integrity of the script by making him believe that he was getting *his* way. Hanna, reader of men and of text. She and Sybille had fallen in friendship the instant they met.

Hanna was forty years old, a lesbian. She reached for the suitcase, prised it loose from Sybille's grip and set it down.

'Liebchen?'

At this, Sybille began to sob, spluttering: 'I'm sorry, I'm sorry, I'm sorry.'

Hanna put her arms round Sybille, laid her friend's head on her shoulder, caressed her neck. 'Shh, shh, no need to be sorry, there, come on, just cry, you can tell me when you're ready, don't worry, darling, you're safe here.' Sybille slumped against her. Hanna soothed her back with a circular motions of one hand. 'Come,' she whispered, 'come and sit down.'

The two women sat, side by side, on the settee, Hanna held Sybille's hand, stroked her shoulder, listened, as in gouts of muddled phrases, the story trickled then poured out. As it did, the acuteness of Sybille's despair subsided into a weariness of defeat, her sinews and nerves letting go of the tension strung into them. 'It's a mess, a mess,' she said.

Hanna raised her friend's hand and kissed it. They sat a long while in silence, Hanna holding Sybille's hand. Then she said: 'Yes, it's a mess, but…I don't know. Nothing happens in isolation, honey. There's always a reason why things get shaken up. Maybe a subliminal reason, but a reason.'

'I don't know what you mean.' Sybille's eyes were swollen with crying, her cheeks puffy and stained with tears. She blew her runny nose.

'Oh, some niggling doubt that you weren't aware of,' said Hanna. 'Something that, well, just forced this to happen because…' She paused. 'Maybe something had to happen.'

The face that turned towards her was like that of a child smitten by the first large horror life had visited on her. 'I don't understand. I didn't want it. I wasn't looking for it.'

'Sybille, at risk of appearing unsympathetic, you may not have wanted it but you did do it. Now, listen. Hard as it may be, perhaps, deep down, you *did* think you wanted it.'

'What?'

'Just tell me.'

Sybille wrestled to find any coherence. 'I can't bear it. Everything in me hurts.'

Hanna brooded for a while, holding Sybille's hand tighter, stroking the wrist.

'There are questions you have to ask yourself, darling.'

'I asked Felix questions. It got me nowhere.'

Sybille stared down, twisting at the sodden rag of linen with which she'd tried to dry her eyes. Hanna stood up, went into her bedroom and brought her a fresh handkerchief.

'Thankyou.'

'Has everything been all right between you and Felix?'

'Yes. I have to be away a lot and I know he's not very happy with his work at the moment. Doesn't say much about it but having to do dull architectural jobs isn't much fun, after the excitement of the theatre. You know how it is. The company caught up in the glamour and buzz of the production, and then the play ends and all the emotional heat evaporates. One day up, next day…it's a fickle world.' *Fickle*…the word jolted her. 'It's hard to cope with that, if you're not used to it.'

'As you say. It's why I always kept a bit of distance.'

'Felix doesn't get depressed, just…he's not sure in himself. He's resilient but…I suppose he found it difficult. Everything larger than life on stage and backstage… often rather smaller, when it's all over.' She sneezed. 'You get used to it. You do a job, you finish and you walk away. I think Felix has found that very hard. He's too…' What? Sensitive, gullible, introspective? She didn't know, couldn't decide any more.

There was a long pause before Hanna spoke.

'Why did you tell him?' she said. 'You didn't have to.'

'I felt I did.'

'Why?'

'Oh…' She closed her eyes, her head made a shivering motion. 'I was trying to be honest.'

'Honest? I don't think so. Factual, maybe, but…sounds like an excuse. Because you thought you couldn't carry the guilt of it on your own. Isn't that it? Bloody nonsense, and you know it.'

'But I was scared. How could I have been …been with him

again, when I'd…'

'That depends on what you felt with this other man.'

Sybille dabbed at her eyes, at the slowing stream of her tears, the last juice of her sapped energy… *O to sleep, to sleep and drown all that I've done, in bad dreams.*

'I don't know any more. It's all such a tangle.'

'Sybille, darling, don't be obtuse. You must know. You damned well need to know.'

Sybille drew a deep breath. 'I love Felix, I never stopped loving him. I…this other man. We had to be in love in the play. It spilled over and what didn't get done on stage got done in his hotel room. As sordid as that. A rush of lust, a delusion of romance, it was a lot of things unconnected. Oh, god, I don't *know* what it was. I fell for him, I suppose. I was in a pickle. I don't need to feel lust with Felix. The love and the sex are dependable, always have been. Perhaps I just had an idiotic hankering for something unreliable, and then regretted it almost as soon as it happened, even before it happened. '

Hanna thought for a moment. 'Was the sex good?'

'What?'

'Oh, come on, Sybille, don't play the blushing virgin.' She laughed.

Sybille shrugged. 'Not particularly, no.'

'So, you had dry biscuits out when you've got cake at home.' Sybille didn't listen.

'Oh, god,' she said, swamped in the sheer juvenile transparency of the whole sorry affair.

Hanna paused. 'Cup of coffee? Glass of schnapps?' Without waiting for a reply, she got up and prepared both.

Sybille held the cup with both hands, raised it to her chin as if inhaling the fumes, her eyes fixed on the pattern in the kilim rug on the hardwood floor.

'So,' said Hanna, putting down her own cup, 'why *did* you tell him?'

Sybille shook her head. 'Because I thought he deserved to know. Because I needed him to know.' It sounded so pathetic. What a disastrous miscalculation she'd made.

'Hoping he could push it to one side, no harm done, to relieve you of the guilt?'

Sybille didn't answer at first. She knew what the answer must be and shrank from it, the cowardice. 'Something like that.'

'Then, pardon me, my dear, but you were a bloody fool. And let's keep morality out of it, let's not retreat behind *principles*, and all that rot. Precepts for the feeble-minded.' She reached for the schnapps and poured them both a thimble in the shot glasses and held one out for Sybille. 'Here. Communion wine for the non-believer,' she said.

She clinked her glass with a light ping on Sybille's. 'You can stay here, of course. Till you get yourself sorted out. There are no comings and goings at the moment to disturb the peace, more's the pity. I mean, *faute de mieux*, I'd settle for even average sex. Any work on?'

'I've got rehearsals starting next week.'

'In Vienna?'

'Neunkirchen.'

'There's a theatre in Neunkirchen?'

Sybille looked up, her features relaxing just enough to allow a faint hint of a smile. 'So I'm given to believe.' She finished the schnapps.

'They're giving you accommodation, I assume?

'Yes.'

'How long's the engagement?'

'Two months, all told. I should be back at the beginning of December.'

'That should give you some breathing space.'

Sybille studied her empty glass. 'We were going to go away for the weekend.'

There was a long pause.

'What…what do you think I should do? About Felix?'

'Darling, at the risk of stating the obvious, you've already done it. You told him you were coming here?'

'I left a note.'

'In that case…' She didn't finish. 'Darling, listen. There comes a point where words fail, as they always fail, and there's only time and silence. But, time and silence may take over. Your body and spirit have an innate intelligence. Chances are, they'll work it out. And it won't be for want of my affection, you know that.' At which Sybille broke down again and cried and cried.

36

The evening before she left for Neunkirchen, Sybille returned to Hanna's apartment to find a suitcase with additional clothes she'd asked Felix, in a brief message, to send. She went into the spare room where she slept, the feeling of displacement enforced by the books, photographs, furnishings, the trappings of Hanna's life, constant reminder that she was in limbo, between what she had known and an unknown she hadn't yet the strength to address. She missed her own things, she missed her life, she missed Felix. Her feelings were divided off, in disarray.

November

Winter was coming to Vienna. Frost and dark closed in. The first snow fell. The snow ploughs came out, workers cleared the pavements into the street, pedestrians skipped or plodded. The light in the icy mists of the city was dull, as through smoked glass.

Georg arrived, without warning, from Paris.

'Didn't you get my letter?' he said as he walked into the apartment and put his bag down. 'Where's Sybille?'

Felix didn't answer. A sudden heat of shame rose in him.

'Is she working?' said Georg taking off his coat and draping it over a chair. 'Any brandy?'

Felix made for the kitchen to fetch the brandy and the glasses. Georg was sitting at the table lighting a cheroot. He proffered the box to Felix. Felix shook his head and sat down. The cork squealed as he twisted it free of the neck. He poured, pushed one glass across the table to Georg, and downed his own shot in one.

'So, where is Sybille?'

'Not here.'

'I can see she's not here. Is she away, charming the provinces?'

'I imagine so.' The flat tone betrayed him, the wan look, the averted eyes.

'Felix, what the hell is going on? Something's going on. What is it?'

When Felix had finished telling him, Georg whistled. 'Damn.' He took a long pull on the cigar and blew three smoke rings. The vapours hung awhile and dissipated as Felix tried to fill the glasses once more and couldn't because his hand was trembling and the neck of the bottle jiggled at the rim of Georg's glass. Georg reached out and took the bottle from him.

'Felix, my god. I would never have thought it possible, never. Not you two. I know I wasn't sure about Sybille at first and she was definitely lary of me but...' The expression was rueful. 'Not since. You were so...'

Felix muttered: 'I know.'

'Why, then? For an indiscretion? Hardly serial adultery, was it? Sounds more like a lapse in taste. I know I'm not one to talk on matters of fidelity. What do I know? Changeable is about the most charitable construction you could put on my antics. Something in me, I acknowledge it, and to my constant regret. I've had the luck and the misfortune to know and be with some amazing, crazy women. Delectable but crazy. I'm not talking fault or blame. Not even reason. That's how it's turned out. And I've never got the hang of playing by the conventional rules. I think that's it. Love, so-called, the feeling that sweeps away mistrust, hesitation, uncertainty, doubt, an intoxicating triumph of emotion over common sense...dear me, you think you'd learn. I've done love, without holding back, with a full heart but a weak stomach, if you see what I mean – shallow grounding and top-heavy expectations. And when things don't go as you want, or think they should, when love gets complicated by a need for, I don't know, the other stuff, it's all flattened, swept aside. And when that happens, when love fails, or whatever happens to make love loosen its grip, all you're left with is loss and failure. But, you try again, careless of disaster, which is against the rules – I mean the rules about not giving up on a single failure. A failure to persist. Is that a function of lack of self-knowledge or too much? I never managed it, Felix, but you found your way through. You negotiated what I never learnt to – the vicissitudes, Felix, the clashes of will. I always lacked your equanimity, still do, faced with the always and forever thing.' He huffed. 'Have you heard from her?'

'Three weeks ago, something like that.'

Felix shifted in his chair.

'And?'

Felix didn't speak.

'You haven't replied?' Georg rotated his glass on the table between index finger and thumb. 'Don't you think you should?'

'Probably.'

'Is that the best you can do?'

Felix didn't reply. Georg sighed. 'So, what's to be done?'

'I don't know.'

'Don't know? Christ, Felix, what's got into you? You of all people. You're just going to give up? On yourself? On Sybille? Out of some damned stupid pride. Hm? Because that's what it is and the sooner you accept the fact the better.'

Felix made a *haven't a clue* face.

'You're behaving like a jilted youth. Get over yourself. She does the decent – and completely idiotic – thing by confessing and that makes her a fallen woman? Some forgiveness, maybe? Some understanding?' He saw the stoniness in his friend's face and softened. 'Come on, Felix, I can see the hurt she must have caused you, but…'

'Do you?' said Felix. 'Do you?'

'Actually, yes. Thing is, for all the apparent dalliance, feelings as ephemeral as dew…' He smiled. 'Some of the hurts have been quite deep. Not in my temperament to let them get me down, bright face to the world and all that, but…look, Felix, we've known each other a long time. I'm not completely vapid. I just don't let things show, that's all. I cover it up. I'm not saying that's a good thing, it's just how it is. How I get by.'

He studied his glass.

'Pride, though, wouldn't you say, Felix?'

Felix hoisted one shoulder.

'Are you just going to sit there and not say anything?'

Felix didn't reply.

'You've got to do something about it, haven't you? She deserves that. *You* deserve that.'

Again, Felix didn't respond. Each man toyed with his glass.

'Very well,' said Georg, breaking the long silence, 'if you're not going to say anything, I shall. She made a mistake, and that's a massive pity. But it's no excuse for such lavish *self*-pity.'

'I know and I can't work it out.'

'Don't give me all that. Stop feeling sorry for yourself. She did what she did, but what about you? You're the one who told her to leave, booted her out without the option. What are you going to do, go to a lawyer, divide the spoils, settle out of court? Well, here I am, the lawyer. So…what are your instructions? The clock is ticking.' He lit another cheroot.

'I don't know.'

37

Sweet course

Sybille stared at the picture of the three of them, Hanna, Felix, herself, by the lake, frozen in whatever moment had caught them, each one, in whatever thought or mood or emotion, forever past, forever stuck. Her thoughts veered between utter vacancy and a spinning centrifuge of questions.

Hanna leaned back in the wicker chair by the window. The cane crackled like straw burning. She tilted her head back, drew on her cigarette and blew a thin stream of smoke which hazed the sun filtering through the glass.

'What do you think?' said Sybille. Hanna was looking out of the window. The note from Felix lay on the table. 'Hanna?'

'Sorry, absent.'

'So…what do you think?'

Hanna shrugged and blew out another thin stream of cigarette smoke. 'Depends how you feel about seeing him. Unless you want to interpret it as a summons, in which case…'

Sybille chewed her lip. 'It does sound a bit like a summons.'

'Or maybe not.' Hanna drummed her fingers on the chair arm.

'He probably wants to talk about the apartment. I did write some time ago.'

'And this is the first you've heard?'

Sybille nodded. Hanna's face registered her disapproval.

Sybille got up to pace round the room. 'How on earth did it all get so damned complicated, so damned bloody-minded? God, I'm such a fool.'

Hanna didn't say anything at first. She looked across at her friend and thought hard before speaking. 'Listen, darling,' she said, 'what have you got to lose?'

'Everything?'

'I don't think so.'

'That's what it feels like.'

'So, by the same token, you've got nothing to lose.' She smiled. 'Sybille? Come on, darling, have the grace to scoff at the paradox.'

Sybille nodded, tried to smile, began to cry. '…oh, I'm sorry, damned cry-baby that I am.' She sobbed. 'Why do I cry? Why do I always cry?'

Hanna went over and put her arm round Sybille's shoulders.

Sybille dabbed her nose, the tears slowing. 'Thank you, dear friend.'

'There's nothing to thank me for.'

'For being here.'

They sank into a silence where questions have no purchase.

Sybille and Felix met for lunch, at the beginning of the following the week. Lunch made for a safer ground than supper. After supper, they'd both have to part and go back to the empty beds which were perhaps the most cogent reminder of their separation. After lunch, separate ways had more territory to explore before the lonely vigil that attended sleep.

The conversation was hesitant, polite, inconsequential, a

cautious game of protocols. Then Felix asked, without knowing quite why: 'Where are you staying?' and immediately thought, no, no, no, *Where are you living?* was the right question, wasn't it? *Staying* meant temporary accommodation, matters unresolved, the unspoken question *what next?* And that's why they were sitting in this restaurant, for lunch, wasn't it? Tiptoeing round *what next?*

She answered in a breezy offhand manner that excluded him. 'I've found a nice little apartment off Franziskanerplatz,' she said. *I'm settled* she was saying, forging a new destiny, getting on with my life without you. She'd found a place of her own, to which he, by implication, would not be invited just as she was not welcome at the apartment in Singerstraße.

'Oh,' he said, not able to conceal a faint deflation in his tone. *A nice little apartment.* 'Franziskanerplatz.'

'It's quite convenient.'

'That's good.' *Convenient for what?* he wondered.

She mopped up the residue of her soup with a heel of bread. Then she said: 'You heard, Reinhardt has left for America. You know why. Do you still think they're clowns?'

Felix shrugged. 'He was too visible.'

'Being visible isn't the issue, being Jewish is.'

The beef was tough, the sauce thin and tasteless, the vegetables past whatever best they had once pretended to and each of them gave up on any pretence of their own that the meal was worth persisting with. They did so at more or less the same moment, although Felix was waiting in overplayed courtesy for Sybille to lay down her fork and knife as she was waiting for him to discard his.

They pushed the plates aside. Hunger could wait.

Oh, Sybille, he wanted to say, *how I've missed you.*

She thought of the *nice little apartment* she'd been to inspect that very morning, how poky it was, how dingy, the sour reek of cooked onions and cabbage emanating from the apartment on the ground floor, which made climbing up the stairwell like walking past an overflowing garbage bin.

Suddenly it was all too much. She stood up, knocking the chair over, fumbled in her handbag for her purse, put some money on the table without counting it and said: 'Sorry, I wasn't paying attention to the time. I'm late for an audition. Sorry…' thinking *coward, coward,* and dashed away from this insupportable courtesy.

The waiter arrived with the sweet course.

Felix waved it away, asked for and paid the bill and got up to leave.

He opened the door onto the street and found her waiting on the pavement outside. She said: 'It's not a nice little apartment. It's…' but he wasn't listening, he was saying: 'Come home. Would you, please? Sybille?'

38

Felix and Sybille spoke no more of the intermission, as they called it, in the gust of intense relief and then hilarity which bowled them both over after they made love that afternoon. It did not detain them, the scorpion thought: how often it is that the hurts inflicted in the bedroom are soothed in the bedroom.

'I'm sorry,' she said.

'No, I'm the one who has to be sorry.'

'I was so stupid. I didn't think, it meant nothing.'

'Sybille, darling. You think I wasn't stupid, too? I behaved like a stupid pompous fat-arse idiot. You didn't deserve that.'

'I did. What else could you do?'

'All those things I said…good god, the thought.'

'Don't, my love, there's no need.'

'I was so bloody self-important, so bloody…bloody.'

'Yes you were. But I shouldn't have done what I did to make you…let's just forget it, shall we?'

'Do you forgive me?'

'There's no need.'

'But do you?'

'Of course. What about me?'

'You?'

'Do you forgive me?'

'How ignoble it would be, how ungenerous, in all that I've done ignoble and ungenerous, not to forgive anything. Oh Sybille…'

'Shhh…'

'I couldn't bear to be without you.'

'You were, for three months, pretty well.'

'And I didn't function, I didn't function at all.'

'Nor did I. It was…'

'Horrible, horrible.'

'Make love to me again, stop my tongue, flood me.'

'Sybille, you…'

'Come inside me, come inside me, take me.'

In the pulse of their once more being, in the stroke of their joined rhythms, the breath of their moving together, they dispersed the starved haunting that had brought them back to themselves and all they had locked away…shared utterance…I yearn for you, in this nowhere place, in this time, in this world, I yearn for you. So often in bed, in the street, in endless moments, I miss you. In speaking and in silence, I miss you. But oh, now, my heart, my spirit, peace, peace, enough, that is enough. Memory be still. I am here. Even so, I am here…

As they lay together in the sweet stupor of their bodies' contentment, she said: 'Let's not talk of fresh starts, renewals, anything like that, let's just *be* again.'

'I love you. I never stopped loving you.'

'You were very angry.'

'More with myself than with you. I see that. But it's gone and that's not a promise, darling, a promise is too self-regarding. It's just a fact.'

She reached across to him. 'Hold me. I never stopped loving

you either. Not for a moment.'

'I know. That's what made being so angry so intolerable – there was no logic in it, only a sick dumb sense of being wronged, but…'

'But you were.'

'No. What we went through was on both sides. And the longer it takes to admit that, the harder it becomes to admit it at all. Isn't that true? Except that you admitted it straight away and I couldn't and I'm sorry I couldn't.' He sighed. 'Thank you, darling.'

'For what?'

'Your generosity.'

'Just *be* Felix. Just *be*, as will I. We are more than what happened between us, much more and we will always be more, won't we?'

She spoke with the finality and confidence that begged no discussion.

They celebrated New Year's Eve at Hanna's apartment. Hanna introduced her new partner, a mousey little creature with enormous blue eyes and frizzy blonde hair, called Gisele, much younger than her. Hanna was clearly besotted and Gisele, too. She looked startled as if she'd been hoisted out of deep-seated shyness into adoration.

'She's an absolute pet,' Hanna told Sybille in the kitchen as she basted the roast chicken. Sybille leaned against the sink, a glass of seltzer in one hand, a cigarette in the other.

'Where did you meet?' she said.

'At the grocers.'

'The grocers?'

'She dropped her change, I stooped down to pick it up and, as I handed it back to her, our…'

'Eyes met?'

'I know. It sounds dreadfully corny, but it's true. They met and they stayed met.'

'What does she do?'

'She works at the linen counter in Knize's.'

'Very grand.'

'Well, *it* may be, but she isn't, not in the least. She's homely, thoughtful, and just what I needed. Very inexperienced but…' She looked up and smiled. 'She has to be worn in, of course. That's part of the excitement, though what she sees in me…'

'Exactly what I see in you, what we all see in you.'

Hanna paused, discomfited. She'd never found compliments easy.

'She's an orphan, poor dear,' she said.

'So she's found a home.'

'I hope so. I do so want so.'

In the main room, Felix sat with two friends of Hanna's, Fritzl, a journalist of known louche character, a bachelor, somewhat nicotine-stained, who, at the age of fifty, to general surprise, had taken up rambling, he who'd spent much of his entire life in smoke-filled rooms – bars, where he sniffed out talk on the ground, offices where he did the rounds of informants by phone, theatre lounges where he wrote play reviews for filing at the editor's desk en route to a nightcap at his favourite drinking hole. Typically, Fritzl passed off this change of direction not as anything serious but as a joke – 'Never know what exotic wildlife you'll run across in the Vienna Woods, hey?' – although there'd been his doctor's stern warning vis-à-vis the perilous state of his heart, lungs and liver, about which he kept quiet. He'd brought with him an old friend, a sub-editor who'd never aspired to any grander role. He'd not long since lost his wife to tuberculosis.

'Not even forty,' Fritzl told Hanna. 'Terrible shock, all at sea, poor man, mind if I bring him, Hanna, take him out of himself?'

Fritzl, brandishing a half-full bottle of Riesling, came into the kitchen. 'Now then girls, all hugger-mugger. No secrets. Top up? What's the gossip? Glass of the grape that can with logic absolute the four and twenty jarring sects confute, in exchange for a titbit?'

Hanna, reaching for a saucepan, gestured with her chin at a glass on the table. 'Food'll be about twenty minutes.' She reached for the wine and took a swig.

'Sybille?' Fritzl said, wiggling the bottle.

Sybille debated, then finished the seltzer and held out her glass.

As he poured, the last of the bottle, Fritzl said: 'It's all going to go pop pretty soon, mark my words.' He finished the rest of his own wine and plucked another bottle from the ice bucket. As he unscrewed the cork, he said: 'The whole bloody lot. The tottering republic. Collision course with disaster.'

'Hasn't Schuschnigg…?'

'Schuschnigg? Do you really think the puppy Schuschnigg's any match for that damned Nazi Rottweiler?'

Sybille stubbed out her cigarette. Gisele came into the kitchen, went over to Hanna, stroked the small of her back and turned, blinking, to take in the others. The sudden call to engage with people who knew Hanna so well, made her blush.

Fritzl was in his stride. 'For every syllable of reassurance our bumbling Chancellor utters - autonomy, national sovereignty, the glorious flag, Red White and Red unto Death, blah blah blah - there's a gun being loaded across the border in Germany. You see if I'm not right.'

'Where are the cutting edge articles in the newspapers, then?' said Hanna. 'You should speak out.'

'I've tried to. But what's the point? Cassandra told the truth and no one believed her. It's talking to the deaf and the moronic. Who'll listen? Who ever listens? Kraus has been saying it for years. Truth's a negotiable commodity, on sale to the highest bidder. What these weasels of misinformation vend as *truth* is what sells best to the masses and the masses believe what they're told to believe, or told not to question. The truth is not fact, it's how things go, the record of the biology of humanity's general incompetence and very occasional stroke of genius, the continuing saga of the single impregnating sperm reaching its target as the thousand others founder in the attempt. As the man said, strain to succeed and you'll always come unstuck. As for the purveyors of this mendacious version of what's really going on, what's more important to them: their integrity or the profit they make out of warping it?'

Now Hanna took over. 'Right, you two, out of the kitchen. I need some space. Not you, darling, I need a hand.' Gisele hunched her shoulders, a fond shiver of pleasure coursed through her. She was wanted.

Fritzl and Sybille went into the main room to join Felix and Ernst. Ernst had tried to be light-hearted but all he could manage was a vague expression of bewilderment. Felix didn't know what to say. The poor man's grief couldn't be shared or assuaged. And what price sympathy? Such delicacy of touch we need. Our sensibilities are like those solid tears of melted glass solidified in cold water, impervious to heavy blows at the larger end, fragile at the tapering tip: those feelings in us that have always proved immune even to hammer blows, can suddenly be shattered by even light pressure.

'I'm sorry to be so gloomy.' Ernst forced a smile. 'I don't mean to be a dampener. It's really kind of Hanna to let me come.'

Fritzl, who'd come into the room ahead of Sybille, overheard and went across to put his hand on his friend's shoulder. 'Come on, Ernst, I told you. Any friend of one of Hanna's friends is welcome, you should know that.' He poured his friend some more wine and, without a word, looking at him with obvious affection, raised his glass in salute.

Sybille came over to sit next to Felix. She looped her arm through his. Fritzl turned to her.

'And what's the news backstage at the Varieties, Sybille, dear?'

'Nothing, I'm sure, that you haven't heard already and many times before.'

'No back stabbing out of the ordinary? No mental break-downs, tantrums, blow ups? No juicy affairs?'

Sybille and Felix looked at each other and kissed. Sybille turned back and smiled at Fritzl. 'Hear no evil, see no evil, speak no evil.'

Gisele came in with the cutlery and started to lay the table. Hanna called out from the kitchen. 'Fritzl, wine duty, please. Sybille, darling, come and give me a hand with the vegetables, would you? And Felix, chairs round the table, if you don't mind, then see if there's any music on the radio that is halfway listenable to.'

'Hanna, a royal feast. What sumptuous delights. Ladies and gentlemen, our hostess and chef.' Fritzl's cheeks glowed with bonhomie and ample sloshes of burgundy.

'Hanna,' they all chimed, 'Hanna.'

'And, as the pitiless clock ticks on towards the doom of a new year, whatever grotesqueries it may bring, a wish everyone.' Fritzl pulled out his watch from his waistcoat pocket. 'Damn. Would you believe it? Too late, doom has just come and gone. It's already happened. The tumbrils are rumbling towards us.'

'How could we have missed it?' Ernst asked. His mood had lightened. For a while he'd been allowed, or allowed himself, to escape from the enclosure of grief, mainly because of an animated conversation with Gisele about porcelain. They'd been seated next to each other and, by way of initiating conversation, Ernst indicated a small bowl, coated with pale violet lustre, on the mantelshelf, and asked where it had come from.

'Hanna bought it for me, for Christmas,' she whispered, with a fond glance at her lover.

'It's exquisite. Meissen, isn't it?'

'Yes.' Her eyes widened. 'You know about porcelain?'

'A little. It's not a Böttger, is it?'

'I don't think so. I'm sure not. His colour, of course, but probably not an original. It doesn't matter, though, does it?'

'Of course not. It's beautiful. Quite lovely. And you know about porcelain? More than me, I'm sure. How nice.'

She reddened. 'Oh, a little. From my mother. She collected it. She died three years ago.' She broke off. 'Oh, I'm sorry, I shouldn't have said…'

'No, no. It's all right. It happened. It's better said than not. Really. So Fritzl keeps telling me.' He gave a weak laugh.

Gisele's guileless charm, her unaffected manner, her youth, warmed Ernst through. Her smile was like balm, her innocent delight captivating.

'She, my wife, had a small collection of porcelain. All we could afford,' he said, 'but she was very learned, read and read about it, knew how it was made, everything. It was impossible not to get caught up, she was so enthusiastic. We went to museums, antique shops, together. It's what I'll miss most. We did everything together. That's the hardest part. But...' seeing the dismay in her face, 'no it's all right. Not everyone you can talk to, you know. Some people have a natural sympathy, it helps. And now I can let you into a guilty secret: we found it was wonderfully satisfying to covet pieces, you know? To see a really fine piece you couldn't possibly buy and think how it would look in the glass cabinet, with the other altogether humbler things.'

Gisele giggled. 'Oh, utterly sinful. I do the same. I wander through the china department in the shop sometimes, just to gloat, deciding what I might sneak down to steal when the shop is shut.' She giggled again. 'But I love the temptation.'

Fritzl, putting his watch back in his pocket, said: 'Midnight and three minutes past, unless my timekeeper is fast, but we can make our own time, can we not, *shall* we not? Happy New Year to one and all...if any of you is optimist enough to believe in that unlikely prospect.'

'Enough of your infernal cynicism, Fritzl,' said Hanna.

'You prefer "eat drink and be merry, for tomorrow we die"? No no no. I sketch your world exactly as it goes, as the man said.'

Hanna took over. 'Come on, everyone, charge your glasses, past midnight or on the dot, what difference? Love and friendship,' squeezing Gisele's hand beneath the table.

And Felix recalled that time, impossibly long ago, when Georg, now back in Paris, had proposed the same toast. He looked across at Ernst who, of them all, had most to weigh him down and, for the moment at least, was relaxed, consoled by good fellowship. And, Felix thought, it's what got them through, wasn't it, through the bad times? Love and friendship? Got them through and levied on them all its infallible cost: loss.

39

J ust over a month later, on 14 February, Felix looked up from the *Wiener Zeitung* and called out: 'Sybille? Listen to this. Sybille. Are you listening?'

She came in from the bathroom, drying her hair. 'What is it?'

'It's about the tea party Schuschnigg went to in Berchtesgarten.'

'Was summoned to.'

'It says Hitler greeted him on the steps of his chalet.'

'The pigeon inveigled into the Eagle's Nest?'

'Quote "frank and friendly discussion in a cordial atmosphere…reached agreement on the *status quo*…" unquote.'

Sybille gave a snort of laughter. 'Cosy *entente?* How very apt. It *is* Valentine's Day. The wolf lies down with the shorn lamb?'

'Just listen to the guest list: *General* Keitel, Chief of the Supreme Command of the German army, *Luftwaffe General* Sperrle, *General* von Reichenau. Plus the Führer. All in army uniform, I don't doubt.'

'Generals discussing *détente* is no more than Napoleon telling the Pope that God is on the side of the big battalions.'

The following Sunday, they sat by the radio to listen to a relay of Hitler's address to the German parliament.

After half an hour, Sybille went into the kitchen to replenish the coffee pot. She returned to her book, blanked out the monotonous voice and Felix started to doodle on a sketch pad, preliminary designs for the lay-out of a town-house garden. The owners were looking for something "unusual, not overly elaborate, pleasing to the eye, easy to maintain, classical but at the same time contemporary". The usual vagary. People in earnest search of good taste, whatever that was, to impress the neighbours.

As the pages turned, one by one, under his pencil, he thought of Domenico and marked a place in the dressed stone party wall, six feet high, for an inlaid plaque. Then he jotted down possible mottoes to be engraved on it. *Even in Arcadia, I am there*…bit serious…*I number only the serene hours*…rather po-faced…*We must cultivate our gardens*… philosophy? Stuffy and plain…Goethe ? 'I learned to love amid the flowers'? That has a ring, he thought, and turned another page…

Hitler droned on.

After nearly three hours, Sybille put a marker in her book and said: 'Are you hungry? I'll make some lunch.'

'Lovely.'

She got up and went back into the kitchen. Suddenly, Felix called out: 'Sybille, he's talking about Austria.'

'Coming,' she said and went on peeling the hard boiled eggs from that morning after breakfast, then sliced them onto the plate and washed her hands. She walked back into the room even as Hitler concluded and the assembly erupted in a raucous applause that came across like a mush of static interference as if the radio tuner had slipped station.

'I thought you said he was talking about Austria.'

'You missed it. Can't have been more than five minutes. Sort of afterthought, tacked on at the end.'

'What did he say?'

'Nothing much. An awful lot about the wonderful efficiency of the Nazi system, booming manufacture, under the Nazis, the Nazi care of its people, the huge triumph of Nazi industrial production, heavy industry in particular.'

'Code for rearmament. Anything about the Jews?'

'Not that I heard.'

'The less he says, the more he's hiding.'

'I was only half listening, may have missed something.' He shut the sketch book and got up to turn off the radio.

The phone rang. Felix answered. 'Georg? Georg…good to hear your voice…Yes, fine. You? …Of course. Listen, we're just about to eat…no no, come…' He put his hand over the mouthpiece. 'Sybille?' She came to the doorway. 'It's Georg? Have we enough food?' Sybille nodded. 'Sorry, Georg. Join us…please, do…of course…of course…See you shortly.' He replaced the receiver, Sybille went back into the kitchen and, not more than half an hour later, Georg rang the doorbell.

'Sybille, Felix, dear friends, it's good to see you.'

He plonked the ox-leather Gladstone bag on the table and opened it. 'Toot sweet from Paris,' he said, taking out two bottles of Lalande-de-Pomerol, two pots of paté de foie gras, a box of Belgian chocolates, a tin of calissons d'Aix, a jar of cherries in brandy, a bottle of cognac. 'And for Madame…' He held out a slender packet of black tissue paper tied with violet ribbon.

Sybille pulled loose the bow in the ribbon and laid the silken band almost reverently on the table. The tissue paper rustled seductively as she unfolded it to reveal a fine, lawn linen handkerchief trimmed with a delicate filigree of…

'Breton lace,' said Georg as she smiled at it with delight.

'It's lovely. Thank you very much.' She kissed him.

'Absolutely my pleasure. And, for Monsieur…I know, only an occasional indulgence but…' He pulled from his inside pocket a slim metal tube and handed it to Felix. 'Havana. I have its twin,' patting the pocket. 'Perhaps for later…'

'Georg, thanks. How good to see you. Have you been back long?'

'Direct from the station. Couldn't wait to see the two of you. Now, how about a glass of that claret?'

'Thank you for a delicious lunch.'

'What's the view from Paris?' Felix asked as he drew on the freshly lit cigar. The aroma laced itself into the room as if the room had been impatient to smell it. Georg poured the first thumb of brandy into the glasses.

'The view from Paris? Good health.' He raised his glass. 'Chin.' He sipped. 'The *official* view in Paris is that, after a period of turbulence and uncertainty, civil unrest, economic stagnation, Austria has achieved and signed up for a remarkable rapprochement with Germany which portends not only renewed prosperity but harmonious communication, neighbourly rapport, between the two Germanic nations in mutual parity of interest and goal. All Teutons united in one great big happy family, at last.' He sipped the cognac again, rolled the cigar between thumb and index finger, glanced at them both.

'How's the cigar, Felix?'

'Excellent. Sybille?'

He handed her the cigar she took a puff and handed it back. 'I do adore the smell of a cigar but can't match the taste with the aroma.' She lit a cigarette. 'And what, pray, is the *unofficial* view from Paris?'

Georg swirled the brandy in his glass. 'The unofficial view is that what Hitler chooses to do he will do, whatever he says, in public, he won't do.'

'And what, in the unofficial view, will Hitler choose to do?'

'In my opinion?'

'In your opinion.'

'In my opinion...I think Hitler intends to gobble up Austria. And soon. The meeting he had with Schuschnigg? That was the embrace of the assassin who swears lifelong friendship before the stiletto blade goes in.'

'What about the referendum?' said Felix.

Georg laughed. 'Do you honestly think a referendum will make a scrap of difference? That would predicate a government with any shred of authority. It's Schussnigg's last show of defiance. "Come on Austrians, stand up and be counted. Free and independent Austria, the hour has come for the people to decide, jabber jabber"...it's all he's got left, isn't it? Hitler's not going to pay any attention to their referendum.'

He drew on the cigar and, pensive, stared at the brandy in the glass.

'Are you back for good?' said Felix.

'No. Official business. Not sure for how long but I shall use the time to settle my affairs here.'

'That sounds ominous.'

Georg frowned. 'It is ominous, Felix, and in my opinion, I think you and Sybille would be well advised to do the same.' He noted the bleakness in Sybille's face. 'To put it bluntly, I mean leave. Why do you think Reinhardt upped sticks? And he's far from being the only one, either.'

'I said just that. He wouldn't listen. Felix?' Felix said nothing.

Georg cleared his throat. 'Listen, I do urge you both to consider most closely what is going on, right now. And, grim as the prospect of having to leave may be, I understand that and you must know I'll do anything I can to help. All right? Good. And now I must tell you about Francine. She's the most wonderful woman. I'm bewitched, enchanted.'

On the evening of Friday 11 March 1938, Felix and Sybille arrived at Georg's apartment on Nußdorferstraße for supper. On the radio, the Wiener Philharmoniker was playing a Beethoven symphony.

A radio announcer interrupted the music:

'We have just received news from the Chancellery, that the national plebiscite due to take place this Sunday has been cancelled. Will you please continue to listen. The Chancellor himself will address the nation in the next few minutes.'

Georg raised his eyebrows. 'Well, well. I wonder who called it off…'

The music resumed. The announcer interrupted again and introduced the Chancellor.

'People of Austria,' he began, 'it is my heavy duty to tell you that we are faced with a grave, a critical situation.

'A representative of the government of the German Reich this morning delivered an ultimatum to our President saying that if he did not appoint a candidate, chosen by the German Reich, to the office of Chancellor by eight o'clock this evening, German troops would begin to cross our frontiers. That time limit has now expired.

'You will no doubt have heard or read reports that the

workers, urged on by their Marxist leaders, have risen in revolt, that streams of blood have flowed and that the government is powerless to take command of the situation to restore order. These reports are a complete fabrication.

'The Federal President has instructed me to tell you although our nation is confronted with naked aggression, we nevertheless refuse to shed German blood, and we have ordered our armed forces to withdraw, to offer no resistance and, instead, to be prepared for any decision that may be made in the hours to come. The Federal President has asked General of Infantry Schilhawski, to assume overall command.

'At this dark moment in our history, I bid the people of Austria farewell and, from the bottom of my heart, say: God be with you, God be with Austria.'

The national anthem followed the momentary silence after he left the microphone. Felix, Sybille and Georg looked at each other without speaking.

Within minutes, they heard the noise of wild shouting and the growl of diesel engines down in the street outside. Georg went to the window. 'Quick, turn off the lights,' he said.

From the darkened room, the three of them watched as a cavalcade of open-backed lorries snarled along the street in first gear, each one packed with men chanting: '*Ein Volk, ein Reich, ein Führer*... One people, one kingdom, one leader.' Some wore Storm-trooper brown-shirt caps, others, steel helmets, most had swastika brassards. Swastika flags flew above the cabs. Now they shouted 'Death to the Jew-boy, death to the Jew-boy.'

For twenty minutes the lorries trundled past, the chanting went on.

Pedestrians shrank in fear, huddled in doorways, flattened

against walls. Alongside one lorry marched an Austrian police-man, a swastika armband on the sleeve of his forest green uniform. A man running along the pavement tripped and fell off the kerb. The policeman rushed at him, and began to beat him with his truncheon. The man twisted and rolled in a futile attempt to avoid the blows. The policeman shoved his inert body into the gutter with his boot and marched on behind his new masters.

As the last lorry disappeared out of their view, the radio struck up with the Nazi marching hymn.

'How dare they play that filth.' Georg strode across the room and switched off the radio. He turned the lights back on. 'My God, what next?'

Felix and Sybille went to sit at the table. Georg stood next to the radio.

'Do you think it might be wiser to stay here tonight?' he said. 'I can make up the bed in the spare room.'

Late next morning, Felix and Sybille walked back to Singerstraße, mute and sunk in thought through half empty streets. Windows, walls, doors had been daubed with crude swastikas. *This, Austria, is your future,* they read. *We're here now. Your day has come.*

As they approached the apartment, they heard the groan of aircraft in the distance. Soon the sky was filled with a vast armada of Luftwaffe bombers, squadron after squadron, skeins and skeins of them. A white blizzard of propaganda leaflets spewed from their bomb doors, calling the Austrian people to their true destiny, union with their German cousins.

That night, the streets were crowded again with hordes of

Nazi supporters marching in a triumphal torchlight procession, parroting the slogans, chanting the sentimental anthems of the brown shirts.

The night brought a late snow, too, and, in its wake, early on Sunday morning, instead of the municipal army of men clearing the streets and pavements, came, slow as a hearse, the tanks and soldiers of the German army.

The people of Vienna watched, in silence. The soldiers in field grey overcoats and coal-scuttle helmets on board the camouflaged vehicles paid them no heed. It was as though they were passing in sombre processional towards the altar of victory and those watching were caught up in a speechless ceremonial of mourning.

At strategic crossing points along the border, divisions of the Austrian army stood aside to allow the invaders to pass unhindered into the heartland. In towns and villages along the route, the inhabitants watched the Wehrmacht legions roll by, like a great transhumance of cattle and flocks in search of fresh pasture. The grumble of the engines, the metallic jingle, grate and clack of the caterpillar tracks, jarred in the stillness of this Sunday morning, in a quiet dampened by the snowfall and the thick, frosty air.

Church bells pealed summoning the flocks to eucharist, somehow incongruous against the ground bass of the military vehicles. From one belfry, in a hamlet, a single bell tolled a slow monotone from its melancholy throat, like a death knell. It rang, it echoed, it faded away as the tanks and lorries drove on eastwards towards Vienna, into the consumptive light of a watery sun.

As Georg put it later: Austria just laid back, opened her legs and beckoned the German rapist in.

Later that afternoon, marauding Nazi gangs roamed the streets, smashing the windows of shops owned by Jews, stoving in door panels and window frames. Posses of them rampaged into apartment buildings, hammering on internal doors, screaming 'Jews out.'

The mezuzah, the sacred scripture in a box fixed to the door post of orthodox households became less a promise of sanctuary than a brazen invitation to the thugs – crashing into the house, the door splintered off its hinges, furniture, crockery, glass smashed, the family huddled in terror at the dining table, holding hands, mumbling prayers, a few final sweeps of the bludgeons on their heads, backs, shoulders before the ritual cleansers moved on to the next fetid cesspit of Hebrews.

Jehovah, the ancient guardian of Israel's people, was being trampled on his own hearthstone.

From behind the drapes at their first floor window, Sybille and Felix watched one of the smaller groups entering their building as another broke into the apartment block across the street. Loud voices inside the stairwell echoed, as the men scoured the place, door by door, floor by floor.

Sybille stood up and fumbled at the buttons of her skirt, let it drop, then the buttons on her blouse till it was loose on her shoulders. She tossed her skirt onto the back of a chair.

'What are you doing? Sybille?'

'Go into the bedroom, rumple the sheets, then go into the bathroom, hide.' She was fiddling with the clasp of her bodice under her slip.

'Sybille…?'

'Just do it.'

Mystified, he went. She tugged the bodice loose, pulled at the décolletage of the slip so that the swell of her breasts showed. Heavy boots clumped up onto and along their landing. She pinched at her cheeks to make them flush. Her hands shaking she lit a cigarette, even as there came a violent hammering on the door. She breathed in and opened the door.

He was about twenty years old. On one sleeve of the leather overcoat, the red, white and black Nazi armband. He was carrying a policeman's truncheon.

She leaned against one door jamb, holding onto the edge of the door with her other hand. She took a deep puff on the cigarette, hoisting her breasts, and exhaled a breathy mock kiss of smoke.

'Yes, officer? Can I help you?'

'I'm not an officer.'

'Not an officer? Handsome boy like you?'

'Shut up.'

'Oh, impatient. All that noise, running up the stairs.' She smiled. 'Got a hard on? Greedy?'

He flinched.

'Who recommended me?'

'We're looking for Jews.'

'They do special tricks for you, do they, Jewish girls?'

He squirmed. She coquetted her eye-lashes.

'Nice Aryan girls do tricks, too.'

'Fucking whore.'

'You looking for a whore that doesn't fuck? There's a thought.' She gestured over her shoulder with a furtive toss of her head then leaned forward and said, in a low voice:

'Thing is, I'm busy at the moment…one of your chaps, actually. He couldn't wait, either. He's very…' She ran the tip of her tongue between her lips. 'Oops, client confidentiality.' She giggled. 'If you come back in, say ten minutes? Can you wait that long? It'll be worth it.' She took another draw on the cigarette, bent forward, her cleavage in full view, and whispered: 'Well worth it.'

His face went taut. 'We're looking for Jews,' he said, with a grimace of disgust, his eyes glassy, sweat glistening on his glabrous face.

She blew out another stream of smoke, 'We're all looking for something, sweetheart. Not sure what, know it when we find it, isn't that it? Maybe you'll find what *you're* looking for here. Now, if you'll excuse me…' She wrinkled her nose. 'I'd better get back. Time is money.'

The youth hesitated then swivelled and headed for the stairs. Sybille struggled to close the door as if its weight was beyond her. As soon as it was shut, she propped herself against it, her heart thumping. She listened to the sound of the boots clumping down the stairs, the hectoring cries dwindling, the front door to the building slammed shut. One of the gang marked a white cross on it: job done.

She stumbled into the bedroom and sat on the side of the bed, took up a corner of the top sheet and wiped her face. Felix came in and sat beside her.

'Darling…?'

She shook her head, sniffled and leaned into him. She didn't speak.

'Darling, I love you,' he said.

Her whole upper body heaved, she gasped for breath.

'I love you,' he repeated. 'We'll…'

He didn't finish. She was crying.

Georg came later that day. 'Bad news, I'm afraid. No don't upset yourselves. Only, I've been called back to Paris at the end of the week.' He braced himself. 'So, what are you going to do?'

Felix knew there could be no discussion now. He carried in his passport the single most cogent reminder that in this crisis of their lives, he no longer had a voice. Against his name was written *Jew*.

'Sybille, my love,' he said. 'I'm sorry to have been so stubborn.'

She reached for Felix's hand, closed her eyes, tightened her lips, took a deep breath and sighed.

But where to go? South to Fascist Italy? East to soviet Russia? West to Nazi Germany? Some buried corner in what was once part of the empire?

Georg stood up and began to pace. 'Very well. My advice is to go to France and from there, England, maybe, America. I think the safest route may be through the Tirol. There isn't anywhere right now that isn't at some risk. Best to try to get ahead of it. Sybille, you've played there?'

She nodded.

'Innsbruck?'

'Yes. I don't remember when.' She felt dizzy, faced with the enormity of what they were going to have to do. The leaden fact of having to pack a suitcase – what to take, what to leave behind, for ever, in all likelihood, home, possessions, career, language, made her falter. She saw it in Felix, too. He leaned forward to stroke her hair. Georg pressed on.

'So you still have addresses? Boarding houses? Digs? Hotels? Names? Telephone numbers?'

Too much to think about, too much to absorb, too many things at once. 'Somewhere.'

'As many as you can find.. You're an actress, you're going for audition, meeting directors, perfectly legitimate. They can't object to that…in principal.'

She looked up, her eyes penetrating.

'Don't worry,' said Georg. 'I have a contact in Linz. He can help you on your way, give you *bona fide*.'

Felix listened in mute distraction. Jew. The mark of Judas.

'Felix,' said Georg. 'Felix?'

'Yes,' he said. The weakness coursing through him, body and mind, worked like anaesthetic.

'You'll be what you are.'

'And what's that?'

'A theatre designer.'

Felix snorted. 'Ah, yes, of course, the celebrated fabricator of sets, the dreamer up of false worlds made out of cardboard and canvas.'

Georg snapped at him. 'That's enough of that. If you have to play the part – which you do – then, godammit, play the part like a professional.'

'Yes, yes, I'm sorry…' Sybille squeezed his hand.

'All right, this isn't going to be easy for either of you. Just try to think of the worst moment being when you snap the case shut on all you're going to be able to take with you. Now: money. You ought not to risk taking any amount out of the ordinary with you. They'll charge you with smuggling and confiscate it. How much can you sew into your knickers,

Sybille?' He laughed. 'All right. Who do you bank with?'

'Arbeiter.'

'Both of you?'

'Yes.'

'Good. It's best if you leave by the Swiss border. Get to Switzerland and then as far away from Europe as you can. That's my advice. Whatever it entails. I know the president of the Länderbank. He's a Jew. Transfer everything there – I'll prime him, but we need to be quick. Can you do it tomorrow, first thing?'

Caught up in the turmoil of details, the finality of it struck them: tomorrow. The journey into exile had all but begun. No time to think, to stop, to waste, to waver.

'What happens then?' asked Felix.

'The money will be paid into a Swiss bank. That's about as safe an option as you have.'

'Are you sure?'

Georg shrugged. 'I don't know. But the choices on offer are very limited, I'm afraid. Unless you have another suggestion?'

What did they know about any of this? Who did? They stared into blankness, into the overthrow of everything they'd ever known, into an entirely new and baffling logic.

'It's all so unreal,' said Felix.

But they came to the decision in the same moment: to surrender to circumstance, and it was a relief. Since nothing felt real any more, why not, then, yield to the absurd?

Next morning, Monday 14 March, the snow now churned to slush was replaced by a blizzard of flowers, the drone of the aircraft giving way to a jubilant roar from the densely packed crowds along the streets of Vienna, instead of the grinding of diesel engines, church bells rang out in jubilant chorus across Vienna, as he came, in the open-topped Mercedes, saviour, messiah, the man who would restore their dignity, conquering hero, smiling, waving, saluting, brimming with pride, come to reclaim his birthright, the land of his birth, German Führer, now their Austrian Führer, too. *Sieg heil, Sieg heil, Sieg heil...*

Later, on his way back from the bank, Felix passed the café Josef Mantler. Fixed to the windows on either side of the glazed front door, were two stickers franked with the swastika, forbidding Jews entry. *Protect yourself against Jewish proprietors. Only German shops.* Next to the door, a wooden signboard, at ground level, in range of a kicking boot, read: *No trespassing.*

As he walked on, he saw, coming towards him, von Fessl. They passed with bare acknowledgement, strangers and not strangers. Felix stopped, turned round and watched as von Fessl went into the café from which he was now barred. A chill of awful recognition ran through him. For a brief moment, it was as if he were dead.

40

Georg left on Friday morning. They waved him off at the station. Their suitcases were packed – clothes, one or two smaller valuables, one book each. Other precious moveables they stored in Georg's apartment.

Georg was standing by the open window of the compartment. 'Come to Paris. We'll arrange things from there,' he said.

Paris....It was an infinity away.

'Safe journey. I'll think of you.'

The guard's whistle shrilled. Georg leaned forward to kiss their outstretched hands, stood back and waved as the train moved off.

They spent that evening, their last in Vienna, with Hanna and Gisele, and said goodbye with brave resolution as if the separation would be for weeks, only, a month or two at most, an excursion.

We'll think of you, here.

We'll think of you. Travel safe. Send a card.

Take care of yourselves. We'll be back.

Make sure of it.

When would they return? Would they, in truth, ever return? Return to what?

We will. Thank you for a lovely evening.

And thank you, for everything.

We should go. Early start.

Yes, a long journey.

Think of it as an adventure.

(An adventure…would that make it feel any better? It's what you'd say to a child, isn't it?)

Take care my lovely darlings. Go, go on, else we'll all cry and I don't want to remember you in tears. Go. Go. God with you.

The train laboured through the wintry landscape of the Inn valley, between the snowbound massifs of the Austrian alps.

Felix and Sybille sat side by side next to a window. Three of the passengers in their carriage had travelled, like them, all the way from Salzburg. The others had joined at Innsbruck. All refugees like them? On Georg's advice, they didn't enquire.

'Say nothing. If anyone asks what you're doing, where you're going or why, say something innocuous – stick to work.'

'But the train's heading for the border. It's a bit obvious, isn't it? Won't they make the assumption?'

'Let them. Be tired out, too exhausted to talk. Offer food round. Complain about how slow the train is. Gawp out of the window. Read. Anything casual. Act normal.'

'Act *normal?*'

'Sybille, Sybille…' Georg clicked his teeth. 'Should be meat and drink to you. Come on, bear up. Don't let the nerves show. You should be practised enough in that.'

They'd left Innsbruck early that morning with enough food and drink to sustain them. They pecked at it like misers. Unscheduled stops extended the cheerless drag on their spirits of the three hundred kilometres at what felt like a crawl. Night fell. They were still a long way short of their destination. The lights in the compartment flickered and went out. It was biting cold. Darkness closed in on the train like a tunnel. Ice webs patterned the glass of the window. Felix wiped away the frosting and gazed out at thickets of black conifers rooted in a frozen drift of glacial white. The moon appeared intermittently from behind shutters of cloud. The stillness of the icy waste, the empty prospect of their immediate future, the creeping shadow, all reinforced the chill of foreboding. The silent landscape in the grip of intense cold formed an impenetrable barrier behind which they were trapped.

Sybille began to shiver. Felix took her gloved hands between his and tried to rub some warmth into them. Some of the passengers dozed or, unable to sleep, shifted, squirmed, fidgeted on the hard bench seats. Cramps and cold pinched their limbs, their lips were bruise blue, their cheeks drained of colour, their breath like spurts of thin mist.

Some time after three in the morning, the train slowed into a station and came to a stop with a noisy belch of steam. Felix wiped an eyelet in the window and peered out. He could just discern a station sign: BLUDENZ.

Sybille asked where they were. Felix fumbled in his coat pocket for a fold of paper on which he'd written details of their journey. He held it up to the window. Not enough light. He asked her to light her lighter. In the flame he read, sotto voce: 'Bludenz, then Feldkirch where we change for Buchs…just across the Swiss border.'

The man sitting opposite was craning to hear. Felix caught his eye, he looked away.

'How far is it?' Sybille whispered.

The train snorted more exhaust steam.

'Twenty kilometres.'

'To the border?'

'No, to Feldkirch.'

'Twenty kilometres,' she muttered, pulling the lappets of her coat tighter about her neck. *Twenty is better than two hundred, not as good as two.*

Felix looked out of the window again. He spotted a single light way off at the far end of the platform near the front of the train. It came nearer - a man carrying a lantern. He stopped every so often, knocked against the side of the train, spoke and moved on.

He reached their door, rapped on the glass of the window. The voice was muffled: '*Alight here*. Everyone alight here. Bring your luggage.' He walked on to the next carriage.

The passengers in the compartment were baffled. Alight here? One or two stood up and began to lift their cases down from the racks.

Felix turned down the catch of the door and pushed. It wouldn't open, the seams had frozen tight. He pushed with his shoulder now, the door gave and he almost tumbled out. He stepped onto the platform and made after the man with the lantern.

'Excuse me, excuse me…'

The man turned round. He held up the lantern in Felix's face. 'What d'you want?'

Shielding his eyes, Felix said: 'I don't understand. Isn't this train going to Feldkirch? We were told that…'

The man interrupted. 'It was going to Feldkirch. Now it's not going anywhere further than this. Here is where it stops and here is where you get out.' He started to trudge back along the platform, the way he'd come. Felix followed.

'Why isn't it going on?'

The man didn't answer.

'Will there be another train?'

The man carried on walking. 'No idea,' he said.

'Where are we supposed to go?'

'Unless you want to go back to Innsbruck, you stay, here.'
He shuffled on, flat-footed on the frozen surface.

Felix watched him go. At the end of the platform, the man
opened a door, a blade of light shot briefly out from the room
into which he disappeared, then he closed the door on darkness
once more.

All along the length of the train, carriage doors were being
forced open, people disembarking, some slipping and teetering
like drunks on the treacherous pads of ice, cases handed down
onto the platform.

There was little haste. People reached for their luggage with
submissive apathy. Their senses dulled by the tedium of the
journey and the invasive cold, they had little fight in them for
objection. Explanations were otiose, protest too much effort.
Many of them, jittery and fearful at the start of the journey,
were drained, now, sick with nervous exhaustion.

The overhead racks emptied, the benches were vacated,
carriage doors opened onto an icy draught that cut to the bone
and the passengers shuffled grim-faced along the platform of a
deserted station in a nowhere called Bludenz. Why were they in
Bludenz? Who among them had ever heard of Bludenz? Who
cared about Bludenz?

Felix stood outside the compartment while Sybille reached
up for the first case and swung round to hand it out through
the door. She reached up for the second case as the whole train

317

lurched backwards a few metres. She swayed and grabbed for the seat to steady herself.

The steam whistle gave out an eerie, shrill wail. All the lights went out. In the pitch black of the empty carriage, Sybille held out the second case to Felix, but lost strength in her arm. She dropped it before he could catch hold. It fell down into the gap between the platform and the train. She yelped in dismay.

'Damn, damn.'

'Come on. Quickly.'

The train jolted again with a shudder of wheels, a gasp of the boiler. Sybille clung to one post of the doorway, stepped down, felt Felix's guiding arm about her waist and let herself drop. He pulled her away from the edge of the platform, she slipped and fell. The train coughed out another gout of steam and began to move, back in the direction of Innsbruck.

Sybille clambered to her feet and they watched it pull out of the station, a ghost train, empty and dark. As the engine went by, there was a brief flash of inferno as the stoker shovelled coal into the furnace and then kicked the door shut.

Felix embraced Sybille.

'Are you all right?'

'The case…'

'I'll get it. Are you all right?'

She nodded without speaking.

Felix knelt by the platform's edge, dropped backwards onto the line, located the case and heaved it over his head to where Sybille was reaching down to take it.

'Have you got it?'

'Yes.'

He gave it another push as Sybille hauled it to safety.

He began to walk along the loose stone gravel of the track towards the end of the platform.

'Felix,' she called out, 'be careful.'

He held one hand against the platform's under wall to guide him. It was caked in soot. He stumbled, nearly fell, stumbled again and did fall, barking a shin, before he reached the end of the platform and the ramp leading back up to the level.

The other passengers had already commandeered what few benches there were in the unlit waiting room and at the side of the platform when Felix got back. He smiled at Sybille. *See? I've retrieved the case. A small triumph. Take heart.*

They went over to an angle between the main building and a projecting wall, crouched there, huddled together, to wait for daylight. Darkness. Silence. Cold. Desultory flukes of wind moaned in the struts of the platform roof.

Night slowed the hands of the clock to bare movement. Night had nowhere to go, no appointments to meet, no promises to keep.

A sullen light began to filter in at last and broadened into grey dawn. Now they could see, against the blank, colourless sky a line of mountains, the defined outline of buildings, a black cordon of pines.

Sybille, who had hardly even closed her eyes, now slipped into a profound sleep - a dream of standing in the wings of a strange theatre, waiting to go on stage in a play she didn't know with actors she'd never met before, to perform a script she'd never read.

Felix stood up to stamp some life back into his numb joints

and stiff muscles, then walked along the platform, looked out into the town beyond the station buildings. Lights marking what must be houses winked on here and there in the bank of shadows. He walked through a side gate onto the station forecourt, looking for any likely source of warmth. Across the road that lead up to the station, above a doorway, just visible in the early murk, a sign read *Kaffee*.

He went back to where Sybille sat hunched against the wall. She murmured drowsy syllables, still half asleep, as if protesting that she'd blundered into the dream by accident, it was all a mistake, she shouldn't be there. Her muscles twitched. Other people had stirred and begun to hobble around, stiff-legged. Some remained crumpled on the benches, stupid with cold and long sleepless hours. No one spoke.

Felix leaned over Sybille and stroked her cheek. She muttered, blinked, stared in confusion through half-shut eyes at the blurred grey line of the wall stretching along the station's perimeter opposite, the dull wash of paling sky above and beyond it. She couldn't focus. *Where are we? What am I doing here? What happened to us?* Felix crouched beside her.

'Sybille?'

She stirred into a dim consciousness, her body feeling like a great lump of immoveable weight.

'Sybille?'

She yawned, licked at her dry, numb lips, shifted her aching arms and shoulders, forced a smile.

'Can you stand up? We should walk around a bit, restore the circulation. Come on. Give me your hand.'

He bent down to grasp her hand. She breathed in, tried to get up, her knees buckled, she sat down hard. She tried again,

320

struggled to her feet, and, cramped and dizzy, held onto Felix's arm as they walked the length of the platform. They plodded back to collect their cases and went out onto the station forecourt. The Kaffee showed lights now and a queue of other passengers had already formed, at the door.

The Kaffee doors opened at 8am. The first in line entered to the light and warmth of the interior and quickly filled the place. Felix and Sybille waited outside.

Inside, the coffee machine gurgled, the waiter and waitress filled and ferried cups of bitter, boiled coffee. The cash register yodelled. The room was clammy with a fug of thawing clothes.

When the first passengers had finished their coffee, the waiter shouted: 'All right, folks, let the others in, your cups back to the counter, please. Thank you.'

At last, Felix secured them two cups of the coffee. They held them and sipped, the heat of the cup working into their benumbed hands.

And so the population of the entire train tramped around, stood about or sat with their luggage, a jetsam of frazzled strangers tipped into this town of Bludenz, itself not yet fully awake. They were stranded, in limbo. Where to now? What now? Would it be the grim sound of motor vehicles up the hill bringing police patrols, militia? Units of the German Wehrmacht on detachment to hunt down fugitives? Another train? No train? Perhaps the Bludenz authorities marching up to tell them:

You can't stay here.
Where else can we go?
Not our problem but not here.

321

Felix and Sybille walked back into the station. Felix put his arm round her shoulders. 'Let's go and ask the man what's happening, see if there's another train coming.'

'He said there wasn't. You told me he said there wasn't.'

'That was last night. Maybe there's been a change, he may have news.'

'You go,' she said. 'I'm tired. I'll wait here.'

'You sure?'

'Yes.'

'All right. I won't be long.'

She reached for his hand. 'I'm scared. What if the police come?'

'Nothing we can do about that. Let's hope they don't.' He held her face in his hands. 'Try not to think of that, just wait, be strong. There'll be a way out of this. There has to be.'

'Felix?'

'Yes?'

'You do love me? You won't leave me?'

'I love you beyond calculation and I will never leave you. I won't be long.'

The station master, unshaven, bleary with sleep, opened the door. Felix saw, inside the frowsty room, a table, next to it, a wall-mounted telephone, a single wooden chair, a low cot, the bedding tousled.

'What d'you want?' The man coughed.

'I wonder if you could help.'

The man scratched his cheek and said nothing.

'We need to get to Feldkirch. The train last night…'

'Stopped here because someone in the powers that be said it

had to stop here. Don't ask me. I don't make the timetables.'

He made to close the door.

Felix fumbled in his pocket for some money and held it out. 'Please? If you've got any information, any idea whether there'll be another train coming through today. I'd be very grateful.'

The man pocketed the money. 'Don't hold your breath.'

'Thank you.'

The door closed.

'What do we do now?' Sybille asked. They were sitting on the floor in a corner of the crowded waiting room. The other passengers, too, by and large morose and silent, resigned to waiting, to ignorance, to doing nothing.

Felix blew his nose, sneezed, three times, dislodged his spectacles. 'I don't know. What do you think?'

'That station creature must know something, mustn't he?'

'I'm not sure he does. He probably resents us as much as he resents the people who boss him about.' He sneezed again. 'What about getting something to eat?'

'I can't even think about it. I've gone beyond hunger.'

'I asked at the Kaffee, there's a bakery somewhere at the bottom of the hill and a grocery.'

'What if a train comes?'

'Well, yes, but what do you think?'

She shook her head. 'I can't think any more. My head's seized up. I don't know where we are, where we're going, what…'

'Sybille, listen. We're *here* and we're going to Switzerland.'

'But how? How do we get to Switzerland?'

'Somehow. We'll do it. We'll do it. I'm going to run down to that shop and get some food.'

'What if a train comes?'

'I'll hear it and come straight back. You need some food inside you.'

He leaned down to kiss her and walked away, out of the station, past the Kaffee and on down the hill. To either side of the narrow road, houses showed a single light in a window. Bludenz was picking the sleep out of its eyes and brushing away the night's torpor on waking. A cyclist rode by with a rattle of loose mudguards. A man in a thick overcoat plodded up the road on the other side. Felix rounded a slight bend and saw the sign for the promised bakery some eighty metres distant.

He could just see two women standing at the door, talking. As he approached, another woman emerged from the shop, a basket on her arm, and one of the women waiting shuffled inside. Another woman exited, the second woman disappeared.

Felix got to the door and took in the warm, yeasty aroma of fresh-baked bread, sponge fingers, pastries. There was a separate counter for various sorts of sausage and cheese. Inside the shop, a line of three women waited at the counter whilst a fourth packed the loaf handed to her by the man serving into her basket and left. The next woman in line began her order and there came the noise of a motor vehicle advancing up the road, the motor at low revs. Neither customers nor man serving reacted but Felix felt his chest and stomach clench with angst.

He turned to look out of the window as the military car drew up outside the shop. The woman at the head of the queue handed money to the baker, he passed her a loaf and some cheese.

All four men in the military vehicle wore the black uniform with silver insignia, the black caps with silver skull and crossbone badge, of the German SS. Two of the men got out of the car, pulled their tunic taut under the leather belt, corrected the set of the cap and moved towards the shop entrance as a woman left. They stood aside in an elaborate show of politesse, clicking heels, saluting, half bowing, stiffly from the waist. They came into the shop and walked up beside the counter where the last woman was packing what she'd bought into her basket. The two SS men marched straight up to the counter. The baker braced himself for what was coming. It wasn't the first time they'd plundered his stock. Felix felt his pulse thumping. Whilst one of the men began to reel off an order to the baker, pointing to items in the racks behind the counter, the second men stared at Felix.

He was no more than a boy, his unblemished face already hardened by unquestioning belief in the doctrine of superiority, unswerving loyalty to the Third Reich, which the pastors of the new faith had preached at him since late childhood. He eyed Felix. Felix felt his head swimming as if he were on the verge of fainting, his heart rate accelerating.

'What are you doing here?' said the young SS soldier.

Felix blinked and, his voice cracking, said: 'For bread and…' He didn't continue.

'For bread. You hear that, Wolfgang. A man here who's come into a bakery in search of bread.' He caught a laugh in his throat and strangled it. The other SS man turned to appraise Felix. The baker had gone out into the back room for more bread.

'And what else? What else are you doing here, in Bludenz, apart from buying "bread and…"? So far from home, perhaps? Or do you belong here? Is Bludenz your place of residence?

Of domicile?'

Felix couldn't think what to say. The SS man walked right up to him and spoke into his face. Felix breathed in the sickly scent of the man's pomade, quailed at the steely eyes boring into him.

'You speak German? You seem to speak German? Good, very good, because we're all Germans, now.'

'Yes. I speak German,' Felix muttered.

'Heil Hitler.' The young SS man gave the Nazi salute.

Felix didn't respond.

'You say nothing? You are disloyal?'

'I'm Austrian. We…'

The man put his arms akimbo and hissed: 'You *what*… Austrian?'

The man Wolfgang was packing four loaves of bread, a large paper bag of sponge cakes, waxed paper parcels of sausage and cheese into a linen flour sack.

'We aren't yet used to it,' Felix said.

'It is an order.'

'I'm sorry. I came in to buy bread for a picnic.'

'A picnic? In winter?' He jeered.

'That is, for the train.'

'You think there are trains from Bludenz today?'

'I was told there were.' Damn damn, he thought, that was our lifeline, the train out of here, to safety, oh, pray god, not a bad omen, pray god I haven't betrayed us. Damn, why do I so lack cunning? Think, Felix, *think*.

'And in which direction are these imaginary trains pointing?'

Felix couldn't think. 'Salzburg?'

The SS man's head jerked back in a gesture of mock

326

astonishment. 'And from where, then, will these trains that are going to Salzburg come?'

Felix was off balance and mumbled: 'I don't know.'

The SS man's tone flattened. 'Show me your papers and your ticket.' He put out his right hand, palm uppermost.

Sweat pilled on Felix's brow. The man Wolfgang had slung the sack over his shoulder. 'Come on, Friedrich,' he said. 'Time for breakfast, I'm hungry.' Friedrich hesitated, looked between Felix and his colleague. 'Aren't you hungry?' said the other man. 'See what the kind baker has given us to eat.' He grinned at the baker behind the counter who stood silent and emotionless like a sulky child. Sulky children, that's what these men make of us, he thought.

Wolfgang was at the door of the shop. 'Friedrich. Come on.' He walked out. The man Friedrich snarled at Felix: 'Enjoy your picnic, Austrian,' and left the shop. The vehicle drove off.

As Felix walked back up the hill with the provisions – bread, cheese, half a sausage – he heard the sound of a train in the distance, though from which direction he couldn't be sure. He quickened pace, slipped on a patch of black ice, didn't fall, regained his poise. He looked up the long hill, the station out of sight. It was too far for him to run. He'd get there in time, he told himself, if he took it steadily, he'd get there, the train wouldn't go straight away.

Now he could tell that the train had come from the east, their train, it must be their train, unless, like the first one, it was going to stop in Bludenz and go back the way it had come.

The noise stopped – the train must have drawn into the station. The train's steam whistle blew and several gouts of steam swelled over the station roof, like puffy clouds. Felix was panicked. There was still a long way to go. He couldn't yet see the station buildings. He started to run. It was no good, he couldn't get safe purchase. He stopped running and started to stride as hard and fast as he could. Fear, the chill air and exertion shortened his breath. His lungs heaved and beat at his chest wall, so it felt. The bag of provisions was awkward to carry. He had to clutch it in the crook of one arm. It made keeping his balance difficult. His glasses misted over with his panting. His head throbbed.

The train whistle blew a second time. The car in which the Nazis had come to the bakery stood on the station forecourt. A covered lorry was driving up the hill behind him, to carry away the detainees. Jews. First and foremost, Jews. Soldiers in helmets lined the platform, rifles at the ready. An SS officer passed through the train checking papers. Sybille...what had happened to Sybille? His throat and midriff constricted, every gulp of air squeezed out with painful effort. He sobbed. He cursed the ice under his feet.

He pressed on, to the top of the hill, past the Kaffee and there was the station. But there was no car on the forecourt, no soldiers on the platform, no covered lorry. The train was waiting, and Sybille was there, clinging onto an open door, the only door in the train that was open. She was arguing with the stationmaster with furious energy. The train whistle blew a third time in a huff of steam. The stationmaster shoved at the door in an attempt to close it, pushing Sybille out of the way. She clung to the handle.

Felix staggered along the platform and called out, in a hoarse voice: 'Sybille.' Sybille pointed to him and yelled something at the stationmaster then called out: 'Felix, hurry.'

And he was there, handing Sybille the bag of food, bundling into the carriage as the train belched staccato gusts of steam and began to shunt westward, in the direction of Switzerland. Sybille heaved at the door and slammed it shut.

Felix sat, gasping for breath, opposite her, her expression torn between relief and a remnant of anger. She closed her eyes and leaned back in the wooden bench seat. Felix reached across and took her hand. She opened her eyes to see his glasses trained on her, both lenses opaque with cataracts of his panted breath. She leaned towards him and curled one arm round his neck. They sat like that, head to head, for a long time as the train gathered speed, anxiety draining from them to be replaced by a different sort of disquiet. Ahead of them, nothing was certain. In this, their present limbo, nothing was certain.

Felix picked up the bag of bread and cheese and said: 'Something to eat?'

'Not hungry,' she said, her face wan with distress. 'Later. I'm sorry.'

He folded his arms across the bag.

'Don't wait for me,' she said.

'No. It's all right. I bought it for us.'

They looked out of the window at the passing landscape. The train was moving through a corridor between mountains, a natural causeway, Switzerland over to the left, behind the ridge.

The train drew into Feldkirch. They and most of the other passengers got off. This time, Sybille marched straight across the platform to the waiting room, carrying the bag of food, leaving Felix to follow with the cases. They sat, ate some food and settled to wait.

A policemen peered into the room through the glazed door,

opened it and looked round. He was middle-aged with a sour expression, his eyes hooded with distaste and boredom. He turned to a couple sitting by the door and held out his hand. 'Papers.'

They rummaged for tickets and identity cards. These he scanned with obvious lack of interest. He was making his presence felt, no more. There were better ways of spending his time than quizzing a sad bunch of refugees, warmer places to be. He handed the papers back, glanced once more round the room and left.

The train drew into and then out of Feldkirch five hours later and, for an hour, crept as if in pain to the Swiss border. On one side, Austrian border police, on the other, Swiss police, two of whom boarded the train and made their way through, checking papers. The Austrian guards huddled over the stove in their hut, as if turning their back on what was happening here – nothing to do with them, their responsibility ended at the border, unless the Swiss kicked up a fuss and refused to allow someone entry. It happened.

The Swiss customs officer came to Sybille and Felix, scanned her papers and handed them back, scanned those of Felix, looked over the card at him with a frown and arched his eyebrows. Whatever the doubt was that hovered in his mind, he didn't pursue it. He handed the papers back and moved on.

Sybille sat opposite Felix, slumped against the side of the carriage. Her spirit faded into indifference. A quarter of an hour later, the train snorted the steam out of its boiler exhaust pipes and crossed the border, into neutral Switzerland. Felix reached across for Sybille's hand and squeezed it. It was limp.

Half an hour later, the train pulled into a station and stopped, panting exhaust steam. Felix looked out of the window and saw the sign: BUCHS. 'Darling?' he said.

Faint recognition stirred in her face as he looked at her and squeezed her hand again. She'd had the look of an effigy, lifeless, her eyes dimmed.

'Darling, it's Buchs.' Looking at her, he hesitated, tears pooled. He croaked: 'It's where we change.'

'Change into what?' she said.

41

New York City, 5 May 1955

Felix strolled into Goldfarb's Delicatessen 'n Drugstore, a few blocks over from Ebbett's Field, home of the Brooklyn Dodgers.

'Mr Brightman, how you doin'?'

'I'm well, Mr Goldfarb, and how are you?'

'I don't complain. Could complain, could always complain, but so long as you got your health…know what I'm saying?'

'I know what you're saying.'

'*Suddeutsche Zeitung* just came in.' He reached under the counter and handed Felix the paper, a week or so old, as ever. 'But it's got the news, don't it,' Goldfarb liked to say, 'and in German. You're Austrian? Am I right? I know how you like the old lingo. Me not so much. Okey dokey?'

Goldfarb had blended, as he liked to put it. 'Either you join or you stay out. Me? I blend in.' He'd come across as a refugee from Bavaria, early in the War, and embraced his new life in America, more strictly in New York, more strictly still in Brooklyn, beyond whose boundaries he'd never strayed, as eagerly as he'd left behind *fucken Hitler and his fucken crazies and lowlife bums*, as he put it in the singsong Brooklyn accent that covered for the grammatical irregularities of his English. Brooklyn accents and baseball averages, this was how he blended, plus, all-important plus, the fortunes of *his* team, the Dodgers.

'First team to hire a black player, Mr Brightman. Jackie Robinson. He could play. You ever go?'

'No. I never go.'

'Sheesh, you should have went to the game last week. Humdinger, Mr Brightman, lollapalozza. You oughta go, before they got to absquatulate. Rumour is. Heading off to Los Angeles. Can you believe that? Voluntary exile? Not like us who didn't have no choice. Sad day that's going to be, Mr Brightman, sad day. But, they go, I gotta go on and support 'em, gotta support a team. You're not interested in baseball, you're not American. Couldn't switch to the Giants across from here. Sworn enemies, Mr Brightman,' he said, leaning forward as if it were dangerous talk. 'A giant, yet, could get to the park,' he continued, in a low voice, confidential, 'Staten Island as a stepping stone and, bingo, the other side of the river, one stride. But, viper's nest, Mr Brightman. Catch me I go there? Nah. Never live it down. Anyway,' as if there needed to be a more rational excuse, 'it's too far for me to go and I don't like to travel out of Brooklyn, plus my wife doesn't like me risking public transportation – there are stories, Mr Brightman, crime stories, horror stories - and I wanna stay faithful, first love, last love. So, you know what I'll do? Listen to the games on the radio commentary. I'll still be a gen-yew-ine fan of the Dodgers. And, you wanna know a secret?' He winked.

'What's the secret?'

'The feller giving the spiel on the wireless, he can't see the actual, live, as-it's-happening, game, can you figure that out? He slapped his hands together. 'He just makes up the plays from bits of paper they hand him with bare detail and he turns it into the live speech like he was right there. Can you believe it? That's America. They work things out.'

Felix was perusing the front page of the paper.

'You see where Austria got her ticket? Page four. Big news.'

'Ticket?'

'Get out of jail free. Got signed off by the governor's board. Free to go. No more lock-up. Home run, already. Which makes it *so long* and *goodnight Vienna,* bye bye the doughboys. Capeesh?'

'Sorry, Mr Goldfarb, would you explain, maybe?'

Goldfarb tapped the paper. 'Page four. You can read it. Austria got free is what happened, and that's straight from the shoulder.' He winked. 'Independence is what happened, all the occupant soldiers going home, for good.'

'Occupants?'

'Occupy, occupants. Everybody goes home, slam bang.'

Felix looked at the headline on page four: *Austria, Treaty of State.*

'No more people telling you what to do and how to do it, Mr Brightman. Everybody free to come and go. Independence, already.'

'Well, that is something.'

'Something is right.'

'Thank you, Mr Goldfarb.'

'You're welcome, Mr Brightman. You take care, now.'

Austria was Austria again.

Sybille immediately wrote once more to Hanna without any great hope of a reply. So many letters written and no answer.

She couldn't believe Hanna would have moved, except with reluctance, except – dreadful thought – because she'd been forced to leave the apartment.

'It's the only, the first, place I could ever think of as home,' Hanna had said. What her parents called home, the house in which she grew up, she could never think of as home. She went back to it out of habit, duty, and, as she came to think, cowardice, unwilling, for whatever reason, to confront the reality of her loathing of the place and of the people who inhabited it, the crabbed supervisors of the family blood-line.

After university in Augsburg – as far away from the parental snake pit as she could find to offer her a degree course – she'd moved to Vienna to study for a doctorate, earning a keep by translation work, most of it mundane and tedious. She lived in one temporary lodging after another, lonely and unhappy, ricocheting from one brief, failed affair to another, distraught and unhappy. The brief liaison with one of her lecturers, the only man she ever went to bed with, she described as disgusting.

Then Gudrun arrived, Gudrun announced herself, Gudrun was there and, for the first time in her life, Hanna told Sybille, she'd felt the shock of a consuming passion, love's migraine.

Gudrun had coaxed her out of her bookish, hermit existence – 'that's not living, it's running away,' she said. Gudrun had wakened her to a dimension of life way outside the confines of anything she'd ever experienced. Gudrun was the first lover to whom she'd surrendered her entire being, the first lover who tested her feelings to the limits of abandon and tolerance. Gudrun, lithe as a cat, intense and insistent, her eyes blazing with need, impatience, desire, urgency. But nothing was enough for her, there must always be more – more love, more surrender, more forgiving, to satisfy the jealous rage which possessed her and which she could not control.

Hanna's past was so full of secrets, Gudrun insisted, of other women, of other lovers who still held her attention, still lingered in her, despite all her protests that they were gone, forgotten. And that man…what had she been thinking of? A mistake, she called it. It meant nothing, she claimed. Liar, Hanna, liar. Of course it meant something. Everything you say to me is equivocal if not a direct untruth or evasion. You should go back to him, your man, make your life what the normal people call normal, if you choose to be normal, which is what you're best suited to, normality. The taunt was always the same, *you should go back to him*, and always, as it was calculated to do, unleashed Hanna's exasperation – proof, if any were needed, of her ingrained infidelity. So Gudrun thought and assumed.

'Why did you ever tell me, if it meant so little?'

'Because you asked. You had to know the contents of my head, my heart, my bed.'

'And see how you enjoyed telling me, to rub my nose in the story of your past amours. You wanted to make me squirm.'

'Gudrun, darling, please, please stop it, I love you.'

'I was better on my own, I was always better on my own. You should go.'

Go, then, thought Hanna, but even the thought was intolerable to her. Life had never been so complicated but without this complication of Gudrun, life was inconceivable, so completely had Gudrun occupied her, so completely the idea, the being, the genius of Gudrun, her generosity and her terrible need.

And on and on and on it went, the panic lashing and goading her, until she was exhausted. It was the pattern of her metamorphosis, Gudrun. The wild panic and rage succeeded by the childlike sense of fun that made her irresistible.

One day, she gave in to the panic. She went out, didn't come home and was found, late next afternoon, hanging from the bough of a tree in the woods. In her pocket was a note: *Enough. I love you. I'm sorry. G*

It was in the aftermath of Gudrun's suicide, afflicted by loneliness, by guilt, by inconsolable misery, that Hanna found her home and, in the way of these things, believed it to be Gudrun's parting gift to her. Not an apology, but a gift of the life they'd lived together, a gift exceeding the death that had torn them apart, a gift of the life she could no longer sustain for herself.

Walking to the library one morning, Hanna had seen the sign *To Let* in an apartment window and, in a kind of automotive trance, she'd walked up the stairs of the building, knocked on the door and was, an hour later, the new tenant.

'You see, Sybille, it was here I really found myself. I'd pretty well lost all sense of myself after Gudrun, even though I'd reached the point when I wasn't sure if I could endure the vortex of her moods any more. Poisonous depression, wild gaiety...But, the instant I walked into the apartment I knew I'd found my home. I felt at peace, a wonderful serenity. I can't explain why or how. You see what I mean about her gift to me?

'Up till then, I'd concluded that I was going to end up as a dotty old spinster, burrowing into dictionaries and pretending that it was fulfilment. But, I thawed out. I felt my nerve ends tingling again. I wanted to love someone, to make love to someone, to believe they loved me, even if it wasn't true. Curious, isn't it, how love can fool us into being what we call true to someone. But, to hell with that. I didn't want to hold back any more. I'd done that for so long. Even at the expense of getting hurt. It would be worth the cost, to feel alive again. Damn it, Sybille, don't we all get hurt? Don't we stay children, in a way, like children, vulnerable, and if we don't, where's the truth of our feeling then?

'That's what Gudrun gave me, too. She was impossible, but I'd thought for too long after she died that she was irreplaceable. I'd dedicated the leavings of my life to mourning her. You can imagine what she'd have said to that. I wouldn't succumb to love again, I told myself, because love dies and I could not face another death. And, then, I didn't care. Love was too precious to weigh in the scales of profit and loss, of unthinkable pain and unimaginable joy. I gave in to the possibility of it, I surrendered to it, just as Gudrun had surrendered to whatever demon had hold of her. And then - how long after? I don't know - Gisele, dear sweet innocent Gisele, my lovely bashful elfin charm appeared and I...' Her eyes were wet with tears. She smiled. 'You know...'

And so Sybille wrote once more to her friend, a last letter it had to be, to placate the gods of enigma, but as if it were for the first time, telling her friend that they were both well, that they'd found a home in America, how the train had finally come to that nowhere in the mountains and how they'd arrived in Switzerland, travelled across France to Bordeaux and taken passage on a passenger ship across the Atlantic and...to this place that felt like paradise when they arrived.

The letter went unanswered.

One bright, warm early autumn afternoon the following year,

Sybille and Felix stopped in the middle of the Brooklyn Bridge and took in the view westwards over Upper New York Bay. Sunlight glinted from a clear, blue sky on the flat waters of the estuary. Passing tugs and smaller steam boats hooted as they criss-crossed the busy waters. In the central stream, a passenger ship nosed into the narrower neck of the Hudson river, past the Statue of Liberty, the Mother of Exiles. Sybille felt a stab of nostalgia, remembering their first sight of the city's skyscrapers, thrusting up out of the horizon, that bleak morning in January, the notched high ramparts of Manhattan. The flat-topped towers were like candles with no flame, eloquent of the sombre passage of the journey they'd made out of Europe's gathering night. But there was one flame, guiding them in to haven. They'd watched from the forward taff rail, as the colossus with her beacon torch drew nearer and nearer...

Give me your tired, your poor,
Your huddled masses yearning to breathe free,
The wretched refuse of your teeming shore.
Send these, the homeless, tempest-tost to me,
I lift my lamp beside the golden door.

And now, she'd thought, as they walked out of the immigration station on Ellis Island that day, we are part of that anonymous jetsam, with our two suitcases, the clothes we're wearing, the money that Georg had spirited into Switzerland for us and that nebulous promise of freedom.

Gazing across at the big Cunard liner out of Liverpool, moving at slow speed up the sound, she said: 'Felix...I'd like to go back.'

'Already?' They'd set out from their tiny apartment in Flatbush not an hour before intending to cross the bridge into lower Manhattan and visit one of their favourite coffee shops. 'Are you tired?'

'I mean *back*. To Vienna. To Budapest.'

'Ah.' Of course he'd known, they'd both known, that, one day, they might try to go back. They didn't speak of it. The subject was painful. One of them would break the silence eventually. He'd shied away. The associations of Vienna were still raw in his mind. They'd fled because of him, Sybille had had to forsake her stage career, to find work with a firm of theatrical costumiers, in the city. She'd never complained. Until now, perhaps. Was this what she meant?

'Are you unhappy here?' he said.

'Not especially. Are you?'

'No. Sometimes.'

She pressed forward against the parapet of the bridge. The liner was steaming past Ellis Island.

'What do you miss most?' she said.

The question Domenico had asked him. *And would you give the same answer, now, Felix?* he asked himself. *No, because we're not in prison.*

'Felix?'

'Yes?'

'What do you miss?' and before he could answer she said: 'Ever since we arrived here, it's felt as if our cases were just waiting, our two cases, yours and mine, to be packed, only the essentials, for the next stage of the journey.'

'Does it really feel like that?'

'All the time. Until we unpack them for good.'

340

'But how will we know that?'

She turned round and leaned back against the parapet. 'I don't know. Where, when? I don't know. Let's go for coffee.'

They walked on across the bridge into the city and Schmidt's which wrapped them round with Vienna's warm, cake-sweet aromas laced with freshly ground coffee beans.

'*Quäsertorte, bitte,*' Sybille said to the young waitress, a German Fräulein, who served them. '*Wie geht's?*'

The waitress bobbed a courtesy. '*Gut, gut, vielen dank.*'

Schmidt's was crowded as ever, German mingled with English. The clink of crockery all round made a pleasing tinkly sound, a reduced *Glockenspiel* of welcome. The waitress came back with the tray. Sybille poured the coffee.

Felix, stirring his coffee, said, in English: 'Do you really not like it here?'

She replied in German. 'I like it well enough. But it doesn't change what I miss which isn't here…a world away. Across that great ocean beyond the bridge. Just how this felt once. A world away. And now I'd like to go back. For a while I didn't want to, a long while, too soon, everything too…' She shook her head and didn't finish.

'Do you think you might want to stay? If we do go back?'

'*If* we go back? Why wouldn't we?'

'I don't know. No reason.'

'Anyway,' she said, 'who knows what's left of what we knew? Perhaps it's all so changed we'll hate it. But I'd like to see it, to touch it, smell it, to find out. I'd like to know. I've forgotten.'

'Then let's go.'

She toyed with a portion of the cheesecake, musing. 'What a misery I was. On the train, on the ship.'

'You were sick, worn out, we both were. Don't you think I felt the same?'

'You didn't show it. Do you remember how they couldn't get our name right?' A flicker of a smile passed.

'Yes. *Welcome, Mr and Mrs Brightman, of Austria, you say?* (Had they ever heard of Austria?). *Welcome to America, Land of the Free.*'

'*Displaced person.* I didn't like being a *displaced person,*' she said.

'They meant well. They took us in.'

'So they did, but I didn't want to be taken in, like an orphan.'

'Even so...'

'I know, we had no choice.'

'We escaped. We've made the best of it.'

'Have we? We've never really stopped being outsiders, foreigners, have we? It feels...I don't know, it feels just too big, this world we came to, too big. We're lost in it.'

'Along with half of old Vienna,' he said. 'Home from home, isn't that their phrase?'

She glanced round at the other customers. 'I suppose we've made the best of it. We've "done our best". Perhaps that's what it is, I don't want to go on doing our best. It's so very unsatisfactory. Like making do. It was the same when I first arrived in Vienna. It took an age to settle.'

'But you did, you made it home.'

'After a fashion. Except that home had been Budapest and I think it always will be, somehow, except that...' She didn't finish. She reflected and said, almost to herself: 'You can only ever do your best and if your best is not good enough for the people you're with, you're with the wrong people.'

'And you want to go back? To live?'

She thought for a long while, then without looking up, whispered: 'No.' She sat back in the chair. 'Because I think it's only an idea. Home is where we are, isn't it? For all that it matters.'

'Even if the cases are waiting to be packed?'

'Even if the cases are waiting to be packed.' She smiled. 'Something Hanna said to me once, about feeling at home. I don't think I've ever believed it, *really* believed in it. It's an illusion. Attachment to places, things, it doesn't work.'

'But you said you wanted to go back.'

'I know. I mean I'd like to go back to the old country if only to remind myself why we couldn't stay, to feel something of that. To make sense of the journey.' The smile was unreadable.

Felix's eyes widened in shock. 'My god…'

'What is it? Felix…?'

In the doorway stood a woman of about fifty, with blonde, permed hair. She wore a mouse grey fedora and a long dark brown velveteen coat with a white, rabbit's fur collar. With her was a man in a three-piece, herring-bone grey suit. He held a soft trilby hat in front of his chest in the way a barber will hold a mirror so that a customer can view the back of his own head. It was von Fessl.

As von Fessl and the woman sat down, the two men locked gaze and stared at each other for a long freezing moment. Then, von Fessl spoke to his companion, who was handing her coat and hat to the waitress. As she sat down, he consulted the menu and read from it aloud.

'Felix? What's wrong?'

'Didn't you see? Over there. It's him.'

She cleared her throat. 'As you say, half of old Vienna.'

'You must admit it's damned odd.'

343

She leaned across the table, a cock-eyed smile on her face. 'And so, my dear, is he following you or are you following him?'

'It's not funny. It's…'

'You're making too much out of it. As you say, half of old Vienna, that's all he is. Don't make a thing out of it.'

'One creepy bit of old Vienna I'd happily never see again.'

'Amen to that.' She pursed her lips. He nodded.

'So,' he said. 'Shall we go?'

She pointed to her plate. 'I haven't finished yet.'

'I mean to Europe.'

'Joking.'

'What about the business?'

Sybille had, for the last few years, been working with an interior designer, choosing fabrics, matching colour schemes, searching out antique furniture, modern furniture, objets d'art, paintings and sculpture from a small network of gallery owners and dealers which she had acquired. She worked under her maiden name. The Hungarian carried a certain cachet, an old world kudos, the distinction of old money which drew in the new money.

'Martha can cope without me.'

A little over a month later, they read the news of the uprising in Hungary. The puppet communist government caved in and fell, the Hungarian revolutionaries drove out the occupying Soviet army. An unimaginable miracle had transformed and blessed the ancient kingdom. Hungary was free and Hungarians celebrated freedom with the fervour of a people for so long oppressed.

Their joy was short-lived.

In the first days of November, Soviet tanks drove into Budapest. The resistants took to the sewers, cellars and tunnels from which they emerged to carry on the fight. Thousands died. The street battles went on until 10 November when the Russian army overran and crushed the remnants of the rebellion. Next morning, on the anniversary of that day when, the guns fell silent across the Western Front, in 1918, the guns fell silent across Budapest and Hungary died again.

Sybille did not speak about it. The agony of her distress was too deep. The desolation too complete. She turned away from any thought of Europe.

In late 1958, quite out of the blue, they received a letter from Georg.

Felix said: 'How on earth did he find us?'

'Read it out.'

'My dear friends, I apologise for the long silence but I've been in Australia. Fancy that.'

'Australia?'

'This is how it all happened. After we met in Switzerland, I felt as if my last contact with the old country was severed, and for good. I don't think I have ever felt quite so alone. Anyway. I went back to Paris, and Francine. You remember? After Hitler invaded Poland, I told Francine we should make contingency plans. I knew that once the Germans had marched into France, as surely they would, things would get very unpleasant indeed. Which they did. She said I was talking like a coward, with a vehemence I'd never seen in her. I said she should open her eyes. It was all right for her, she was a citizen. I, on the other hand…But, she refused flat even to consider leaving "in her country's hour of need". Very dramatic. All very commendable. Anyway, I made a somewhat injudicious remark about the idiocy of blind patriotism and Jeanne d'Arc and that was that. I don't know what happened to her.

'I took a train to Calais - the Germans were already in Belgium - and scraped it to England. They looked at my papers and arrested me, said it was nothing personal and I said: "How much more personal can it get?" They said all German nationals were being taken into custody as a matter of course, because there was a war on with Germany, or hadn't I noticed. I said I was Austrian. "You speak German, don't you?" they said. 'That doesn't make me German,' I said.

'I ended up with a bunch of other Germans and Austrians in an internment camp on their Island of Man. Didn't ever see much of it. We were billeted in a terrace of houses. There were barriers about the place but the atmosphere was fairly relaxed if a bit overcrowded.

'Most of us had to sleep two in a bed, head to toe. The food was adequate, the duties weren't so onerous. There was the tea, of course. It tasted vile. They put bromide in it, we heard, to curb the itch.

'It was extraordinary, though. There were intellectuals, scientists, academics, musicians, all manner of artisans. It was like a vivarium of all manner of intelligence and talent, and, you know what? The Brits didn't make use of it. We even had a lion-tamer from a circus that had been on tour. He could dead-head flowers with a flick of his whip. And, there was a Viennese baker who went into full production. But no coffee. Can you imagine?

'We had concerts, plays, revues, university-level lectures

pretty well every night. We got to swim in the sea occasionally, and there was a camp football team. The one thing we all had in common, apart from loathing the Nazis, was that we spoke German and, as far as the Brits were concerned, German equals bad. Maybe there were spies among us. We never found out and I'm not sure the Brits did, either. We were all classified as "the enemy within".

'Halfway through the war, a a lot of us were put on a ship and taken to Australia. Again, no reason offered.

'You know how cynical I've always been about puny Austria puffing herself up like a bullfrog. Well, there was a minor aristocrat on board, spent his entire time holding court with a small clique of admirers. And a pathetic little schoolmaster, a real bourgeois, was desperate to meet this von Whatsit, to touch the sacred hem. He pestered one of the acolytes until the man agreed to introduce him. The moment came. Von Thing was standing by the ship's rail with his cluster of toadies. The schoolmaster was ushered up and introduced. Our exalted nob barely registers him, delivers the full aristocratic snoot, before he turns away, back to his conversation. The schoolmaster was in ecstasies. Austrian aristocracy had gazed upon him. He had, for an endless moment, basked in the presence of greatness.

'After the war ended, we were released. A lot of the men went back. I stayed, became a lawyer again, moved to a small town called Tanunda, in the Barossa Valley, in South Australia, as different from Vienna as you could conceive of, like a country village. But, there's been a large German community here for over a century. There's even a male voice German choir and bowling club. I felt at home, there was work for me, I enjoyed the sunshine, and brace yourselves, here's one for the Viennese head-shrinkers - I got married. To Alexandra. Her husband had been killed in the war in the Pacific. She's a private secretary to the owner of one of the vineyards here. So I've become quite the Antipodean.

'Alexandra has two splendid sons – Duncan, who's a budding novelist, and Patrick, a musician. He specializes in Aboriginal instruments, something called a didjeridu. I bet you never heard of that. It makes a sound like nothing I've ever heard. Deep-throated rumble and strange strange rhythmic melody, though now it occurs to me, it bears some resemblance to an alpenhorn...

'Talk of landing on my feet. They welcomed me into the family and I felt, oh, I don't really know, I felt I'd come home at last. And it cured me of any lingering desire I had – not much, I must say - to go back to live in Europe. And what *is* Europe, now?

'You're wondering, of course, how I found out where you were. You know me, I am a walking *Open Sesame*. I contacted the Austrian embassy here, pulled some strings and... Voilà.

'Now. Alexandra and I are planning to come to Vienna next year – she's never been to Europe and we decided we could kill two birds: show her where I come from and give her the chance to explore the old world a little. Why don't you come while we're there? It would be wonderful to see you and one of the German expatriates here has told us about a lovely place in the south, not far from Munich. When we've done our tourist thing, we aim to go there for a week's holiday, doing nothing, before coming home again. Will you join us there? I'd so love it, we'd love it.'

Felix put the letter down. 'What do you think?'

42

To the end of the world, May, 1959

The liner docked in Bordeaux. Felix and Sybille travelled south by train, through the flat coastal Landes, to Biarritz where they stayed for a few days, went for long walks along the promenade, cheered by the fresh sea air and the soft boom of the Biscay rollers, and on to Pamplona. Felix made sketches of the cathedral, the churches, the Navarra palace. Sybille wandered round the barrio, exploring the heart of the old city, junk shops, fabric shops, antique jewellery emporia.

From Pamplona they travelled to Santiago de Compostela where, basking in warm sun at an outdoor table of a café opposite the cathedral, they watched pilgrims arriving, among them a man toting a long stave with a cockleshell attached and two white Pomeranian dogs each fitted with small pannier bags on their rump.

An elderly couple, wearing identical drab raincoats, tramped up the steps, tread by tread, towards the main portal. The man was unsteady, tired out. The woman supported his elbow. He stopped halfway, removed his hat and wiped his brow. A continuous flow of pilgrims passed the couple, entering and leaving the building. The man put his hat back on and stared for a long moment at the steep flight of steps ahead, a mountain to climb. There was desperation in his tense posture, in the way he viewed this last, daunting obstacle. His shoulders heaved.

Once more, the woman supported his elbow and they plodded, as if every step took a mighty effort, up to the flat pavement in front of the ribbed stone arches framing the main double doorway.

In the central pilaster dividing the archways, at chest level, a semicircle of five dints has, over the centuries, been worn by pilgrims touching the stone with their fingers.

The woman manoeuvred her exhausted companion up to the doorway and bent to whisper something to him. He didn't look at her, but nodded and removed his hat, raised his right arm towards the marks in the stone and laid his palm flat over them. The woman reached out to his hand and guided as his fingers settle, one by one, into the shallow indentations in the stone. He followed what she was doing and, as they settled in the centuries-old marks, his body relaxed, he sagged at the knees, his eyes fixed on his hand. Some power had flowed into him, the blessing of the saint himself, it must be. Then he bowed his head. He'd achieved it, the journey, he'd reached Santiago, all that way, he'd got to the shrine of Christ's brother.

They continued through Spain into Portugal and on down to the far south-westerly tip of the Iberian peninsula, to the town of Sagrès built on a tiny finger of land jutting out into the Atlantic ocean. From here the Portuguese explorers set sail into the wide uncharted ocean. It was the last bit of Europe they saw.

At breakfast on their first morning, Felix said: 'They called it the end of the world.'

'I'm not sure if I care to be at the end of the world. Mightn't we drop off the edge?'

'There's a statue of Henry the Navigator at the bottom of the cliffs.'

'Is there just? More coffee?'

'Yes, please.'

'Oh, there's only a dribble.' She waved for the waiter.

'He never went to sea, himself.'

'Who?' The waiter whisked the empty pot away.

'Henry. The Navigator.'

'Why is he called the Navigator, then?'

'He paid for the expeditions. Masterminded the enterprise.'

'Did he now?'

He looked across at her and said: 'Someone had to.' Dear Felix, she thought, he can always make me chuckle, even when I don't feel like chuckling. 'I thought I'd go down to make a sketch,' he said. 'Would you care to come?'

She laid a hand on his arm. 'If you don't mind, I shall stay in the hotel to read, to have some lunch and a siesta. I've had enough rattling about for the time being. Time just to sit still for a day. And I have no wish to scramble down cliffs even for a wonderful view on the way. I imagine there's a wonderful view. Is there a wonderful view?'

'I think there is, will be.'

'Ah. Nevertheless, I shall remain here and do nothing. Besides, I should only be a drag on you. I haven't got the shoes.'

He set off after breakfast with his small collapsible canvas-topped stool and satchel containing sketch book, pencils, a small flask of wine and a bocadillo of the local ham and unsalted bread.

The path down the cliff side traced a twisting line along a

ledge cut into the rock. It was narrow, part paved, part trampled to bare dust by centuries of passage. A brisk offshore breeze blew in buffets off the sea, scuffing the surface of the water into ruffs of white surf. In a perse blue sky the sun shone full, proud of drifting rags of cloud. The rollers thumped onto the rocks below and splintered into fountains of spray, like exploding glass. The air zinged with ozone.

At the foot of the cliff, Felix settled on his best vantage point to take in the view - the jutting prow of the cape, the battlements of the castle perched on its flat summit, and, near the sea's edge at the foot of the cliffs, the bronze effigy, on a rough-hewn plinth, of Infante Henry, Duke of Viseu, gazing oceanwards, in proprietorial, heroic pose.

Felix set up his stool, took out his sketch book and a pencil, stared at the statue, the cape in the background, drew a rapid outline, shaded it and then folded the book over the pencil. He turned, instead, to gaze at the sea beating on the shore and the rocks. Staring across the vast vacancy, he watched the evolution of waves forming out of the pitch and swell, larger and larger as they surged towards the shore, rolling up and over the under-tow of spent waves flooding back off the beach. And, at the full height of their cylindrical leap, the belly compressed, the dense mass of water thinned and spread, the crest curled over and plunged down, driven on by the relentless weight of the oncoming flood, wave after succeeding wave, in the incessant drive for land, like a watery element of Time itself. Dark water and white foam, a hissing roar overlaid by the low keening of the wind which, like a great harrow, raked the broad furrowed acres of the ocean.

Successive waves heaved and plunged, growing in size as the

submarine turbine spinning the waves up from the sea floor mounted and accelerated. The final wave of the sequence was the mightiest of all, thumping with a hollow reverberation onto the land's shelf.

Lulled by the pleasing crescendo of sound, Felix reflected on the soothing perpetual motion of the sea, and on the lurking menace it fosters, of the latent storm that will dash the continuum in pieces. We are all, he thought, of successive generations of waves forging on without cease, an endless tide, swelling and breaking, seething away to nothing in the pebbles and sand of our eventual oblivion. We can do no more than flirt with the monstrous hidden energy of Time's sea, in its infinite subtleties of form, the paradoxical beauty of both its placid calm and its wild rage. We may contain its savage force by walls and coigns, and some who know its switches of mood may ride its fury out, but there is no taming it. It abides, its mastery guaranteed by the same powers which first bring us to being and then destroy us.

I'm watching the sound, he thought, listening to the motion.

Into his reverie filtered another sound coming nearer, indistinct, at first, then a soft pizzicato of laughter, exclamation, muffled words. He bridled. He did not want to hear human voices, not here, not in this blustery solitude of tide and wind.

And then a crunch of shoes on the shingle, approaching him. He didn't turn to look. A voice, clear and firm, close behind, addressed him in halting Spanish. The underlying singsong accent of its speaker was unmistakeable.

'Sir? If your honour pleases, make excuse of us. It is not our desire to perturbate you.'

Then do not perturbate me, he thought, but half turned,

now, to see a group of six young men in walking boots and Loden jackets, standing in a line. Each carried a satchel slung over the shoulder, a folding stool in one hand. Three wore hats with feathers in the band. Yes, the accent, the attire…all familiar.

'We are coming here to make a depiction,' said their spokesman, a pale, blonde-haired youth, ruddy of cheek with a broad smile and a wide-eyed, boyish candour.

Felix nodded, hoping they'd take the hint and leave him to his meditation. The spokesman, however, added: 'Perhaps that is your ambition also,' pointing to the sketch book in Felix's lap.

Felix made a wry face. They were not going to go away. 'Perhaps you'd find it easier to speak in German,' he said.

The young men, startled, looked at each other in arch surprise and laughed. Two of them clapped. The spokesman's eyebrows voiced his – their – astonishment. 'But you are German, too,' he said, as if it were the funniest thing imaginable, and looked round at his companions, all full of bright wonder, for confirmation of just how funny, how very hilarious, it was.

'Austrian,' said Felix. 'Like you.'

'Austrian? Yes, Austrian,' said the young man with delight heaped on astonishment. 'And you are Austrian too. That is a most strange coincidence, would you not say, sir? A very strange coincidence, worthy of note, would you say?'

Felix made a small gesture of agreement.

Warming to this clear overture to conversation, the spokesman continued: 'My companions and I are from architectural school in Vienna on a study tour, organized by our professor. Who is here also.' His eyebrows arched, his eyes shone, he pointed one index finger vertically as if the presence there of

354

their professor were also a remarkable, if not marvellous, fact, worthy of note. 'We have visited cathedrals and palaces, the truly magnificent Mezquita in Córdoba, the equally splendid Alhambra palace in Granada, and so, eventually, we come here.' He thrust out his chest and cocked his head, the entire group came to attention and bowed, just as an older man appeared behind them and said: 'What is this?'

It was von Fessl.

He and Felix stared at each other, von Fessl at this irritant, this importunate nuisance, Felix at this man who had dogged his steps ever since the dark road out of Gorizia, like a nagging, recurrent pain for which no doctor could find a cause, like an echo threading in the wind. What to say? What was there ever to say to a man with no more substance than a ghost? Memory could not speak. No words worth uttering.

The two men regarded each other as if through glass, the window of a train carriage, the thick pane dividing restaurant from the street outside, the off and on mirror blink of a revolving door.

Von Fessl gave Felix the faintest nod and walked away, Felix, still seated, watching him. The students trailed behind him, their professor, chattering, and took up positions round the statue, his weathered, bronze arm pointing out across the sea, westwards to the New World…its riches, its promise, its risk, a frozen gesture of prophecy. They stood, as directed by their professor, away from the tideline, whilst he himself walked over to a low shelf of rock protruding from the sand of the beach further down.

The incessant thump of the waves, the hiss of the receding

water sucking at the pebbles and sand of the beach, the yelp of the gulls, the hoarse hum of the onshore wind.

The young men, showing their awkwardness at the pupils' task, eager to be taken seriously, knitted brows, stagey concentration, shifting position for a better angle on the subject, von Fessl himself, between the statue and the tideline, perhaps absorbed, perhaps not, but making a professorial show of being so, sketchbook braced in the crook of his left arm, the pencil in his right hand moving as he glanced down, held in poise as he glanced up. . . glanced down, glanced up, line following line on the page whose upper edge fluttered a little where it was loose, where his fingers could not keep it tight against the breeze.

Felix watched. This man. Why here? And why in any of the otherwheres he had appeared? No answer. What does he have to do with me that he has been someone I cannot shake off? An unwanted presence, almost a haunting, though not dangerous, not threatening, not...anything. Just there. Why me?

The waves surged and built towards these men standing on the beach, rose up out from the great hollows of the ocean floor, as a snowball rolls, gathers in size and weight, more and more accretions of volume, rolling, building. The weight of the sea's water barrelled into the waves that crashed onto the beach. Felix watched. The semi-circle of boys, the statue, the statuesque figure of von Fessl on his own plinth, the flat pan of the beach sloping imperceptibly down to the tideline.

The freak wave, when it came, seemed to heave itself up out of the very seabed, towering above the waves uncurling ahead of it, monstrous in size, bearing down on the beach, a wall. Felix saw it, stood up and knocked over his stool. One of the boys saw it, dropped his sketchbook and, as he shouted *Look out, look out,* pointing – the electricity of panic in his arm and fingers – pointing at the wave, the wave overleapt the tide's cordon, raced on and crashed in a blasting force onto von Fessl, swallowed him, spinning in its wicked maelstrom, and, as the bulwark of its waters burst, the wave collapsed, boiling, down, and drew back on the fierce tug of the tide, like a fisherman's net, dragging its prize with it. Of von Fessl there was no sign.

The boy who'd seen it coming was already running towards the water, tearing off his jacket as he went, flinging it to the sand. The others – had they seen it? It seemed not – looked round. What? What is it? What's happening? Felix, running across the beach, now, called out: 'Stop him. Stop him.' One of the other boys, stung to action, chased after his companion, brought him down at the water's edge. Felix got there, grabbed hold of him. 'It's no good. You can do no good.' The lad was struggling to be free, to go in there, into the open jaws of the next waves, the oncoming pelt of them, the tireless endless race of the combers.

Felix and the other boy pulled him out of the sluice of the tide, onto his feet, rough-handled him back, over the sand.

Felix held him by his arms. 'It's no good. Too late. Nothing you can do. Nothing you can do.'

The boy went limp, hung his head, shamed, overwhelmed.

They stood, motionless, Felix and the circle of young men, staring at the break and roll of the onrushing waves, the empty waters. Nothing. Not a sign. He was gone. Except the sketch book, von Fessl's sketch book, washed up at the tideline, sloshing back and forth, like the corpse of a seabird.

Felix was suddenly conscious of them, these boys, young

men, as old, only, as some of the men with whom he'd stood on the dark road out of Gorizia, the living from whom he'd been separated on the bank of the Isonzo, the dead lying in its mud. He looked at them, their faces rent with disbelief, horror, anguish.

They stood watching a long, long time, in hope, in desperate and failing hope, spellbound in their horror. Nothing. The sea had not even spewed the corpse up above the surface, a final act of spite.

It was Felix who spoke, at last.

'Where are you staying?' How mundane it sounded, like 'time to go home'.

One of the boys, his brow furrowed – wasn't he the one who'd introduced them? – stammered. 'In, in, t-t-t-town. In. Town, sir. In…' He gestured towards the cliffs.

Felix touched him gently on the shoulder, as he erupted in tears, great gouts of sobbing. The others slowly clustered round. Felix felt the closing of their circle round him. He looked at them, each one, one by one.

'Come on,' he said. 'There's nothing any of us can do here now.'

They walked away from the sea towards the cliffs. The thump of the waves behind them, the yelp of the gulls, the hoarse, low whirr of the wind.

43

A month later, southern Germany.

The Schloss Schwanheim stood on a rocky prominence, backed by dark pines, with an apron of clipped grass slopes, overlooking the lake of the same name, high in the Bavarian alps. It was a fanciful, neo-Gothic mock castle, constructed of dusty pink stone, the window casements, roof eaves, doorways, detailed in darker brick, with hexagonal turrets at each corner and fretted crenellations along the parapets. Architectural school of mad king Ludwig II.

The waters of the lake ran clear as schnapps, the conifers gave out a perfume of resin, and, in the light of the westering sun, the stone face of the nearby mountains alchemised to gold.

The alpine garden on either side of the main entrance to the Schloss, planted by the wife of a previous owner, made a quilt of tiny jewel-like flowers, intense colours and enamel white, brilliant as the incrustations on a Fabergé egg.

The Schloss, built for a member of that quaint Dodo species of minor Bavarian aristocracy, with whom Bavaria had once been over-supplied, had, after the last of them died, been converted into a hotel. It offered its guests the blessings of pure mountain air outside, de luxe service inside, and untrammelled peace and quiet.

The entrance hall, flanking corridors and main staircase

which swept in a gracious curve to the upper landings, were panelled in glossy mahogany. Chandeliers dripped with crystal. The ceiling cornices exhibited discreet ripple mouldings. Hotel staff glided in deferential silence along the parquet floors on undisclosed business.

The dining room, its round tables laid with salt-white Egyptian cotton napery, fine glass goblets, and ornate silver-plate cutlery, gave onto a ballroom where, on a low raised dais, a palm court orchestra played every evening, and the young waitresses, released from duty, danced together, gay *Mädchen* on bare feet, with braided hair.

Round the edge of the ballroom were dotted small tables and easy chairs for diners taking coffee after the meal, all wearing the formal dress – dinner jacket, long gown – insisted on by the hotel management. At one of the tables, on their first evening together, sat Felix and Sybille, Georg and Alexandra. Georg had a round-shouldered stoop, now - age and a new contentment had loosened him. Alexandra was a tall woman with a trim figure. They were, it was plain, very happy in each other.

Finally, Georg had met a woman to whom he could be open and Sybille remarked on it later. 'Men need to be opened,‘ she said. 'All your bravado is no more than a cover for emotional cowardice.'

'You're right,' said Felix.

'Of course I'm right.' She gave him that smile which so enchanted him, knowing, mirthful, self-deprecatory, as if there were times when she could not quite take herself seriously and didn't expect it of others.

The head waiter approached, bowed, his hands clasped in front of him.

'Ladies, gentlemen, may I ask if everything was to your satisfaction with your dinner?'

Sybille's nose wrinkled. 'The asparagus was swimming in butter,' she said, 'and the Riesling was over-chilled. Apart from that it was fine.'

The waiter all but recoiled in dismay, a dumbshow of exaggerated concern. 'I *am* sorry, madame. I will inform the sommelier.'

Felix was conciliatory. 'I didn't mind, myself.'

'You never mind, Felix. You're too accepting,' said Sybille turning aside to watch the dancers. Not always too accepting, in fact, but it was a long time ago and they'd weathered it.

Georg smiled at Alexandra who said: 'I'm with Sybille on that. Too much chilling suppresses the bouquet.' Her German was flawless, the accent elusive.

The waiter coughed. 'Are you ready for your coffee?' he said, with a glassy expression. 'Petits fours? Chocolates? The chocolatier has quite excelled himself today, I can recommend the petits fours…'

'The petits fours, yes, thank you,' said Sybille glancing round at smiles of agreement.

On the other side of the room, an elderly couple stood to leave the ballroom, the old man fumbling for a walking stick, his wife clutching the back of the chair and, her arm through his, his arm clenched on it in mutual support, they made their way slowly across the room.

The palm court orchestra whisked to the conclusion of a lively galop, the young Mädchen curtsied one to each other and burst into an eager round of applause. The members of the orchestra nodded in appreciation and then turned over pages of their music for the next number.

Sybille turned to Georg. Dreading the answer, she asked: 'Have you, did you have, any word of Hanna?'

He'd dreaded the question that he knew must come and didn't answer at first. He held her gaze, then, all but whispering: 'Yes. When we were in Vienna. She and Gisele died in Mauthausen. I don't know why they'd been taken there. Political? Hanna was never very discreet about her opinions. Perhaps just for being in love. *Sexual deviation* was the ghastly phrase they used. I can't be sure. I'm so sorry.'

Sybille didn't speak. No words would do. How could words cover so final, so complete a vacuum? 'Thank you Georg,' she said. 'At least I – we - know, now.'

The coffee and petits fours arrived. The orchestra began to play Léhar's *Gold and Silver* waltz, always the last number of the evening. The young Mädchen formed couples, the music began, they danced.

EPILOGUE

That is the story, as Felix told the bare bones of it to me, one evening in the Schloss. It was some while after the meeting with Georg and Alexandra and I have no reason to believe the story was any different from how he told it. Felix was not one for self-aggrandisement or dramatisation. He seemed as bemused by it as I was. As for anyone who says that the death of von Fessl is completely unbelievable, what valid grounds do they have for saying so? Reason does not apply. We cannot say of something that it did not happen because we have no experience of such a thing. Isn't *impossible* often the limit we put on our own imagination? Once it could be said, and without contempt, that there are more things in heaven and earth than are dreamt of in philosophy. We can philosophise ourselves into a cul de sac, as Felix did in captivity, but we can also dream ourselves into the infinite spaces of the universe. What else is love but a capacity for dreaming of the infinite and the loss of love the disappointments of reason?

It's true, there may be inconsistencies in Felix's story, but there are always inconsistencies, the inconsistencies which make and unmake us. We are a challenge to definition. Isn't there, at the heart of humanity, a solitude which nothing, finally, can touch or console, not even, especially not, maybe, the truth, any truth? Tell me the truth, says the exasperated parent to the recalcitrant child, when it's not the truth they want but the fact and, with it, an admission which is the excuse for, the justification of, punishment, exercise of power. We are all hungry for confession. That is, perhaps, our moral weakness.

ACKNOWLEDGEMENTS

I have a great deal to thank James Essinger for, above all the very existence of this book in published form. Curiously, at the head of the much that I owe him is the fact of the very words thank you which I had, originally, supposed to be a single word. He put me right on this so that now, those two syllables come freighted with a very different cargo of gratitude. In this case, with an untrammelled warmth and cheerful acknowledgement of his extraordinary generosity as well as recognition of his exceptional devotion to literature, its delights and very existence as a most important part of human endeavour. I have lived with this story for so very long that even the idea of its appearing in more available form than in the recesses of my computer is all but overwhelming. James, THANK YOU. And to Karla Harris for essential, assiduous cleansing of the text. Also, of course, to Charlotte Mouncey for surmounting so many obstacles to design and make such a fine cover for the book. I am also indebted to Bosia Jefford, a Pole, for her help with some of the exchanges in her native tongue.

My debt to David Sharp is deep and in the case of this book, David, whose love of and insight into fiction has proved invaluable to me in so many ways, asked a crucial question which jolted a necessary change in the novel's opening chapter. Asking questions is the hard bit – answers follow and, for the most part, impose an easier task than nailing the elusive query. David felt something was not right, he probed, I pondered, clicked, and the problem was solved. Those who pose the questions may not know the answer themselves but they have a way of eliciting triumphant effort in those of whom they make enquiry. To David, therefore, my profound gratitude.

The late Sir John Keegan, a historian of considerable stature, generously answered questions about vital military intelligence relating to the comportment of the Italian military in WW1 by letter. Graham Upton, in charge of the printing department of Sevenoaks District Council is faultlessly helpful.

George Clare's *Last Waltz in Vienna* was very useful.

I also acknowledge, of course, Rudolf Strauss who knew Felix and heard the story from his very lips in that remote Bavarian Schloss. Rudolf recounted the story to me one evening at supper years ago and I cycled home afterwards with the form of it singing in my head, sat down and wrote it all up in every detail. Thereafter, it lay on me like a responsibility for a long time. Why had Rudolf told me, unless in some unconscious knowing that it would be my task to record it? That's how I see it, anyway. We are here to snatch up, not to discard or ignore and how ever could I let slip such a remarkable narrative? But how to cast it? I did not know. I was technically inept. Research I could do and I did research, in the library of the Imperial War museum, the old asylum, in its early days called a Bethlehem Hospital, corrupted to Bedlam. Visitors paid a sum of money to come to see the antics of the poor crazed inmates and it's not fanciful to say that poring over books and files in what had been the refectory in the upper gallery of the dome of that ancient edifice, one could hear the cacophony of those tormented voices in faint, irrepressible echo. The clutter of research can lie similarly on the memory – incoherent, disconnected, random voices, the garnered detail from archive, campaign maps, historical record, files. Those voices chant a sort of challenge which will not be silenced, in line, perhaps, with the stern comminations of the Ten Commandments emblazoned in a frieze round the interior of that dome, painted there for the spiritual improvement of the unfortunate patients. If I labour the point of the locale, it is merely to stress how miserable I was for so very long that, having collected so much information I was, it seemed, even further sunk in inertia. I could not make sense of this story beyond the bare bones of it, as Rudolf had recounted it to me. James, unwittingly, I think, was a major part of my slow emergence as the writer who finally managed to distinguish a clear voice amid the cacophony, to retrieve the clarity of that first telling and to expand it into novel form as it stands here, not least in his steadfast belief in me and my ability, when I had little of either. Learning how is such a big part of why we are here, after all, and in my acknowledgements, I add, perhaps strangely, the Highgate Mens' Pond on Hampstead Heath, where I met Rudolf and where we swam together each morning. The company of men who gathered there for the daily immersion in cold water – 'dukes to dustmen' so they say – mirrored one aspect of the book, inadvertently: the vivarium of which Max speaks, the happenstance of deportation during the war, when undesirable aliens were carted off from the UK to far-off climes, academics, professionals, artists, musicians prominent among them, a multifarious master class in the making. Those waters gave me, and I hope you, much.

Graeme Fife, Sevenoaks, Kent, UK
November 2023